# dark sentinel

## By Christine Feehan

**'Dark' Carpathian series:**

Dark Prince
Dark Desire
Dark Gold
Dark Magic
Dark Challenge
Dark Fire
Dark Legend
Dark Guardian
Dark Symphony
Dark Melody
Dark Destiny
Dark Secret
Dark Demon
Dark Celebration
Dark Possession
Dark Curse
Dark Slayer
Dark Peril
Dark Predator
Dark Storm
Dark Lycan
Dark Wolf
Dark Blood
Dark Ghost
Dark Promises
Dark Carousel
Dark Legacy
Dark Sentinel

Dark Nights
Darkest at Dawn
(omnibus)

**Sea Haven series:**

Water Bound
Spirit Bound
Air Bound
Earth Bound
Fire Bound
Bound Together

**Shadow series:**

Shadow Rider
Shadow Reaper
Shadow Keeper

**GhostWalker series:**

Shadow Game
Mind Game
Night Game
Conspiracy Game
Deadly Game
Predatory Game
Murder Game
Street Game
Ruthless Game
Samurai Game
Viper Game
Spider Game
Power Game
Covert Game

**Torpedo Ink series:**

Judgment Road

**Drake Sisters series:**

Oceans of Fire
Dangerous Tides
Safe Harbour
Turbulent Sea
Hidden Currents
Magic Before
Christmas

**Leopard People series:**

Fever
Burning Wild
Wild Fire
Savage Nature
Leopard's Prey
Cat's Lair
Wild Cat
Leopard's Fury
Leopard's Blood

The Scarletti Curse

Lair of the Lion

A
CARPATHIAN
NOVEL

# CHRISTINE
# FEEHAN
# DARK SENTINEL

piatkus

PIATKUS

First published in the US in 2018 by Berkley,
an imprint of Penguin Random House LLC
First published in Great Britain in 2018 by Piatkus

1 3 5 7 9 10 8 6 4 2

A CIP catalogue record for this book
is available from the British Library.

Hardback ISBN: 978-0-349-41979-4
Trade paperback ISBN: 978-0-349-41978-7

Printed and bound in Great Britain by
Clays Ltd, Elcograf S.p.A.

Papers used by Piatkus are from well-managed forests
and other responsible sources.

MIX
Paper from
responsible sources
FSC® C104740

Piatkus
An imprint of
Little, Brown Book Group
Carmelite House
50 Victoria Embankment
London EC4Y 0DZ

An Hachette UK Company
www.hachette.co.uk

www.littlebrown.co.uk

*To Martha Nylander,*
*my girls' night out partner in crime.*
*Have many fun memories of us with the others,*
*hope to make many more!*

## FOR MY READERS

Be sure to go to http://www.christinefeehan.com/members/ to sign up for my PRIVATE book announcement list and download the FREE ebook of *Dark Desserts*. Join my community and get firsthand news, enter the book discussions, ask your questions and chat with me. Please feel free to email me at Christine@christinefeehan.com. I would love to hear from you.

# ACKNOWLEDGMENTS

As always there are many people to thank. Chris Tong is amazing and always answers the call for research if I'm stuck on something. Thank you, Chris, for your timely aid over and over, with the language especially. Anita Toste, my sister, who is a little bit Carpathian, for her spells, and for always answering questions even when she doesn't know she's doing it. Sheila English for stepping in when my son couldn't be here for the power hours. Brian, for keeping me on track with those power hours. And of course, Domini Walker: thank you for the tremendous work you do on every manuscript to make it the best it can be before my editor sees it. Also, Denise, what would I do without you? You make certain everything gets where it is supposed to be on time, and you bring me those blended lattes so I can work!

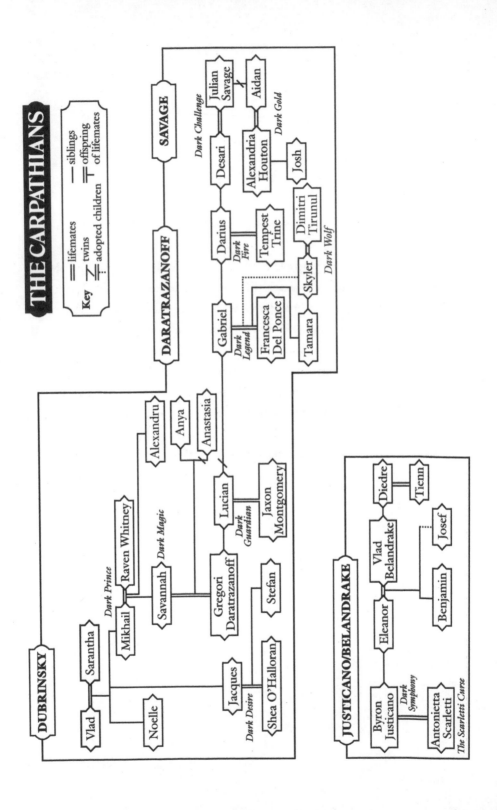

# THE CARPATHIANS

**Key:**
= lifemates
— siblings
⫫ twins
⫪ offspring of lifemates
⫶ adopted children

**DUBRINSKY**

**DARATRAZANOFF**

**SAVAGE**

**JUSTICANO/BELANDRAKE**

Vlad = Sarantha

Noelle

Mikhail = Raven Whitney *Dark Prince*

Jacques = Shea O'Halloran *Dark Desire*

Savannah = Gregori Daratrazanoff *Dark Magic*

Stefan

Alexandru

Anya

Anastasia

Lucian = Jaxon Montgomery *Dark Guardian*

Gabriel = Francesca Del Ponce *Dark Legend*

Tamara

Skyler

Darius = Tempest Trine *Dark Fire*

Dimitri Tirunul *Dark Wolf*

Desari

Alexandria Houton *Dark Gold*

Josh

Julian Savage *Dark Challenge*

Aidan

Byron Justicano = Antonietta Scarletti *Dark Symphony* / *The Scarletti Curse*

Eleanor = Vlad Belandrake

Diedre

Tienn

Benjamin

Josef

# THE CARPATHIANS

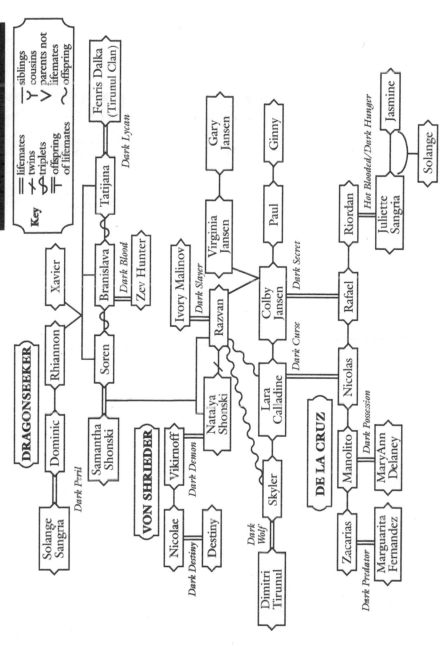

**Key**

| | |
|---|---|
| = lifemates | — siblings |
| ⚯ twins | Y cousins |
| ⚹ triplets | V parents not lifemates |
| ⚌ offspring of lifemates | ⁓ offspring |

**DRAGONSEEKER**

Fenris Dalka (Tirunul Clan)

*Dark Lycan*

Tatijana

Branislava — Zev Hunter

*Dark Blood*

Xavier

Rhiannon

Soren

Samantha Shonski

Dominic

*Dark Peril*

Solange Sangria

Ivory Malinov — Razvan

*Dark Slayer*

Gary Jansen

Virginia Jansen

Colby Jansen

*Dark Curse*

Paul

Ginny

Rafael

Riordan

*Hot Blooded/Dark Hunger*

Juliette Sangria

Jasmine

Solange

Lara Calladine

Natalya Shonski

**VON SHRIEDER**

Vikirnoff

*Dark Demon*

Nicolae

*Dark Destiny*

Destiny

*Dark Secret*

Nicolas

Manolito

*Dark Possession*

MaryAnn Delaney

**DE LA CRUZ**

Zacarias

*Dark Predator*

Marguarita Fernandez

Skyler

*Dark Wolf*

Dimitri Tirunul

# OTHER CARPATHIANS

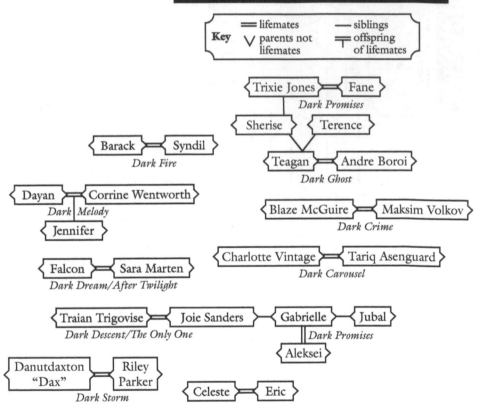

Key
══ lifemates          ── siblings
V parents not        ╤ offspring
lifemates            of lifemates

Trixie Jones ══ Fane
*Dark Promises*

Sherise          Terence

Barack ══ Syndil
*Dark Fire*

Teagan ══ Andre Boroi
*Dark Ghost*

Dayan ══ Corrine Wentworth
*Dark Melody*
Jennifer

Blaze McGuire ══ Maksim Volkov
*Dark Crime*

Charlotte Vintage ══ Tariq Asenguard
*Dark Carousel*

Falcon ══ Sara Marten
*Dark Dream/After Twilight*

Traian Trigovise ══ Joie Sanders ── Gabrielle ── Jubal
*Dark Descent/The Only One*              *Dark Promises*
Aleksei

Danutdaxton "Dax" ══ Riley Parker
*Dark Storm*

Celeste ══ Eric

# Dark Sentinel

# I

ontemplating allowing himself to die made Andor Katona feel
like a coward. He had never believed that sitting out in the open
waiting to meet the dawn and have the sun fry him was an act of
nobility. He—and a very few others—had always believed it to be an act
of cowardice. Yet here he was, deliberating whether or not to give himself
permission to die. The sun wasn't close, but the wounds he'd sustained
battling so many vampires at one time had weakened him.

With the loss of blood, and several near-fatal wounds, the human
vampire hunters hadn't recognized him as a hunter and had attacked
while he'd left his body an empty shell so he could try to heal those
wounds. A stake close to the heart—they'd missed—hadn't felt so good.
They really weren't very good at their self-appointed task. They'd torn
open his chest, and more blood had spilled onto the battleground. He'd
never thought he'd die in a country far from home—killed by a trio of
bumbling humans—but dying seemed a good alternative to continuing a
life of battle in an endless gray void.

The three men, Carter, Barnaby and Shorty, huddled together a distance from him, casting him terrified and hate-filled glances. They were

trying to convince themselves they'd done it right and he was dying. Of course, they'd expected him to die immediately and now wondered why he hadn't and what they should do about it. He could have told them they'd need another stake and a much better impaling technique if they wanted him to die. Did he really have to instruct others on how to kill him? That was ridiculous.

Sighing, he tried weighing the pros and cons of dying in order to make a rational decision. He'd lived too long. Far too long. He'd killed too often—so much so that there was little left of his soul. He'd lived with honor, but there had to be a time when one could let go with honor. It was past his time. He'd known that for well over a century. He'd searched the world over for his lifemate, the woman holding the other half of his soul, the light to his darkness. She didn't exist. It was that simple. She didn't exist.

Carpathian males lost all emotion and the ability to see in color after two hundred years. Some lost it earlier. They had to exist on memories, and after so many centuries, even those faded. They retained their battle skills—honed them nightly—but as time passed, all those long, endless years, even the memories of family and friends faded away. He lived his life far from humans most of the time, working in the night to keep them safe.

Vampires were Carpathians who had given up their honor in order to feel again. There was a rush when one killed while feeding. Adrenaline-laced blood could produce a high. Vampires craved it, and they terrorized their victims before killing them. Andor had hunted them on nearly every continent. As time passed, the centuries coming and going, the whispers of temptation to turn increased. For a few hundred years, those whispers sustained him, even if he knew the promise was empty. Eventually, even that was lost to him. Then he lived in a gray world of . . . nothing.

He had entered the monastery high in the remote Carpathian Mountains, a place where a very few ancients had locked themselves away from the world when they'd been deemed too dangerous to hunt and kill but didn't believe in giving themselves to the dawn. Every kill increased the danger of turning, and he had lived too long, knew too much to be vampire. Few hunters would ever be able to defeat him, yet here he was, nearly done in by a trio of inept, bumbling human assassins.

He had taken the vow to be honorable in waiting for his lifemate with the other ancients. Of course, the situation had been made worse by secreting themselves in a place where there was no hope of each finding the one woman who could restore emotions and color to their lives—but they had known that. They had accepted the truth: their women were no longer in the same world with them.

The whispers of his would-be killers grew annoying. Really annoying. His head was swimming, making it difficult to think. He lay looking up at the sky. Stars were out, but they appeared as blurred lights, nothing more. Their light was a dull gray, just as the moon was. He looked down at the blood seeping out of his body, pooling around him from more than a dozen wounds—and that didn't count the stake. The blood was a darker gray. An ugly mess. How had he gotten here, so far from his homeland and the monastery where he'd placed himself so he wouldn't give in to the nothingness that surrounded him?

Hope had come to the monks, so they'd scattered, looking once again for the women who might save their souls. When they'd realized the world was too changed and too vast and once more they didn't fit and there was little hope, they'd answered the call of their fellow monk and followed him to the United States. The vampires had grown powerful, and Carpathians were behind in the ways of the new world. It had been an effort to catch up when before he had always found it easy to learn newer, more modern things. That had led him to this moment—considering that he'd outlived his time.

Everything was different. He was forced to live in close proximity to humans and to hide who and what he was. Women were different. They no longer were satisfied having a man care for them. He had no idea what to do with a modern woman. Contemplating his demise seemed so much wiser than trying to understand the reasoning of a present-day woman.

It was difficult to think, although the night was beautiful. The humans kept talking, whispering together, sending anxious looks his way. He wanted them to be quiet and considered silencing them so he could continue to contemplate, but it was finally dawning on them that maybe they should have studied anatomy a little better before deciding on their profession.

Carter ended up drawing the short straw. The others sent him over to figure out what had gone wrong. He was shaking, trembling from head to foot as he approached, clearly terrified of the man they had tried to murder. Sweat poured off the assassin, and he wiped it away with the back of his hand as he drew near.

He loomed over Andor, the stink of fanaticism reeking from his pores, his features twisted into a mask of hatred and determination. Andor wasn't quite ready to make up his mind about death. He lifted his hand to push enough air at the man to send him flying backward when a woman rushed out of the darkness and attacked.

The moon was full, scattering beams of light over the battleground. There was no evidence of the vampires he'd killed because he'd disposed of them properly. He wasn't getting a minute of peace any time soon, not even with a stake sticking out of him and his blood everywhere, not with his supposed savior in the form of a little whirlwind of fury attacking his three would-be assassins. He was going to have to rescue her. That meant living longer. He didn't like having his mind made up for him.

She moved with incredible speed, an avenging angel, her long hair flying, her hiking boots crunching rock, dirt and the lightning-scorched grass beneath her feet. She bashed Carter with what appeared to be a saucepot, whirling like a tornado and striking him again. She went under his punch, blocking it upward with one arm: it sounded as if it must have felt like a blow as she clobbered him right in the face with the pot. Carter staggered backward and then hit the ground.

Andor closed his eyes briefly, thinking perhaps he was seeing an illusion. What woman would attack three men with a saucepot when they'd just staked someone? He sighed again and thought about how much blood he was going to lose when he sat up and yanked out the stake. It would leave a good-sized hole in his chest. On the other hand, he could leave it in . . .

"Don't you move," she hissed, not looking at him, but one slender hand came back behind her, palm toward him in the universal signal to stop.

He went still. Utterly still. Frozen. His lungs felt raw, burning for air. It wasn't possible. It couldn't be. More than a thousand years. An endless void. His eyes hurt so badly he had to close them, a dangerous thing to do when she was certain to be attacked.

The other two men hadn't the courage of Carter and had backed away a distance from him, just in case when Carter did whatever he was considering to remedy the situation—in other words, trying to kill Andor again—they thought themselves safe. Both men might not want anything to do with the big man on the ground, but a woman armed with a sauce-pot was an entirely different matter. They had separated and circled around, edging up on either side of her while she had been busy smacking Carter with the pot.

"What is *wrong* with you people?" She was furious, emphasizing each word with a bang of the pot on Carter. "Are you crazy? That's a human being you're murdering."

Andor had been lying in a puddle of his own blood, contemplating death, surrounded by a gray world. Everything had been gray, or shades of it. The ground. The blood. The trees. The moon overhead. Even his three would-be assassins. He had felt no real emotion, detached and completely removed from what had been happening to him. The world changed in the blink of an eye. His burning eyes, his lungs that refused to obey his commands. Everything so raw he could barely comprehend what was happening.

Color burst behind his eyes. Vivid. Brilliant. Terrible. In spite of the night, he could see the green in the trees and the shrubs, varying shades. His blood appeared red, a bright shade of crimson. He made out colors on the three men, blues and true blacks. The moon caught the woman right in its spotlight, the beams illuminating her.

Andor's breath caught in his throat. Her hair was the color of chest-nuts, dark brown with reddish and golden undertones making the thick mass gleam in the moonbeams. Her eyes were large and very green, and she had a mouth that he could fixate on when he'd never obsessed or fixated on anything in his very long existence.

The vivid colors were disorienting when he already was in a weakened state. His stomach knotted. Churned. He felt as if he had vertigo. He needed to sit up. To protect her. The colors flashed through his mind, swirling into a nightmare of soundless chaos. At the same time, emotions poured in, feelings he couldn't sort through fast enough to make sense of or process.

Carter was on the ground cowering as Shorty reached for the woman. She whirled around and bonked him over the head. "Do you have *any* idea how hard it is for me to meditate when you're *murdering* someone?" She glared at Andor over her shoulder. "And you. Lying there, deciding whether or not you've had enough of life? What is *wrong* with you? Life is to be cherished. Not thrown away."

Shorty tried another misguided attempt to punch her. She hit his hand with the pot so hard even Andor winced at the sound. Shorty howled and stepped back, regarding her warily.

"I'm on a journey seeking personal enlightenment, and you are disturbing my aura of love." The pot hit Barnaby on his shoulder hard enough that he covered his head and turned sideways to avoid another swipe. He'd made the mistake of trying to sneak up on her from the other side.

"I'm on a path of nonviolence so that my life can be an example to the world of what it would be like living in a better place. Peace . . ." She smashed the pot against the side of Barnaby's head as he went at her again and then kicked the side of his knee hard enough to send him to the ground. "Love." She turned toward Shorty and began to advance on him menacingly. "Embracing nature."

Shorty grinned at her and shook his head. "You're a nut."

"Maybe, but you're a murderer." She ducked a punch, blocking it smoothly with the pot and bashing his arm while she stepped in and punched his jaw. Hard.

Andor could see Shorty's head snap back. She had quite a punch, but he was going to have to do something before the murderous pack got serious about going after his woman. He forced his body to move. It wasn't easy with a stake protruding from his chest, right beneath his heart. When he moved, blood leaked out around the wood. It hurt like hell and he had to cut off his ability to feel pain if he was going to actually move.

*"Don't,"* she hissed out at him, a clear command. Annoyed.

No one in his lifetime had ever used a tone like that on him. *He* gave the orders, not a woman, and certainly not a human. Worse—a human woman.

"Don't you move. I'll get to you in a minute." She turned her head to look at him over her shoulder, and her eyes widened in horror. "Oh. My. God." Her saucepot lowered and she half turned toward him.

He waved his hand toward Shorty, who was coming up behind her fast. Shorty stumbled and fell, almost at her feet, drawing her attention. She smashed the pot over his head. She became a little fury, rushing Barnaby again.

"Why would you do that to another human being?" There was a little sob in her voice, as if just seeing the cruelty of the stake in Andor's chest hurt her as well. "I'm supposed to be learning to live without anger and you're *torturing* and brutally murdering another man. How can I possibly be okay with that? If this is some kind of test, I'm failing. You're making me fail." She kicked Barnaby in the chest, hard. Her forward snap kick was powerful and sent the assassin flying back so far, he hit a tree and slid to the ground.

"He's not human!" Carter shouted. "That's a vampire!"

She stopped in her tracks. "You're all crazy. He's a man." For the first time wariness had crept in.

Maybe she finally realized she was out in the middle of nowhere with three madmen who had staked another man. Andor could only hope.

"There's no such thing as vampires."

The three men got shakily to their feet and then fanned out, surrounding her. "We saw him. He called down lightning. Look at the scorch marks on the grass," Carter said.

"They're right, in that there are such creatures as vampires," Andor said calmly. He managed to sit all the way up, both hands supporting the stake. He was weaker than he'd realized. Maybe he really wasn't going to make it out of this one. He'd lost far too much blood. "They're also wrong. I'm not a vampire. I was hunting them. The humans saw the tail end of the fight." He had no idea why he was bothering to explain. He had never explained his actions in his life.

"Don't listen to him," Shorty said. "Cover your ears. Vampires can beguile you."

"Beguile me?" She sounded as if she thought Shorty was insane. Her gaze shifted to Andor, and she paled. "For God's sake, lie back down now."

Her skin looked beautiful in the moonlight. His eyes on hers, Andor reached up to grasp the thick stake protruding from his chest. Her eyes widened. She shook her head, dropped the saucepot and ran toward him.

"No. Don't pull that out."

Shorty tried to grab her as she ran past him. The thought of one of these men putting their hands on her brought out something in Andor he hadn't known was lurking beneath the surface. It exploded out of him, a roar of pure rage. It came with the force of a volcano, welling up from somewhere deep and threatening to annihilate everything in its path.

"Do not touch her." It was a decree. A command. Nothing less.

The mandate froze all three men. She made it past them and was on her knees at his side, her face a mask of worry as she touched the stake.

"Don't move." She jumped back up, pulled a cell phone from her jeans and began frantically trying to get it to work. She kept putting her arm up into the air, waving her phone around and moving from one place to another.

"What are you doing?"

"I need to find just one bar. Just one. We're down in this valley and I can't get service to call in rescue." She pushed past Shorty and then stopped. Froze. Very slowly she turned her head to look at the man. He wasn't moving. He stood, one arm outstretched, but he was looking the other way. Not at her. "Um." She backed away from Shorty. "What's wrong with you?" She looked at the other two men. Neither so much as blinked. She backed up even more. "Something's wrong with them." She turned very slowly to look at Andor.

He could smell her fear. It was beginning to dawn on her that no human being could live with a stake the size of the one he had in his chest. Now the men claiming he was a vampire weren't able to move. They looked like statues carved of stone. He considered leaving them like that, but it would raise questions in the human world and he couldn't have that. Not now, when there seemed to be a real war brewing between vampires and Carpathians. More than that, he needed blood if he was going to survive this time, and the three could supply it. He *had* to survive now. There was no other choice.

"I need your help," he said quietly.

She shook her head, but she took several steps toward him. "I'm not good with blood. I need to call someone . . ." Her voice was faint this time.

"There isn't time. If you don't do as I ask, I *will* die, and you will have risked your life for nothing. Thank you for that, by the way." He kept very calm, hoping she would follow his lead.

"When I say I'm not good with blood, I mean I could faint."

"I'll deal with the blood. You just do what I tell you and we'll get through this."

She looked from the three men frozen like statues back to him. Her gaze dropped to the pooling blood. "You're bleeding from more than the stake."

"I told you; before they came, I was engaged in a battle." Hands covering the gaping wound in his belly, because he could see she really might faint, he had no choice but to lie back. Sun scorch his weakness. She was afraid now, he could see it in her expression and feel it in her mind. He was doing his best to keep her from reading his thoughts. She was clearly telepathic. She had knowledge of his pondering ending his life and she wouldn't have that if she wasn't reading him. Keeping her out of his mind took effort.

"Okay." She moved cautiously toward him, her saucepot held like a weapon. "I wasn't kidding when I said I don't do well around blood."

For the first time, he caught a note of shame. Of guilt. He didn't like it. He liked her annoyed. He liked her fighting. He liked her confident. That jarring note put knots in his gut and gave him a need to gather her close and comfort her. It was also getting more difficult to block the pain in his chest. He wanted to grasp the stake and pull it out, but he needed her to have everything ready for him.

"You're going to need to pack my wounds with fresh soil. It can't be burned. If there are scorch marks on the ground or grass, it can't be used." He closed his eyes. He could feel the beads of blood dotting his forehead and running down his face. When she saw that up close, she might really faint, and then he'd have no one to help. It was too late to send out a call.

"What's your name?" At least, if he was going to die, he'd go knowing the name of the woman who had come to save him.

"Lorraine. Lorraine Peters." He heard her take a deep breath. She was that close. "And you're not going to die. We can do this. Are you certain about the soil?" She was already scooping dirt into her saucepot. "It's very unsanitary."

"My body responds to the soil. To the earth. When you have enough, bring it to me." He wanted to see her face, but he was afraid if he opened his eyes and looked at her, she would be the last thing he saw. He would take that vision with him to the next life, instead of enjoying time with her after waiting for so many centuries.

Her body jerked hard, and Andor realized he was drifting. She might have caught some of his thoughts.

"I am sliding in and out of consciousness and having odd dreams. I think these men put weird thoughts in my head." It was the best he could do and it seemed to work. She was breathing again. Not evenly, but still, he hadn't lost her yet. He tried to keep air moving in and out of his lungs.

"I'm sorry I'm such a baby about blood." She knelt beside him. "I just don't see how I'm going to be of help to you. This stake . . ." She trailed off. There were tears in her voice. Misery.

She wasn't worried about him being a vampire. She wasn't thinking about the three men standing behind her as still as statues. She was thinking she was an utter failure as a human being because she couldn't look at the blood seeping around the stake or dripping from any number of wounds he couldn't heal.

"Bring the soil up close to me. I need to mix saliva with it." He hoped she'd be so intrigued she'd forget about the blood. A sense of urgency was beginning to take hold. He knew he was slipping away. Too much blood loss.

"Um . . ."

"Andor. My name is Andor Katona."

"You've lost so much blood. You need a transfusion."

She was still catching partial thoughts but didn't realize it. He had to be careful, but it was impossible when he was trying to keep himself alive. Ordinarily, he would open the earth, shut down and try to allow the soil to heal him, but he was too far gone and he knew it now. Anxiety gripped him. After centuries of hunting her, he'd found her and was slipping away inch by inch, or pint by pint of blood loss.

"I can spit," she offered.

There was a note of hesitancy like she thought he was a lunatic and she was simply indulging him because she was certain he was going to die. He was beginning to think he might.

"Let me." He didn't know if her saliva was powerful enough to help with healing. His saliva contained a healing agent as well as a numbing one.

He scooped a handful of the soil, mixed it with his saliva and pressed it into one of the gaping wounds in his belly where a vampire had tried to eviscerate him. Now that she had something to do besides faint at the sight of him covered in blood, she concentrated on helping him pack his wounds.

Andor closed his eyes and tried to conserve his strength. As an ancient, he had built up tremendous power and control. He had never considered that three humans—not very bright ones at that—might bring him down.

"Don't." She whispered the command. "Tell me what to do next."

"I need blood. I've lost too much. Pack the soil around the stake. I can't take it out until I have a transfusion."

"I'll give you my blood," she said, her voice trembling. "But I'm afraid I really will pass out. Just tell me what to do."

He was *starving*. Every cell in his body craved blood. Was it safe to take her blood? He would have to stop before he took too much from her, and he didn't know if he still had that kind of control. He had to rely on her. If she was weak, she couldn't help him. On the other hand, if he was going to release one of the human males from their frozen state, he would need to be stronger to keep them under his power.

He could feel two of his teeth growing sharp. Lengthening. He breathed deeply and kept his head turned from hers. "I can help you through it if you let me. I'm telepathic as well. You know we have shields, barricades in our minds, so to speak. Trust me enough to let me make it easier for you. I don't have much more time."

There was a small silence. He lifted his lashes just enough to see her chewing at her full lower lip with small white teeth. She nodded. "Yes. But hurry. I'm already feeling dizzy. I'm trying not to look but it's nearly impossible. And my hands are covered in . . ."

"I'll take care of it." He reached for her mind immediately. There was no sense in waiting. She was either going to let down her barriers and he was going to live, or she wouldn't and he wasn't going to make it.

He reached for her hand, and just that act sent pain crashing through him, driving the air from his lungs in a brutal rush of agony. Her skin was soft, like silk. His thumb brushed over her pulse, where it beat so frantically. She was afraid of him. Of giving her blood. Of fainting and making a fool of herself. Her phobia of blood made her feel foolish and weak. She detested it and tried very hard to overcome it.

He forced himself to stop reading her and took complete control, using the last of his strength to take over her mind. He was very lucky in that she had taken down her shields herself, giving her trust to him when he had yet to earn it. He didn't delve deeper into her mind to find out why. He sank his teeth into her wrist.

Her blood burst into his mouth like bubbles of the finest champagne. Nothing had ever tasted so exquisite. So perfect. He knew he would always be obsessed, would always crave her taste. He savored every drop, feeling his cells reach for the nourishment, soaking it up, desperate to replace what was lost.

For the first time that he could remember, Andor had to fight himself for discipline. For control. He didn't want to stop. He *never* wanted to stop. He was desperate for blood. Her blood. Very gently he swept his tongue over the two holes in her wrist and turned his head toward the three would-be assassins.

Shorty came to life, one slow inch at a time. His body jerked and took a step toward the Carpathian. Terror was written on the man's face. Andor ignored it. He didn't want to waste his strength on calming the man; after all, he'd help drive a stake through Andor's chest.

The moment Shorty got to him and knelt obediently, presenting his neck, Andor sank his teeth deep. The blood was good. Not tainted with alcohol or drugs. He took as much as he dared and then sent the man back to his campsite after wiping his memories. He planted an encounter with wild animals, something that would definitely spook him and make him uneasy enough to want to break camp and go home.

He brought Barnaby close next, instructing him to kneel beside him and grasp the stake with both hands. Andor took the remainder of the soil, mixed it with his saliva, took a deep breath and told the human to remove the stake. Nothing in his long life had ever hurt as much as it had when that stake had been driven into his chest. It hurt nearly as much when it was removed.

Blood welled up and he shoved the soil deep into the hole, gritting his teeth, grinding them together to keep from striking out at the helpless man. More blood spilled around the wound, soaking into the dirt. He couldn't breathe for a moment. Or think. He just lay there, gasping, staring at Lorraine's beautiful face, telling himself she was worth everything that he had endured, including this.

His vows to her were carved into his back—tattooed there in the old primitive method, the ink made by the monks in the monastery. They had to scar the skin deliberately with each poke from an array of needles. He had the vows in Carpathian going down his back. He'd meant every single word.

*Olen wäkeva kuntankért. Olen wäkeva pita belső kulymet. Olen wäkeva— félért ku vigyázak. Hängemért.*

He had other tattoos, but none meant as much to him. The code he lived by was scarred forever into his back. He was Carpathian and it took a lot to leave a scar. He had suffered to put those words into his skin, but they needed to be there—for her. The code was simple.

*Staying strong for our people. Staying strong to keep the demon inside. Staying strong for her. Only her.*

Those last two words of his code—his vow—said everything. Every wound he had suffered in battle, every time he'd had to kill an old friend or relative, every night that he'd risen and endured the gray void, was for her. Now he knew her name. Lorraine. He loved the sound of it. He loved the look of her and her grit. She had courage, even if she needed to temper it a bit with wisdom.

While he took Barnaby's blood, he thought of the monastery and those long, endless years without hope. They had spent nights practicing their battle skills and then working on their tattooing techniques. All of those residing in the monastery had become brothers—although they had known they might have to kill the others. The difference was it would be an honorable way to die.

He sent Barnaby on his way with the same memory of wild animals getting too near their camp. He planted a memory of them all running in different directions and then one by one making their way back to camp with the idea of breaking it down and heading to their homes. They no longer sought to hunt and kill vampires, nor did they believe in them.

Now that he was a little stronger, he directed Carter, the one who had actually driven the stake into his chest, to start digging into the soil. Andor knew he couldn't move. He was too heavy for Lorraine to help him get out of the sun. He had to get into the ground, had to have Lorraine pitch a tent right over top of him.

Carter couldn't dig very deep without tools. He used Lorraine's saucepot. He dug right next to Andor so the Carpathian could shift his body enough to slide into the shallow depression. It was no more than a foot deep, but it was long enough and wide enough for his body, which was saying something. He wasn't a small man.

He forced Carter to help him and then took his blood before sending him on his way with the same memories as Barnaby and Shorty. It was the best that he could do. Just that small movement had him leaking blood. He needed time to let the soil rejuvenate him enough to gather the strength to begin healing himself. Carpathians as old as he was were incredibly strong. He could overcome this, he just needed a little luck on his side and Lorraine.

He released her mind, and she blinked at him, still kneeling, but now he was about a foot from her in the depression. He should have had Barnaby dig it deeper, but he couldn't take the time. He attempted a smile at her, going for reassurance, but just looking at her hurt nearly as much as the hole in his chest.

On her, the colors appeared even more vivid. Her hair, with the moon shining down on it, was a beautiful mix of hues. Her skin was nearly translucent, she was so pale. He knew that was from him taking her blood.

"Are you feeling all right?"

She blinked several times, calling his attention to the sweep of thick, long lashes. "Where's the stake? How did you get it out?" On her knees, she shuffled closer to him and let out a little feminine gasp that caught him somewhere deep when she saw the hole in his chest packed with soil. It wasn't a small hole. It hadn't been a small stake.

"I didn't want you to have to deal with it. I do need your help. I'm weak. Really weak."

She looked beyond him and then turned around fast, clearly looking for the three men.

"They left. Ran."

"Cowards, but I'm glad they're gone. Still, having them where I could see them made me happier because now I have to worry they might come back to try to kill us."

"They ran out of here and I planted a suggestion, one that if it takes means they won't even remember us."

"You're an extremely strong telepath," she said. "And I can't believe you're still alive, but we need to call for help. Get a helicopter to get you out of here. I'm going to have to hike up to the top of the mountain and see if I can get cell service."

He shook his head. "Are you camping with a tent?"

"Of course." Her fingers brushed at the stubble on his face. She had a little frown as she rubbed at something along his jaw, determined to remove it. He was certain it was a bloodstain. Her gaze studiously avoided any other part of his body where the wounds had bled, leaving wet, red stains behind.

"How long will it take you to break down your camp and bring everything here?"

She frowned at him. "Not long at all. I camp a lot, but seriously, Andor, I'm not good at taking care of injured people, and you don't seem to realize how bad off you are. We need a helicopter."

"My body doesn't respond to regular medicine."

"Does it respond to a surgeon repairing holes in it? That gash in your stomach was horrendous. And that stake . . ." She trailed off, going even paler if that was possible.

"No, I told you, although you're trying hard to make me human. I hunt vampires. My body makeup is different. I know you thought I was going to die and you humored me by allowing me to put soil in my wounds, but the earth really has healing properties." Sun scorch him, he was exhausted. "Please. I'm asking for your help. Get your things and come back. Wild animals will find me and I'm helpless."

She regarded him with a small frown. "I didn't think about the animals, but you're right. I have no idea what to do." She sank back onto her heels. "If I leave you to hike up the mountain, you could really be in danger. If I stay, seriously, Andor, you could die. You should already be dead."

He was beginning to really fall for that frown, or maybe he was just so light-headed from the pain. Keeping it at bay was becoming difficult in spite of the infusion of blood. He was still leaking far too much, and right now, blood was at a premium. He had been careful not to leave the three vampire assassins too weak. He wanted them out of the area.

"Just hurry and get your camping things."

"The scent of blood will draw wildlife. There are bears and coyotes in these mountains. For all I know, there could be wolves, but I don't think so. I can't leave you alone."

"You have to. We need your tent. I can't be out in the sun. Not even for a few minutes. You have to cover me with your tent and the soil through the daytime. I'll sleep and hope the soil starts the healing process." It was going to be a long process at the rate he was going.

He knew the moment he'd won. Her expression changed from worry and indecision to determination. "It's going to take about twenty minutes. I'm not that far from here, but it is a little bit of a hike." She was already on her feet, anxious to go now that they had a plan.

"Lorraine, thank you for not asking questions and arguing."

"What would be the use? I can't leave you, and I can't raise anyone from down here in this valley. You're either going to live or die, and you're the strongest person I've ever met, so I'm betting you're going to live."

He hoped she was right. He didn't feel very strong. In fact, he just wanted to close his eyes and let the night take him for a little while. Just to give himself a few minutes where he didn't have to block the pain. It was taking so much strength. He was trying to slow the steady leaking of blood. Once she was back with the tent and had set everything up, he could take more of her blood, but he needed her fit, not weak.

"I'll need water," he reminded as she started to turn away.

"I have plenty, and there's a stream not too far from here. I have a filtration system." She was backing away, her eyes moving over his torn body for the first time since he'd been in her mind. She swallowed hard and shook her head again. "I'll be back in a few, hang on."

Andor watched her go. She seemed to take his strength with her. His lungs continued to burn for air, telling him he needed to shut down soon. There was too much damage to his body. He had destroyed seven vampires. Two were very close to being master vampires. They'd lived long enough that he should have run across them, but he seldom remembered names or even faces of the undead.

He closed his eyes. She would come back, although she really detested the sight of blood. He'd read the revulsion and the way it had made her ill. Her stomach had churned and she'd fought not to be sick. She'd really had to work not to faint. It was a testimony to her courage and tenacity that she'd stuck around to help him.

She was his lifemate. He knew she was, yet he was so wounded he couldn't bind them together, he didn't dare. That meant she could still walk away from him, and he'd be more dangerous than ever. He could only hope that he had read her correctly and she was everything he believed her to be. She was coming back. She had to, if he had any chance at all of surviving.

# 2

Lorraine was absolutely certain when she returned to Andor she would find him dead. No one could live with wounds that horrendous. They just couldn't. It was impossible. She felt like a coward leaving him so she wouldn't have to witness his death. God knew she'd seen enough blood and death for a lifetime. She was certain when she returned it would be over and he would be dead.

She stood by her tent, shaking, her hands over her face. Her stomach heaved. She had to breathe deeply to keep from being sick. All that blood. She hadn't looked at the ground other than the one time, but when she had, the dirt under and around the man had been wet and slick with blood. His clothes had been covered in it, so stained she'd thought he was wearing red. Everywhere she'd looked on his body, he'd had wounds. And that stake . . .

What was wrong with the world? Were people really so cruel and ugly as to drive a stake through a man? The circumference of the wooden rod had been about that of a broom handle. How could someone actually drive that through human flesh? Her stomach heaved again, and she felt the familiar rage churning in her belly.

She had no idea where the three men had gone to, but she was angry with herself for not taking their pictures so she could describe them accurately and give the photos to the police when she had the chance. She was also very concerned that because she'd seen their faces, they would come after her to kill her.

Lorraine forced herself to move, to begin breaking camp. She was an experienced camper and, although she was on automatic pilot, she was fast. Her camping gear was minimal because she had to pack everything in one backpack and carry it wherever she went. She was walking across the mountains, on a journey of self-discovery—at least that was what she told anyone she came across. In reality, if she was being strictly honest with herself, she knew she was running away.

All that blood. She pressed her hand to her forehead and looked up toward the mountain peak. Up there, she could probably call for help. If she hiked up the mountain, it really would be too late, and Andor would die alone, probably at the teeth and claws of a wild animal rather than just bleeding out. She'd helped pack the wounds with dirt. She'd probably be charged with murder, because if the wounds didn't kill him, the bacteria would.

"Damn it!" She shouted it aloud. The night carried the sound of her voice to the other side of the valley. "Just damn it." She whispered that one, because she knew she wasn't going to let the man die alone. She couldn't.

Shouldering the large pack, she headed back to him. She had been telepathic all of her life. As a child, she'd thought everyone could hear what others were thinking. When she'd realized they couldn't, she hadn't wanted to be different and had tried to turn off her ability. She'd been unsuccessful. Then there was the period of time she'd embraced it as a gift, as something she could use, especially against her parents and brother. That phase hadn't lasted very long, either. If only . . .

She found her vision blurring. Tears ran down her face as she jogged back toward Andor. She thought she'd cried every tear possible, that she couldn't have a single one left, but they were back. If only she hadn't gone off to college. If only her parents had asked her to come home and talk to her brother. If only Theodore had called her himself.

She nearly stumbled and that made her swipe angrily at the useless tears. They didn't do any good, no matter what grief counselors said. Tears gave her a headache, but they didn't bring back her parents or her brother. They didn't stop the newspapers or tabloids from reporting or asking questions. Tears didn't stop her so-called friends from ostracizing her.

She started down the hillside, weaving her way through the trees to come to the wide meadow where Andor lay. She could see him lying very still, as if he were dead. He was in a shallow depression of freshly dug earth—like a grave. Or a partial grave. When she'd first arrived, swinging her cooking pot at the man standing over Andor, she hadn't noticed that they'd dug out the ground. They clearly had planned to bury him. What if they'd made him dig it and that was why it was only a foot or so deep? She'd heard of that kind of sadistic behavior in serial killers.

Her footsteps slowed. She didn't want to go up to him and find him dead. She'd found enough people dead, their bodies soaking in bright red blood. Who knew there was so much blood in the human body? Or that it could be so sticky and get everywhere? She stopped for a moment to catch her breath and take the time to compose herself.

*Lorraine?* The stirring was in her mind. Her name a soft whisper. Talking telepathically felt intimate. She hadn't known that because she'd never known another being that could do it. She'd never even thought she could push her voice or thoughts into someone else's mind.

*I'm here. You're alive, then.* She didn't know if that was a relief or not. She forced her feet to move again, to walk toward him.

*I'm alive. Just barely. I need water. I cannot take your blood again so soon and I need something to help keep me alive until you are strong enough again.*

*I've brought you some.* She picked up the pace, hurrying to his side. She shrugged out of the backpack and caught up her water bottle.

His eyes were intense, fixed on her face. She had never seen eyes the actual color of indigo, but that was the only true color to describe his eyes. A cross between a midnight blue and a deep violet. In the darkness, his hair and eyes both appeared inky until she got up close. There was only the briefest of hesitations and then she lifted his head gently, holding him as she pressed the water bottle to his mouth. For a moment she thought he might not drink, his face rippling with what appeared to be disgust, but she saw the moment he made up his mind and then drank.

"I'm sorry it took so long. I was . . ."

*You thought I was dead and were afraid to come back to me.* There was a twinge of humor in his voice as it brushed against the walls of her mind.

"Well . . ." There was no denying it, not if he could read her thoughts. "Yeah. The thought of finding you dead out here in the middle of nowhere—" She broke off.

It was difficult to hold his head up and not look down at his body covered in bloodstained clothes and dirt.

"I shouldn't have packed your wounds with dirt. I honestly didn't think you had a chance of surviving, but you've lived this long, so maybe I was wrong. I should try to clean out the wounds." Her stomach lurched again at the idea. "I'm not much of a medical type. I don't even put Band-Aids on other people's wounds."

*I know this is difficult for you.*

That made her feel small. Guilty. Ashamed. He was the one suffering. She was acting like a baby. "What do you need me to do? I don't have any painkillers with me." She had aspirin but was afraid to give it to him. It was a blood-thinner, at least she thought it was, and the last thing he needed was to lose any more blood.

"Can you put your tent up around me? Over the top of me, so that I'm inside it? It is large enough?"

Because she was traveling distances and hadn't known what kind of weather she'd be running into, Lorraine had brought an all-purpose tent, one that was larger than a single overnight tent. It was heavier and she could spend several rainy days in it, moving around if she had to.

"Yes. I can set it up."

"The sun can't touch me at all." He issued the warning aloud.

She lowered his head back to the ground and stepped away from him, trying not to think of the implication of those words. Lots of people had allergies to the sun. His skin wasn't exceptionally pale, nor had she seen evidence of vampire teeth, but just the fact that he was still alive after being brutally assaulted and left with so many wounds that should have killed him made her think about what the three men had accused him of being.

*I'm not going to hurt you, Lorraine.* Again, there was soft amusement in his tone.

Her body clenched for no reason, deep inside, a purely feminine reaction to the sound of his voice brushing along the walls of her mind. It was truly intimate and every individual note felt as if he was stroking velvet over her skin.

She didn't answer him. Instead, she put the water bottle close to his hand and began to lay out her tent. It was easy to pitch, an extreme, rugged, mountaineering tent. Almost at once, she saw the problem. She couldn't put the tent over the top of him with the floor in it. "I'm going to have to pitch the tent a distance from you and then find a way to get you inside."

"You'll have to cut out the floor where the tent is positioned over me."

Her heart stuttered. "I can't cut the floor out. It will ruin my tent. This wasn't cheap, and I still have a long way to go."

"I'll repair it for you."

She didn't say he'd be dead by morning because that would have been rude. Instead, she touched her favorite camping knife to make certain she was wearing it on her belt and proceeded to lay out the tent for easy setup. She was going to cut the floor out exactly around him. It would be the dumbest thing she'd ever done, but she consoled herself with the idea that she was giving a dying man his last wish.

It took a very short period of time to set up the tent, a giant hole in the floor surrounding him. She sank down onto the ground beside him. "I think we're good. This is a heavy tent. It's made to withstand wind and rain and lower temperatures. I think it will keep the sun off your skin. Do you have allergies?" She sent up a silent prayer that if he didn't, he'd lie to her.

He managed a small smile, and her heart nearly shattered. In spite of the blood and wounds, he was valiant. He fought to stay conscious. She could see it was an effort, but he did it for her. She wanted to tell him not to, but then if he let himself go to sleep, she feared he'd slip away and she'd be there in the close confines of the tent with a dead body.

"I need you to dig out more of the soil around me and cover as much of me as possible."

Her heart accelerated. She found herself staring at him—at that face with all those angles and planes. All that stark male rawness. He was extremely masculine. He looked as if he could be quite dangerous even lying there with so many terrible wounds. He wasn't threatening her in the least, quite the contrary. He was being quite gentle when he spoke to her, and she somehow knew he wasn't accustomed to it.

"I'm not burying you while you're still alive." She poured resolution into her voice because she had the feeling he was used to getting his way. The three would-be murderers had said he could beguile with his voice, and she believed them. Not because she believed he was a vampire, but because his voice was so powerful a weapon he could cast spells with it. The timbre and pitch were so perfect she wondered what he would sound like singing. Most certainly, he wouldn't have trouble hypnotizing or mesmerizing an audience.

"Not burying me alive," he countered. "Just covering my body with soil. I told you, the composition of my body allows the soil to heal me. The more natural minerals, the faster I heal. This ground hasn't been touched. The soil is particularly loaded with elements I need."

She thought he was a New Age nut. Newer than New Age. She'd never heard of any of her friends who were into that sort of thing believing in partially burying their bodies so the earth could heal them. How far should she go to humor a dying man?

"Just please do this for me."

"I cut up my tent for you," she snapped and then was ashamed of herself. Lorraine pressed the heel of her hand to her throbbing head. She had the headache from hell now and she couldn't complain, not when he was lying there with giant holes in his body.

"I'm sorry. It's just that you're asking me to do things that I believe are going to harm you more than help you. I don't want to carry the responsibility of your death, and I would. I put dirt in open wounds. If you're in what amounts to a shallow grave and I dig it deeper and you die, the authorities are going to think I killed in you in a terribly brutal way."

"Lorraine." He said her name softly and just waited.

She counted the beats of her heart. The air moving in and out of her lungs. Crickets sang. Somewhere a coyote howled. He remained silent, and the compulsion to look at him grew until she couldn't stand it. Her gaze met his and her heart nearly jumped out of her chest. Those eyes were every bit as hypnotic as his voice.

"I'm not going to die. What makes you so certain the authorities would believe you would kill a man? You don't have a mean bone in your body."

She couldn't face him, not that gentle look, not his innocent questions. She caught up the saucepot. It was a little dented from hitting one or all of the men she'd fought. She began to dig around him, scooping up the soft soil and tossing it over his body. It kept her from having to look at him.

"I have a bad temper." That was a confession. A true one. "I'm working on it, though. I took a year off from school and am traveling in the mountains, living immersed in nature as best I can in order to conquer the worst traits in me. Especially my temper."

Andor watched her. She didn't have to look up from her task to know. She felt the impact of those indigo eyes on her. It was like a physical touch. There was something so compelling about him she couldn't seem to resist him. She knew his wounds should kill him—one was enough, let alone all of them—but there was a part of her that believed he wouldn't die.

"I have no idea whether or not I have a temper."

Her gaze jumped to his face before she could stop it. "Of course you know. How could you not?"

"I have been in a place for a very long time where I didn't feel emotion. Now that I do, I suppose I will find out what kinds of traits I have, good and bad."

The tip of her tongue moistened her upper lip while she considered what he'd said. "It's hard to feel again after being numb." It was the best she could do. She didn't want to pry into his life because if she asked questions, he would return the interest. She couldn't have that. She'd come to the mountains to escape the spotlight.

"When you haven't felt anything for a long time, any emotion, good or bad, is welcome. The problem is figuring out how to control feelings when they seem so wild and out of control."

"I didn't think of that. Take another sip of water. You lost so much blood and need the fluid." She bit her lip and then sank back on her heels. "Andor, I'm going to be honest with you. If you're going to make it, I should strip you, wash you and try to sew up these wounds. I don't have a clue how much damage has been done to vital organs. For all I know you're still bleeding internally."

He shook his head, his eyes on her face. That look. It was impossible to ignore. He made her feel as if he saw everything about her.

"Come here."

"I am here." She was closer to his bloody body than she wanted to be. The scent of blood was strong. It looked as if he'd bathed in it. She was fighting every moment not to vomit. That would be wonderful, add that smell to the already nauseating scent now almost overpowering in the confines of the tent.

"I can't come to you, Lorraine, so I need you to get closer. Come up by my head and you won't have to be near the blood."

She detested that he knew she was struggling. He was dying, and instead of her being a help and comfort, she was still too immersed in her past to get beyond the blood. "I'm sorry, Andor. I wasn't always a baby." What did it matter if he knew? The entire world knew. He was dying, and when he was gone, she'd be alone in the wilderness again, surrounded by silence.

"Come up here, by my head." He patted a spot with just his hand. His long lashes lowered and she noticed they were the exact black of his hair.

She scooted until her knees were just under his wide shoulders, facing him, keeping her gaze steady on his so she wasn't tempted to look down and see the hole packed with dirt in his chest. He was incredibly good-looking. Not handsome. He was too unrelentingly masculine to be called that. Still, he was beautiful. A man of raw power, even cut down as he had been.

He lifted his hand toward her face, his fingers finding her temples.

Very gently he touched them. Pressing. His touch felt light but firm and his palm spanned her face in order to allow him to reach both sides. Strangely, the headache that had refused to leave her was suddenly gone. His hand dropped to her stomach. Once again, his fingers spread wide and his palm pressed into her. Through her shirt, she felt heat spreading, and the terrible sickness churning there was gone as well, just like the headache.

He removed his hand and waved it in the air. At once a slight breeze seemed to go through the tent, removing the foul stench of blood, pushing it through the screened windows. He slumped back down as if that effort had cost him.

Lorraine knelt beside him, her mind spinning. Chaotic. In turmoil. "You're a healer." She breathed her sudden realization aloud, in total awe. He *had* to live. She knew they existed. When she'd researched telepathy, she'd also looked into other psychic gifts. True healers were very rare. And needed. "Can you heal yourself? Is that why you're so certain you won't die?"

He rested his head against the dirt. She hated seeing him like that, but he seemed to want—or need—to be surrounded by the soil. Those long lashes closed down so she was no longer looking into his fathomless eyes.

"When I'm stronger, I can do it. Right now, I'm worn out."

"You need more blood, don't you?" Even suggesting it to him made her heart go crazy, but if she was going to be any help at all to him, she would have to give him the tools he needed to heal himself. He'd only taken a few sips of the water. Blood had to be one of the tools he needed.

"Yes. But not yet. You keep digging around me, make the hole deeper and throw more soil over me. Right up to my neck. Just leave my arms and head out. While you do, tell me when you began to have such an aversion to blood."

She scooted backward until she was beside her very dirty saucepot. She began to dig, understanding that he wanted to be deep in the cool soil. While she dug, she began to notice how the soil was richly black and sparkled with veins of minerals. Once she got down to that layer, she dug with more strength and speed, working her way around him, as close to his body as possible. She widened the long hole so he could move to one side while she dug deeper.

"Before I tell you why I have such a hard time with blood, you have to know a few things about me."

"That's good, *sívamet*, because I want to know everything there is to know about you."

"You could look into my mind."

"You could look into mine."

"That wouldn't be polite," she denied.

"Exactly."

She liked that he didn't want to rip explanations from her, even though he could. She liked the sound of his voice and the way, for such a big man, his touch was gentle. She didn't want him to know any of those things.

"I grew up in a family of martial arts practitioners. When I say that, I mean for generations. My parents believed in the lifestyle, and we lived it. I will say, both had tempers, especially my dad, so the discipline was considered essential. When you grow up in that world, everyone you know practices some martial art—most learn several. I can't remember a time I wasn't working on learning some discipline from various countries around the world."

"I wondered why you were so confident when you attacked my three would-be murderers. You moved so well, and your kicks and punches were very powerful."

She didn't want him to know that a simple compliment uttered so casually by him could affect her as it did, could please her so much. She didn't even know why herself. "My parents were very loving. We might have been disciplined, and we were expected to work hard, but they were loving, demonstrative parents."

She couldn't keep the tears out of her voice. No matter how many times she went over what had happened, she couldn't stop the horrible emptiness that sat in her like a giant, gaping hole. She dug hard for several minutes. The only sound in the tent was her labored breathing. Andor barely made a sound, and the few times she snuck looks at him, his chest was hardly rising and falling. That scared her, but now that she knew he was a healer, she was going to put all her hopes into that.

"You say 'we,' as if there were more of you."

Again, his voice was so gentle it turned her heart over. Not prying. Not acting as if she owed him an explanation or that he was in some way entitled to one. He didn't even try to hurry her. She knew, because she dug for another few minutes.

"Can you scoot to your left just a foot or so? It's deeper and you're going to get jarred when you slide into it, but the soil is very rich in minerals."

"I need to remove my clothes."

Her gaze flew to his. Now he had his eyes open, and he didn't blink. His gaze held hers captive. It was impossible to look away.

"I need to be completely immersed in the soil to heal myself."

She licked at suddenly dry lips. It wasn't as if he could do anything. He was practically dead. She took a deep breath and nodded. "I can cut them off. Just keep me from throwing up on you."

"Cut them off?" he echoed, one dark eyebrow arched.

She unsheathed her favorite knife. "The blade can cut through any-thing. The material shouldn't be a problem."

"I can rid myself of my clothes. You keep digging. I just don't want you to think I'm about to demand anything of you. Sexually, that is."

She burst out laughing. She was thankful he made her laugh because just the thought of him naked made her body heat up unexpectedly and laughing eased the sudden clenching in her deepest core. "I would have to think you were a zombie, with as many holes as you have in you, if you were suddenly to start making moves. I'll pour dirt over you while you remove your clothes."

He nodded, his hands going to his chest. Lorraine turned her back to give him some privacy. She knew it was going to hurt him. He didn't seem to ever acknowledge that he was in pain, but she could see it re-flected in his eyes and the deep lines on his face.

"The 'we' you hear is my brother. Theodore. Teddy. I used to call him my Teddy bear. He was so sweet. The best brother ever." The ache in her grew and she rocked back and forth, pressing three fingers against her lips as if that could keep the rest of the story from being told, let alone happening. The tent seemed to revolve, spinning like a whirling top. There wasn't enough air to breathe. Her lungs felt raw and burning. Her throat closed until she was gasping, trying to get air.

"Lorraine. *Sívamet.* Breathe with me. Turn around." There was command in his voice. Steel. One didn't dare disobey.

She turned, and his hand caught hers. He brought her palm right over the top of the dirt smashed into the hole in his chest, and settled it over his heart.

"Feel me breathing. Feel my heart beating. Let yours follow. In. Out. Just like that. Your body knows how to do it."

Her body followed his until they were in perfect sync, and the lump was gone as well as the terrible burning sensation. "I'm sorry." What else was there to say?

"Do not be sorry. You have nothing to be sorry for. And yes, this soil is very good, very rich in nutrients. If you could continue to dig it a little deeper and cover me with more, I would appreciate it."

She knew he was giving her something to do so she wasn't thinking too much about the fact that she'd made a fool of herself. She looked down, expecting to see him naked, but he was covered in a thin layer of dirt already. She began scooping.

"My brother killed my parents and then himself." It was better to just blurt it out, the elephant in the room no one wanted to talk about yet everyone was *desperate* to talk about. She kept her head down. "He wanted to bulk up so he began using steroids. I was away at college, so I had no idea. Mom and Dad began to suspect because he was particularly susceptible to the side effects."

"Did they talk to you about it?"

She shook her head. She didn't want to hear the sympathy in his voice. That would just bring on the waterworks. "I didn't find out until after. They talked to some of their friends about it and apparently decided to confront him. You know—like an intervention. There were three couples: Mom and Dad; Dad's brother, Uncle Walter, and his wife, Aunt

Janey; and Paula and Lincoln Steanor, two friends who were the parents of my brother's best friend. He apparently flew into a rage, went into his bedroom, got a gun and came out and opened fire."

She stopped shoveling, her hands shaking. She couldn't look at him. "It was two days before Thanksgiving. I came home about three hours after he shot them all and then turned the gun on himself. I opened the door and walked into a bloodbath. Mom, Dad, Aunt Janey, Paula, Lincoln and my brother were all dead. Uncle Walter lived another five hours. He told me and the police what happened."

"Lorraine."

Just the way he said her name nearly was her undoing. She jumped up, flinging the dirt in the saucepot over him and then rushing out into the night. The moment she was out of his sight, she put her head down, hands on opposite knees, and tried to breathe. Her life had been ripped right out of the headlines. Theodore would never be known for all the good things he'd done. The groceries he'd bought for elderly neighbors. The lawns he'd mowed for them, and porches he'd fixed. He'd never taken money, not even for gas.

No one would remember that he'd taken a job at the local movie theater when her father had broken his leg and couldn't work as a carpenter and they'd needed to pay bills. Or that he'd gotten up on Saturday mornings and worked in the soup kitchen to give meals to the homeless. So many memories. So many good times.

He would never be remembered as an incredible athlete, or for all the trophies he'd earned for the dojo where the family had trained. The football he'd played, so successful as a receiver he'd helped bring their high school to victory over and over.

He would forever be remembered as a mass murderer. He was her beloved brother, and he had killed everyone she'd had in her life. Everyone she'd loved in her life. He'd left her with nothing, and no amount of counseling would make it right. No amount of counseling could change what had happened. No amount of meditation would ever give her answers.

She straightened slowly, tears blurring her vision as she looked up at the stars. No amount of tears was ever going to make her heart stop hurting. She glanced over her shoulder toward her tent. She'd fled the city and come into the mountains. She was an experienced camper, both in very hot weather and extreme cold. It wasn't that she planned to stay in the wilderness forever, but she needed to feel whole again.

She was so angry. Angry at her brother. How could he have done such a terrible thing? But he'd been out of his mind. She was angry at his decision to start a drug that had such bad press. He'd known the side effects of taking steroids, yet he'd done so in spite of the risks. He hadn't been out of his mind when he'd made that choice. Her parents. The moment they'd known, why hadn't they called her? Why hadn't they taken the steroids from him, gotten him out of the country if they'd had to? They'd had friends, resources, choices.

She wanted to scream until her throat was torn and no sound would emerge. Until it was raw and bloody, just like the bodies of her family and friends. She'd done just that on some nights when the nightmares came and all she saw was a river of blood. Where had her friends gone? All the students she'd trained with from the time she was a toddler running around in the dojo with her mother and father—where were they? Somehow, she was tainted by what her brother had done. They smiled and said how sorry they were, but they refused to come near her. It was the same with high school and college friends. And then there were the reporters.

*Sívamet. Come back to me. The tent is as refreshing as the outdoors. You are safe in here. I am completely covered. Bring in your sleeping bag and lay it beside me.*

She closed her eyes against the need welling up in her—the need of comfort. Someone who didn't blame her. Someone who had never said a word against her brother. The whispers. The looks. The questions. She hated them. She'd run from them, just gathered her camping gear, took the best tent and as much cash as she could safely carry and gone to the place where she most remembered happy times for her family.

*I don't know how to be okay anymore. I don't even know who I am.* It was such a silly thing to say to a man who might be dying. She slowly turned as realization dawned on her. Three men had attempted to murder Andor

Katona in the most brutal and sadistic way possible. Instead of raging, instead of anger, he was calm, even courteous and looking out for her feelings. What kind of man was he?

She had come to the mountains to try to find peace. She had tried meditation several times a day unsuccessfully, but she was determined that she would eventually find her zen. Maybe some of Andor's peace would rub off on her if she was around him enough. It was worth a try.

*Why aren't you angry with those men? The ones trying to stake you?*

*They are rather inept at their self-appointed job. I felt sorry for them. They are misguided. Although, now, giving it some thought, believing in vampires, purporting to see one—and of course the undead are the very epitome of evil—mistaking me for one is an insult, but it can be overlooked.*

She frowned. She had made up her mind that she'd stay out in the wilderness until she could overcome her anger and learn to take the high road no matter what anyone said or did regarding her family. There were dozens of unlearned lessons she needed, and she'd brought the most important books on meditation and the way to achieve inner peace. Three idiots believing they saw the very epitome of evil in what turned out to be a nice guy had made her anger worse.

She'd been chanting her mantras in singsong, hoping she would eventually achieve the ability to better listen to others. To improve her energy. To allow her to gain peace from her surroundings, no matter what those surroundings were. To have better sensitivity toward others. She had a list, and it took a long time to go through that list as she chanted.

First Andor's thoughts had disturbed her. She heard him clearly weighing the decision to live or die, and it had smacked too close to home. Had her brother done that? Sat in his room and considered whether or not to shoot his family and friends and then himself? All the chanting in the world hadn't overcome those thoughts. Then she became aware of the *feeling* in the air. That stench of fanaticism. Of *murder*. She'd been furious all over again. This time she could do something about it. This time, those wanting to kill another human being weren't going to succeed. She'd stopped them, but she hadn't done so peacefully.

It wasn't that she minded kicking or punching or hitting the three killers over the head with her saucepot to stop them from killing some-one, but she should have been able to do it without anger. She should have been calm, like Andor.

*Lorraine. Come inside. I am only peaceful because when you first felt me, I was not feeling any emotion. I was incapable. Come back inside.*

She wanted to go inside. She actually didn't want to be alone anymore—at least when she had the opportunity to be around Andor. He was an intriguing man. She honestly didn't know how he could survive, but if he was a powerful healer—and she'd read that some could cure all kinds of things—then maybe he really could repair his body.

*Give me a minute.* She spent a few minutes looking up at the stars. One of the things she loved most about camping was the night. She rarely made a fire, not unless it was very cold or she had to cook something. Mostly she didn't cook. She didn't leave anything behind, wanting to leave every site even better than the way she'd found it.

Lorraine walked around the tent, widening her circle, needing to get a feel for this campsite. It was lower than she would have liked, but there was no dragging Andor up the small hill at the base of the taller mountain. Still, it was defensible, although, again, they weren't near water. She always liked two escape routes and water close just in case of an emergency. Defending a wounded man from idiot vampire killers or the epitome of evil—a vampire, providing there was such a thing—needed careful planning.

*Lorraine.*

The way he said her name got to her in places she'd forgotten she had. The notes brushed along the walls of her mind intimately. Not just her mind, other places. That brought her up short. What the *hell* was she thinking? Andor was nearly dead, his body riddled with terrible wounds. She hadn't even seen him. Not really. She couldn't look at him with his body covered in blood. She shuddered. The fact that for a moment she went to another place was just wrong.

*There is nothing wrong with you.*

Great. He was reading her mind. Now she really couldn't look at him.

*This form of communication is very intimate. When you speak to me, I have the same reaction.*

She was able to breathe easier. At least she wasn't alone. *So, it's common to feel this . . . connection? You've had it with others?* She honestly didn't know if she wanted him to answer her in the affirmative or negative.

*I have only spoken this way to other males, and I assure you, I do not have the same reaction with them that I have with you. Come back inside.*

She wrapped her arms around her middle and took another slow look around their campsite. *If we're attacked again, this place isn't very defensible.*

*I will place safeguards to prevent anyone from coming near. Please come back inside. You are staying away because you are upset and you do not want me to witness your tears. I feel them, Lorraine, and I cannot come to you to comfort you.*

Was that what she was doing? Hiding? She knew she was. That was what she'd decided to do, at least until she felt she was strong enough to face everyone again. She needed to find that place of peace Andor had found.

*How do you do it? How can you be so calm when you might be dying and those men robbed you of your life?*

*Come inside, lie down and rest. I'll tell you.*

She wanted to know his story, and the pull to be with him was stronger than she first thought and growing in her the more they communicated telepathically. She decided it would be far better to be closer to him physically than talk to him mentally. She was in more danger from the intimate communication. There was just something about the way he filled those empty places inside of her that she couldn't resist.

# 3

"Are you comfortable?" Andor kept his gaze fixed on Lorraine's face. She clearly had no idea how beautiful she was, or what danger she was in. She was confident in her skills to protect herself, and he understood why. She had training. She was far better than average when it came to defending herself, man or woman. The problem was, she was dealing with a Carpathian, not a human, and he had no intentions of letting her get away.

"Yes. I should ask you the same thing." She turned her head to look down at him.

She had finished covering him up to his neck in rich, dark soil. Already he could feel the healing properties working on his wounds. He wasn't out of the woods, so to speak. He needed more blood and a good healer. He had sent out the call to his brethren, using their common path, not the one used by most Carpathians. Vampires would have been able to hear that one as well.

"I am as comfortable as possible." He was, as much as he could be under the circumstances, but he needed to shut down his heart and lungs to keep from losing any more blood. He had definitely slowed the leaks, but until he could get a healer there to help him, he was still in trouble.

He sent her a small smile. "You're indulging me."

She turned on her side and propped her head up with one hand. "Yes. I figure if you're right, and the soil helps, it's all to the good. If you're wrong and you get some raging infection, at least I granted your last wish before you died."

"I have decided I want to live."

"The great debate you had going earlier. It didn't make sense until I saw all those wounds on your body. You really were in a battle before the three stooges showed up."

He picked up from her mind that the reference to "three stooges" was from a long-ago television show. Her natural shields were lowered because she'd started to grow comfortable with him. He knew he would have to work on that with her. They could never take the chance that a vampire nearby might read her thoughts, or creep into her mind.

"I was in a battle. I know I look like I didn't do very well against them, but in my defense, there were several of them. I managed to defeat them, and while I was trying to heal the wounds, the band of assassins showed up." There was just the slightest bit of ego in telling her the truth. He didn't want her to think her lifemate couldn't take care of her.

"I wondered how they managed to sneak up on you and do so much damage."

"To heal a body, one has to shed their own body and become pure spirit. I didn't have anyone guarding the empty shell I left behind. That gave them their opportunity."

Her eyes widened. "Could you do that now? I could guard you. I wouldn't let anything happen to you." Her tone was skeptical but hopeful.

He nearly groaned. He wasn't making a good showing as a potential husband or mate. "I'm too weak."

"I'll give you more blood."

It was a generous offer considering she didn't like anything to do with blood and she would have to remove the shields completely from her mind as she'd done before. "Thank you, *sívamet*. I appreciate your offer and certainly will take you up on it later, but at the moment, I wish to hear your voice. It soothes me and keeps the pain at bay."

"What is *sívamet*? You call me that often. What language is it?"

"I'm from the Carpathian Mountains and *sívamet* is a word used in my world for a woman a man . . ." He had to be cautious. "Cares for," he settled on. He couldn't very well call her "his heart" when she had no understanding of their connection. "I do not know how to give you an exact translation that would make sense to you."

"But it's a good thing?"

"Yes, Lorraine. A very good thing. You think I was debating whether or not to end my life because I was wounded and in pain, but that wasn't the reason. I had given up all hope of finding the woman meant for me. I was no longer certain I could endure loneliness without her."

She frowned. His heart clenched hard in his chest. He had never thought in terms of *cute* or *adorable*. They were silly words humans came up with to describe children. Lorraine was not a child by any means. Nothing about her suggested a child, yet that frown, to him, was adorable. There was no other word for it.

He was fascinated by every expression that crossed her face. Every thought she had in her head. He wanted to know every single thing about her life before he was with her. More than anything, he wanted to comfort her and take away the pain he felt radiating from her every second she breathed. He was ashamed that he had considered ending his life, even for a moment. Had he done so, had he allowed the humans to succeed in killing him, she would have suffered alone.

"Andor, you don't give up on life over a broken love affair."

He could tell she wanted to say a lot more but had carefully chosen her words not to offend him. He couldn't stop himself from reaching out and catching the thick strands of chestnut-colored hair between his fingers. It felt as silky as it looked. As soft. "So beautiful." He murmured the words aloud. He thought them in his head. Tucked them somewhere close. Her hair was beautiful, but so was her soul. That half that she unknowingly held for him, it was beautiful as well. So much light in so small a package.

"Andor? This is important."

So was feeling the silk of her hair and admiring the color. He hadn't done such things in centuries. They were simple to her, but to him such things were miracles. "I'm listening, but you got it wrong, *mica*, I was looking for my woman. I hadn't found her, and I was giving up. You're absolutely right, though, I should never have even thought of giving up." He was passing that advice on to his brethren. They needed to know their women would come to them in their darkest hour, or at the most unexpected time.

Relief softened the glint of temper in her eyes. He liked that fire in her. She would need it, dealing with their life together. She might want to stamp it out, but he knew sometimes the flare of heat, directed in the right way, could win battles.

"Tell me about your life, Andor."

He had known that question had been coming and didn't want to lie to her. He didn't want to scare her off, either. "My people are few and scattered. Most live in the Carpathian Mountains, but a few live here in the United States. I was scouting for any threats when I ran across the ones I . . ." He searched for a benign word, but couldn't find one. He sighed. "Hunted. I was hunting for the enemy. I didn't expect so many and that is how I was wounded so severely."

She was silent for so long he wasn't certain she was going to speak. Her eyes stayed glued to his. She didn't look away, nor did she look as if she didn't believe him. "You don't believe in the police." There was no sarcasm in her eventual comment, merely a statement of fact.

He couldn't stop himself from playing with her hair, running it through his fingers and bringing it occasionally to his face so he could inhale her scent. She was out in the wilderness camping and she still smelled feminine and good enough to devour. He tried to figure out the scents. Grapefruit for certain. Something else. It was faint. Elusive. A little wild.

"No. We have to handle things ourselves."

"When you said you cleaned up the battlefield, did that mean you buried the bodies?"

Her eyes were steady on his, but he felt her holding her breath. There was that first touch of fear in her.

"*Sívamet*, I am no murderer. There are things you need to know, things that will frighten you. I will open my mind so you can see for yourself and then, once you have, I'll answer your questions." It was a gamble. A huge one. He couldn't stop her if she chose to run. If he survived, he would go after her, and he'd tie them together so she couldn't run from him. He had no doubt that he would be able to win her over. She was his true lifemate, and no one else would do for her any more than another woman would do for him.

"Tell me about your tattoos. They're very unusual. I saw them when you rolled into the depression of soil I dug out. They drift up your neck and over your shoulders." She touched one of the rigid scars just behind his shoulder.

Andor just offered to open his mind to her and she hadn't responded. He refused to cheat and touch her mind or influence her in any way. If she wanted to move to a different topic in order to have time to think about it, he would happily give her that. Talking to her distracted him from the pain. He needed her blood to find the strength to set safeguards around them. The vampires he had defeated had to have sent word to their masters and it would be common knowledge by now that he had been wounded. They would send others to kill him.

*We are on our way to you, Andor. Ferro travels with me.*

Andor's heart leapt and then settled. The voice in his mind, on that path the brethren had forged, was still a good distance away, but they had heard his call. Sandu and Ferro were monks and had passed two centuries in the monastery with him.

Ferro was considered the most dangerous of all of them. He had lost his family early and with that, his emotions. He was an efficient killing machine and would be nearly unstoppable as a vampire. He had hesitated leaving the monastery, determined to keep his honor, but the lure of a lifemate was too strong for any of them to resist.

That hope given to them had been a lifeline to desperate men. Their lives had loomed in front of them endlessly and this last hope had been grasped at, even if it might not have been the wisest choice for all of them. Yet, he had found Lorraine. Even Ferro had the chance of finding his lifemate—he just needed to be watched very, very closely.

*I am not alone, Sandu. My wounds are very severe. I am safe for the moment and with me is my lifemate. She is unaware of the fact that she belongs with me, nor can I bind her to me.*

There was a moment of silence while Sandu digested that and what it meant. *Your injuries are mortal?*

*Yes. Several of them. I will take her blood and set safeguards, but I cannot go to ground. I am partially immersed in the soil, and my wounds are packed with it, but I will not survive another rising. Once I shut down my heart and lungs, she will think I am lost to her and she might leave my body to call for officials to come. If she does that . . .*

*We are making our way toward you. We will push it as long as we can before we go to ground and rise as early as possible. I have sent word for Gary to come. He is the strongest healer we have available to us. He is a distance away as well, but says he has already started toward you.*

Andor didn't know what to think about that. Gary Daratrazanoff was unknown to him. The prince had sent him to be Tariq Asenguard's second-in-command. He was a Daratrazanoff, a member of one of the ancient lines of guardians and healers. Andor had no choice. He knew it would take not only Gary, but also his two fellow monks to save him.

*I ask that you watch over my woman.* He sent the image of Lorraine to Sandu and Ferro.

*She will be safe.* Sandu made his promise.

Their word was their honor. Sandu wouldn't fail him.

*She will be safe.*

Andor closed his eyes briefly. Ferro giving his word was extraordinary. As a rule, the man didn't speak. When he did, it was to issue an order, and even that was extremely rare. It was a relief to know that he'd given his word to protect Lorraine. Ferro, like Sandu, would never go back on that word, which meant, no matter how close Ferro was to darkness, how much that stain had spread through him, as long as Lorraine lived, so would Ferro and he would hold to his honor.

"Are you talking to someone?"

Andor's gaze jumped back to Lorraine's face. "How did you know?"

"I'm catching a word here and there. Why are you so uneasy speaking with them?"

How did he answer that? "Our species is older than yours." There it was. She was either going to believe him or not. He had offered her the chance to look into his mind, and that offer was still open. "When we have lived too long, life can become intolerable."

Her small white teeth sank into her lower lip, but her gaze didn't waver from his. "The reason you're still alive is your species is different than mine? Because no human being could possibly survive those wounds, healer or not."

"Precisely the reason," he agreed. "But even I cannot hope to live without aid. I need healers to help me and I put out the call. It is a toss-up to see who will arrive first, enemy or friend. Whoever went to ground closest to us will get here first."

She pulled back just a little. Not enough to be worrisome, but she was analyzing what he'd said and she was an intelligent woman. The things he'd told her had to seem far-fetched in her modern world.

"Explain *going to ground*."

"Are you certain you would not prefer to look into my mind and see the things I am telling you about?"

"I'm very certain. You tell me. I can always look if your explanation becomes too ludicrous to even contemplate."

He figured that would happen very soon. He tugged on her hair and brought the strands against his mouth, rubbing them back and forth across his lips. Again, he expected her to pull away from him, but she didn't. That meant something to him. He needed to touch her in some way, to stay connected. It gave him more pleasure than he had ever imagined just to feel the silk of her hair against his skin.

"I am Carpathian. We are an ancient species with many powerful gifts. With gifts comes balance. Always. The sun will burn us. We must sleep in the soil to rejuvenate, and during the midday, when the sun is at its highest, our bodies go into a paralyzed state. If you were to see me during daylight hours, you would think I was dead, when in fact, I am not."

He waited. She just watched him closely without making a comment. He couldn't tell by her expression whether or not she believed him, but he resisted the urge to touch her mind.

"When a male is born, his soul is split in two and the other half goes into the body of a female. Sometimes she is born immediately, other times not. Sometimes she lives a complete life cycle and is not found by her lifemate—her male. When that happens, she dies and is reborn again and again until he finds her. We thought, for centuries, that she had to be Carpathian. Our prince discovered by accident that a psychic human female could hold the other half of our souls."

She frowned. "You're saying that this woman you're looking for, and have been looking for, might not be of your own species."

He nodded slowly. "We had no idea. None. Too many of our males were lost because we did not have that information."

"Lost to suicide?"

"Some met the dawn, yes. Others chose to give up their souls and embrace evil."

She shook her head slightly, and this time, he could read her. She didn't believe him.

"You're back to vampires. If there were vampires in the world, don't you think we'd know about it? Come on, Andor. They wouldn't just be in the scary horror films, or the romance films, they'd be out feeding on and scaring the crap out of the public."

He conceded the point with a nod. "That is true, unless hunters are sent out to destroy them and erase the memories of anyone who has seen them. Most who have witnessed them are now dead, so the mop-up on removing memories doesn't occur that often."

"Where do these vampires come from?"

"They are Carpathians who have chosen to give up their souls." He wasn't going to lie to her or soften the blow. "*We* have the potential to become vampire. I do. Every male must find his lifemate or eventually must end his life in the sun, or every night that he exists, he poses a danger to everyone around him."

"You included."

He nodded. "Me especially, although at the moment I am far too weak to harm anyone."

"Why you especially?"

He was beginning to fall for her hard. It had nothing to do with her looks, and everything to do with her intellect and brightness. She had no idea how truly calm and disciplined she was to listen patiently when the things he was telling her had to sound completely absurd. Even so, she was paying attention and trying to suspend disbelief in order to judge for herself whether or not there was a possibility of realism in his statement.

"I have lived far too long. When the males of our species reach two hundred years, they lose all emotion. They feel nothing. Not good or bad. They simply exist. At first memories sustain them, the memory of how they felt with loved ones, that sort of thing, but after years go by, those memories begin to disappear. Around the same time that we lose emotions, colors fade to a dull gray. We hunt the vampire, and those vampires are often family members or friends we grew up with. Killing takes pieces of one's soul until little remains but honor. Honor must sustain us until that day we choose to become evil, or to leave the world."

She took a deep breath and let it out. "That's a pretty bleak life you're describing, Andor."

He nodded. "It is."

She was silent again, her eyes steady on his. Her fingers beat out a little tattoo on her sleeping bag. "If I look into your mind, what am I going to see?"

"Things that will terrify you." He was honest.

"Things you've done to others?"

"Things done to me. Things done to innocent humans but not by me. And things done by me in retaliation for what was done to humans and to my people."

"Aren't you afraid that your telling me these things might make me leave you here alone to die? You're taking a big chance."

"You asked me and I answered honestly. There is the possibility that you will think I'm completely crazy. There's also the possibility that you'll run, but that isn't too likely."

Her long lashes swept down and then back up. The impact of those green eyes on him was enormous. He crushed the silky strands of her hair in his hand, holding them tightly as if he could hold her to him.

"Why do you say that?"

"It isn't in you to leave a helpless person to die. Even if you thought I was a bad person, you wouldn't leave."

She didn't argue that point. "Were you looking for this woman when you met these vampires?"

"I had foolishly given up on her. I was an advanced guard for a man named Tariq Asenguard. Have you heard of him?"

She nodded. "He owns a string of nightclubs with partners. He has a big club in San Diego. I don't know a lot about him other than that."

"He is Carpathian. Like me. He found his lifemate, and they have a compound—an estate—surrounded by other Carpathians. On every continent, Carpathians have been sent to hunt vampires to keep others safe. Tariq was named as the voice of our prince here in the United States. One of my brethren from the monastery, Dragomir, had come here, found his woman, and needed our help. We answered his call. That's how I ended up being in this area."

"Tariq Asenguard, the very hot millionaire or billionaire or whatever he is, is Carpathian?" There was disbelief in her voice.

"If one lives a long time, it is not difficult to acquire a fortune. I am uncertain why you refer to him as 'hot,' but if that is a compliment, I am not happy with you for giving it to him."

She flashed a small smile, and a few of the knots he'd thought were pain from his wounds unraveled. "You think I'm her."

"Her?"

"The one. Your lifemate. You think I'm that woman, the one with your soul."

"One does not think; one knows. I know. It is impossible to make a mistake."

"Enlighten me."

He tugged on her hair until she yelped and glared at him, but she still didn't pull away. He liked her little glare. It made him feel as if they were a couple who had been together for a long time and she felt comfortable with him. If he didn't live through the following day, he had this with her.

"I have been without colors or emotions for centuries. Far, far too long. Long enough that I had given up hope. Then you charged to my rescue and I felt once more and saw colors so bright they hurt my eyes. They still do. It took a little bit of time to sort things out."

She was silent again, her gaze drifting over his face. Finally, she shook her head. "I think you're a little delirious. Drink some water, and I'll make a run outside to take care of business and then you can give yourself another transfusion."

"You aren't going to look into my mind?"

"No. I'm going to let you have your fantasy and I'm going to stay sane a little while longer. I have to set up your protection just in case."

"I have to set up yours. You cannot fight vampires. They have to be killed a certain way, and even with your impressive skills, you would be unable to succeed."

"Hey, I've seen the movies."

"The movies got it wrong."

"Well, perhaps you'd better instruct me."

He found it interesting that she didn't sound sarcastic. She didn't even sound as if she thought he was crazy. He had the feeling there was a big part of her that believed him. "You really cannot fight them."

"Even so, Andor, if they come and I have no choice, at least if you tell me what I'm doing, I'd have a fighting chance. Without knowing, I wouldn't have any chance at all."

There was logic in what she said, whether he liked it or not. He might not wake up, and if that happened and the vampires arrived before his brethren, they would kill her for certain. If one came, and he was newly turned, a pawn for the master vampires in the area, there was a small chance she could stay alive.

Andor nodded slowly. He was tiring and that made him worry even

more that the blood was leaking out of his body too fast. If he tried healing himself and used up all his strength, there would be no time for the
others to come. On the other hand, if he didn't and he bled out, Lorraine
would be as lost as he was.

"The heart of a vampire must be removed and burned. He can regen-
erate over and over if you do not burn the heart. He can take any shape,
including those of your loved ones he picks out of your mind. His voice
can rule you, compel you to do his bidding, even things abhorrent to you.
You are telepathic and know about shields, so you have to have yours up
and strong at all times in his presence. You can't be deceived by his lies or
the images he creates."

"So, I'd need something to burn him and his heart as well."

He liked that she sounded thoughtful. A part of her was actually
thinking about the possibilities. She wasn't certain if his information was
the truth, but she was still giving it consideration.

"Yes. But even if he appears to burn, you have to make certain the
heart is destroyed, completely incinerated."

She nodded. "You're right. I wouldn't want to have to fight such a
creature, but if I had to do it, I want to know how. What about insects
and rats, like you see in movies?"

"He can create an army of both, the same with bats. He can create
human puppets." He gave a small sigh. "There were so few of us, but I
think Carpathians thought that we would eventually win the war on vampires and just have to occasionally destroy one here and there."

"Why didn't you enlist the aid of humans if they were in danger, too?"

"You know why. Men like those three. There are always fanatics, and
we would be persecuted and forced to defend ourselves. Most of us stayed
away from humans. Tariq is one who didn't. He liked humans and embraced their technology. That gave him an insight the rest of us didn't
have. The vampires were making a stand, here, in the United States,
building their armies and learning to use computers and software to track
hunters, and also to find psychic women."

"How did they do that?"

"They have a psychic testing center, the Morrison Center. Men and women go there either for fun or really believing they have talent. As soon as it is determined that someone really has psychic ability, they're targeted."

She was silent a moment. She shifted her weight off her hip, turning over onto her back and staring up at the ceiling of the tent. "The Morrison Center?"

"Yes. They have them all over the world now."

"Representatives came onto the college campus where I was going to school. I almost went, but decided against it. I didn't like anyone knowing my business. That was something my father drilled into me."

He remained silent. It had been that close. Had she filled out their forms and been tested, she might have been lost to him.

"They were there during the sunny part of the day."

"Because the men and women who work in those places have no idea that their system has been hacked."

She frowned, but kept staring up at the ceiling. "Can you heal yourself? If I give you a lot of my blood, can you heal yourself?"

He shook his head. "The best I can hope for, *sívamet*, is for your blood to keep me alive and to give me the strength I need to set safeguards my brethren can unravel but vampires cannot. That way, if the enemy gets here first, you will be safe."

"I'm going outside for a few minutes. Is the ceiling on this tent heavy enough to keep you from burning during daylight?"

"I will shut down my heart and lungs, and you will have to finish burying me." He kept his eyes on her.

The breath exploding from her lungs in protest was audible. Her body snapped around so she was facing him. "I am *not* going to bury you alive. It isn't going to happen. I semi-believe you but I don't at the same time, so if you're insane, then too bad, I'm not helping screw you up." She leapt up and nearly ripped the door to the tent getting out.

She was fast. Very fast. *You will need that speed if you have to fight a vampire. Hitting them with your saucepot will not kill them.*

*Don't talk to me right now. I'm upset and I need time to think.*

*You cannot be out there too long. I cannot stay awake much longer. That* much was true, but it wasn't because the dawn was creeping slowly toward them. Nor the fact that he didn't like her where he couldn't see the enemy coming at him. He couldn't move, his body already beginning to succumb to the pain he'd kept at bay through sheer effort. That effort was costing him.

She didn't respond, and he closed his eyes and allowed himself to think about finding her. How it was so simple. One moment his world was the same, and the next it was entirely different. One moment. That was all it had taken. He remembered searching. Looking for her from continent to continent. He had known then it was like looking for the proverbial needle in a haystack, but there was the theory that fate would eventually throw her in front of her lifemate. That belief came from the fact that the two halves of the same soul would forever be reaching toward each other.

He didn't know if the theory was true or not, but she had come out of nowhere. Her quest for peace, wrapped up in whatever terms she called it, had brought her to him right at the very moment when he'd considered giving up.

*Csecsemō, thank you for staying even if you are having a difficult time believing me.*

*The problem, Andor, isn't that I'm having that difficult of a time believing you, it's that I do believe you. I don't want to look into your mind because I'm afraid of what I'll see, and that makes me a coward.*

*You are no coward, Lorraine.*

*I have to look if I'm going to protect us. I'm working up my courage.*

*I despise the fact that I have met you at my weakest moment. In my world, it is my responsibility to protect my woman. Not the other way around.*

*Welcome to the new world, Andor. Right at the moment, if you're not crazy, I would much rather be living in yours, where you have to fight some hideous creature capable of tearing your body apart the way something did.*

Was she weeping again? He didn't think so, but he put his hand over his aching heart just in case. The agony was no longer as physical for him as emotional. He really felt useless lying in the ground, his strong body so weak he had to rely on his woman—his human woman—to protect him.

That just wasn't done. It was sobering and very humbling. It was possible he needed a lesson in humility, but not right then, not when she was in danger.

*I can do this.* There was determination in her voice.

She was returning. He could feel her. He wanted to make one blood exchange so he could find her no matter where she was in the world. They didn't need it to forge a telepathic bond, but it would make their connection even stronger. The problem was, he needed every single drop of blood he had.

She pushed open the tent door and then zipped it up behind her. She had her backpack and she opened the flap and began pulling out items. She set them close to her sleeping bag, on the far side where he couldn't see them clearly, but he could smell them.

"Weapons? Gun oil?"

"I'm out in the middle of nowhere. I expected wild animals, but figured I wouldn't have that much trouble with them."

"You had a gun but you brought a cooking pot to a site where you knew someone was attempting murder?" He spoke quietly, for the first time anger beginning to stir. He recognized the emotion, although it was foreign to him. She had a weapon but hadn't armed herself before exposing herself to danger. That was unacceptable.

"I was at the stream with my saucepot when I heard your thoughts and then realized someone was trying to kill you. I didn't have time to run back to my camp and get out a gun. I thought you'd be dead by then."

"What about you? Did you think someone might kill you?"

"No. I thought I was going to bash someone in the head. I didn't realize there were three of them, and even if I had, I wouldn't have gone back for the gun. It would have taken too long."

*I want to shake you right now.* He didn't say it aloud because he couldn't. He needed the more intimate form of communication so she would feel his emotions. Feel the way he felt so helpless.

*Please don't. Give yourself a transfusion instead.*

*Remove your shields.*

She sat close to him and extended her arm. "No, this time I'm going to watch you." There was pure challenge in her voice.

"Lorraine. Be very careful what you wish for."

"I didn't see how you did it last time. I want to see this time. You stay out of my head."

He knew what she was doing, proving to herself one way or the other that he was as crazy as a loon, or she was really in trouble and he was telling the truth. He also knew she had carefully analyzed everything he'd told her about himself and the Carpathian people.

Having grown up reading vampire stories and watching the films, she would acquaint the things he'd told her with vampires. Sleeping in the ground. Paralyzed during the day. Burning in the sun. She was demanding to know if he drank blood, or if he had somehow, in that short time, in his weakened state, managed to give himself a transfusion without tubing and needles. She'd put it all together and realized giving himself a transfusion the way humans would was impossible.

"Lorraine." He tried again.

"Just do it. I mean it, Andor. If you need blood, take it."

He took her hand very gently in his, his thumb sliding over the pulse thudding in her inner wrist. "I would ordinarily, since it is your blood, the blood of the woman who is mine, take it differently, but since I cannot, this will have to do."

He brought her wrist to his mouth. Kissed that now frantically beating pulse. His tongue slid over her skin. She gasped, a small sound he felt in his heart. His teeth scraped. Teased. She bit her lip, her eyes going dark with heat. He didn't look away, refusing to allow her to pull her steady gaze from his. He used his tongue a second time, making certain the skin was numb before he sank his teeth deep. She cried out and tried to jerk her arm away, but he held her firmly.

Her breathing was suddenly erratic. Too fast. Her heart accelerated. He reached for her, needing their more intimate connection and knowing she did as well.

*You are safe, Lorraine. You will always be safe from me. You are the one person in this world I could never harm for any reason. The things I told you about myself are the truth. I am Carpathian, not vampire. I hunt the undead.*

She didn't fight him, but he could feel her withdrawal, the way she curled into herself.

*Sívamet. I do not want you to fear me.*

*Is that what you think I'm feeling?*

He had been careful, even talking to her telepathically, not to push into her thoughts. He knew she didn't want that. She'd told him to stay out of her mind. He stared into her eyes; all the while her exquisite taste burst through his mouth and into his cells. He had craved this—had been denying himself for what seemed an eternity—and now that her blood was sustaining him, he savored every drop. He didn't want to stop. Not ever. The way she tasted was unlike anything he'd ever experienced.

*What are you feeling?*

Her breathing had changed again. Heightened. Her face was pale, but a soft flush had stolen up her neck to tinge her cheeks. Her green eyes had darkened. She shifted positions again, stretching out on the sleeping bag, her arm relaxed as it lay across his chest, her wrist to his mouth.

*This is the most erotic thing I've ever experienced and I can't even tell you why.*

His woman. So courageous to admit what she was feeling. He heard the curiosity in her voice as well as the guilt. She didn't want to have any kind of sexual feelings toward a man she knew was so badly injured.

*You are supposed to feel that way when your lifemate takes your blood. It would be terrible if it hurt you.*

*This isn't nearly the sacrifice I thought it would be. The good part is, I didn't see any blood.*

*You thought it would be a sacrifice to give me blood?* Amusement welled up. They were in dire circumstances, and she still could make him find moments of pure happiness.

*Yes. But I just think I will sleep for a while. Take what you need, Andor. It's all right.*

# 4

Lorraine woke, turned her head and looked at the mound of dirt beside her. Her heart slammed hard in her chest and she sat up fast, her breath coming in an agitated frenzy. She gulped air and then realized that made the dizzy sensation even worse. She put her hand over the soft dirt right where she knew Andor's heart should be. He had convinced her to cover even his head. His mouth. His nose. There was no rise and fall beneath that blanket of dirt, but he'd told her not to expect one. He said he was shutting down his heart and lungs to give himself more of a chance, hoping his friends would arrive in time to save him.

She wasn't going to look for two reasons. If he was already dead, she wouldn't be able to take it. She knew that. Losing him would have been too much for her. She told herself he was a stranger, but somehow, in the night, speaking so intimately, talking together, afraid he might be dying and struggling to find a way to make every minute of what was left of his life count, she'd bonded with him. She'd connected with him in a way she never had with another human being.

More importantly, if he was alive, she wanted him to stay that way. She wanted him to have every chance to live. With his heart and lungs shut down, he couldn't lose more blood. She'd given him quite a bit the night before. Enough that she woke up thirsty, so parched she was already gulping water. She'd been dizzy and weak after he'd taken her blood and had barely been able to cover him after he'd woven what he called "safeguards" around their camp. He'd claimed it was an invisible barrier that would keep out vampires and even human campers if there were any close by—which she doubted. Unless the bumbling vampire hunters returned.

She had to get up and check things out. She also needed to go to the bathroom. She'd been so parched the night before she'd drunk nearly half the water in her canteen. Very carefully, she eased her body away from the mound of dirt. She'd slept close to him. She'd told herself she was guarding him, but she knew it was more because she'd needed to feel close to him.

She tucked the gun inside her jacket and added the large can of wasp spray she carried, just in case she had to set a vampire on fire. Wasp spray was a very good weapon, and she nearly always had a can handy. Night was falling when she stepped out of the tent, the last rays of the sun slipping dramatically from the sky. She took a careful look around and then made her way to the bushes. Andor had been very precise about how far from the camp she could get and she followed his instructions to the letter.

She wasn't certain how she knew he was telling her the truth about his life and his people, but something in his voice, the strong connection between them, allowed her to listen to his explanations. Every word he uttered resonated with her, as if she already knew the truth and had just needed him to confirm it.

Lorraine stood beside the tent, running her hand over the side of it, needing to hear the sound of Andor's voice. She had always been independent. According to her parents, unusually so. She liked her own company. If she was somewhere quiet with a good book, she was happy. She could spend hours in the dojo training without a partner. Her brother had always wanted to have a partner to spar against or compete with during training. She was content and even preferred to work by herself.

It was strange to crave the sound of a voice. To want to feel another person's heartbeat. She told herself it was because she'd been through such trauma and everyone had ostracized her, so she'd learned to be lonely, but she knew that wasn't the truth. It was Andor. Something about his quiet acceptance drew her. He knew he was close to death. He wasn't angry at the vampires he'd fought or the three men who'd managed to stake him. He just quietly fought to survive.

Through no fault of her own, fate had taken her family and made her a pariah with her friends. She wanted to find Andor's inner peace, that place of acceptance and peace that was so ingrained in him. Harmony with the world around him ran like the deepest part of a river in Andor.

She moved around the campsite, setting up her defenses. Andor had set the safeguards, but she wasn't positive they would hold. She had forced herself, after he'd taken her blood, to look into his mind specifically for encounters with vampires. She'd asked him to bring those memories to the forefront so they would be easy for her to tap into.

She looked up at the moon, trying not to hyperventilate. She hadn't been able to sleep very well, the nightmare battles far too close. She'd never imagined such an evil creature, or one so powerful. Andor's last battle, the one where he'd defeated seven vampires, had been her last vision. She couldn't take any more after that. Heart pounding, stomach churning, she spent a few bad moments with her hands over her face, fighting the urge to run away.

How had Andor managed to get up every evening and go out looking for such evil? It was madness. Sooner or later—maybe even this time—he would be defeated. He would die a horrible death. No one even knew he existed. Or if they did, such as his brethren, they weren't capable of emotion and wouldn't even mourn his passing.

She hated what had happened to her family, and she hated Andor's life for him. She had no idea why terrible things happened to good people. Her brother had been a good person, her parents wonderful. Her aunt and uncle and Theodore's best friend's parents had been giving and kind. They didn't deserve what had happened to them. And Andor . . .

Lorraine sighed. Looking into his mind, even just to see battles, connected them even more. She didn't need or want that. He touched something deep in her and just stayed there. Inside. Where she couldn't get him out. He was in her head, and now, she thought, he was branded deep in her bones. She understood their connection. Talking telepathically and being in each other's minds was a strong link between them.

She only had so much in the way of ammunition to fight off vampires and she had to place it in the most strategic positions—the ones that made sense. She studied the various battles between Andor and the vampires, each separately, to try to find patterns. Similarities in the way vampires fought. When she was pitted against an opponent in the ring, or in her martial arts class, that was what she did. She watched for weaknesses. She found out their favorite methods of attack. What the knockout punch was.

At first, as she sat outside the tent and watched the sky darken, she could only see how powerful and clever vampires were. They took on various forms, used soft, gentle voices and then commanding, compelling ones. They whispered to Andor, tempted him, all the while cunningly plotting his death.

She watched Andor in action, replaying the scenes over and over in her mind, learning the way he moved. She was used to watching fighters. They had bodies honed from years of training, working the bags, sparring with opponents. None could compare or even come close to the blurring speed and fluid movements of Andor. He was breathtaking. Beautiful. Every muscle was honed to perfection. He was a pure fighting machine.

She pulled her legs up tailor-fashion and began to breathe deeply and evenly. She had ideas now on how to defeat a vampire if she had to fight one alone. It could be done if she didn't get one that was really, really good. Some of them were so powerful she hadn't believed even Andor could defeat them—and he had. She found herself feeling inexplicably proud of him. It would be pure luck to get the right one—a newly turned vampire still getting used to being undead. She sent out a silent prayer to the universe that if she had to protect Andor, that was what she was going to go up against.

Finding out about Carpathians and vampires might have freaked her out at any other time, but after what had happened to her family, nothing compared. Nothing would ever compare. She had walked into a room full of blood and death. Every family member gone. The destruction caused by the vampires in villages and small towns was horrendous, but no more than what she'd walked into.

"Andor." She murmured his name aloud. She didn't want to lose him. The world needed him and his skills. She admitted to herself it was more than that. He had filled those lonely places in her and soothed the raw edges of her memories. He couldn't take away the pain, but he did bring her the first comfort she'd felt since her family had died. She wouldn't let Andor down. She would guard him, and if he had lived through the day, he would live through the night and be alive when his brethren came for him.

In the distance, an owl screamed, and when she looked in that direction, a tall pine tree shivered. No, it was more like shuddering. Her heart skipped a beat. She kept her eyes glued to the tree and the brush surrounding it. Darkness was falling, but the moon was throwing enough light for her to make out the way the needles on the pine suddenly went from green to brown. A bush a few feet from the tree shriveled, pulling in its foliage.

Lorraine stood up slowly and stretched. She had to get this right, place herself in the exact position so the vampire would take the spot she needed him to be in. She faced toward him, staying loose, breathing evenly. There was a pause in the shivering brush, and she knew the vampire had become aware of her.

Within seconds, she felt the first oily touch of his mind seeking to probe hers. She had worked part of the night on strengthening the shields in her mind. Andor could pick thoughts out of her mind, just as she could his, but neither could probe deeply without the other's consent. She told herself the vampire wasn't stronger than Andor. She could hold out against him.

Soft whispers touched her mind, brushing gently, insistently, looking for entry. The tone was almost tender, like that a lover might use, but she felt its foulness. She began to hum to drown out the voice. She didn't want to hear his entreaty or his commands. He tried pushing a compulsion into her mind, but her shields held fast.

The vampire burst through the foliage, rushing her, red, pitiless eyes glaring at her as he came. She held her ground, her fingers around the bottle of whiskey she had brought to warm herself on cold nights. One small sip, maybe two. The bottle almost hadn't made the cut when she was deciding what to bring with her. She had to carry everything while she was hiking through the mountains. Now, that bottle might save her life.

The vampire ran into an unseen force. Sparks danced through the sky. Red and white and yellow, the flames licked at the rotting flesh of the vampire. He leapt back and howled. His curses were barely intelligible. He snarled and paced along the edge of the campsite, occasionally testing the safeguards Andor had constructed from where he lay inside the tent, so badly wounded.

Lorraine deliberately held her ground, just turning to face the monster. She hoped if she stayed in position, he would eventually choose to stand in front of her to communicate with her. From what she'd seen in Andor's mind, all vampires seemed very susceptible to flattery. They appeared to be vain, egotistical creatures.

The vampire eventually came back to stand directly in front of her, right on the little rise of soil she had prepared. Her heart gave another leap of joy, but she slowed her breathing and pulse so he wouldn't be able to use the signs against her. When he stood still, his looks changed completely. He was no longer a rotting corpse, with flaming red eyes and a mouth that was no more than a slash with jagged, stained teeth. He was dressed in modern clothes and was young and quite good-looking.

He bowed to her. "Lady. I believe you are harboring a fugitive. He has committed terrible crimes against his country and I've been sent to bring him to justice."

Deliberately, Lorraine stalled. The longer this played out, the more time Andor's friends had to get there. If she didn't have to try to kill this creature, she would be much happier. She glanced over her shoulder toward the tent, looking as nervous as possible. Since she truly was nervous, it wasn't difficult.

"Do you mean Andor?"

The vampire nodded. "That is his name, yes. I have tracked him for a while. He's a very dangerous criminal."

"Is he?" Again, she looked over her shoulder, her uneasiness transmitting itself to the vampire. "He's very . . . commanding."

"Are there others in the camp with you?" he asked.

She shook her head. He would know that if he walked around the campsite. "What's your name?"

"Dartmus."

She wrung her hands together. "I don't know what to do." She tried to sound very scared and very young.

"There were three other men here." It was an accusation, nothing less.

She nodded. "He ran them off, but he did something weird first." She stopped there, making him ask. Each second was a second she'd gained so Andor's brethren could get that much closer.

"What did he do?"

She felt the oily probe at her mind again. It was like thick fingers, scratching and clawing to find a way in. She had to work to repress a shudder of revulsion. Just the touch made her feel sick.

"The men were like statues, over there." She indicated the spot where the three men had suddenly gone motionless, frozen in time, arms outstretched, knees bent as if they were caught in mid-motion taking a step. It had been the first time she'd realized the things she'd stumbled across were far deeper and worse than they'd seemed. She'd done what she always had, stayed as quiet as possible to learn as much as she could in a short period of time. She'd needed to make an assessment of the situation fast.

The vampire glanced in the direction she pointed but his eyes were narrowed and his brow furrowed. She thought she saw a bug crawling up his face, but it had grown a little darker now and it was impossible to be sure. She knew he was wondering why he couldn't get into her head.

"He told them to leave after he took their blood, and they ran away."

"Let me inside."

"How? I don't know how. He's still in the ground. I think he might be dead, but I don't know and I don't want to find out."

"Invite me inside."

She shook her head. "He said I can't do that. He said if I invited any-one inside the camp, the moment they touched that barrier, they would burn." She gave another shudder. She told herself it was for effect, but the truth was, he creeped her out.

His eyes were glowing in the dark, a fiery red he couldn't seem to control. He had managed to put himself together, to make himself look human, but his skin cracked, and now she was very certain bugs slipped out. His teeth one moment seemed normal, the next they looked spiked and stained. His lips were thin, and they looked stained, too. Once his tongue came out, a long purplish-red thing that scooped up one of the bugs near his mouth.

"You will invite me in *now*." His voice was shrill.

It hurt her ears. She resisted covering them, forcing her body to stay relaxed. He was getting angry, just the way the other vampires had in the images in Andor's head. If they were thwarted in what they wanted for too long, they threw tantrums. She knew they became lethal at that point.

"I'm sorry, but no. I think you'd better go now." In contrast to him, she kept her voice very low and soft. Almost gentle, the way one lover might speak to another.

That threw him for a minute. He hesitated and then howled his rage and raced to the barrier again. His chest hit and a thousand tiny embers lit the air all around him. Sparks raced up his shirt and snapped against his chin. He screamed and hit at his face and clothes to keep any flames from burning out of control. Several licked at his chest, but he stamped them out with the heel of his hand. He glared at her, pacing back and forth like a wild animal, but he stayed right in front of her, just as she'd hoped. Now he was much closer, right along the invisible barrier Andor had created.

He stopped abruptly and tried staring into her eyes. She immediately dropped her gaze to his chest. Low enough not to meet his gaze, but high enough to still see his face and any signs he inadvertently gave before he tried his next attack. He was studying her, and she tried to keep her mind as blank as possible. From being with Andor, she knew she could hold a barrier between the vampire and her deepest thoughts. He couldn't command her. But he could most likely catch any random thought that moved in and out of the front of her brain.

"You were expecting me." His hand began to tap a rhythm against his thigh.

"Of course. He told me that a little toad might show up and I was to keep that toad out at all costs. He said a human woman as puny and defenseless as I am could keep the likes of something as slow and insignificant as you out. He told me to expect you to be as inept as the bumbling vampire hunters sent to kill him."

She saw the fury her words unleashed in the way the skin of his face cracked and peeled off, leaving rotting flesh below the mask. He looked hideous with his face partially gone and his eyes receding deeper into the pits in his skull. He didn't seem to notice that his mask of civility was slowly peeling away.

"He said that?"

"Yes, he did."

She felt the ground move slightly. Waves appeared in the dirt all around him and then under the barrier right into the campsite, coming straight at her. Her heart accelerated but she didn't move. She forced air in and out of her lungs, one slow, controlled breath at a time.

"I saw this one. Bugs crawling out of the dirt, but they aren't real. They can't be. The bugs couldn't make it past Andor's safeguards. He's in the ground and he would never fail to safeguard his resting place. This is an illusion. You're going to have to do better."

That rhythm he was tapping on his thigh was now sounding out in the forest, in the trees where she couldn't see. Branches creaking to that same beat. He was up to something, but she didn't know what. She just had to stay alert.

"Let me in! Invite me in!" He screamed the words at her and hurled himself at her mind, this time slamming into her shield over and over, battering at her hard enough that she felt bruised. Her head hurt so bad it felt as if it might explode.

She refused to let him see he had succeeded in hurting her. This was a tantrum, but it was also for show. He stepped back and raised his hands. He began to murmur words and moved his hands around. She knew immediately he was trying to figure out what the safeguards were. That scared her.

Andor had explained that a mage had taught the ancients spells to guard their resting places and that all safeguards were based on those earlier spells. That meant vampires knew what Carpathians used, because at some point in their lives they had used them as well.

"Hurry," she whispered aloud.

A rustle warned her. She glanced up and saw the migration of bats. Thousands of them coming out of the forest, heading straight toward her. Dartmus cackled like a witch in a horror film and then put his arms in the air, directing the bats. She realized immediately he was finding the weak spots of the barrier, places he couldn't pass through; the bats might be able to make it through at his command.

Taking a deep breath, she ran toward him, holding up the bottle of whiskey. She lit it on the run and hurled it over his head, pulling the gun and firing, breaking the bottle right over his head. She'd gone over the procedure a hundred times in her head, praying she could do it. Her parents and brother loved trick shooting as much as she did, and they'd spent hours on end thinking up things to challenge each other with. She'd never tried this particular one, but she thought she would have enough time to get a shot off if she threw the bottle high enough into the air. Andor had assured her anything could go out of the campsite, just not come in.

The whiskey fell over the top of the vampire, soaking his clothes. The burning piece of flannel she'd used hit his shoulder. She caught up the wasp spray, hit the trigger and held her lighter to it, turning it into a flamethrower. She knew she had to get close, the range wasn't very far, but the wasp spray lit beautifully. She lit Dartmus up, holding the steady stream of flames right against his chest, right over his heart. Instantly the whiskey there caught fire and flames spread over him.

Dartmus dropped his hands, screaming while he twisted and turned as if that would somehow put out the flames. The bat migration stuttered in the sky, all of the creatures suddenly disoriented and unsure where they were going or why. The vampire shrieked loudly, the sound carrying on the night. She sent up a silent prayer there were no more of his kind in the woods close by.

All the while she concentrated the spray on the place she knew the vampire's heart to be. He was so engulfed in flames now, she was unable to see his head and face. She used spurts, to save fuel and keep the pressure on. This was all the defense she really had and if it was gone, she wouldn't have anything to fight him with if he got through.

Dartmus stumbled back away from her and the barrier. She moved as close to it as she dared. She knew exactly where it was. If she stayed inside of it, she couldn't ensure the vampire's heart had incinerated. If she left the safety of it, she might not be able to get back inside. Dartmus kept moving backward as he stumbled and twisted, roaring his pain and then abruptly going silent.

Lorraine thought the silence was far worse than the high-pitched shrieking. She made the decision to let him go. She couldn't take the chance of getting outside her circle of protection. Clutching the near-empty spray can, she sank onto the ground because her legs wouldn't support her anymore. They just turned to rubber.

The wind picked up, fanning the flames so that they towered toward the sky in a fiery funnel. She gasped and pressed her hand to her mouth. She didn't want to start a forest fire. She would have to go out of her safety zone if he approached the foliage.

He dropped to the ground, and suddenly there was another man there. He was tall, dressed in a tight tee and loose pants that didn't hide the fact that he was ripped. She could see the muscles in his back rippling beneath the shirt. He waved his hand and the flames were gone. He slammed his fist deep into the charred chest and extracted the heart.

She wanted to look away, but it was impossible. Lightning forked across the sky, lighting up the night. It was early, so the dark veil hadn't completely fallen, but the lightning was so bright it hurt her eyes. She could hear it sizzling and cracking. Her hair stood up on her head. On her body. She actually felt a vibration through her heart.

Even as she watched, peeking through her fingers to shield her eyes, a whip slashed across the sky and hit the heart where it lay on the ground a distance from the charred body of the vampire. The stench was so foul her stomach rebelled, but she held it together even when the lightning whip was directed at the vampire. Then the man stuck his arms and hands in the white-hot energy.

He turned his head toward her, and the breath left her lungs in a long rush. He was the most terrifying man she'd ever seen. Much scarier than Andor. Of course, Andor wasn't scary to her, but still . . . She wasn't letting this man near him. He had the widest shoulders, and he was tall. His hair was long, just like Andor's. He came toward her, and she scrambled to her feet and backed away, holding up one hand so that he'd stop.

"Don't come any closer." Her heart pounded very hard, and this time she couldn't stop it. He scared her more than the vampire had. Maybe it was because there was death in his eyes and she'd seen the lightning bolt he'd handled. She knew Andor had done the same thing, but watching the images like a movie was far different than having to witness it. She knew she was still reeling from having to fight off the vampire attack as well.

"I do not have time for your fear. Andor is dying and he must be helped." He lifted his hands, much like the vampire had done, and began to speak ancient words as he unwound the intricately woven barrier.

She found herself gripping the gun and the wasp spray. He had to be Andor's friend. He'd killed the vampire. He knew Andor was in trouble, and the vampire hadn't mentioned that. Why was she so afraid of this man? His eyes were the strangest color, like iron, but with rust running through them. They didn't look in the least bloodshot. His features were hard. Intense. She wanted to run into the tent and beg Andor to wake up so she could ask him what to do.

The moment the man's hands dropped, he strode toward her, his face a mask of determination. Before she could speak, he moved past her straight to the tent. The next thing she knew, her tent was no longer there. Andor's body lay in the shallow depression, covered with the dark, rich soil. He was still unmoving. Lorraine wanted to throw herself over top of him to prevent the stranger from getting anywhere near him.

It was too late. He waved his hand and the soil opened, revealing Andor's naked body. He lay as if dead. She heard the stranger's swift intake of breath.

"Can you save him?"

He glanced at her. "I do not know. He is far from us. His thread to you is all that has kept him alive."

"There were supposed to be two of you." She still was a little worried that she was doing something wrong. She should have asked Andor to show her images of the two men he expected.

"Sandu is in a fight just south of here with two of the undead. They were answering the call of that one." He jerked his head toward where the fight had taken place. The wind had scattered the ashes of the vampire throughout the forest. "I am Ferro."

"Lorraine. Tell me what I can do to help him."

"I must go now into his body and try to heal him from the inside. You will have to keep any enemy off us. If something comes, you call out to me, touch my body, otherwise, do not get near me. Be ready to give me your blood."

"Not Andor? Shouldn't I be giving Andor my blood?"

"I will be weak when I return, and there is no way the first time will heal much. I must be at strength." His eyes swept over her, dismissing her. "Your blood will not be sufficient, but it is all we have."

She didn't even care that he was a jerk. "Hurry." There was a sense of anxiety she couldn't get rid of. She felt that with every second that passed Andor drifted further from her.

Ferro sank to the ground beside Andor, his touch shockingly gentle as he brushed dirt from Andor's face. He plunged both hands deep into the soil. Then he was gone. Just that fast. She hadn't even blinked. She was looking right at him and yet he was gone. She could tell his body was an empty shell. He looked every bit as dead as Andor did.

Lorraine closed her eyes and put both hands on Andor's chest. *If you can hear me, Andor, know that you have given me more than I've had since my family died. I laughed when I didn't think I ever would again. I was excited and happy and surprised. So many emotions. You gave them all to me. I don't want you to die. I want you here, because I believe the world needs you. There's a part of me that knows I do as well.*

She was grateful he couldn't hear her, because she didn't want him to think she was one of those women who saw a man for the first time and decided he was the one and she had to be with him. She wasn't needy as a rule. She liked her independence. She'd always liked her time alone and had never been lonely—until the death of her family. After that, she'd felt lonely all the time—until Andor.

They'd only been together a short time, hours really, but those hours had been very intense, and she'd learned a lot about him. More than she knew about any other person, because he'd allowed her into his mind.

She forced herself to leave the two men, hoping Ferro was good at his job. He wasn't the healer Andor had mentioned just before she'd buried him completely. Ferro was worried. Well, concerned, not worried. Like Andor, he seemed matter-of-fact. Either his brethren would live or he would die. She walked slowly along the outside circle where she imagined the barrier had been placed before Ferro had taken it down. She kept the wasp spray in her jacket and the gun in her hand.

Two men came striding out of the darkness straight at her. She took a two-handed grip on the gun and brought it up, aiming right at the taller man's heart. "Stop right there and tell me who you are."

The taller man kept walking. He had the same long hair as Andor and Ferro. His shirt was off and his chest was a wall of muscle. Tattoos drifted down his arms and over his shoulders just as Andor's did. His eyes were blacker than night but burned with red flames. There was blood on his belly, as if a razor-sharp claw had tried to rip him open. She recognized that wound. It was like Andor's, except this man's wound was shallow and Andor's belly had been ripped open. She lowered the gun.

"I am Gary Daratrazanoff," the other man greeted. "That is Sandu." He continued walking as well.

"I'm Lorraine. Which of you is the healer?"

"All of us are capable of healing," Gary replied.

"Andor said one of you was a healer. Ferro said the same."

"They were referring to me." Gary's gaze was already moving over Andor.

There was no expression on his face, but she saw the look that passed between Sandu and him. Her stomach dropped. "He's a really good man. He fought and killed seven of those hideous things." She felt like she was pleading for Andor's life. "You can't just give up on him. He stayed alive this entire time waiting for you."

"No one will give up on him," Gary assured. "You keep watch. Sandu will be needed for blood."

Like Ferro, Gary dropped down beside Andor and pushed his hands into the soil. She didn't take her gaze from the healer because she wanted to make absolutely certain she saw him as his spirit left his body. For one brief half second, she thought she saw a brilliant flash of light move from Gary's body to Andor's but then it was gone and the night closed in around them.

"Are you his friend?" Lorraine asked in a low voice.

"I am his brother."

She studied the expressionless face. These men wore masks. They were dangerous, and if everything Andor had told her was true—and at this point she wasn't about to quibble over details—then his brethren didn't see in color or feel emotions.

"I don't want him to die." She didn't know if she said it as a test or she needed to admit it to herself. She had no idea when she'd become so dependent on the man.

"I do not want him to die, either. You are thirsty. And hungry. You have to take care of yourself in order to help supply blood. We will need quite a bit in order to save Andor. Ferro and the healer will need it as well as your lifemate."

She didn't argue. The last thing she wanted to do was eat, but Sandu was right. She was thirsty, and she had to be ready to give blood. She sat beside her backpack, gun in her lap, the spray can beside her knee, facing out toward the forest, and drank from her water bottle.

"You managed to defeat a vampire," Sandu said. "Ingeniously."

She shrugged. "I'm not certain he would have stayed down. I didn't want to risk leaving the safety of the guards Andor set up to check to see if his heart had actually been incinerated. I think Ferro is the one who actually killed him."

"I am not sure many people would have thought of making their own flamethrower. And it was smart not to have left the safeguards. Vampires can be very tricky. They often will make replicas of themselves so you cannot choose the correct one. Then they attack. Until the heart is destroyed, you have to always know they are deadly."

She nodded, taking in every word carefully, just as she had with Andor. "I see one of them tried to eviscerate you."

"A common practice. He did not succeed."

"I could clean it the old-fashioned human way."

"It is unnecessary. I do not feel it. When this is done, we will worry about the small things."

She didn't think being nearly eviscerated by a vampire was a small thing, but then she was going to have nightmares about the lightning and Ferro. She supposed that wounds were nothing to Carpathians unless they were like Andor's, massive and many.

"Can you start healing him from the outside while they're healing him from the inside?"

"The best use of me is for my blood and my strength to protect both of their bodies while they work to save our brother."

She wanted to argue with him. She just wanted Andor healed, and the anxiety in her wouldn't go away. Jumping up, she shoved her gun in her waistband, grabbed the water bottle and left the group to walk around the campsite again.

Now that the gruesome battle was over, one would never know any such thing had taken place. The cicadas were singing, and she could hear frogs calling one another. Bats dipped and wheeled overhead, going after a multitude of flying insects. She could hear the sound of the stream rushing over rocks. A cool breeze touched her face and ruffled her hair. She kept walking, restless energy preventing her from sitting.

It was obvious to her that Sandu didn't want to talk. She understood that. Maybe these men didn't feel anything, but somewhere, they had to care about a man who had spent several human lifetimes with them. They felt it somewhere deep, somewhere lost to them. She paced back and forth, watching the sky and the surrounding forest. She didn't forget the ground. Dartmus's lesson had taught her that.

"Lorraine," Sandu called to her. "We need your blood."

She turned and hurried back. Ferro was swaying with weariness. His body was pale. There were tiny beads of blood on his forehead, and her stomach lurched. He was feeding from Sandu's wrist. She didn't look— she couldn't. She kept her gaze on Andor.

"Can you save him?"

She felt the impact as Ferro's eyes jumped to her face. She still didn't look at him because she knew he continued to take blood from Sandu's wrist.

"Ferro says he is very bad. Three of the wounds should have killed him outright. Two more are borderline. One he would have been able to heal."

"That doesn't tell me anything."

"It tells you it's going to be a very long night. I'm going to take your blood so I can provide for the healer. Then I will go hunting to find another source."

None of it sounded good, but at least she wasn't alone with Andor, trying to save him when it would have been impossible.

# 5

Andor was cold. He had never been so cold in his life and he couldn't seem to regulate his temperature. He tried opening his eyes. Everything was dark, bleak, bitterly cold. He was blind. His heart should have reacted with a jump. Something. He couldn't hear his heartbeat. He wasn't deaf. He knew that. He could hear voices. Musical. Chanting. They had chanted often in the monastery. Perhaps he was there. He opened his mouth to call out. No sound emerged.

Andor stayed very still, analyzing what was happening to his body. He was blind and couldn't speak, but he could hear. There was no heartbeat that he could detect, yet he was aware. He felt the cold. The voices were soft but persistent and he listened, trying to discern what they said. Which chant they were using. He could join in. Silently, maybe, but the words would ground him. He was Carpathian. He belonged to the Earth. Chanting aided his people in many things. He could be of some use in spite of his strange situation.

*Ot ekäm ainajanak hany, jama.* My brother's body is a lump of earth, close to death. *Me, ot ekäm kuntajanak, pirädak ekäm, gond és irgalom türe.* We, the clan of my brother, encircle him with our care and compassion. *O pus wäken-*

*kek, ot oma śarnank, és ot pus fünk, álnak ekäm ainajanak, pitänak ekäm aina-*
*janak elävä.* Our healing energies, ancient words of magic and healing herbs
bless my brother's body, keep it alive. *Ot ekäm sielanak pälä. Ot omboće päläja*
*juta alatt o jüti, kinta, és szelemek lamtijaknak.* But my brother's soul is only
half. His other half wanders in the nether world. *Ot en mekem ŋamaŋ: kulke-*
*dak otti ot ekäm omboće päläjanak.* My great deed is this: I travel to find my
brother's other half.

Andor heard the words of the chant and recognized the Great Healing Chant of his people. A soul was lost to them. A warrior of great im-
portance and a healer risked his life to follow his brethren down the great
tree of life into the other world to bring him back. He knew that others
would be gathered in a circle around the fallen warrior chanting to help
aid the healer.

It was a great risk to follow the fallen into the other world. Both souls
could be lost. It was only when that individual was needed, or when his
lifemate . . .

He shivered, something important moving in his mind. He needed to
get warm. His body felt like a block of ice. He couldn't quite catch the
thought that pushed at the back of his mind so persistently, so he concentrated on the words of the healing chant. His native language was only
spoken among Carpathians, and it was rare for the words to be interpreted
into another language, yet English was added so someone non-Carpathian
could understand what was said.

*Rekatüre, saradak, tuppadak, odam, kaŋa o numa waram, és avaa owe o*
*lewl mahoz.*

We dance, we chant, we dream ecstatically, to call my spirit bird, and
to open the door to the other world. *Ntak o numa waram, és mozdulak,*
*jomadak.* I mount my spirit bird and we begin to move, we are under way.
*Piwtädak ot En Puwe tyvinak, ećidak alatt o jüti, kinta, és szelemek lamti-*
*jaknak.* Following the trunk of the Great Tree, we fall into the nether
world. *Fázak, fázak nó o śaro.* It is cold, very cold.

Andor heard those words. *Fázak, fázak nó o śaro.* It is cold, very cold.
He shivered again. He couldn't call out, even now when he recognized the
voices chanting. Two of his brethren. Who? He tried to think. Sandu for

certain. Sandu had a beautiful singing voice. The other? Ferro. That surprised him. Ferro was a born leader. He could have been a gatekeeper had he not been so far gone. He could stop a vampire just with his voice alone. It was that compelling. He never raised his voice. He didn't have to. The urge to obey when Ferro commanded was too strong to ignore, even for the undead.

He shivered again. Ice seemed to pierce through his body. Hundreds of shards. Ice surrounded his heart so that he finally knew why his heart couldn't beat—it was frozen. *He* was the warrior lost in the nether land. A great warrior was risking his life to retrieve him. That was the only answer to the glacier-cold. Who had risked his life? And why?

*Juttadak ot ekäm o akarataban, o sívaban, és o sielaban.* My brother and I are linked in mind, heart, and soul. *Ot ekäm sielanak kaŋa engem.* My brother's soul calls to me. *Kuledak és piwtädak ot ekäm.* I hear and follow his track.

His soul, however, was lost. They all knew that. He had been locked behind massive gates with safeguards woven by eight of the most ancient of all Carpathians. Why would they retrieve him when he finally was seeking peace? The need had to be great. But there was no way to find his soul. The warrior risking his life would be lost as well.

He listened intently, all the while trying to call out with his voice. It suddenly occurred to him to use telepathy. These were his brothers. They knew him. They knew his mind. They could find him, tune to him in all the darkness.

*I am here,* he called to them. Shivered. The ice grew colder.

Something moved again in his mind, brushing the walls gently. So softly. The touch was barely there but strangely intimate. He felt instantly comforted as if he was no longer alone. The touch had been disturbingly feminine, and he knew he should recognize it.

*Can you hear me?*

If his heart wasn't a block of ice, it would have gone into overdrive. He knew that voice, from long ago, somewhere far away. He knew her. He forced every bit of strength and discipline he had acquired over the years to open his mind. He didn't have a body, but his mind was working—somewhat. Slowly. Everything was difficult.

*If you can hear me, Andor, sielam sieladed—my soul to your soul—find me. Reach for me.*

The more the voice called to him, the more he felt her in his mind. She had found him in this ice-cold, dark place. He was blind, but he could reach for her. He was speechless but determined to find her. *My soul is tattered and split. There is nothing left.*

*I am left. Én olen hän ku pesä sieladet—I am guardian of your soul. You are not alone.*

The feel of silky hair brushed over his face. He felt her. Breath to breath. Inside. Along the walls of his mind. She was there with him in that freezing, dark place and she shouldn't be. Everything he was rose up to protect her. He knew her. She was truly the guardian of his soul. She held the light to his darkness.

*Lorraine.* He whispered her name. A talisman. *You cannot be here.*

*There was no other way to find you. My soul sought yours. He is here. The warrior, the healer who will bind himself to you.*

The warrior/healer would bind himself to Andor's soul and fight for him to come back from the land of the dead, but that would mean he would bind himself to Lorraine as well. The other man was there, pouring into his mind with Lorraine. He was strong. As ancient as Andor or Ferro. Andor still couldn't place him, but the healer was extremely powerful.

Voices called to him now. They came from below him. From either side, as if a great circle of warriors were surrounding him. All male. Ancient. Long gone.

The most powerful voice came into his mind, blending with those ancient warriors chanting in their singsong voices. *Sayedak és tuledak ot ekäm kulyanak.* Encounter I the demon who is devouring my brother's soul.

Andor felt the terrible wrenching in his body. The pain was shattering. Lorraine cried out, a soft protest that was heartbreaking. He tried to reach for her, but he couldn't move his body. He could only shiver and try to swallow the pain. Devour it. Take it in and embrace it. There was no other way or he would have abandoned his woman, the *hän ku kuulua siela*—the keeper of his soul—and let go, although the abyss called to him.

*Nenäm ćoro, o kuly torodak.* In anger, I fight the demon.

The pain worsened, and Lorraine cried out a second time. His chest was on fire. His belly twisted and burned. She felt that terrible agony with him. He tried to shield her, but he could do nothing. His power seemed to be gone and he was left helpless while his lifemate suffered.

*You must go, Lorraine. Be safe.*

*My soul keeps your soul. It is the only way we can hold you to us, Andor. I know there is pain.* There were tears in her voice, and it was far more torment than the pain tearing at his physical body. He couldn't hold her in his arms. He'd never held her. He'd never had the chance to comfort her. All those long years he'd waited, and now, in the end, he hadn't had his chance with her. She needed, and he hadn't provided.

*You comforted me more than any other. Hold fast, Andor. Stay with me.*

He took a breath, and all that came into his lungs was piercing cold. Ice. Freezing him from the inside out.

The voice in his mind continued. *O kuly pél engem.* He is afraid of me. *Lejkkadak o kaŋka salamaval.* I strike his throat with a lightning bolt.

The warriors surrounding him chanted louder, their song adding to the strength of the great healer fighting for his life. He fought now as well. He couldn't leave Lorraine. She had the courage to bind her soul to his and follow him down the great tree of life to the nether world where he would be judged, risking her own life. The healer had also risked his life by binding his soul to theirs.

*Molodak ot ainaja komakamal.* I break his body with my bare hands.

If he could have, Andor would have screamed at the pain crashing through his body. It felt as if the vampire had succeeded in eviscerating him. His internal organs seemed to be wrenched from his body, torn in two, ripped and shredded. He couldn't scream, but Lorraine did. At once he focused on her rather than the agony of torture he endured.

*Sívamet, you must let go of me. I do not want this for you. I command this of you.*

There was a moment of silence. Something velvety brushed along the walls of his mind. A caress. The beauty of it was in such stark contrast to the ugliness of the torment he suffered. He felt her there with him. To his shock, there was amusement.

*You can't command modern women, Andor. We don't obey. I made the choice to bind our souls together. Ferro, Sandu and Gary explained exactly what would happen and how once we were tied together, our fates would be the same. I knew what I risked.*

That made her—extraordinary. He hadn't bound them together. There were no blood exchanges between them. He'd taken her blood, but not given his in return. She didn't know his world, yet she accepted him. She chose to save his life at the risk of her own. If the healer couldn't repair his wounds enough to retrieve him, she would die as well. So would the healer.

*Then we will live.* He decreed it. He would never allow her into this land without him by her side.

*Yes, we will.* She breathed her decree.

The healer's voice slid into his mind once again. *This will not be easy. You have to endure this last before the fight is finished.*

*I can endure.*

*Lorraine?* The healer made the inquiry.

*I can endure.* She repeated Andor's exact words.

*Once started, I cannot stop,* the healer warned.

*I will not let go,* she assured.

The healer didn't wait. *Toja és molanâ.* He is bent over, and falls apart.

Fire spread through Andor, a terrible storm burning every part of him. Every organ. Burning him up. He could almost see the ashes in his mind, whirling with that force that rushed through him. Lightning, white and hot, crashed through him, striking his flesh repeatedly, each lash worse than the last. The whips of lightning tore open skin and muscle to strike his insides, those deadly wounds, burning away the dead and stimulating new growth.

There was no way to endure without sound. Without his silent gasps and groans. Without adding silently to Lorraine's screams. She felt every lash with him. That terrible fire. The force breaking him apart and the tornado-like wind whipping around him in an attempt to stimulate his body back to working.

*Hän ća δa.* He runs away.

There was a sudden silence. Andor took another breath. This time he pulled air deep into his lungs—lungs that felt raw and burning as if they hadn't had air for a very long while. He was no longer so cold, yet he felt the night air touching his bare skin. He tried once again to open his eyes and to his shock, his lashes lifted.

The first face he saw was Sandu's. His brethren looked tired and pale, as if he hadn't fed in many long nights. Sandu gripped his forearms. *"Én jutta félet és ekämet*—I greet a friend and brother. You have been long gone from us. You need blood. Take what I freely offer." He cut a long line over his wrist and pressed the drops of blood welling up to Andor's mouth. "It was a hard-won battle. Gary is more of a healer than I have seen in all my long existence."

Andor didn't think Sandu could spare the blood, but he was starved and knew he wasn't nearly healed. Gary had saved his life, but the wounds still needed attention. He still needed blood. More of it. So did the others. His gaze shifted around, looking for one person. His heart clenched hard in his chest. Lorraine lay between his body and that of Gary Daratrazanoff.

He jerked Sandu's wrist from his mouth. Sandu shoved it back to his mouth before he could speak. *Is she alive? What is wrong with her?*

"She is fine. Exhausted. It took a good deal of the night to get you back. She is strong, that one."

Andor could hear the respect in Sandu's voice. Sandu and the others, Andor included, respected few people. He jerked his chin toward Gary. The healer had been a question mark for all of them. They knew his history. Unlike the brethren, Gary had been born human. He had dedicated his life to the Carpathian people, working to come up with a solution to the problem of their women being unable to reproduce. In doing so, he'd fought alongside the Carpathians over the years he was with them, changing as he did so from all the blood exchanges and the knowledge he'd acquired. Still, all that hadn't made him into what he was now.

The healer had been mortally wounded aiding another great warrior. Gregori Daratrazanoff, the prince's bodyguard and healer of their people, had befriended Gary years earlier and refused to allow him to die. The human male was taken deep into their most sacred cave where they could call to their ancestors. If Gary were accepted by them, he would become a true Daratrazanoff. The ancient warriors had poured their memories and fighting skills into that single body. The toll on him was tremendous, yet the prince had asked that he take up the role of protector and body-guard to Tariq Asenguard, the prince's choice to lead in the United States.

*He is bound to Lorraine.*

For the first time, Sandu's steady gaze slipped away and touched the two lying side by side. "That is true. It was the only way to find you. Gary went into the other world repeatedly, but you were too far gone. Had she not gone after you, Andor, you would have been lost to us."

*Who told her of this possibility and taught her the words of our language?* He kept the question mild and made certain his face remained expressionless, but for the first time in centuries, he was truly upset. Whoever had told her a lifemate could bind souls and find him had knowingly risked her life.

"It was necessary."

*You? You risked my lifemate? Do you know what she's suffered?*

"He didn't." Ferro was there, looking as dangerous as ever. Like Sandu, he was pale, although not quite as much. He nodded to Sandu. "Go feed. If necessary take animal blood. The others should join us by tomorrow night. They are on the way." His strangely colored eyes bored into Andor, making him uncomfortable. "We have been unable to wake you for several risings."

*Several risings?* He glanced again toward Lorraine's sleeping figure. She'd been alone with his brethren and Gary for several risings. She looked exhausted. Had they been giving her their blood? Taking hers? He had to get up, get his strength back. Heal.

Andor politely closed the wound on Sandu's wrist before letting go. He started to sit and instantly realized it was impossible. Most of his body was covered in soil. More, he was far too weak. He glared at Ferro.

"You had no right to risk her."

Ferro shrugged. "She asked if there was another way when the healer returned and made it clear you were lost to us. There was another way, and she wanted to try it. We fortified her as best we could. She was brave and would have made a great warrior. Do not take that from her, Andor."

"She lost her entire family. She was committing some form of suicide."

"She was not. Do you think any of us, Sandu, Gary or I, would have allowed such a thing? She thought only of you when she made her decision. I took a vow and I will keep it. She was safe. We bound our souls to hers as well. Sandu and I, at your request, made certain your woman was safe. We would have pulled her free of that land."

"She doesn't know what the two of you did," he guessed.

Ferro shook his head. "We had little time. She needed to learn the language."

"That is how she could speak Carpathian so fluently and perfectly."

"Yes. She had to understand, and she had to be able to appeal to what you would most understand."

The fact that Ferro and Sandu had bound their souls as well to Lorraine was both touching and shocking. Warriors, especially ancient ones, would never, under any circumstances, bind themselves to another Carpathian male's woman. In doing so, they, too, had risked their lives when she had traveled to the nether world to retrieve him.

"Why?" He didn't understand. "I have lived my lifetime. Far more than my lifetime."

"She has not," Ferro said simply. "It is possible that we might find our lifemates in this century, but you *did* find her. She is a good, worthy mate. She deserves happiness, and she hasn't had that in a while. We might never have the chance to achieve that for our women, but we could for yours, and you are *ekäm*—my brother."

There was a sincerity in Ferro's voice that humbled Andor. Ferro had rarely spoken to any of them, but he'd seemed different these last few weeks, more willing to communicate. The modern world was changing them all in some subtle way. Andor hoped it meant that all of the brethren would have more time to search for their lifemates so that they would have a better chance to find them, rather than locking themselves away as too dangerous for society.

*"Ekäm."* They clasped forearms in the age-old greeting of warriors as Andor made his reply. Ferro had been his brother for over two hundred years.

"You did not bind her to you," Ferro said. "Why?"

"I was too weak, but also, I knew the chances of me surviving were very slim. I did not want her to live a half-life here on earth. She is human. If she remained human without ties to me, she could eventually find another to go through life with." The thought didn't sit well, but he knew he didn't want his woman to be alone, pining for a man she'd never had until the day she died. "I would not be a true lifemate if I had not looked out for her."

Ferro nodded. "That is true, although it would have been easier to retrieve you." His gaze moved slowly over his brethren. "You are pretty torn up. Did you know any of them?"

Andor shook his head. He was exhausted. He knew he had been given ancient blood and the healer must have worked on him, but the truth was, he didn't feel much better than he had when Lorraine had buried his body in the hope that he would be alive when the others came. Ferro had said they had been fighting for him for several risings. He had assumed that meant he had been back in the land of the living for those risings. If he hadn't . . . He glanced again at Lorraine.

"Did she hold me to this earth while all of you slept?" Because if they hadn't rescued him in a single rising, he would have slipped back no matter how much headway the healer had made in bringing him back from the other world.

"She did," Ferro answered. "She is worthy of you, Andor."

He was astounded. She was human and not tied to him. How had she managed such a feat? "The question might be, am I worthy of her?"

"I believe you are." Ferro turned his head and looked out into the night. His features had changed subtly. He looked more dangerous than ever. "We cannot stay here much longer."

Realization came to Andor. "The vampires are continuing their attacks."

Ferro nodded. "We have fought off three attacks, but our fear is they will send puppets during the day against Lorraine."

"Bury me deep with safeguards and take her back to the Asenguard compound where she will be safe. They will think I have been taken with you."

Ferro shook his head. "She will not leave you."

"That does not sound like you. You would force your woman to go to safety."

"Perhaps *persuade* is a much nicer way of putting it, but yes, she would go. I am a different man and my lifemate would be a different woman."

Lorraine sat up, her chestnut hair tumbling madly in every direction. Andor watched it fall around her shoulders and settle down her back. Somehow, the silky strands were as shiny as ever. Her skin was very pale but looked as soft as ever. Those large green eyes of hers moved over his face, anxiety in them. She smiled at him as she came up on her knees beside him. "You're awake. Oh my God, I can't believe you're awake." Her gaze shifted to Ferro, moved over him, taking in every detail. "You're healed again this evening. It's such a miracle how you do that. I was worried when you went to ground." ·

Ferro shrugged his axe-handle-wide shoulders. "There is no need to worry. I will heal or I will not. Worrying does not change the outcome."

She rolled her eyes and then looked back at Andor. "I'm so glad you're awake."

"We are going to have to have many discussions about what is acceptable and what is not," Andor said, his voice as stern as he could make it while he feasted his eyes on her. She was beautiful to him, glowing from the inside out. He knew her outer shell would be considered attractive by humans, but that mattered little to him. It was what was inside her that counted, that and the fact that she was his other half. She was his. He belonged to her.

"Yes, I couldn't agree more," she fired back. "Because getting yourself torn up like this is entirely *unacceptable* and not very wise. Whatever reasons you have for having no regard for your well-being aren't good enough."

"I will leave you two to your reunion. Andor, I caution you, do not try to move or come out from under the soil. The healer has worked every night with one of us as well. Until the others arrive, we cannot risk more damage." Ferro stood, facing outward. "Stay in camp close to them and be prepared. The enemy is close."

"How close are the brethren?" Andor asked.

"They come," Ferro said. "They do not give away their positions." He turned and strode away.

"He is amazing," Lorraine said. "I don't think he ever gets tired. He's like a machine. Sandu and Gary are as well." She reached out and brushed his hair from his face. "You really scared me, Andor."

"You know that if the healer had been unable to retrieve me from the other world, you would have died as well. By binding yourself to me and following me to that other place, you risked everything."

"So did they."

"They are not you."

"Andor, would you have gone after me?" She settled back on her heels.

He wanted her hands back on him. In his hair, on his jaw, just touching him. He needed that touch. "Of course. I am your lifemate."

"Exactly."

"You have no idea what that means. You were not searching for centuries for me. I deliberately did not bind us with the ritual words so if I died, you could continue on."

Her smile was slow in coming but when it came, his heart clenched—it was so beautiful. "Perhaps you did bind us, you just didn't know it, because when your brothers couldn't find you in that cold, dark place, *I* did."

He couldn't reprimand her anymore. He was too proud of her. "Thank you, *sívamet.* I would have been lost without you."

"It was a joint effort." She brushed her hand down his face, her touch lingering. "Being locked in your mind, it's amazing how much one learns.

I think those few nights were a lifetime of learning, maybe several lifetimes."

"You have the advantage. I was unconscious."

"I think you were a little more than unconscious. You really scared me," she reiterated. "You can't do that again. What were you thinking, taking on seven of them? Two were considered master vampires, at least that is what Sandu told me."

"He should not have."

"If you were feeling better, I might kick you. I don't have girlie kicks, either, Andor. When I kick you, you're going to know I did, so refrain from ever treating me like an idiot. Of course, I have to know the difference between a master vampire, a lesser one and a pawn. I'm going to be living in your world. That means I'm going to encounter them, and if we have children, they will encounter them. My sons will need to learn to fight, but so will my daughters. I don't believe in being helpless. I shoot. I can use a knife. I have practiced with a flamethrower and I'm deadly accurate. The others have helped me learn the things I need to know and I've found your mind, which is filled with battle tactics, extremely helpful."

Andor shook his head. "I cannot believe that my own brothers have encouraged you to be a little hawk. I doubt they would be quite so lenient with their own lifemates."

"You don't understand, Andor." She leaned closer to him. "I lost everyone, my entire family. Everyone I loved. I couldn't save them. It was already too late by the time I got home. I wasn't about to lose you. Can't you understand?"

"I understand," he said gently.

Her grief tore at him, and then she gave a little shrug, pushing her greatest sorrow down so she could function.

"We've had to fight off a few attacks and everyone is exhausted. We needed everyone to be able to help if we were to succeed. Women are capable of fighting these things if given the proper training. I'm not saying all women should, but neither should all men. We're all different, Andor. I found that out when I trained in my parents' dojo."

When he shook his head, she framed his face with both hands, insisting he really hear what she needed to say. "I was raised on martial arts and I loved it. My family lived that life. Others came to learn various degrees of self-defense, or wanted to train to fight in a ring to get trophies. Some of the people that came through were very gentle creatures and couldn't find it in themselves to attack no matter what. Others were eager for the challenge, for the battle." She let go of him and sank back to her knees again.

"What are all these weapons?" Andor nodded to the various items that surrounded him, laid carefully out in a circular pattern about six feet from him.

"I have to fight from a distance, so I needed several flamethrowers and ways to kill a vampire should they get past Sandu, Gary or Ferro." She shuddered. "They really are disgusting, vile creatures. Ferro and Sandu have really helped me build up my shields to make them stronger. I do the exercises all the time. Two of the vampires nearly penetrated them and got to my memories. I couldn't believe how powerful they were. I could feel the compulsion in their voices. I didn't want them to be able to find you there, just in case. You were in the ground, and they didn't know you were even alive or anywhere near here. If they'd managed to kill me . . ."

"Stop. Do not say it." Real fear gripped him. After centuries of searching, if they brought him back only for her to have died, he feared what could happen. "It is frustrating to know I cannot aid the four of you."

Her face changed instantly. Softened. Her eyes went to a sea green. "I know it must be horrible for you to just have to lie quietly."

"It is far more than being uncomfortable, Lorraine. It is the fact that the four of you, my woman and my brothers, are in danger and cannot leave because of me. I have never been in such a position before."

"I know that," she replied, her voice soft with some emotion that tore at his heart. "I've seen you, inside your mind, your memories, the way you protect everyone. You're the guardian, the one who would stand for all of us. Now you have to allow us to stand for you."

"It is so much more difficult than one would think."

"I have to take care of business. Unlike Carpathians, who have only to wake up and clothe themselves to look completely refreshed, I have to wash up, brush my teeth and use the bushes for business."

"I can help with the washing and brushing of teeth," he offered.

"No," another voice chimed. "You can't."

Andor glanced over at the healer. Gary sat up. He looked so exhausted, Andor wanted to order him to go to ground. A Daratrazanoff was not the kind of man to be ordered. They gave orders. Gary spoke in a soft voice, but it carried, and with it, authority.

Andor had never been one to recognize authority. He had sworn allegiance to his prince so many centuries ago he could barely remember. Like his brethren, he believed his prince, Vlad, had betrayed them. Instead of destroying his firstborn son, he had allowed a series of events to unfold that nearly destroyed their people. Vlad, through his inability to cause his lifemate sorrow because of her love of their child, had brought the Carpathian people to the very brink of extinction. Andor and the other ancients living in the monastery had not sworn their allegiance to the new prince, the second son of Vlad.

Lorraine leaned close to Andor, her silky hair brushing his face as she kissed the side of his mouth. "I'll be right back. You two can posture at each other." She smiled at Gary. "Good evening. I see you didn't go to ground again. Ferro said that is very dangerous and that you need the healing soil."

"I was too exhausted to open the earth," Gary admitted.

"Perhaps, but I think you were guarding me as well as Andor, offering your body in exchange for ours." She stood, dusted off the seat of her jeans, which called attention to her bottom, and sauntered away, toward the trees.

Andor watched her go, but his mind was reeling with the implication that Gary had been too tired even to open the earth. He had slept out in the open, just in a shallow depression beside Lorraine. They were all at the very end of their strength, even the healer. That told him far more than he'd realized about how dire the situation was. If the ancients couldn't even get into the soil by the end of the night, they were expending too much energy keeping him alive.

Andor felt the healer move in his mind. He was strong. Ancient. A formidable man with insane fighting skills. He was a powerful healer, one very much needed in the United States, especially now that they found the vampires had slowly, over the centuries, fortified their position and had a good foothold already.

*You will not live if you move too much. We have been unable to heal those wounds. Three are worrisome. I need to be able to concentrate on them, but the vampires know we are here and we're hiding something. That something is you. Lorraine won't go with an escort to the Asenguard compound without you. If we are to save her, we must save you.*

*I will order her to go.*

*All the orders in the world will not work on her.*

*Then she must be forced.*

*We are all tied to your fate. The four of us and you, Andor. She will not leave you. You may not have bound her to you with the ritual words, but the bindings are tighter than any I have seen without them. Part of that is her. She has a will like iron.*

*Ferro indicated that he felt the presence of vampires. I could see the darkness begin to take him over,* Andor cautioned. He wanted Gary to realize the danger to Lorraine was very real, iron will or not. The others might have provided her with weapons, but if the vampires sent a concentrated force after them, especially during the day when they couldn't aid her, she might be lost to them all. *They must be close.*

Gary nodded. *They harass us continually. Sandu and Ferro sent for the others. I cannot begin to heal you properly until they arrive. They were also under attack. Sergey has become quite a battle strategist.* Gary named the master vampire who had formed a plan centuries earlier and then methodically carried it out. He had shown himself only when he was at his greatest strength and was certain he had the ability to be victorious. Now, his army was nipping at the heels of the Carpathians, weakening them on a nightly basis.

"Call Lorraine back closer to us," Andor said. "You can shield her from any eyes while she does what she has to do."

Gary shook his head. "In truth, I cannot spare the energy. I have to get you to the point that you can travel. We need to take you to the healing grounds Tariq has built up. We also need the reinforcements of ancient blood. You have to stay very still and keep your body buried under the soil. You can't move. I've managed to remove the poisons from your body that were injected into you as well as their parasites. I cut out the dead tissue and have stimulated some growth. There were so many places leaking blood, I couldn't get to them all, so as fast as I stopped one, another seemed to spring up."

"Lorraine has yet to understand that a hunter seeks to end the vampire when he finds one. I had no choice but to fight them." It was no apology. He stated a fact. Hunters sought out the undead, tracking them from lair to lair. It was their job to destroy them wherever they were. In this case, he had been drawn into a trap. Three lesser vampires had been used as bait. It had mattered little to him, they all needed to be terminated.

"I understand," Gary conceded. "But it doesn't make the healing any easier."

Gary's head snapped up at the same time Andor felt the dead space in the night's air that indicated the unseen presence of the enemy.

*Lorraine. Get back here now. Are you within the safeguards?*

*Of course, I feel it. The four of you have shared your minds so much, you've trained mine. He thinks I'm all alone out here.*

*O jelä peje terád, emni—sun scorch you, woman, you are not bait for the undead.* He was going to wring her neck when he was able to move again.

Her soft laughter flooded his mind and then it was cut off abruptly and she was gone. Behind her, along the walls of his mind where she had just brushed her amusement, pouring into him and making him feel whole, he felt a piercing pain, like a knife jabbing. It was the lingering sensation when all else vanished.

# 6

One moment Lorraine was laughing, amused by Andor's archaic way of thinking, and the next something stabbed deep into her mind. She had the presence of mind to shut herself off from Andor, recognizing the attack of a vampire. This one was strong, stronger than anything she could imagine. The stab went deep, the pain radiating outward to encompass her entire brain. It was painful enough that she went down to one knee, dropping her head into her hand. Something had been ripped out of her mind before she'd managed to slam down her shields.

She took in several deep breaths and willed her mind to stay blank. She would not betray the fact that Andor was so injured and that all of the Carpathians were weak. They didn't want to leave her alone during daylight hours, so they slept in shallow depressions, rather than sinking deep in the earth where they would have been safe and could recuperate. They did take turns, with Gary insisting he take a turn as well. She thought he should always go to ground, but no one listened to her. The ancients were still living in the dark ages as far as women were concerned.

The jab hit her shields and bounced back, leaving an oily residue behind. The feel of it made her gag. She knew she had to get back to camp. The Carpathians had constructed a shelter to prevent any ray of the sun from reaching them. They had also built a strong safeguard around their camp, the three ancients weaving it so that the invisible barricade would be nearly impossible for even the greatest master vampire to unravel.

She reached for the flamethrower she kept close to her at all times as a flutter of wings told her she wasn't alone. Intellectually, she knew the hideous creatures couldn't penetrate the barrier the Carpathians had woven, but that didn't make it any easier emotionally. She wanted to run. She swallowed hard and slowly rose to her feet, looking up at the surrounding trees.

There were five crows sitting on the branches overhead, looking down at her. Their eyes looked evil as they stared steadily at her. She forced herself to look away from them to the foliage around her. From the many battles she'd studied in each of the ancient's heads, she knew not to be deceived. If she could see the undead in any form, it was because they wanted her to see them, and most likely the attack would come from another direction.

Out of the corner of her eye she caught sight of movement and she turned to face the new assailant. A man strode out from the trees, walking with a confident stride and a smile on his face. Her heart pounded and clenched hard. Her mouth went dry. They'd warned her. All of them had, but she still wasn't prepared. The last time she'd seen him, her brother had lain in a pool of blood on the floor. Now, there he was, looking like he always had.

Theodore had been an athletic man. Really good-looking. He had the same chestnut-colored hair that she did, the same green eyes and easy smile. "Little sister."

That greeting stiffened her spine. Ferro and Sandu called her *sisarke*, which meant "little sister" in their native language. Sometimes they called her that in English, but Theodore had never called her that. She moistened her lips and watched him come closer. She stepped back, taking a firmer grasp on the flamethrower. This replica of her brother was perfect. That easy stride that showed with every step that he was a fluid, perfect fighter. She had always admired the way his muscles flowed when he moved, giving him such an advantage over every opponent.

She'd been thinking of Theodore just minutes before. How much she loved him. How well they'd gotten along. He was older by several years and had never once seemed to resent having a baby sister come along. He'd always seemed proud of her, not jealous. He'd helped her learn difficult moves and train when she'd needed someone to work against. He'd always been patient with her. She preferred being alone in the wilderness where she could have those beautiful memories of her brother, rather than the lurid headlines people remembered him for.

Now her stomach lurched as he walked right up to that invisible barrier with Theodore's confidence. He ran into it, and it flung him backward so hard he landed a good twenty feet away on his butt. He sat there a moment, shook his head and burst out laughing. Even his laugh was the same. Exactly. That laughter hit her hard. She had to fight not to cry. Tears burned behind her eyes but she refused to shed them.

"You don't get to use my brother like that," she reprimanded.

The replica of Theodore stood up, dusted the seat of his jeans off and grinned at her good-naturedly. "Invite me in. I have so much to talk to you about and unless you invite me in, I'll have to go away."

She wanted him to leave, yet perversely, she didn't. Seeing Theodore happy, grinning that old familiar smirk of camaraderie when it had been the two of them against the world, made her happy. She knew that was dangerous. This was a trick. An illusion. Still, it was a perfect one.

"Say my name."

The clone of her brother frowned at her. "What game are you playing? Invite me in."

"You have to say my name."

At once there was that powerful jab at her brain. This was concentrated, like an ice pick seeking to poke a hole through her shields to get at the information the replica of Theodore needed. She pressed her palm to her temple and shook her head. "Teddy, you can't get your way like that. Don't you remember my name?"

She had to find the courage to lure him close and then destroy him with the flamethrower. That would start the war. While she was distracted with the clone of her brother, the others would work to get the safeguards down. They would work together. Gary, Sandu and Ferro had gone over it with her a hundred times.

The clone of her brother moved closer, looking a little wary of the invisible barrier that separated them. He stretched out a hand to her. "You are my beloved little sister."

"I am," she agreed. "Why did you do the terrible things you did, Teddy?" She knew this image had no idea why, but she had always wanted the opportunity to ask him and he was standing right in front of her. Close now. She was going to have to do this. She had no choice if she was going to protect Andor and the others. They were in it together.

She had saved Andor when she couldn't save her brother or parents. She wasn't going to allow a replica of Theodore to kill him or one of the others. She already thought of Sandu, Ferro and Gary as family. They might not feel anything for her in the same way she did, but she knew their souls were bound together. That meant their fates were.

Theodore stepped closer. "I had no choice. They gave me no choice."

"Who gave you no choice?" She needed him a couple of feet closer to ensure accuracy. She leaned toward him as if to hear him better.

At once the vampire pawn took the bait and came almost right up to her, stopping just short of the safeguards. She heard the rustle of wings as one of those watching grew restless and shifted his position in anticipation of success. The crow's wings spread wide and then settled once more against his feathered body.

Steeling herself, Lorraine took a deep breath and let it out slowly. She kept the flamethrower along her thigh, waiting. The clone stepped right into the space where she had practiced hitting and she whipped it up and hit him with the one thousand degrees Celsius of heat and flames. The clone exploded into a fiery blaze so that his entire body was enveloped in orange and red. She kept the flamethrower trained on his chest in the exact spot where his heart should be.

The crows raised their voices with his to a shriek that clawed at her insides. They left the branches in a diving attack, swooping low and at the last minute rising, not as birds, but as their truer forms—the undead. They looked terrifying and hideous with their stained teeth and rotting flesh. They came directly at her face. She didn't make the mistake of switching targets, although self-preservation demanded that she do so. She hung on grimly to the canister they'd given her, that ever-flowing flamethrower the ancients had constructed for her protection.

The sounds were so awful it hurt her ears. She knew she was crying because her vision was blurred, but she held steady. The five vampires spread out, making a semicircle around her, just outside the invisible line of defense. They were swaying, tapping out a rhythm. She'd seen that before. The sound of the branches in the trees picked it up. Tap. Tap. Tap.

The clone, on fire, began to make gruesome noises, each shriek in time with that odd rhythm. Her heart began to thud with the sound so that her pulse beat with that strange rap, rap, rap. She felt it echo in her mind. Rap. Rap. Rap. Like a knock. They were seeking a way into her mind. She couldn't change her heartbeat. Now her breath exploded from her lungs on each tap of their fingers against their thighs, each click of the tree branches. Still, she kept her finger on the trigger of the flamethrower, refusing to back off.

The clone went to his knees, writhing, screaming, the sound punctuating that same drumming beat. He pitched forward facedown. She snapped off the flamethrower and stepped back from the barrier, staring defiantly at the vampires facing her. None of them spoke, but they continued to keep the same beat. She was afraid it might drive her mad. More than anything, she wanted to reach for the ancients, but she knew she couldn't open her mind.

Other than the tapping sound, the night went silent. At once dread filled her. A terrible ominous sensation that raised the hair on her arms and at the back of her neck. She felt fear creep down her spine. Her mouth was dry, and the urge to step forward, to move out of her place of safety, was strong—so strong she knew it was a compulsion.

Lorraine forced her body backward a few steps at a time. Her boots dragged in the dirt, unwilling to obey her. It was only because she was disciplined that she was able to manage. It only took her a few feet from the barrier, but it gave her a sense of triumph that she'd managed to.

This was what they had all been waiting for. Not this. Who. The ancients had known a master vampire had been harassing them, sending his pawns. No one believed it was the head of the army, the undead so cunning that he had fooled everyone; there was more than one master vampire. Each was extremely dangerous.

Sergey Malinov, the master vampire commanding all others, would not travel or attack without pawns, and also some of his best fighters. The ancients also believed he would show himself eventually. He couldn't wait too long, because circumstances would change and their little band might grow stronger.

"Come to me," the vampire whispered, gesturing with his hand, his fingers moving over and over to the sound of the tapping.

He was beautiful. Far more beautiful than Andor, Ferro, Sandu or Gary. His skin was smooth, without a single blemish. His beauty seemed almost blasphemous beside his hideous companions.

She shook her head and managed to stumble back. He didn't take his eyes from her, all the while those fingers beckoning her at that same rhythm. It was nearly impossible to resist him. She took her first step forward, and he smiled, his teeth gleaming white. Pristine.

Movement behind and to the left of the semicircle of the undead caught the master vampire's eye. He swung toward the movement. Gary stepped out of the tree line. Ten feet from him was Sandu. Another ten feet was Ferro. A fourth man she didn't know was there and then a fifth. Relief hit her knees so that she nearly crumpled to the ground. As it was, she went down on one knee, breathing deeply to try to clear her head.

"The plan worked, *sisarke*," Sandu said. "You did very well. Go inside. This slaughter will not be for your eyes."

Lorraine wanted to watch, not for the gore, but to learn. The master vampire spun around to face the five ancients. Each of those faces was grim and scarred. He spat onto the ground, and she saw something wiggling in the dark matter. He pointed to the maggoty creatures, and they replicated over and over and began to grow. She gasped, scrambled to her feet and backed farther away.

"I know none of you," the master vampire stated, as if by claiming that, all of them were inferior to him.

"You have no need of knowing us," one of the two men she didn't know answered.

"Have you no names, then? I am not afraid to tell you I am Karcsi. Perhaps you have heard of me." As he spoke, the tapping got louder, more insistent.

Lorraine realize it was affecting her. She had moved back, but now she was close to the barrier again. Karcsi was targeting her in the hopes that she would come out from behind her shield of safety and he could use her against the ancients. She could have told the vampire it would do him no good. None of those men would stop what they were about to do. They had been born to fight vampires. They had spent centuries honing their skills with battle after battle. Nothing would dissuade them from their ultimate goal—destroying the master vampire.

The man who had spoken before bowed slightly. "I am Dragomir, a monk from the monastery high in the Carpathian Mountains. Now that we have that out of the way, let us proceed."

The words were barely out of his mouth before he moved, his speed so fast he blurred as he attacked, not the master vampire, but one of the lesser ones. Sandu and Gary also joined him, along with the man she didn't know, each targeting one of the vampires tapping.

Ferro went after the master vampire. She hated that it was Ferro, although he looked far more fit than he had before. Presumably, the ancients had given him blood before they had sprung the trap. Now that Karcsi was completely engaged in a life-and-death struggle and the other vampires had been unable to continue their hypnotic tapping, she was able to pull out from under the spell completely.

She ran along the barrier, keeping her eyes on the last of the lesser vampires, the one who was circling around trying to come up behind Ferro. The ancient and the master vampire rose into the air, hurling fiery spears at each other. The undead hit some kind of impediment and sank toward earth. A lightning whip found his ankle as he dove toward Sandu's head. The whip jerked the vampire back toward Ferro.

Ferro and the undead crashed together as they hit the ground, lightning sizzling all around them. The wiggling creatures rushed toward their master and his attacker, some instantly incinerated as they came into contact with the lightning whip. The stench was foul, making her retch. She kept her eyes on the lesser vampire with difficulty. There was so much happening at once, it was difficult to follow all the action.

She needed to get back to Andor. He would be going insane, worried about her and wondering what was going on, unless one of the ancients was keeping him informed, and she didn't see how that was possible. She was getting anxious, although Ferro, Gary and Sandu had all three assured her over and over that nothing would get through their safeguards above- or belowground to threaten Andor while they sprang their trap.

She also knew Andor wasn't going to be happy with any of them for using her as bait. It wouldn't matter that she had come up with the idea. They knew they had to have time to heal Andor. He was still in jeopardy. After the terrible fight for his life, she wasn't about to lose him now. She'd known that fighting a master vampire would be impossible for her, but she hadn't had any idea of how incredibly powerful that undead was. She never would have been able to resist his compulsions, even with the safeguards up.

The lesser vampire circled around Ferro, who had his back to her. The vampire was stealthy, stepping through the wiggling maggots as they squirmed toward the ancient. Some had already reached him and were swarming up his leg. She could see a blood trail circling his ankle. The lesser vampire, in order to get behind him, moved right in front of her, almost in position. Ferro stepped to his right to avoid an attack by Karcsi.

Lorraine realized Ferro had inched around, bringing the fight back right in front of her so that the lesser vampire, doing his master's bidding, would be forced to creep up on the ancient using the path closest to her. It shocked her how skilled these men were, that they were able to know where everyone else was on the battlefield.

She had to figure exactly where the vampire's heart was, something a little more difficult when his back was turned. She sent up a silent prayer that she got it right and hit him with the flamethrower. It occurred to her that she'd come into the wilderness to find peace. She really had been on a journey of personal discovery, hoping to find a way to subdue her temper and make herself into a better person. Instead, she'd found a group of people far more violent—out of necessity—than her family had ever been. They didn't fight for glory, fame, trophies or medals. They fought to save lives.

The smell of burning flesh, rotting as it was, disgusted her. She hoped she could just destroy him and his heart quickly, but he spun around and threw the flames back at her. She dropped the flamethrower as she stumbled back. The flames hit the defensive obstruction and roared back at the vampire.

He screamed, rushing toward the barricade as if by his anger alone he could break through it to get at her. She managed to get her hands on the canister and hit him with another steady stream, this time directly over his heart. He hit the barrier over and over, that invisible line of woven safeguards. Each time sparks and embers flew into the air.

The wind intensified and the flames engulfed him completely. Gary came up behind the vampire and whirled him around. *Get to Andor. We've got this.*

She'd never been so happy to hear anything in her life. The horror of what she was witnessing was too much. All the blood covering the ancients from where the vampires had ripped open their bodies made her physically ill. She couldn't help them anymore. Her job had been to be bait and then, if possible, take out the last vampire who they knew would try to do his master's bidding to kill Ferro.

Lorraine rushed back to the invisible structure that was over Andor. His indigo eyes were an inky mixture of midnight purple and blue. He was furious. There was no getting around that fact, not when he'd never been angry at her before.

"You used yourself as bait to lure the master vampire in." It was an accusation, nothing less. "You knew I would not approve of such a thing, but you did it anyway."

She couldn't exactly deny it. "It was necessary."

"It is never necessary for you to put yourself in danger. I would not have been able to get to you, although I would have tried if Karcsi had managed to lure you beyond the safeguards."

The fact that he knew the master vampire's chosen name meant someone, or all of them, was sharing information. "I know you're angry, but I did what I felt was right." She tried not to sound defiant. She wasn't a child and had every right to make her own decisions based on what she thought was right for all of them, but he looked more than angry, he looked hurt. Guilty. Ashamed. Shame was the last thing she wanted him to feel.

"You knew, had you discussed this plan with me, I would have forbidden it."

Just hearing the word *forbidden* made her see red. She tried to tell herself he came from a different time, when men ruled women. An entirely different culture. She even reminded herself he was a completely different species and their society, out of necessity, was different, but the fact remained, they were in a mess and needed all hands on deck.

"You don't have the right to tell me what to do."

Something very dangerous flickered in his eyes. He might be near the brink of death, but he was an extremely powerful being. "I have every right as your lifemate." Suddenly he sounded calm, too calm.

"We aren't lifemates yet," she snapped, her temper getting the best of her in spite of her desire to be reasonable and calm with him. She was shaking, sick to her stomach and still upset over having set the clone of her brother on fire. Seeing so much blood had brought the images of her family far too close. Knowing a battle raged just a few yards from her with hideous, vile creatures wanting to kill them all in a very brutal way had her shaken.

"We are lifemates," he assured in a very low voice. "Apparently, you do not feel like my lifemate, although you are bound to me soul to soul and you have been in my mind for several risings. That must not be enough."

Her heart gave a little leap. "It isn't that. I'm human, Andor. First, you didn't go near humans for all those years and then you locked yourself away in a monastery. Time marched on, and with it, women changed."

"A lifemate is still the same."

"You don't know that. How would you know that?"

"You do what it takes to make me happy, and I do the same for you."

"Sometimes, Andor, it's about keeping someone safe. I'm alive. So are you. We needed to get rid of the vampires and to do that, we had to draw out the master vampire."

"It was too much for three of my brethren to clone you when Karcsi managed to conjure up an illusion of your brother? They thought nothing of risking you. I assure you, Lorraine, they would never risk their own lifemates."

"We did what we thought was right. They were weak. There was no one in the vicinity to give blood. They wanted to do something like that, but I could tell they were worried about the vampire somehow knowing. I made the decision I thought was right."

"If you thought it was right, you would have talked it over with me," Andor said. His gaze never left her face.

He looked too calm. Andor was almost always calm, but now, with all signs of his temper gone, she was very concerned. She opened her mouth to try to get him to understand her reasoning, even though she knew he wouldn't accept her explanation.

"*Te avio päläfertiilam.*" She had learned enough of the language just by being in his mind, but he interpreted for her anyway. "You are my lifemate."

"I'm working on wrapping my head around that." She tried to be conciliatory.

"*Éntölam kuulua, avio päläfertiilam.* I claim you as my lifemate."

The moment he uttered the words, something inside her responded. She actually felt ties threading from Andor to her. She held up her hand. "Wait. Andor, wait."

He ignored her. "*Ted kuuluak, kacad, kojed.* I belong to you. *Élidamet andam.* I offer my life for you."

Lorraine could barely breathe. "I know you're upset with me, but we have to talk about this. Andor, we have to discuss it."

"In the way that you discussed your decisions with me?" Those indigo-colored eyes never left her face.

"I know, I do. I get your point. It's just that what you're doing feels permanent. You're saying vows, right?"

He nodded slowly. "You are correct. The ritual binding words are imprinted on the males of our species before we are born. They only work with the woman who is a true lifemate. You are uncertain if you are my lifemate, so we are testing that theory." His eyes didn't so much as blink, and he reminded her of a predator. "*Pesämet andam.* I give you my protection. *Uskolfertiilamet andam.* I give you my allegiance."

"Stop it. I mean it. You can't do this because you're upset with me. This is something that could potentially affect both of us for the rest of our lives."

"You getting killed would not have done that? Do you know what happens when a male Carpathian loses his lifemate? When you were in my mind, or sharing the mind of males who are not your lifemate, did you find out that very important piece of information?"

She shook her head, suddenly very afraid of what he might tell her. To be strictly fair, Andor wasn't the kind of man who would be angry because she had done something she believed was right. He would be upset, but not angry. Had she missed an important piece of information that might have affected her decision?

"The male will go into what is known as a thrall. In other words, he is insane. During those few moments after her death he must choose to suicide, or during the thrall, he will become vampire. I am an ancient. I am extremely powerful. Those who hunt me must be either my brethren, which will send them closer to their destruction, or most likely I will kill many Carpathian hunters and an unknown number of humans. All because you chose to do something without first discussing it with me."

Okay. None of that sounded good. No one had volunteered that information to her. Had she had that, perhaps she would have made different choices, but truthfully, she thought a lifemate was a wife to their people. Maybe much more important since they had to search centuries for her, but still . . . To become vampire because they lost her seemed extreme.

"*Sívamet andam.* I give you my heart. *Sielamet andam.* I give you my soul. *Ainamet andam.* I give you my body. *Sívamet kuuluak kaik että a ted.* I take into my keeping the same that is yours."

"You're making me crazy," she objected. "Just give me a few minutes to think about this. I need you to better explain what a lifemate is."

"I did explain it to you."

"Well, I didn't understand exactly. Clearly, it is far different than a human finding a life partner. Andor. You can't say ritual words that might tie us together . . ." She knew the moment she said "might" she'd made another mistake. It was just that she was very nervous. With every word he spoke, and each was very beautiful, she felt those ties binding them together, as if their souls really had been one, torn apart, and now was being cemented back together.

"*Ainaak olenszal sívambin.* Your life will be cherished by me for all time. *Te élidet ainaak pide minan.* Your life will be placed above mine for all time."

"I was in your mind, Andor, but I was specifically looking for battles to better learn how to protect you while you were so horribly wounded. When the others came, I asked them for help as well. When it became apparent that you were so far gone you were in a coma and Gary couldn't bring you back, they explained that my soul was bound to yours and they could use that tie between us, to find you. I didn't know enough about your species to know what I was doing, but I did know I had to find a way to save you."

"You think you did so because you wanted to save someone after what happened to your family, but if you look deep down, Lorraine, you will see that it was far more than that."

He didn't need to tell her that. She knew. There was a huge pull between them. "I'm sorry I didn't have all the necessary information to make good decisions."

"Had you turned to your lifemate, instead of to others who are not capable of feeling emotion, you would have been told all the facts. *Te avio päläfertiilam.* You are my lifemate. *Ainaak sívamet jutta oleny.* You are bound to me for all eternity. *Ainaak terád vigyázak.* You are always in my care."

Whatever he did was irrevocable. She knew it immediately, the moment that last word was uttered. The power of those ritual words was consummate. She scooted away from him. "I think we just had our first real fight."

"There is no need of another."

"Maybe you don't think so, but this world of yours is overwhelming as it is, Andor. You can't take away my free will like that. I might have come to you because I wanted to—now I'm rethinking everything I thought I knew about you." She stared out toward the forest. Lightning forked the sky, long ribbons of sizzling white-hot energy. She watched as Ferro controlled it, slamming it at something gruesome on the ground.

She turned her head to look over her shoulder at Andor. "What else?"

"I do not understand."

"What else haven't I been told that is important? For instance, you mentioned children, but you're Carpathian and I'm human. How does that affect the child?"

"You must become Carpathian."

She stared at him for a very long time, unable to fully process his quiet, utterly calm statement. She blinked as if that would change everything. Instead, it brought him more fully into focus so that she noted the lines so deep in his face. A part of her protested that, was alarmed. Nothing could happen to him. "I'm sorry?" she said, unable to believe she'd heard him correctly.

"You must become Carpathian."

"How is that possible?" She lifted one eyebrow, but regarded him steadily. Her heart was in her throat. Nothing made sense to her, not the way she was feeling about him. Not the way she needed to smooth those lines from his face, or the worry from his eyes. She wanted to tell him it didn't matter what she had to do to make him happy, she'd do it; but she wasn't that woman. She would never be that woman. She had to think things through before she impulsively made decisions. And that meant she needed all the facts.

"Come here."

It wasn't an order. Andor said it softly. An entreaty, because he couldn't move and she could. Lorraine took one more look outside at the night that was now lit up with flames and lightning. Thunder rolled. She heard it, but didn't know if the sound was her blood roaring in her ears from sheer fear or if there really was thunder to accompany those long sizzling strands of lightning whipping across the sky in dazzling displays.

"You're going to tell me something I don't like." But she went to him. It was almost a compulsion because she couldn't stand those lines of pain and weariness carved deep on his face. They had all been so determined to save him, and no one, least of all her, had thought of the cost to him. She smoothed her hand over his face, down his jaw. Just touching him made her feel better.

"It depends, *sívamet*. Do you understand what it means to be a life-mate with the way I explained it? My soul was split in half at birth. Each person contains both dark and light. The darkness went into me, the light into you. Now that we are back together, I feel that light. I see in color. I feel emotion. You are an unbelievable miracle to me. Without you, I would go back to darkness. The loss of emotion and returning to that gray void would most likely send me over the edge. You've seen those soulless creatures. You know how vile and horrific they are. I have spent my life hunting them. To lose my honor, to become the thing I detest the most, at the end of my long life, after honor was everything to me, would be the worst."

Lorraine nodded. She understood what he was saying. She felt his sincerity and she understood. He had lived a lifetime with only his honor to sustain him. She'd been in his mind and had seen that. Honor was everything to him—and to his brethren.

"It is an impossibility for me to become human, Lorraine, or I would do so if that was what you wished. I could age with you and choose death when you die, at least there have been rumors that it is possible. There is still the risk of the thrall . . ."

"Andor, tell me what it takes to become Carpathian."

"Three full blood exchanges. We have not even had one. I have taken your blood, but you have yet to take mine. To bind you, soul to soul, Ferro, Gary and Sandu must have exchanged blood with you, yet you have not turned."

She tried to keep her heart rate under control when it threatened to beat wildly. "Three blood exchanges? What does that mean?"

He frowned and reached for her hand. "They didn't take your blood?"

"Yes. Like you did." What was he talking about, an exchange? How could she possibly take his blood? Did he mean a transfusion? She didn't have teeth like his. She didn't understand why she suddenly was afraid, but she was.

Andor brought her hand to his mouth and pressed a kiss into the center of her palm. "They took your blood from your wrist?" He pressed his lips over her wrist, right over her frantically beating pulse. She should have known she couldn't hide her fear from him. He would hear the crazy, alarmed beat of her heart and he'd feel it beneath his mouth and the slide of his tongue that felt too much like seduction.

"Andor," she cautioned uneasily. "You aren't supposed to move at all, not even your arms. Gary didn't want you out from under the soil."

"Answer me, *csecsemő*, was the blood taken from your wrist?"

She nodded. He was dangerous to the woman in her. She hadn't ever been that attracted to a man, mostly because she was training and going to school, both of which she took very seriously. Now, with this man, completely covered in dirt right up to his neck, wounded, holes in his chest and belly, she was so attracted she wanted to kiss him. It didn't matter if a war raged outside. It didn't matter that he was Carpathian and she was human or that he had come from another time when women were told what to do and they obeyed. She was so far from that kind of woman it was frightening, yet she wanted to know the way he tasted.

His mouth moved up the inside of her arm. Tiny kisses. Each one made her sex flutter and her stomach do slow somersaults. His teeth scraped occasionally along her skin, and that felt so erotic it was scary.

"I have tied us together," he murmured, lifting his head, but retaining possession of her arm. His eyes met hers. "The three of them are bound to us, soul to soul. To *both* of us. Can you feel them? Feel their injuries? Reach out to one of them now, Lorraine. Let your mind expand."

She had practiced telepathy for years and had gotten stronger the more she'd worked at it. She'd often caught the thoughts of others as she'd passed them in the hallways at college. In a way, it was different than what he was asking her to do. She wasn't certain why he wanted her to reach out to feel the others, but she would if he needed that.

Lorraine closed her eyes and leaned into Andor automatically, as if she'd been relying on him for a hundred years. His fingers moved on her inner wrist, tracing little circles while his eyes remained steady on her face. She could feel his stare, it was that intense. She reached for Ferro because he had fought the worst of the creatures. She used the lightest of touches and gasped when she felt his pain. So much. His wounds were severe. Her eyes snapped open.

"He does not feel it, Lorraine, only you do. I can stop pain. Gary can. Sandu will not feel it. Pain is a liability to us when we fight. We sacrifice our bodies in order to get to the prize—the vampire's dead heart. You are tied to each of us now, as they are tied to us. You are a light for them, not in the way you are for me, but they feel it and it lightens their burdens. It does not, however, lighten yours. If it became too much, you would be unable to block it out."

"Why am I not feeling your pain? You have to feel it, Andor, I know you do."

"I am your lifemate. I keep you from feeling what is painful to me."

"You're expending energy, which Gary said was dangerous to you."

"He does not have a lifemate."

"If they took my blood and somehow put their blood in me, if there really were these exchanges, why am I not Carpathian?"

"There must be a certain volume of blood exchanged. Gary would know this, and he most likely cautioned the others against taking or giving too much."

"So, you have to give me so much of your blood in exchange for mine three times."

He nodded. "That is correct."

His fingers were moving up and down her arm, featherlight. It felt intimate and right. She couldn't imagine being without him, but she didn't quite understand the full ramifications of having three blood exchanges.

"I don't have your teeth."

"I would aid you. Distance you so you are able to take my blood and it would feel . . . erotic."

Just his fingers felt erotic. His lips on her skin. "Then what would happen?"

"Your human body would die and you would be reborn Carpathian."

# 7

Andor regarded his brethren as they joined Lorraine and him. Each man had wounds, and blood dripped steadily. He waved his hand toward them. "Lorraine has difficulty with blood."

Ferro sank onto the ground. "Forgive me, *sisarke*, I should have cleaned up before joining you."

Lorraine pressed three fingers to her lips and nodded, avoiding looking at the warriors crowding close. Even with Andor waving his hand to create a breeze, the scent of blood was very strong.

"We destroyed one master vampire. I tried to pull information from Karcsi's mind before I slew him," Ferro said, "but he was resistant. Just before he succumbed, I saw someone staring at me through his eyes." He leaned closer to Andor. "I believe Sergey was there for a moment, watching us. That could mean that he has been spying this entire time, using anything from the birds to deer to his lesser pawns."

Andor tightened his hold on Lorraine. He could tell he had shocked her by revealing that her human body would have to die prior to her becoming Carpathian. Now she had a look of horror on her face, and a shiver had gone down her spine.

"He can do that?" Steadfastly, she kept her gaze fixed on Andor's face, not looking at the warriors with various degrees of vicious wounds.

Each was removing signs of blood and attempting to heal himself. She knew Ferro would need blood and have to go to ground. Fighting a master vampire took a toll on their bodies, no matter how skilled in battle one was.

"He can use animals to spy on us?"

"A master vampire can use any living creature to spy," Andor said. "Sergey Malinov was considered the weakest of the Malinov brothers, yet he was the one all along that should have been targeted. Even his own brothers did not realize the extent of his planning and treachery. He has at least two splinters of Xavier, the high mage, in him, which means he has access to Xavier's memories and spells."

Lorraine held up her hand to stop him. "I can't deal with this. It's all too fantasy for me. Mages, vampires, men surviving on blood and sleeping in the ground. I have to get away for a few minutes. Go for a walk or something."

Andor gripped her hand tighter. *Sívamet. You know you cannot. If I could, I would walk with you somewhere quiet and beautiful. I would point out the stars and carry you across the sky so you feel the peace of the night. It is beautiful beyond all imagining. Give me a few more days and I will make this right with you. You have my word.*

Speaking to Lorraine so intimately stirred feelings in his chest that were growing deeper each time he was in her mind. Her face softened and she lay down beside him, turning to just face him as if she could block out the rest of them. He glanced at Ferro and Sandu and immediately both men sat on the other side of his lifemate, protecting her from the gazes of the other men.

"Dragomir, it is good to see you. Isai, thank you for heeding the call."

"You are a mess," Dragomir said, crouching beside him. "Tariq was not happy that he was kept from coming in person. He is guarded day and night. At night by ancient hunters, and by day, his well-trained, human army." There was a trace of amusement in his voice. "I have given blood to the healer, and he will do his best to get you fit for travel."

Andor nodded. More than anything, he wanted to get Lorraine to a safe place. He tugged on her wrist and brought her hand back to his mouth, biting gently on her finger. "Perhaps you should go to the compound, Lorraine. There are women there who were human at one time and now are Carpathian. They will be able to make you feel less alone."

*You make me feel less alone. I just need time to think things through. Everything has happened so fast and every time I think I understand the dynamics of your world, it expands or changes. It is a very frightening place.*

He reached for her hair, that silky mass of chestnut strands he loved to rub between his fingers and crush in his fist. Even with all the warriors surrounding her, as ancient and skilled as they were, during the daylight hours, she was alone. They needed to get to the compound. He cursed the fact that he was the one putting them all in jeopardy. Still, even if Tariq sent a helicopter for him, it wouldn't solve the problem of getting through the gauntlet of Sergey's army. They didn't want to take the fight to the compound, where there were more women and children to protect.

"They are coming at us fairly hard and steady," Sandu said. "It makes no sense, Andor."

Andor was always their thoughtful one. He worked things out step by step. Very logically. When one separated emotion from decisions, the right decision was almost always made. All of them were the same in that they didn't feel, but most simply didn't bother with anything but battle. They looked to Andor to figure out the whys.

"It does make a kind of sense, considering at this point, Sergey has only one goal. He doesn't want anything else but Elisabeta back. He seems to have abandoned everything and is looking for ways to get her. She has been with him for hundreds of years."

Lorraine's eyes opened and fixed on his face. "A master vampire has feelings for a woman? I didn't realize that there could be female vampires."

"She isn't a vampire. It is impossible for a Carpathian woman to become vampire. Sergey captured her and found he could feel through her. There is no way he wants to give her up," Andor explained. "She is safe within the compound at the moment, but he will be desperate to reacquire her."

"She is healing in the earth, although it is only her mind we hope to heal. He punished her, but he didn't harm her," Dragomir said.

"He harmed her," Andor said. "You just cannot see the scars."

"She will seek to go back to him."

Every head turned to regard the healer. He had taken blood from Isai, Andor's brethren from the monastery. Gary looked closer to his full strength in spite of the few lacerations Andor could see on him.

"Why do you say that, healer?" Sandu asked.

"She has had no one but Sergey Malinov in her life for hundreds of years. He has been her everything. She is submissive to him and only responds to orders. Didn't you see her? Observe her as she was put into the ground? She is lost without him. She cannot make decisions for herself, and once she is aboveground she will be lost. She has never made a single decision for herself. She depended on him for sustenance, for company, for every single thing."

"Why would he do that?" Lorraine asked, sitting up slowly and looking at Gary.

"Vampires want to feel," Gary explained. "They were once Carpathians and they wanted to feel so much that they willingly traded their souls in order to feel a rush when they fed while killing their victims. You can imagine what a treasure Elisabeta would be to him. She is of the light and that light would shine into his rotted soul. He would feel the things she does through her mind. He kept her as pure as possible in order to never lose that. No one, not even his brothers, knew he had her."

Gary moved to Andor's other side. "Stay still. Your arms were supposed to be under the blanket of soil."

The healer glanced at Ferro, looking him over in a single perusal to ensure the ancient could heal his wounds or one of the others was capable of doing it. Without another word, he shed his body, and Andor could feel that white-hot light moving through him.

"We cannot have a traitor in our midst," Sandu said.

Ferro turned his head sharply. "Elisabeta is no traitor."

"She was taken as a very young woman and has had no contact with anyone other than Sergey Malinov," Dragomir said. "Some thought Emeline was a traitor because Vadim Malinov had taken her blood and forced her to become pregnant, but she fought valiantly against him. Who knows how many centuries went by before Sergey gained complete control over Elisabeta."

"When she was taken from the cage, there were signs of punishments, and we were told he had hurt her and threatened to harm any who sought to aid her," Isai added.

"I misspoke," Sandu corrected immediately. "It is true that she is not a traitor. What happened to her is unfortunate. Perhaps she should be escorted back to the Carpathian Mountains."

*Unfortunate?* Lorraine was horrified by their choice of words.

"He would only follow," Isai said. "I have been watching for signs of him. He has spies surrounding the compound. Sergey will know the moment she has risen. He will fight to get her back. I think he will send an army after her."

Andor had the feeling he knew why Sergey was so interested in his own woman. "Lorraine is very vulnerable. He thinks she is Carpathian. She fought off his pawn. She has now stopped a master vampire from ensnaring her. If he wants Elisabeta so badly, he will continue to go after her. Having had complete rule of her for hundreds of years, he is just as much bound to her as she thinks she is to him, but he will try for another woman. Lorraine is out here in the middle of nowhere and several ancients have come to protect her. He would never conceive that she is still human."

Lorraine gasped and tried to pull her hand loose. Andor tightened his hold on her. "*Csecsemő*, he will not be able to get near you. Look at my brothers. Look around you. They are here to help keep you safe."

Andor's chest was on fire, and he had to work hard to keep that from his lifemate. The healer was extremely powerful. Over many centuries, Andor had been wounded, at times suffering a mortal wound, which meant others had had to aid in healing or he would have succumbed, but nothing had ever felt like it did with Gary working on him from the inside out. It felt like a blowtorch was being applied.

"I don't understand how he had this woman and no one was able to get her back." There was a small note of anger threading through Lorraine's voice.

"In those days, when she was taken," Andor said, "there were human wars being fought. Our people were scattering, some sent out by Vlad to other places. Many people, both human and Carpathian, disappeared and there was little to be done about it."

"Elisabeta has a brother, Traian," Dragomir added. "Tariq told me Traian searched for his sister, or any word of what happened to her. She disappeared without a trace. No one suspected the Malinovs. It was speculated, much later, when it was discovered that Xavier, the high mage, was working against our people, that he had taken and killed her as he did Rhiannon."

"What will Tariq do once Elisabeta rises?" Lorraine asked. "Would he send her away? If he does, Andor, we have to help her. It sounds as if she's been conditioned to do whatever this Sergey has told her. She needs someone to talk to, to help her get over that."

"How does one get over hundreds of years of training?" Isai asked. "It is impossible. She has been shaped by these endless years with a sadistic vampire."

"Her lifemate will know what to do, what she needs," Dragomir assured Lorraine. "And Tariq would never turn her away, any more than he would have turned Emeline out of the safety of the compound. He just knows he has to be more watchful."

"If her lifemate held out," Sandu said. "It is entirely possible he has turned or is long gone. In any case, if Sergey cannot get to her physically, he has a blood-bond with her."

Dragomir looked at his brethren for a long time. "Emeline had a blood-bond with Vadim. He attacked her nightly, but she held out against him and she was human. I know you believe Elisabeta will give up vital information on the compound and our defenses to Sergey, but she will not want to return to him. She may feel she has no choice because she knows no other way, but she will not betray us."

"You are so certain of this you are willing to risk Emeline and your child?" Sandu demanded.

Lorraine's fingers threaded through Andor's. He looked up at her face. She was definitely upset over the unfortunate Elisabeta. *Sívamet, no one will turn away from this woman. She is one of ours and will be cherished as the treasure she is. If her lifemate were to find her, he would know how best to help her.*

*How? How can he know?*

His heart lurched unexpectedly. There was no trace of tears on her face or in her eyes, but it was there in her mind. She really hated what had been done to the absent woman. She didn't know her, had never met her, yet she was very upset on Elisabeta's behalf. He fell a little more in love with her. He knew the intimacy of their mind-to-mind contact allowed him to see into who she was and what she stood for. They were surrounded by so many of his kind, yet it was just the two of them right then.

*A lifemate takes a vow to cherish his woman. To see to her happiness. Just as we can see into each other's minds, he will be able to do the same for Elisabeta. Her happiness will be placed above his for all time. She will feel the same about him. She will want to make him happy in all things. It is the way of our people. Elisabeta may be even more determined to see to her lifemate's happiness, but even if that is so, he will balance those needs for her.*

Andor wanted to be healed. To be alone with her. To be able to take Lorraine into his arms and hold her close. She needed comfort.

"Do you think he's out there right now watching us?"

Ferro's head came up sharply. "*Sisarke*, he is not close, but his spies surround us. We will be in top fighting form when we leave this place. Andor will be ready soon. We needed fresh blood supplies. Have no worries. We will get you safely to the compound."

Sandu nodded. "All this talk of Sergey has made you uneasy. That was not our intention. Elisabeta is one of our women. Even if Malinov managed to brainwash her to the point that she would think to betray us, we would never abandon her. We would have to think of ways to counter the harm he has done to her. I know I sounded harsh to you. I felt your disapproval when I misspoke and called her a traitor, but you have been inside my mind enough to know I would not abandon one of our women."

Lorraine tightened her grip on Andor's hand, and he closed his fingers around hers so she would know he was right there with her. She wasn't alone in the midst of all the others. He would always champion her. "I know, Sandu, it's just that I'm human. I'm very modern. You're talking about a woman who never had a chance and all of you are so very removed and distant, as if you're talking in the abstract. That hideous monster took her at a young age and forced her to live a certain way with him."

"He tortured her into submission," Isai said helpfully.

Andor wanted to throw something at the man. "Truly? You could not have tried to put a little sympathy in your voice when you imparted that information to her?" He glared at his fellow monk.

"What? I was telling your woman that none of us believe Elisabeta is to blame for whatever she has become. Was that not being sympathetic?" He looked to Lorraine. "Was that not sympathetic?"

Dragomir gave a little sniff of disdain. "And you say great songs have been written about you."

"They are of a great warrior," Isai reminded.

"Clearly not a compassionate warrior," Dragomir insisted.

"*Compassionate* and *warrior* are mutually exclusive, and you failing to understand the two do not belong together explains why you have no song," Isai said.

"What are they talking about? Songs?" Lorraine asked.

"The Carpathian people tend to have songs sung about great warriors," Andor explained. "Dragomir is upset because he has no song."

"If he was not so compassionate," Sandu said, "he might have gotten one."

Lorraine glared at Sandu. "Compassion is what makes a great warrior. You have to temper your murderous skills with kindness, or you might find yourself looking like a terrible bully and brute."

Andor kept every vestige of humor from his face, but it was impossible to keep it out of his mind. Lorraine turned her glare on him, and he hastily tried to change the subject. Before he could speak, Gary was suddenly back in his body, swaying with weariness, looking extremely pale, as if he had spent far too much time separated from spirit and body. The moment Gary appeared, Dragomir was there, offering blood.

While he did so, Isai shed his body and entered Andor. Lorraine observed the smooth transfer. "I find it amazing how much all of you are so unselfish. You offer one another blood and you heal one another, in spite of the dangers surrounding us."

Andor smiled at her. "We hunt alone as a rule, and often hunters do not like to share or exchange blood because should we turn, the other can always track us. Speaking of which, has anyone heard how Aidan Savage is faring?"

"Who is Aidan Savage?" Lorraine asked.

"He is Carpathian, lifemate to Alexandria. She has a younger brother, Joshua, who is getting up there in age, I think," Dragomir said. "I have had to catch up quickly with all those Tariq has to call on. Aidan resides in San Francisco and has his hands full with a very large territory. It was Tariq's bad luck that the Malinovs targeted Southern California for their stronghold. Aidan is alone unless the Dark Troubadours are performing and then he has help if he has to hunt the vampire."

"What is happening for him to have need of help? Aidan Savage is renowned for his abilities. Even I have heard of him," Sandu said.

"There were two master vampires wreaking havoc in San Francisco. They were aware of his presence, and they trapped him. He fought them both, and I believe it was Alexandria who came to his aid. She fought with him when he was mortally wounded. I have no idea how they were able to drive the two off when Aidan was hurt, but they did, and Alexandria was able, with the help of young Joshua and a human male who works for them, to get Aidan back to their home and into the ground."

"I would have thought the prince would choose him as his representative here in the United States," Andor said.

Gary politely closed the slash in Dragomir's wrist and sank back onto his heels. "He is moving to the East Coast as soon as he is well enough to travel. He is used to living in cities now and so establishing residency in several larger cities in the East will be easy enough for him. Others will be joining him. It was Tariq's bad luck to have established his businesses here, and he has always been a part of human society. He understands them. Aidan has learned to do that as well. Like the De La Cruz brothers in South America, he has always had a human family looking out for him during the day. That same family looks after Joshua while Aidan and Alexandria sleep."

"Are you all right?" Lorraine asked him, anxiety betraying the fact that she was tied to Gary and could feel his fatigue.

Gary nodded. "I just need a little time to recover. All of us will take turns working on the worst of Andor's wounds. We hope to have him ready to travel by the next rising."

Andor shook his head. "That gives her another day to get through without a guard. If Sergey is looking to acquire her, he will eventually strike during the time we are underground."

"For all intents and purposes, Andor," Gary said with a sigh, "you were dead. You have three mortal wounds. *Three*. Not one. Three. Each of those wounds would have killed you. They have to be dealt with before you can travel. If you tried to shift, everything we've done would be undone. We will be flying you home on the back of a dragon."

Lorraine burst out laughing. "Oh my God. Now you're adding dragons to the mix."

"We can shift into any shape," Andor told her.

When she looked around at them all, the brethren nodded. "It's true," Sandu assured. "From a dragon to a moth. You will be able to do so as well after Andor converts you."

Andor's gaze was fixed on his woman and he saw her discomfort immediately. Her small white teeth bit down on her lower lip and she gave a slight shake of her head. He wasn't the only one who noticed. Gary's head went up alertly as did Sandu's. Ferro turned to look at her. Lorraine's color deepened.

"You do know you must be converted," Gary said, his tone very gentle.

Andor realized immediately that because Gary had been human, he had an advantage over the others. Shaking his head slightly to keep the brethren from speaking, Andor kept his gaze fixed on Gary. Having that bond between the three men, Lorraine and him had bothered him on some level. Now he realized it was a good thing.

"I don't know that at all," Lorraine denied.

There was no defiance in her voice, and that told Andor more than anything else that she really hadn't made up her mind. Lorraine thought things through. No one was going to force her to do anything, not without a fight. He was patient as a rule, and that was a good trait to have when his lifemate needed to work things out for herself.

"Lorraine," Gary said. "A male hunter is extremely dangerous, especially one as ancient as Andor. Those locked away in the monastery were there for a reason. Should any of them turn vampire, it would take several of our best hunters to track and attempt to destroy them, most likely at a great cost. Without you fully with him, he will always be vulnerable to turning, even more so than usual, because now he will feel unfamiliar emotions that will rule where his logical judgment once prevented him from making terrible mistakes."

She frowned. "How is that part of the lifemate ritual? The vows? I listened to them very carefully, Gary, and he promises to put my happiness above his own. If I'm not happy being Carpathian and want to stay human, that makes no sense."

"Carpathian males were imprinted with the ritual binding words in order to prevent them from turning vampire. They found their lifemate and recited the words, binding the two together. A woman was raised knowing, and excited about finding, her true lifemate. She had no problem being tied to the man who would spend an eternity devoted to her."

"I'm not Carpathian, and I wasn't raised in your world."

"I wasn't raised in the Carpathian world, either," Gary said. "I was born human. I am no longer human, not a single part of me. Even my past is different, but I still understand what you fear. I had those same fears when Gregori told me he was going to convert me. I'd seen a conversion. It isn't easy on the one undergoing it."

"That is true," Dragomir said, "but we also have found a way to make it easier. Tariq had to convert a child recently and to make it easier on her, the entire community helped and she barely felt the pain. We sent the news back to the prince."

"Pain?" Lorraine echoed. "I really have to know every detail beforehand if I'm going to make an informed decision. I'm not just going to accept that I have to do what everyone expects. The binding ritual was intended for a Carpathian woman . . ."

Gary shook his head. "It was intended to bind a lifemate. Soul to soul. You hold the light to Andor's darkness. You have already restored emotion and color to his world. There is no mistake. If there had been, Lorraine, we couldn't have followed him into the shadow world. I am a modern man. I know he would have been considered in a coma and have slipped away with modern medicine. In the Carpathian world, a soul can still be retrieved. You know how far gone he was from us. I couldn't track him on my own. Even with Ferro and Sandu, I couldn't find him. It was your soul reaching to his that allowed us to find him. We just boosted your strength, allowing you to follow him further when it was needed. You know that. You were there."

She conceded with a small nod and another, much harder bite of her teeth into her lower lip. "I don't doubt the things you say are true. I'm not arguing that I'm Andor's lifemate. I'm just not certain I'm ready to become fully Carpathian. I want to take my time and really look at it from all angles."

Andor brought her hand to his mouth and brushed a kiss over her knuckles. "I want you to take your time, Lorraine. We are bound together, soul to soul, and as long as you realize we are lifemates, meant to be together, I want you to do whatever you need to in order to come into our world with your mind fully made up."

"If you're weighing the pros and cons," Gary said, "consider the skills you will have. You will be faster and stronger. You will be able to shift and assume any form. You will be able to shed your body and become pure spirit in order to heal others when needed. You already have incredible skills. You will not only be an asset to your lifemate, but to all of us. All of the Carpathian people. We have women and children to protect. Tariq is very forward-thinking. I believe that our women should know how to protect themselves against any danger. You, along with some of the other women, are a perfect example."

Andor made certain to keep his mind blank. He had the ancient's resistance to the idea of his lifemate being in danger of any kind. Being

Carpathian meant adapting. Acquiring knowledge very quickly. He wanted to take a page from Lorraine's book and look at everything from every angle instead of making snap decisions and laying down the law to his woman. Everyone was different and would have different needs. That meant he had to know his lifemate and give her the things that would keep her happy. She had been right when she asked to learn to fight a vampire just in case one would happen along. She learned fast, and she had done well against them.

"I was wrong to be upset with you for allowing the others to use you as bait before I let you explain. I am proud of your abilities, Lorraine," he conceded. "Gary has a point, that the women should learn to defend themselves. Perhaps if Elisabeta had known how, she might not have been taken."

"She might have had a better chance to escape," Gary said, "but I doubt she knew when Sergey approached her that he had chosen to give up his soul."

"She would have known," Sandu said.

"Not if he had made up his mind but hadn't done so yet." Ferro sank down into the soil as if he was too tired to keep his frame upright. "I have thought on this more than is necessary. Dragomir told us that all the Malinovs turned at the same time. It was a decision made with much thought, not, as in most cases, when they were at the end of their endurance. If that was so, Sergey could easily have plotted to take Elisabeta. She knew him. She would have spoken with him, gone with him if he said the right thing, maybe claimed someone was injured. He would have overpowered her and secreted her away. If they were in league with Xavier, they would have known his spells. That meant Sergey could use that knowledge to prevent her from reaching out to her brother or any of our people."

"I *hate* that this man could do this to her," Lorraine said. "I want to help her."

"We'll be returning to the compound as soon as Andor can travel," Gary said. "She will be able to rise in a couple more weeks. I have been attempting to heal some of her old scars and lessen Sergey's influence on her each time Tariq feeds her. If you're there, Lorraine, she will need a friend, a very patient friend. You will have to remember, she is from an ancient time and has been programmed by her captor to be a certain way. She most likely will never be very much different, but your influence and the influence of the other women will help. You can't try to just thrust modern ideas on her, though. You will have to be gentle."

Lorraine nodded. Andor felt that same flutter in the region of his heart he was becoming accustomed to. She listened very carefully to every word Gary said. She had more compassion in her than most humans he'd observed, which was why he'd avoided them. They judged one another so harshly. Women, he found, seemed to be worse in their judgments than men.

*I am still in your mind.*

The way she poured into him, filling every lonely space, each crack or hole, made him feel complete. There was a trace of amusement in her voice.

*Am I wrong?* He loved that it was the two of them speaking, mind to mind, in the midst of so many others, even men who had bound their souls to hers. She still reserved that one telepathic path for him alone.

*No, I can't say you are, although not all women are judgmental. Some are worse than others, some not at all. I don't know why some women build themselves up by tearing down others, especially if those others have had unfortunate situations to deal with. It has always been beyond me, and I grew up in a family competing for trophies.* She sent him an image of an actual trophy with her name on it. *My brother and parents did what was referred to as "trash talking." I didn't. I always felt a little bad for my opponent after I defeated them. I preferred to let my skills do the talking, not my mouth.*

Andor liked that, too, about her. At least she had indicated she was willing to return to the compound with him. *I will go with you wherever you wish to go, even if that means back to your former life within a city.*

*You wouldn't be able to breathe in a city.*

He wouldn't, but it mattered little to him. *If that is what it takes to make you happy, I will do so gladly.* He knew she was reading his mind and would see he told her the truth.

*I'm done with living there,* she assured. *I'll try to live within the compound and see if life there suits me.*

*Many of the Carpathians are buying up property around Tariq's and es-*
*tablishing their own homes. Each house and property adds to the defensible*
*territory. We weave the safeguards together, which means they are stronger than*
*ever and there is less chance a master vampire, even one such as Sergey, well*
*versed in the high mage's spells, could bring them down.*

Isai emerged, pale and needing blood. It was Sandu who gave to him
immediately. Andor detested that his brethren were making themselves
weak for him—that they were in danger on his behalf. Dragomir shed his
body and went into Andor's. Isai had been powerful enough, just as Dragomir was, that Andor could feel them repairing the terrible damage done
to him, but neither was anywhere near Gary's abilities, his spirit so hot
with energy it was almost painful.

He looked at the healer. His features were now very reminiscent of
those of a Daratrazanoff. That lineage was very distinct. He wasn't one
man, born with power; the ancients had poured memories and strength
into him, which was why he was so incredibly formidable. "When you
were reborn as a Daratrazanoff, did you retain your memories from your
former life?"

He had been told by Tariq that prior to Gary being reborn, he was
already revered among their people, almost a legend for his tireless work
to help their women carry babies. More, he fought alongside them, and
guarded children unable to go to ground. He was a genius willing to give
his time and energy to a people that had not been his own.

"I have retained everything," Gary said. "I have retained my abilities
to understand modern chemistry and physics from my old life as well as
strategize any battle when needed from my new."

"And healing?"

"The Daratrazanoff line has a long history of healers. I was given their
abilities. I did not have them before."

"Your lifemate has been born in France," Sandu said, giving his blood
to Isai. "Have you located her?"

"She is too young. Until she reaches puberty there is no hope whatsoever of finding her. Once I know she is near the age, I will attempt to find
her." Gary shrugged his shoulders. "If I do, I will ensure she is watched

over until she comes of age. I have observed the way Dimitri was with Skyler and Valentin is with Liv. Dimitri made contact with Skyler and was there for her any time she needed it. Val does that now for Liv. I will do the same for my lifemate."

"I am told that takes a tremendous toll on the male," Andor objected. "You are one of us. The same as the brethren, far too close to the end. If you add such a burden . . ." He trailed off.

"As you have done?" Gary countered.

"Wait. What do you mean by that?" Lorraine demanded. "How has Andor added to his burden? My understanding was once a hunter found his lifemate, he was safe from turning."

"That is not entirely true," Sandu said.

Andor shook his head, scowling fiercely at his fellow monk. Lorraine came up on her knees and caught his face between her hands. "I want *all* the information, not pieces of it you think I'll like. *Everything*, both good and bad."

"*Csecsemő*, I want you to make your decision based on what you want, not what you think is best for me. I am a man. I will do whatever it takes to make you happy. If you prefer to live as a human, I will make that decision as well."

She shook her head. "That isn't fair to me. You tied us together through your ritual vows. I felt them take hold, Andor. I can't leave you. I don't even want to. If staying human or becoming Carpathian is a choice, then I need all the information, not just part, to make the best decision for us. I'm not just alone anymore. You made certain it was the two of us. Now, you have to live with that."

Sandu grinned at him. "I think I like this girl. I cannot feel, Lorraine, not with my emotions, but my soul is bound to yours, and I can feel through you. That was brilliant, and my affection for you is as Ferro's, that of a brother. You are far too good for Andor."

Andor leveled his gaze at Sandu. "Very funny. You are supposed to be championing me, not persuading her she should leave me."

"I just said she is too good for you, and she is."

Andor couldn't exactly argue with that. "Because we are tied together, but we are not formally bound through blood, the toll on me grows. I would not turn because your soul lights mine, but it is a heavy burden."

*That sounds like a watered-down version.*

He remained silent. What was there to say? She understood, he could tell by the way she got that pensive look on her face. *I tied us together, Lorraine, because I had no choice. My blood compels me to bind us. My soul demanded it. This is your decision. Do not let the others influence you. This choice should be yours.*

She studied his face a long time. "I think it should be ours," she said aloud. "Your brothers, in the short time I've known them, have given me back a family when I thought I would spend my life forever alone. You've offered me a world where I can matter, where my life has meaning. I've been told about a woman in need of friends. Perhaps I can have the chance to help her. There are children needing protection."

"Dragomir's woman is pregnant," Sandu said. "It is a very tricky circumstance. She was impregnated by a vampire, the first we knew that it could actually happen. Dragomir was able to replace the acid-like blood with his own for both mother and child, with the help of our healer."

"And others," Gary said.

The healer had his eyes closed, and Andor knew he would take the next session to try to have Andor's body repaired enough to travel the next rising. He still was worried that Lorraine would be alone during the daylight hours.

"She needs friends," Sandu pointed out. "Women friends. And there is Charlotte and Blaze. Blaze is much like you. I suspect by the time the two of you are finished, you will have started an army of women vampire hunters."

Lorraine glared at him. "I hear the amusement in your voice, you chauvinist."

Sandu put his hand over his heart. "*Sisarke*, how can you say such a thing?"

"I heard it, too," Andor said decisively.

# 8

Lorraine woke at least two hours before sunset, her heart beating too fast, as if something other than she was in control. Vestiges of nightmares were in her mind. Images of her brother and parents on the floor. Her aunt and uncle. Theodore's best friend's parents. So much blood. She'd been wading in it. It was everywhere, all over her clothing. Her hands. In her hair. She'd tried to get through it to reach her mother, but no matter how many steps she'd taken, she hadn't been able to get closer.

She sat up, gasping for air, her lungs raw from trying to breathe. She wanted the nightmares to stop. She had them every night. Sometimes she wasn't asleep, she just had to close her eyes and the images were there, as if they were burned behind her eyelids.

She looked around her. She appeared to be alone. There was no tent, but she knew the men had woven a strong shield overhead and below-ground where they all slept. The perimeter of the camp was safeguarded as well. She drew up her knees and rocked back and forth, grateful she was alone. She didn't like anyone seeing weakness, and the tears tracking down her face and the tremors she couldn't stop, to her, were weaknesses.

She couldn't change what Theodore had done. She could keep him in her heart, the big brother no one else would ever remember. Someday, she might even forgive him. Living with his crime, meeting people who would always judge her, and so much worse, judge her parents, that was far more difficult.

If she was very honest, there was a tiny part of her that was angry with them for not telling her Theodore had been having problems. When had he started? The last time she'd been home, and granted, it had been months earlier, he'd seemed fine. He'd been upset that he hadn't won nationals, but he'd been fine. Once she'd gotten him out of the house, and his bedroom—the cave, she'd called it, because sometimes he disappeared into it for weeks—they'd laughed and talked just as they'd always done.

She got to her feet and stretched. She tugged on her jeans and hiking boots and then added a navy T-shirt. The air was turning brisk so she pulled on her jacket as well. If she was Carpathian, she wouldn't need to go find a tree or bush to use. She wouldn't have to worry about food out in the middle of nowhere. She still had plenty in her backpack, but nothing appealed to her anymore.

She walked out of her shelter. It was strange to know she could see out of it, as if it wasn't there, but no one could see into it. The sun shone down and she reached up toward it. If she became Carpathian, she would lose that. She'd always liked sunshine. She loved camping and being outdoors. Andor had said to let him show her his world. The night.

She drummed her fingers on her thigh as she walked toward the brush the Carpathian hunters had included in their circle of safety. They thought she was silly for preferring bushes, but she wasn't about to be out in the open, just in case some human hunter or vampire's puppet could watch her.

Andor. What was she going to do about him? He was so unexpected. She liked being with him and talking to him. She felt at peace when she was close to him or in his mind. When they spoke telepathically, she couldn't help but feel a deep emotional connection to him. More, she felt a physical one. She'd seen his body torn to shreds, his belly opened and a massive wound in his chest. He had another in his back, down low toward his spine where one of the master vampires had nearly torn him in two. Gary had said his spine was missed by a hairsbreadth.

She lifted her face to the sun again as she emerged from the bushes. The rays felt good on her face and skin, although a little prickly, as if she were in danger of getting burned. She'd given her blood to Sandu, Gary and Ferro as well as Andor. Each of the ancients had given her a small amount of their blood, but she hadn't done a blood exchange with Andor yet.

Gary wanted her to at least do two blood exchanges with Andor, to be prepared. She hadn't asked what he meant by that because she knew. If she were wounded in the ongoing fight with Sergey's forces, Gary wanted them to be able to convert her. Andor hadn't done the first blood exchange before Gary had put him deep in the ground. She knew the others planned to sleep around him, above, below and to either side of him. She'd heard that discussion as well.

No puppets had come. Quite a few wild animals, but no humans or anything else. She'd been a little surprised at the number of animals. Ordinarily she would have expected to see a few deer, perhaps a rabbit or two, mice maybe, but there had been a curious fox and several raccoons along with the deer. Each had come close to the safeguards and then veered away.

Lorraine paced, trying to make a decision. She knew she wanted to be with Andor and the others. She liked them. She especially liked that they considered her family. She needed that. She needed to know she had worth and meaning. Andor certainly gave her that. What was it she needed from him to take that last step?

She wanted to be loved. Her father had loved her mother. Really loved her. She knew, from the way the men talked, that a lifemate was cherished, that he would always be faithful, that there would be no other. She'd heard it from all of them. The part about being a lifemate she found difficult was that Andor hadn't chosen her. She'd been chosen for him.

Could she fall in love with him? Hell yes. There wasn't a doubt in her mind. Each of his brethren were good-looking, intimidating men. Powerful. Dangerous. Funny in ways. Very intelligent. She wasn't in the least attracted to them. She thought of them as big brothers, but she hadn't had so much as a flutter in her stomach when they came near. It was Andor to whom she responded, and he'd been covered in blood and dirt most of the time. He'd been unable to get up or help fight off the vampires. That hadn't mattered. She liked him. A lot.

She would have taken a chance with him had he been human, and that was saying a lot when her life had been turned upside down and she was grieving. Would he have looked at her twice if she hadn't been his lifemate? He wouldn't. She knew that. So, she wasn't his choice, she was more his obligation—okay, not obligation, more like destiny. He couldn't escape being with her even if he wanted to. Maybe by death . . .

"Damn it." She muttered it aloud, picked up a rock and tossed it back onto the ground. She wanted the life he was holding out to her. She wanted the man offering it to her. She'd be a fool not to go for it. More, she didn't want him suffering in any way. How did the women these men claimed feel as if they were really their men's choice?

She had confidence in herself. Or she had until her family had been annihilated. Everything she'd ever believed in had been yanked out from under her. The friends she'd had for years, some since kindergarten, had turned their backs on her as if, because her brother had done such a thing, at any moment she might. She'd been made to feel as if his guilt was hers by the very people she'd counted on to get her through it.

She'd tried going back to school to finish her degree. The stigma had followed her. She heard the whispers behind her back and the hush when she entered a room. She wanted to scream at everyone that she wasn't to blame, but deep down, a part of her thought she was because she hadn't seen what her brother was doing to himself.

She didn't want to choose Andor to run away from her problems. She wanted to choose him and the life he offered her because she loved him that much. It shouldn't be an obligation, or because she wanted to hide, or even fate or destiny. Andor was a man who deserved to be loved whole-heartedly. She hadn't considered she would find a man she could love that way until she found him.

A rustle of leaves warned her and she spun around, her mind quickly going to where every weapon the ancients had created for her was hidden. She catalogued them, from the ones she was most experienced with, the most lethal, and then what she had to do to kill a vampire's puppet.

Two men came out of the trees and slipped down the hillside on their butts. One laughed, the other looked embarrassed. Neither looked like a flesh-eating puppet. They both looked totally human with their backpacks and hiking boots.

"Hey there." The embarrassed one spoke first. "What are you doing out here in the middle of nowhere? I'm Herman, by the way, and this is Adam."

"Lorraine." She edged over until she was close to her pack. She should have been carrying her gun at all times. There was one right next to where she'd been sleeping and another in her pack. She knew better than to walk anywhere without a weapon, but she'd opted for a flamethrower. A gun would discourage a human a lot faster. "I'm looking to be alone out here, to just contemplate life."

"We're doing the same," Herman said. He glanced over his shoulder at Adam, who was dusting off his backside and still grinning.

"We're not very good at camping," Adam offered. "It's our first time. So far, we couldn't put up the tent or start a fire to cook anything."

That part might be the truth. The backpacks looked new and Herman wore his too low, which would make him very uncomfortable as they hiked longer distances. Neither of them had hiking boots that appeared broken in. That would make their feet hurt and cause blisters. As if to prove her point, Adam sank down at the edge of the slope and began to unlace his boots.

"I hate these things. I should have just worn tennis shoes."

"Stop complaining," Herman advised and took a few steps toward her.

"Stop." Lorraine believed in giving fair warning. "I'm not comfortable with you any closer. I do have weapons on me and I'm very skilled in their use." Not that she thought either of the two men were much of a threat. They certainly didn't look it. On the other hand, she'd been fighting hideous creatures with amazing powers so the two men were bound to look harmless in comparison.

Herman was much more muscular than Adam. Adam was slender with sandy-colored hair and a perpetual smile. Herman, on the other hand, had a perpetual scowl and he was giving it to her now as he all but skidded to a halt a few feet from the invisible line separating her from them.

"What the hell do you think we're going to do?" he demanded belligerently.

"Herman." Adam stood up slowly, one shoe dangling from his hand. "She's a woman alone out here. Back off. You don't have to be on top of her to talk to her." He sent an easy smile toward her and sank back down onto the slope. "Herman hasn't had anything to eat today and he gets testy. Low blood sugar. We really thought we'd be able to do this. All our friends constantly tell us how fun camping is, but so far it sucks. They dared us to try it and we did, mostly because they bet us a lot of money we wouldn't."

She rummaged in her pack until she found a couple of bags of trail mix. "Here, this might help." She tossed one to Herman. Anything or anyone could go out of the circle, but nothing could get in—not without an invitation. That safeguard had been factored in just in case she accidentally forgot the exact lines of defense. She could reach for any of the men bound soul to soul to her and they would hopefully wake enough to invite her back inside. She wasn't the kind of woman to forget exactly where the safety lines were.

"Thanks," Herman said, sounding a bit mollified. "Sorry I snapped at you. I can see how you might consider a couple of men a threat."

"Do you have any water?" Adam asked.

She frowned. "How could you come out this far without water or food?"

They looked at each other and then back at her. Herman sighed, stuffed a handful of trail mix into his mouth and then offered some to Adam. "We're lost. We got turned around and thought we were heading back but nothing looked familiar."

She pulled her pack close, turning slightly so her body blocked the movement of her hand as she pulled her gun out and shoved it into the waistband of her jeans at the small of her back. She took her largest water bottle out, turned back to them and tossed it to Adam. He caught it in midair, just as Herman had caught the bag of trail mix.

Her heart jumped and then settled. "Where do you live?"

"San Diego," Adam answered and then took a long pull of water from the bottle. He wiped his mouth with the back of his hand. "We're much more at home in a nightclub than the wilderness. I work as an advertising exec. Technically, Herman could be my boss, but since we both own the company, he's not."

Herman scowled at him. "You're not a partner."

"That's up for debate. You got the money, honey, and I've got the brains and talent." Adam laughed at his singsong delivery.

Herman's scowl disappeared and he smiled and shook his head. "He's ridiculous."

"But truthful."

"Yeah, you're truthful," Herman agreed. He looked back at Lorraine with an easy smile. "What are you doing out here? Are you alone?"

She felt the delicate probe in her mind. A touch. Barely there, but it was a push for her to tell the truth. She saw no reason not to, at least partially. "I'm Lorraine Peters. Nine months ago, my brother, Theodore Peters, killed our parents, aunt and uncle and some family friends. I was having a difficult time with the notoriety and decided to come out here alone to try to heal a little. It's a pretty open wound." That was strictly the truth and she even managed to get the word *alone* in there. She shrugged and tried to look as if she wasn't in the least suspicious, but she was. They already knew the answer to their last question—whether she was alone or not—they'd acknowledged she was alone earlier.

They hadn't hiked for four days into the wilderness. They had to have flown a plane and landed somewhere in a field nearby. Why would they lie? There was no way these two men had actually gone through brush and forest. They were definitely human, but they possessed psychic abilities, or at least Adam did. She just wasn't certain what those psychic abilities were.

Herman seemed the more dominant of the two, but Adam raised her suspicions more. It was Adam who'd made the delicate probe. He was no master vampire, able to stab at her barricade. She was even stronger than she had been with all the exercises the ancients had her doing.

They looked very hip. They wore skinny jeans with a rolled hem. She didn't know anyone who hiked in skinny jeans. Their clothes looked new in spite of the men sliding down the slope on their butts. They had admitted they'd never hiked before. She could buy that they were two men with a little more money than they knew what to do with who'd taken a dare from their friends and ended up lost—except she couldn't. It was all too pat, and then there was Adam's ability. She hadn't known anyone else like her—not even at college—so what were the odds that he would go hiking, get lost and stumble on her?

She glanced up at the sun. Another hour until sunset? Andor would know exactly. Carpathians seemed to always know when the sun set and when it rose.

"I'm sorry about your brother and family," Adam said. He looked and sounded genuinely sorry. "That must be terrible for you."

"There aren't any words," Herman agreed. "I'm sorry, Lorraine."

Their sympathy was unexpected. She was more than confused. They looked so sincere she felt grief rise, the fierce, debilitating grief that could overwhelm on a second's notice. She pushed it down and gave them a halfhearted smile. "No, there aren't any words. I was away at college. One day I had them all and the next, my family was gone."

Adam shook his head and looked down at the water bottle in his hand. "That's why this says Theodore."

Of course, she'd brought part of her brother's camping equipment because it was better than hers and it made her feel close to him, as if she'd brought part of her big brother—the one who had loved and protected her—along with her into the wilderness. She nodded. "Yes."

"I'm really so sorry," Adam reiterated. "I can't imagine."

She didn't reply, but she did take a slow, careful look around. The ancients had said Sergey sent spies in the form of animals. That he sent human puppets. She'd looked for images of such things in the hunters' minds so she would recognize them. There had been nothing in their memories that she'd accessed like Adam or Herman. There was a crow staring at her from the branches of a pine tree. Another sat with folded wings and sharp, beady eyes several feet from the first bird, higher, up near the top of another pine. An icy shiver crept down her spine.

When she looked back at Herman, he'd followed her gaze to the bird. "Do they always do that, just sit and stare?"

"Yeah," Adam chimed in. "It's creepy."

"He's probably looking for a free handout. Crows are intelligent birds. If other hikers or campers have fed them, they learn to follow the campers to get a free meal."

Herman looked away from the bird, shrugging his shoulders. "That makes sense." He glanced at his watch. It was a quick look and one she probably would have missed if she hadn't been trained from such a young age to see every nuance, every gesture and every facial expression. He glanced over to Adam.

"Are you feeling more comfortable with us?" Adam asked.

She gave them a little smile, shrugging at the same time. "Not yet. I'm out in the middle of nowhere by myself. Besides, you're just passing through, trying to get home, right?"

Herman nodded. "We want to get the hell out of here."

She pointed to a faint trail just at the beginning of the slope. "That will take you to the stream. You'll find a fork. One trail is very well traveled, the other not so much. Take the well-traveled one and it will lead you, eventually, out of here. It will take a couple of days, but if you stay right on that path, you'll get home."

The two men looked at each other and then at her. "Can you come with us to show us?" Herman asked.

She shook her head. "Not happening. You'll make it, but I'm not going off alone with two men. That would be foolish, and I'm not a foolish person."

The crow sitting very high up in the pine tree spread its wings wide and flapped them. At the same time, the bird opened its curved, sharp-looking beak and croaked loudly. The sound grated on her nerves. She rubbed her arms up and down to still the goose bumps.

Herman sighed and stood up slowly. A noise, much like a growling bear, had Adam leaping to his feet. Both whirled to face the thicker tree line. Lorraine slowly got to her feet, her heart beginning to pound. That noise hadn't been a good one. The crow squawked again, the sound like nails on a chalkboard. It seemed as if the creature lumbering toward them answered with another deep bellow.

*Andor, something is going on. I have no idea what to do. Can you wake?*

There was a brief moment when all she could hear was her own heartbeat. She held her breath, never taking her gaze from up the path above the two men.

*I am here. I am reading the two men from the memories in your mind. Do not trust them.*

That wasn't helpful. She didn't trust them. But something far worse than two human males was in that forest coming toward them. Brush swayed. She caught the faint difference in color as if something foul had tainted the vivid greens. Fronds curled in on themselves.

*Do you see that?*

*I am looking through your eyes. Keep looking there.*

*Can you see Herman and Adam?* The two men were looking up the slope as well. Both had abandoned their backpacks and were walking backward away from the slope. Adam still had Theodore's water bottle in his hand, and she wanted to run and snatch it away from him.

*Do not leave the circle, Lorraine.*

It was the first time she'd really heard complete command in his voice. A shiver went through her, but she couldn't tell if it was a bad one or a good one. Something about that tone in her mind set her on fire in a way she didn't understand.

*I hadn't planned to.* She was intelligent enough to know whatever was coming her way was not something good. "You two need to get out of here now," she warned. "That doesn't sound good. You're out in the open."

"So are you," Herman pointed out. He kept backing up until he hit the safeguard. Sparks flew into the air, and he yelped. His shirt was singed, the smell of burning cloth lingering. He whirled around, slapping at his back and glaring at her. "What the hell was that?"

"It's a safety boundary. No one can pass through it."

The roar went up again and a hideous creature lumbered out of the trees. It walked slowly, ambling from side to side. The face was distorted, one eye drooped. There were pits in the face and the eyes flamed red.

"Holy shit!" Adam yelled and stumbled backward. He tripped and went down on his butt. He just sat there in the dirt, staring.

*He has to move. He is fully human and that is a vampire's puppet. It will attack him. It has most likely been programmed to acquire you.*

*I thought it would want to eat me.*

*I am only guessing, Lorraine, but you are most likely off-limits to it. Anyone else it stumbles across is not, including Adam and Herman.*

"Get out of here!" she called. "Hurry!"

Fortunately, the puppet moved at a relatively slow pace. If Adam and Herman ran, they would be safe, but neither was moving. They seemed transfixed on the creature, so shocked they were frozen in place.

*Lorraine, concentrate on the puppet. He cannot get to you. He cannot pass the safeguards. You would have to issue him an invitation.*

"You have to run," she said again to the two strangers.

Adam, eyes wide with fear, shook his head. "We can't leave you here alone. We might be amateurs in the woods, but we aren't cowards. Come with us and we'll run."

"I'm safe where I am. It can't get to me. If you get out of here, you'll be safe."

Herman had once more backed right to the barrier, so close she could see his singed shirt where the back had come up against the thickly woven safeguards. He looked at her over his shoulder, his face distorted with fear. "How do we get to where you are, so that thing can't get us, because evidently we aren't leaving."

The puppet continued to the very edge of the slope, looked down at them and roared again, its red eyes fixed on the three of them. For the first time, Lorraine felt a bond with the other two men. All three were human, a common denominator.

*If they won't leave, I'll have to invite them in, Andor. I can't let that thing get them.*

*You will not. Take a deep breath. Feel me breathing with you.*

*You're under the freakin' ground, Andor, you shouldn't be breathing.* She knew she sounded a little hysterical. She hadn't been frantic when the vampires had attacked, why now? What about the puppet had her reeling so far out of control?

*I'm not like this, Andor. You can count on me.* But she was like that. She was *exactly* like that—nearing hysteria.

*Sívamet. Breathe. You are holding your breath. It makes perfect sense. What is a vampire's puppet? It used to be a human being. Two other human beings are standing in its way to acquire you. You are human, and more than anything, you have suffered the worst of traumas. The last thing you want to see is any human being torn to pieces.*

Her heart thudded wildly. Her lungs burned. She gripped her gun to try to ground herself. *Is that what that puppet will do? Tear them to pieces?*

For the first time, Andor hesitated.

*Tell me.* She nearly screamed the two words in her mind. *You have to tell me right now.*

The puppet stepped off the slope. Not down, but off, as if it thought it could walk on air. It tumbled down, rolling, grunting, its arms flailing, legs working as if it might still be walking. When it got to the very bottom, it lay for a minute as if stunned, but its head was turned to face them and its red eyes stared without blinking straight at its prey.

*It eats flesh, Lorraine. It craves it. If it gets to either of those men, you cannot watch. You must turn away.*

"Herman, Adam, that thing *eats* people. Get out of here. You have to go. Right now, you have to go."

Both men turned toward her and raced straight at her. Simultaneously, they hit the barrier and yelled, the sparks rising like tiny flames all around them as they bounced off. They fell to the ground, but scrambled up, looking toward the puppet. It had climbed to its feet and was lumbering toward them. It was slow, but it was steady and its intentions were very clear.

The closer it got to them, the easier it was to see details. The creature was horrifying. Lorraine could identify that it had once been a man. She could see him under the rotting flesh. His mouth was a ragged slash. His teeth were brown and there were stains on his chin and clothing. It looked to be a suit he had worn.

Herman suddenly stiffened. "Ethan? Oh my God, Adam. I think that's Ethan."

Even though Herman faced away from her and she couldn't see his expression, she'd been trained to read body language, and he appeared to be genuinely shocked. He even took a step toward the hideous puppet and stretched one hand toward him.

Adam caught Herman's arm and pushed it down. She caught a glimpse of Adam's horrified expression. It was genuine. There was no faking that. Both men backed closer to the barrier.

*Andor, I have to let them in.*

*Lorraine. Sívam és sielam. You are my heart and soul. You need to use your head, not your heart. Why would these men not run? At least run behind the barrier, or around to one side of it? Why would they wait right in front of you when moving would save their lives?*

"Get around to the other side, out of his line of sight!" Lorraine all but screamed it. *I don't understand. What would be the purpose?*

*Just as the puppet is programmed to certain behaviors, so are they. They are under the influence of Sergey. If you invite them in, they will invite the puppet in or force you out to him. The puppet will kill both of them and take you to his master. They don't know that because they don't understand what is happening. They are pawns to be sacrificed. Bait.*

The world tilted as a wave of dizziness rushed over her. *I can't watch them die, Andor. I can't. I'd rather go with him and hope you rescue me.*

*You cannot save them, csecsemö.* There was so much compassion in his voice she nearly wept. She pressed the hand gripping the gun to her heart.

*No, I can't. But you can. Please, Andor, for me. Do this for me. I can't watch them die. I can't see this thing, obviously once a friend, kill them and then eat them.*

*He will not kill them first. They prefer their victim alive and filled with adrenaline for as long as possible, just as a vampire does.*

Lorraine took a deep breath and let it out. She could feel sweat beading on her forehead and trickling between her breasts. *We're only an hour or so before sunset. Can the others rise and kill it?* She knew they were still too far away from sunset. These Carpathians were ancients and had a particular sensitivity to the sun.

The puppet was so much closer. Too close. Adam and Herman screamed, terror mounting, but they couldn't make themselves run from the man who'd once been a friend.

*If I shoot him with arrows or the flamethrower, will that take him down?*

Andor sighed. *Invite the two men inside the safety circle, Lorraine. I will strike at them and put them out so they cannot invite the puppet in. I am nowhere near full strength so you will need to keep an eye on them at all times. If necessary, you will shoot them, do you understand? They cannot speak.*

*Thank you, Andor.*

For one moment, she debated. He still sounded weak. Would forcing him to save these two men push him back to square one after all the concentrated work the others had done to get him ready for travel? Still, the puppet came closer, and she wanted to scream in fear for the humans and also for Andor.

*I am here*, Ferro said. *I will join with Andor. He will not have to use much energy to control these men.*

*Sisarke*, Sandu joined them. *I am here.*

*As am I, little sister*, Gary joined in.

Lorraine let out her breath. "Herman, Adam, I invite you in. Come into the circle of safety. Now. Hurry."

Both men whirled around and rushed the barrier. The moment they were through it, the puppet bellowed in triumph. Both men opened their mouths to invite the puppet inside, Adam grabbing at Lorraine's arms, yanking at her, to try to force her out of the zone deemed safe by the Carpathians.

"Come . . ." Herman froze in midsentence, his mouth open, one arm outstretched toward the puppet.

Lorraine hit the back of Adam's hand hard with the butt of the gun, slamming down on it with enough force she might have broken bones. The adrenaline they wanted in victims rushed through her like a fiery stream. One word escaped Adam's mouth before he froze in place as well. "Bitch."

"You have no idea," she whispered. But she wasn't. She was terrified for them. She hadn't touched their minds, before, but now she did, backing away from them and the barrier, putting distance between her and the puppet.

She found the exact spot where the ancients had gone to ground and sank down onto the soil, still holding the gun and pulling a flamethrower and a spear closer to her. The puppet roared his rage and kept coming. He hit the wide ribbon of safeguards and tried to bulldoze his way through in spite of the fact that it stopped him.

Sparks danced in the air, a million of them, flicking all around the puppet. He tried to put his hand through the barricade and flames raced up his arm. He screamed and stumbled back. His face contorted. One of the birds flew from the tree with savage ferocity and shrieks of rage, dove toward the puppet, that wicked, curved beak slashing his face open. Blood and worms poured out.

Lorraine's stomach heaved. She couldn't stop the little cry escaping. This had once been a man. He hadn't chosen to serve the vampire; he'd been made into what it wanted—a servant to do its bidding. Just as Elisabeta had been made to serve the master vampire. Her gaze went to Herman and Adam, two men frozen in time, their bodies locked into position.

The puppet rushed the barrier again, this time right in front of Adam. He'd yanked Lorraine to the very edge of the circle where the barricade was. One arm was outstretched. She saw immediately that he was in danger. She leapt to her feet, firing several shots in rapid succession at the puppet, as she ran toward Adam. The puppet jerked hard with each penetration of the bullets, his chest exploding in five places, one right after the other. Each hole leaked a dark, oily-looking liquid with a multitude of wiggling white worms in it.

She caught Adam by the waist and yanked hard, trying to pull him over as if he was a statue rather than a flesh-and-blood person. The moment she wrenched at him, they both went down, Adam landing on top of her. Immediately his eyes focused on her, and one hand clamped down on her wrist to pin her hand to the ground so he could wrestle the gun from her.

Lorraine was already in motion. She didn't care about anything but stopping him calling out an invitation to the puppet. She smashed her free hand as hard as possible into his mouth and then continued to his throat. As his head reared back and came forward, she hit him again, this time in his nose, slamming her palm hard enough to break it. Blood sprayed at her. It trickled from his mouth where she'd knocked out teeth.

*Andor.*

Stomach lurching, she twisted her wrist to free it. Adam had relaxed his hold just enough to allow her to break free, gun still in her fist. One leg trapped his, and she brought her heel down on his groin.

Beneath her, his body went still, frozen once more. She dared one look at his ruined face and then crawled away from him. Several feet from him, she vomited. She spit several times and rinsed her mouth out with water from the smaller bottle in her pack. All the while, the puppet kept slamming into the barrier, testing every few feet and raising tiny sparks that looked like little fireflies.

The sounds he made were horrible. He would roar and then bellow. He would shriek and then whimper. Several times he wiped at his chest, smearing the blood and insects all over him. That made her sick all over.

*Lorraine, you must not look at him. It is making you very sick.*

*I can't stop myself.*

*We can end his misery right now, but you will have to participate. That way you do not have to watch his suffering until the sun sets. It is not much longer, but all of us are uncomfortable with your pain and misery.*

She covered her eyes but peeked through her fingers as the unfortunate creature flung himself against the safety net and bellowed his rage. *Why do I have to participate?*

*We must see what we are taking aim at.*

She wiped beads of sweat from her forehead. She wanted to crawl into the ground with Andor. She needed someone to hold her, to comfort her.

*I will be rising soon.*

She heard the frustration in his voice, and felt it in her mind. There was comfort in knowing he wanted to hold her.

The puppet whimpered, drawing her attention. The bird beat at it with its wings, driving it back toward the barrier. When the puppet shied away from it, the bird pecked at its head with its cruel beak.

Lorraine's cry was broken. Tears streamed down her face. *I hate this world. I hate what people do to one another. These vampires are even worse. When does it end? You've been doing this for so long, Andor, and what good did it do you? Any of you? It feels so hopeless.*

*Look at him, sívamet. Keep your eyes open and focus on him.*

She heard compassion, and that should have been soothing, but instead, it made her cry more. She couldn't imagine his life. Any of their lives. They had survived too many years of watching wars. Watching human beings murder one another over petty things. Watching them kill loved ones because they were no longer in their right minds and there seemed to be no help for them.

*Can you wipe your tears? There can be no mistake, Lorraine.* That was Gary. He was a healer and he had to participate in killing this man.

*He is already, dead, sisarke,* Ferro explained. *He is no man. The shell you see is held together by a vampire's will.*

*Let us do this,* Sandu added.

She took a breath, laid the gun in her lap and steeled herself. One hand closed in the dirt, holding it tightly as if she could hold on to Andor. She lifted her chin and forced her eyes open, forced them to stare directly at the puppet.

Almost instantly he burst into white-hot flames. The heat was so intense the fire actually burned blue. It didn't spread along the grass, staying right on the unfortunate creature. He screamed and shrieked until she thought she'd never be rid of the sound. He fell to the ground and rolled around, but it seemed forever until the sound stopped and all was quiet again.

Lorraine lay down and curled into the fetal position and closed her eyes. She wasn't moving until Andor and the others rose, no matter what else came at her.

# 9

ndor rose the moment he was able, moving through soil and around the ancients guarding him to burst through the surface dirt and out into the air. It felt good to be upright and out in the open. The last rays of the sun had faded, giving him the opportunity to get to his woman. She was lying with her knees drawn up into her chest, her hands curled under her chin, making her look small and vulnerable.

His heart nearly stopped. He had stayed in her mind, feeling her pain, trying to make things better from beneath the ground. Seeing her so distraught was heart-wrenching.

*Too many traumas, Andor,* Gary said. *We are not out of the woods yet. Sergey sent these men to try to get her for him. He could be close by with an army. He could also be attacking the compound right now, looking for Elisabeta. I sent word to Tariq to be watchful.*

Andor didn't reply. He doubted if Sergey would try to find Elisabeta's resting place. That would be safeguarded well. He knew Tariq and several others had woven strong safeguards together to ensure Sergey couldn't find her. The master vampire would wait. While he waited, he plotted. He had his eye on Lorraine.

He crouched beside her. *"Hän sívamak,"* calling her beloved. Meaning it. His heart contracted hard. Nearly seized. His woman was hurting, and he had been in the ground. "Come to me." He gathered her into his arms, shielding her from the others' sight, knowing it would embarrass her to have them see her in such a fragile state. He cradled her to his chest, trying to shelter her in his heart and with his body.

She turned her face up toward his, her long lashes lifting. The beautiful green of her eyes took his breath. "You're here. Awake. With me." One hand touched his jaw, and he felt the tremble of her fingers.

"I am always with you."

"You shouldn't be up. And put me down." For the first time, she seemed to realize he was out of the ground, no longer lying prone and helpless. His arms were around her, holding her to him, his body protective of hers.

"I am feeling much better." He nuzzled her neck and inhaled her scent. Her skin was the softest thing he'd encountered—unless it was her hair, that mass of silk.

The pulse in her neck called to him. He knew the others waited to feed, but they wouldn't wait long, not with two fit, but very tainted males right there within their circle. With long strides, he took her into the relative privacy of the trees and sank down, keeping her on his lap.

She slipped her arms around his neck and leaned into him, giving him her weight, and the feel of her breasts pressing into his chest. "I've never really seen you, Andor. Not up close like this. You're . . . large. Your chest, your shoulders. You're a big man."

He smiled, his lips against that steady rhythm pulsing in her neck. He kissed her there. "I am. Most Carpathians are tall. Male or female." Her pulse called to him. Beckoned. He found he was starving—needing the taste of her again. He remembered it.

*I am craving your taste, Lorraine.*

She knew all Carpathians fed on rising. She started to turn her head as if to look toward the circle of safety, where the others were using Adam and Herman for sustenance. He prevented the head turn with one hand, forcing her to look into his eyes. "You are my lifemate, *hän sívamak,* we provide for each other. The others sustained and attempted to heal me, but on rising, I wish to have your taste in my mouth and moving through my veins."

Her eyes searched his for a long time. The more she looked at him—with a mixture of emotions that made his heart hum and the blood in his veins heat—the more he wanted to explore what emotions and feelings with her really were.

"Yes. The answer to you is always yes."

His lips traveled over her neck. Teeth scraped gently and teased at the skin right over her beating pulse. His tongue soothed that small ache. He sank his teeth deep. Her body jerked hard in his arms. She threw her head back and gave a soft erotic cry, her arms pulling him closer to her as he took her blood.

She tasted like he expected heaven to be. Or some mythical place he'd never found on earth where the world was beautiful. He knew he would never forget this moment, with his woman surrendering to him, giving him such a gift. There were already so many—the most—the gift of herself and of life for him. She was extraordinary.

*Take enough for an exchange, Andor.*

His heart leapt. *You are certain?* He had to ask, even when everything in him wanted to do just that.

*I want to know what it feels like.*

*The others shared with you that it would be safer to have two blood exchanges just in case of an emergency.* He wanted his brethren to stop interfering. She needed time to process. That was her way.

*Yes. It makes sense, Andor.*

*O jelä peje kaik hänkanak,* he hissed softly into her mind.

*That doesn't sound nice. What does it mean?*

*Sun scorch them all,* he interpreted. He meant it, too. He was going to beat them within an inch of their lives—once he was up to it. And that would take some time.

*Don't you want to do a blood exchange with me?*

Was there a small hint of hurt? *Sívamet. I want you to make the decision yourself, free of those meddlers and their influence. I want to be your choice. Me. My way of life. I do not want them to pressure you into something you will regret.*

Even wanting her to make the choice with every cell in his body, with his complete heart and soul, he couldn't pull back. For the first time, he held his woman. He loved having her in his arms and feeling the silk of her hair and satin of her skin. The scent of her was in his lungs as he breathed her in with every inhale. He had the taste of her in his mouth, flowing through his veins and spreading through him like a wildfire.

*Funny you would want that*, she whispered into his mind. *I was think-ing the very same thing, wishing that I was your choice.*

There was something he was missing, a little catch in her voice gave her away. *Why would you think you are not my choice?*

*You didn't choose me, Andor. You had no choice whatsoever in this. You encountered a woman who restored emotions and color to you. One who was born with the other half of your soul. If another woman before me had lived and died carrying it, when you met her, she would have been your lifemate, not me.*

He was silent. She didn't understand the concept yet. What she thought was true, yet not true. He forced himself to stop taking her blood. It was difficult when her taste was designed for him alone, when it set up a craving for her.

He opened his shirt, one hand at the nape of her neck. She avoided his eyes, looking instead at the thin line he drew across his heavy muscles, making certain to do so above his heart. His wounds were not yet healed, but were doing so from the inside out. Blood beaded along the line, bright drops of ruby red.

*Look at me, hän sívamak. Into my eyes. See only me.*

He waited to command her to feed until those green eyes met his. There was hurt there, just as he suspected, just as he found in her mind. He gave her the soft command to feed, distancing her enough that she could manage the act without becoming upset by it before their life-mate bond took hold. He knew the exact moment: he felt the jolt through her mind.

The moment it was there for her, he allowed his body and mind to process his own feelings. The way her lips felt on him. The way fire raced through him. The brush of her hair on his bare skin causing strange electrical sparks to arc from her to him and back, so strong he thought he could almost see them. His body stirred. Reacted. Went hot and full and demanding.

He savored every reaction to her. He wanted to feel. He *needed* to after so long without remembering what it felt like to have emotions. And this—with Lorraine—was paradise. He held her to him, his palm cupping the back of her head, feeling those lips moving on him, her tongue, touching her mind so he could taste himself in her mouth.

*Had I found you in another century, it would have been you, Lorraine. If this is not your first life cycle, you would have been reborn over and over. Did you feel attraction toward other men? Did you want to spend your life with another man?*

*It isn't the same thing.*

*Yes, it is. You were born for me. I was born for you. I carry the other half of your soul. This is not possible with humans. I have been alive a long time and I have never come across another species where this happens. Do you understand, csecsemō, I was born for you? To cherish you. To love you. To protect you. To give you a family. All of that, just as you were born for me. That choice was made long ago, by someone far wiser than the two of us.*

It took effort to find words when his body raged at him for the first time that he could remember. He had never felt on the verge of being out of control. Hunters were about control. They had no emotion so when tracking, there was no anger toward their prey. When running across an entire village decimated by a vampire, even in his earlier days, he hadn't felt sadness or anguish. It had been there, buried inside him, but he hadn't been able to tap into those emotions. Now that he was able to feel, he could find the deep sorrow for lives lost associated with each memory.

*I am trying to understand, Andor. I know I don't want to be without you. I know I am not attracted to any of the others. I can't seem to get past the feeling that what you feel for me can't be love. You didn't get to know me . . .*

Her body moved against his restlessly, sending hot blood pooling in his groin. Her breasts felt exquisite against him, and he longed to feel the silk of her skin in his hands. He hadn't known the taking of blood or the giving of it could be so erotic.

He stroked his hand down the thick mass of chestnut hair. It was his favorite color and always would be. He liked the golden and reddish tones deep in the darker browns. He had realized, looking at it for the first time, that she was his. The one. The only. Born just for him.

*I am in your mind. I can call up every memory from the day you were born. I have access to every minute of your life. I probably know you better than you know yourself. How can you say I don't know you? You have access to my memories. You know me better than anyone, even my brethren and I have spent centuries with them.*

*I know nothing of Carpathian life.*

*You know everything of Carpathian life. You choose not to acknowledge what you fear. Those memories are there, and you can access them anytime.*

*I prefer you to tell me aloud. I can . . .*

*Process.* He heard the smile in his voice and knew it was there because she made him happy. Everything about her. Just the way she was. The way her mind worked. She liked to have all the information, but slowly, not all at once in the way she would learn from his mind.

*You think you like everything about me, Andor, but you didn't like me making decisions independently of you.*

*That is true,* he readily acknowledged. *I am still working to catch up with your century. You also were placed in positions that compromised my honor and your life without having all the information you needed. That was unfair to both of us. We have gone past that.* At least he hoped they had. He hoped that even though she was a modern woman and he was from the past, their connection was strong enough to overcome any real problems.

He inserted his hand between her mouth and his chest with some reluctance. They had both taken enough for a true blood exchange. He couldn't afford to be weak, not with the trip back to the compound coming up and a possible fight against more of Sergey's army. With a wave of his hand his shirt was done up so that she wasn't looking at his mangled chest.

Lorraine didn't move for the longest time, her face buried against his chest, her breath coming in ragged pants. She fought for control. He held her, his arms tight, wanting her to feel safe after the trauma of the day. She was as unfamiliar with sexual hunger as he was and the intensity of that was overwhelming. And there was the fact that she had just taken his blood, known she was doing it, and enjoyed it. His woman had to process all of that. He was very grateful that she could do so in his arms. He loved holding her.

After a few minutes, she leaned into him even more. "I'm afraid. I'm not normally a person who lives in fear, but suddenly I'm very afraid. I wake up afraid and go to sleep afraid. I've been doing that since I lost my family. I have nightmares. I can't get the images out of my mind, and now I have more. Vampires. Human puppets. That was so terrible. I could tell that Adam and Herman were good people. They recognized the puppet and were horrified. I'll never get that out of my mind, either."

"I can distance you from it." He made the offer, but he already knew her answer. He hadn't told an untruth when he said he knew her. She would not allow him to soften those memories of her family or the things she had learned about his world.

"Thank you, Andor, but I'll keep my memories. I just need a little time." She lifted her head from his chest and looked up at him, her palm cupping the side of his face.

There was tenderness in her touch. So much so that he wanted to capture the moment for all time and hold it close so he could pull it up often.

"What about you? Are you able to travel?"

"That is the plan, *sívamet*. We will go back to the compound as soon as we're all ready. Each must feed and be in top fighting order."

"You expect an attack."

"I do not know." Andor frowned. "Sergey is a master planner. He was overlooked because his brothers seemed more powerful and much more ruthless. According to all information on the Malinovs, it was the older brothers making decisions, but clearly, Sergey was scheming all along. How he ended up with pieces of Xavier, as well as taking over the armies, I cannot imagine, but that alone allows him access to the high mage's memories, making him doubly dangerous. It would make little sense to attack our group as we travel. Too many warriors. It would be a suicide mission."

He wanted her to continue stroking his face and jaw with her fingers. Every brush was a touch inside him, deep, where he knew he could hold on to it for all time. He liked the way her eyes drifted over his face with almost a physical touch. Each look. Each time the pads of her fingers smoothed the roughness of his jaw, the caress made his heart clench and his blood surge hotly.

"But you think he will," she persisted.

"I think this vampire will nip at our heels continually to weaken us. Tariq was to send out warriors to meet us, but Gary fears Sergey is waiting for that. He has requested that the others stay close to the women and children. He acts as Tariq's second-in-command, but his true position is more. He would make the decision to protect Tariq if necessary."

"Tell me about the other women who are lifemates at the compound."

He nuzzled the top of her head and dozens of strands of her hair caught on the dark shadowy stubble on his jaw, tying them together in the way the ritual binding words had tied their souls together. He liked symbols and to him, the small entangling was very symbolic.

"Charlotte is Tariq's lifemate and she was human. She restored carousel horses, and Tariq had carved them a few centuries ago. He made an effort to collect the ones still around and when he heard her, he knew she was the one. It was interesting that both shared a love of carousel horses."

"Is Charlotte like me? Will she fight?"

Andor thought that over. "Charlotte will fight, but it isn't her nature. Blaze, Maksim's woman, is much more like you. Her father raised her in an apartment over a bar. Her family was targeted, we think, in order for Sergey's brother Vadim to acquire Blaze's best friend, Emeline. Blaze was human and chose to come into our world. She's a warrior through and through and has been working with the children to teach them to better defend themselves against our enemies."

He indicated Adam and Herman, who were seated on the ground, heads down, while they clutched the water bottles from Lorraine's pack.

She sat up a little straighter when she realized someone had recovered Theodore's water bottle and it had been given to Adam to drink out of.

"Emeline was human and does not have a warrior's instincts, but she sacrificed everything in order to save the children. She knew what would happen to her and yet she still went after them when Vadim had them. She is Dragomir's lifemate."

Andor rubbed at Lorraine's lips, tracing her mouth, that sweet curve and the small dimple to the right. His heart beat harder as he did so. His body stirred and images slipped into his mind. His mouth on hers. Tasting her that way.

"Stop." She whispered it and glanced toward the two men seated some distance from them.

"They cannot see us. We are hidden from them by the trees. If you prefer, I can shield us even more."

"When you kiss me, I want to be only aware of us. You. Me. No one else."

There was an ache in her voice his mind, heart and body echoed. "You are right, of course, but waiting for that after all the time being soul to soul and mind and to mind is difficult."

For the first time since he'd risen, a genuine smile curved the rose of her lips. His stomach had a strange reaction to that, as did his heart.

"Are there other lifemates?"

"I am not as familiar with the women as Gary. He might have that answer. I have met Charlotte, Emeline and Blaze. There is another human woman there, but she does not have a lifemate. She is psychic and could be a lifemate, but so far, no one has arrived who would claim her."

"You don't know her name?"

He remained silent for a long moment, thinking how best to answer that. "I come from another century. We did not even name lifemates, Lorraine. Names hold power to us, and we did not allow other men too close."

She sat up straight, looking shocked, but she didn't let go of him. "But that isn't logical, Andor. It is much safer for everyone if there is more than one warrior to protect women and children. Obviously, you need children in order to have more lifemates. Why wouldn't you allow someone trusted to live close and know your woman?"

He could see she was genuinely shocked. "You have to remember, vampires didn't band together. Normally, a hunter tracked an individual. A male with a lifemate would not want another male without one to know his woman or her name."

"Growing up, didn't you know the names of other children? Even if they were female?"

"Yes, of course, but names changed often. We did not use surnames. We stuck to the old ways of protecting ourselves because if a male chose, at any time, to give up his soul and become vampire, a female lifemate would draw him. Actually, any female. It would be worse if he knew her name."

"Like Sergey did Elisabeta's."

Andor could see she was trying hard to understand. "Ferro and some of the others believe Sergey plotted to kidnap and keep Elisabeta prior to his turning. Xavier had kidnapped and kept a Carpathian woman. Sergey knew that and did not tell his prince or any of the other Carpathians; he was a traitor beyond any other."

"I don't think I like Sergey."

A slow smile tugged at his mouth. He felt a little rusty, but it was becoming easy to smile around her. Her brightness fed a need and hunger in him he hadn't known existed. He was a warrior. He had been for centuries. He didn't need others—in fact, they had always been a detriment. Now, this one woman had a light in her that shone so brightly, it spilled over him, and all the darkness that had taken him over, one shadow at a time, threatening to consume him, was pushed back with one of her statements, delivered in a snippy tone.

"Are you laughing at me?"

Her hands dropped from his neck to fit on her hips, instantly calling his attention to those curves. He caught her wrists and brought her hands back up to him so her arms were forced to slide around his neck. He fit her hands to the nape of his neck, and then pressed hard for a moment as if he could force them to stay there. Technically, he could do that, but he preferred to allow his woman to get used to him before he did anything that might scare her off.

The moment Lorraine threaded her fingers together and leaned her body against his, he dropped his hands to her hips. He curled each palm around an enticing curve. Feeling her. Wishing neither of them had cloth between them. He just wanted to actually feel the way her skin felt all over.

She laughed softly. "You're still wounded, you know. The others told me you wouldn't be fully healed until you were in the ground for a few days, maybe even longer. They repaired enough of the damage to get you to fly home, but that's all. You still have three gaping wounds in your body, yet the first thing you're thinking about is getting me naked. You're *such* a man."

He inclined his head. "Thank you for the compliment."

She laughed again, and the sound teased his groin into a hard ache. The notes danced up and down his cock like the touch of fingers, robbing him of breath. Need exploded out of his lungs. Happiness stabbed at his heart, embedded deep and left him—hers. Only hers. Just like the tattoo on his back, painfully jabbed deep into his skin so his body couldn't remove the vow.

"That was no compliment, you goof."

His eyebrow arched instantly. "*Goof*? What is *goof*? And of course it was a compliment. I may be Carpathian, but I am a man."

She shook her head, her green eyes dancing. In that moment, all trace of fear and sorrow was gone. Her features were lit with amusement. He shared that with her. He'd done that for her. Lorraine was a strong woman. She needed his comfort, and he was grateful for that. He liked caring for her, just as she'd taken care of him, and she stood back up every time she got knocked down.

She'd done so at a young age when her parents had entered her in tournaments. Sometimes she'd been the victor. Sometimes she'd been defeated. Always, she'd gotten back to her feet when an opponent had knocked her down, swept her legs out from under her or pinned her to the ground. She'd been born with that trait and she'd developed it almost daily in the way her parents had raised her. They lived a life of discipline and expected her to do the same.

"The others are returning. Those that did not feed from Adam and Herman had to go hunting," Andor said reluctantly.

He wanted more time with her. He needed more time with her alone. He was forced to block pain from his woman. Even so, if she looked too close in his mind, he knew she would find it there. He silently cursed the fact that he'd taken on all seven vampires. He had known going into it that he would be torn to shreds and possibly killed, but it hadn't mattered. Only destroying the undead mattered. He had no idea he was fated to meet his lifemate and would come close to taking her with him.

Once she had bound her soul to his, and the others had joined, in order to save him, all their lives had been at risk. He knew Sandu and Ferro had done so because he was their brother—not of blood but as close or closer. Two centuries could produce that kind of loyalty. Gary had joined them. A healer so skilled, so rare, it would be a huge loss to the Carpathian people, and yet, like Gregori, his older brother, he was a warrior and hunted the undead. To save another Carpathian, Gregori would have gone to the lengths Gary had, risking his own life.

Andor was certain there was another reason altogether as well. Gary had the fighting skills of a long line of ancient warriors. Few would be able to defeat him in a battle. He also had an enormous IQ and was a battle strategist. By tying himself to Andor, Ferro and Sandu, he was assured that there were ancient warriors who could track him should he ever succumb to whispers of temptation. He had now exchanged blood with all of them. They would be able to find him wherever he was in the world.

"Why are you frowning?" She slid off his lap and stood up slowly. Almost reluctantly.

Andor appreciated that she didn't want to end their time alone together. He felt the same way. "I was not frowning." He wore a mask on his expressionless face. He kept his features looking like stone so none could read him, yet she had so easily.

"I'm in your mind. There was a frown."

"Technically, *sívamet*, that is cheating. You have to learn to read my expressions."

"You don't have expressions. Nor do you have 'tells,' little movements you make before you say or do something. I'm very good at reading my opponents. I trained myself to stay out of their minds and just read body language. You don't give anything away."

He stood as well and saw her eyes widen in shock. She hadn't noticed how tall or muscular he was until that moment. He liked the look on her face. She was easy to read right then—she liked what she saw. He held out his hand. She took it without hesitation, and he threaded his fingers through hers. She waited, not moving. He didn't move, either. Once they took that step that brought them out of the brush and trees, it was no longer just them.

He pulled her farther into the shelter of the trees. "I need to kiss you."

"I know. I feel it, too," she said, but he didn't hear agreement in her voice. There was trepidation, not agreement.

"*Csecsemő*, what is it?"

The tip of her tongue touched her lower lip. "If you kiss me, there isn't any going back."

Now he did frown. Openly. "Back from what, Lorraine? I have claimed you as my lifemate. There is no going back from that. I will always need to be with you. You will always need to be with me. One cannot take that back. Our souls are woven together."

She nodded, that adorable frown on her face matching his much more scowling one.

"I'm aware of the ramifications of what you did. I felt the difference when you said your vows. How you could manage to weave our souls together just by your one-sided vow, I don't know. If things were equal, a woman should have to recite them with you."

He tugged her a step closer. "A woman in our world did not need to say the vows for the binding ritual to work. It is the male who would turn vampire and lose all honor after centuries of hunting and keeping his people safe. Of course, his woman would want to bind herself to him in order to save him."

"I don't know," she said. "If he's an arrogant man who wants to boss her all the time, maybe not, and don't tell me some of your brethren aren't a bit—or a lot—like that because I know two who are."

He threw his head back and laughed, because he knew more than two. He might even be counted among that lot, although he wasn't going to enlighten her. She'd learn that soon enough. "I will concede your point, Lorraine, but you haven't told me what will happen when I kiss you."

Her tongue once more moistened her lower lip, stirring his body beyond belief that just that small action could affect him so deeply. He had to suppress a groan of need. His skin felt too tight, his cock ached and every nerve ending seemed alive. She gave a shake of the head. Her hair went flying, swinging in all directions and then settling down her back and around her shoulders like a living cape.

He dared to tug her a step closer. He had managed to gain a step toward her as well so now only inches separated them. He felt the heat of her body and inhaled the fragrance that was all Lorraine. On waking, he had waved his hand to give her the same freshness that he had when rising. He remembered the first scent of her, the first touch of her hair against his fingers. Every detail of her. He paid attention to those things because she mattered to him more than anything or anyone else on the earth.

"Tell me, *sívamet*."

"I want to kiss you, Andor. I think about it a lot. But, I know when I do, I will want you to bring me into your world because I would want more than one lifetime with you."

His heart jumped in his chest, began to beat faster. He wanted that, too. A thousand lifetimes wouldn't be enough for him. "Is this a bad thing?"

"I thought if I talked to the other women, the lifemates who had chosen to become Carpathian, they could tell me if they felt they'd made the right choice. It isn't like I can go back to being human, right?"

"No, once you make that decision, it is done. Your human body dies and you become fully Carpathian. I know the other women will say they made the right choice. They love their lifemates. You know they will say it as well."

"It isn't about that, Andor. I know I've fallen quite hard for you. It's difficult to see into your mind and not fall for you. I also see the repercussions of the sun on you. I love the sun. I lie out in the sun without my clothes and sunbathe. I swim without clothes, letting the sun kiss me through the water. I love the way it looks on the plants during the day. Some flowers don't even open at night. I spent time in my garden, planting and weeding and waiting for spring so the flowers would come up and open. The blossoms are spectacular in the daylight. All those colors."

"You will still see in color."

"But they don't shine like that at night."

He pulled her all the way into his arms. "You are just scared, and I do not blame you. I am going to kiss you anyway. You know you have made up your mind. I see it. I see your resolution."

"Then you see that I have a tiny part of me still holding back. This has to be a one hundred percent, all-in decision."

He caught her chin in his palm and lifted her face. Those green eyes haunted him. So beautiful. He hadn't known he loved the color green so much. His thumb slid gently over her cheek because he needed to feel the softness of her skin. He ached to taste her lips, the color of a wild rose, not quite a red, not quite a pink, but inviting. Tempting.

"I am one hundred percent all-in, Lorraine. I belong with you. To you. All of me. Whether I live as a Carpathian or a human, I choose to live beside you." He meant every word. He knew others of his brethren would bind their women to them and take this choice for them. Lorraine was not a woman to accept that. Ever. She needed to go through her process, even if that meant he had to wait. He had waited centuries. He had bound them together with the ritual words and after learning why, for him, it had been necessary, she had accepted it.

She had accepted the fact that he was upset with her for becoming bait for vampires, to lure them in so the ancients could destroy them. Once he had explained, she had understood the reasons for his objections. She had even conceded she might have made other choices if she'd had all the information.

It had been Lorraine who had insisted on the first full blood exchange, stepping one foot into his world. She was coming to him slowly. Making those decisions and feeling in control. She had to know that her opinion mattered to him and that any conclusion she came to would be honored by him. That was what *lifemate* meant. Other women would be different because they held other men's souls for them.

Ferro, he knew, could never live with a woman like Lorraine. It was clear he respected her, but she would never be his lifemate. Sandu was more like Ferro than Andor, which was always odd to Andor. They had shared the monastery for centuries and had come to know each other very well. In another life, Sandu would have a sense of humor far more than any of the others, but he would be stricter with his woman—his protective streak dictating what was acceptable to him and what wasn't. Isai was always an enigma to them all. He was much more difficult to read. Dragomir was somewhere in between Sandu and Andor. That left the two brethren helping to guard Tariq. Benedek and Petru. He shook his head. Modern women would have a difficult time with any of them, Andor included.

"*Csecsemő*, I need to kiss you." They both knew he was going to kiss her.

Her lashes fluttered, drawing his attention. The breeze was cool on the heat of his skin. Somewhere close, a mouse scurried in the leaves, and the flutter of wings told him an owl was close. He heard a fox bark a distance away. Overhead, stars broke through the faint light as darkness settled a midnight-blue color over the sky. He would never forget anything about this night, not even the smallest detail.

He bent his head and brushed his mouth with exquisite gentleness over hers. His cock jerked hard and unexpectedly. His heart clenched in his chest and then accelerated, beating hard. Hot blood rushed through his veins, pooling low. His lips kissed hers, one corner, then the other. His teeth found her bottom lip and nipped, using the same gentleness.

Her lips were soft. Firm. Cool. Heating fast. When his teeth nipped and tugged, she gasped and opened her mouth. His tongue slid in, tasting her. It was there for him, just like in her blood, that miraculous flavor that was all Lorraine. He wanted to define it, but couldn't take the time; he was swept away, exploring, claiming, leading so she would follow.

She answered him tentatively, her tongue chasing his into his mouth, sliding along it, tangling and teasing, exploring just as he had done. He touched her mind, wanting to feel what she was feeling. That taste of his, so perfect for her. She liked kissing him.

*I love kissing you,* she corrected.

He pulled her closer, his arms locked tightly around her. His mouth taking command again, kissing her over and over. His hands slid up her back and then framed either side of her face, holding her there, while he savored every touch of her fingers, the taste and texture of her, and that wondrous taste that would forever be only his.

*I didn't know it would be like this.*

He hadn't known, either, otherwise, as wounded as he was, he would have been kissing her earlier. *I will never have enough of this. Kissing you is amazing.*

*Apparently, it is also distracting.* Sandu's voice could be heard by both. *We have to go. And we need your votes on what to do with these slaves of the undead. So, stop doing what you are doing and come back here.*

Andor didn't pull away immediately. His woman deserved more than that. He cooled the kiss from burning to hot and then brushed a dozen kisses over her mouth and down her chin to her throat.

*Shouldn't we go?* There was a hint of amusement in her mind.

*Sandu is an ass.* Because she had a sense of humor about their kisses being interrupted, he found his, too. *But I suppose we should go help them figure it out. We might be the only ones with brains.*

*Clearly yours has short-circuited,* Sandu persisted. *You might wait to kiss your woman in the safety of the compound, not out here where the crows gather.*

# 10

Andor was intimidating up close and he could kiss like an angel—or devil. The man was temptation itself. She was used to men who seemed powerful and maybe even a little dangerous. She lived in the world of martial arts. The men were physically fit, often in jobs that put their lives in jeopardy, and could definitely protect themselves and their loved ones. Andor was in an entirely different category—a scary one.

As long as he'd been lying prone, his chest and belly torn open, she hadn't really been nervous. She'd been the one taking care of him. Now, even though she knew those injuries were not fully healed, she could see his raw power and the danger that clung to him with every move he made. She'd seen that in the others, but not him, not really.

He was all muscle. Authority. A clear threat. She knew he was a predator. She'd seen it when she'd first met him, but now it was stamped into every line of his body. She'd tied herself to that—to someone capable of things she had no real idea of. Watching battles unfold like a movie in his mind was far different than experiencing the real thing.

On top of everything else, he was seriously hot. Not just gorgeous.

Not just good-looking, he was so hot she could barely look at him. He had a quality she couldn't put her finger on, but it was powerful and drew her like a magnet. To her, he was spellbinding, mesmerizing. With Andor around, she would never see any other man.

He kissed like a creature from another world. She'd been kissed—or thought she had until that moment. No one compared to him. To his taste. To the way he held her. The way his mouth was so commanding. He wasn't even one hundred percent healed and he already had stolen her body with just his kisses. She couldn't imagine kissing another man after him and being satisfied.

He tugged on her hand until she fit beneath his shoulder. She put one arm around his waist and the other hand—the one he'd been holding—very lightly on his waist. She was afraid of pressing against one of his injuries.

"Is Gary going to work on you this evening?" She knew the healer hadn't had a chance. The moment Andor had risen, he'd come to her.

"No. He will do so when we reach the compound."

That made her uneasy. Andor was on his feet, but his wounds should have killed him. They'd fought to bring him back from that place between the living and the dead, and he wasn't healed. Traveling would be difficult, especially if a fight ensued.

"Maybe he should try now."

"He would be too weak to travel," Andor said. "We would not attempt this if I was not ready, *sívamet.*"

They reached the others waiting by Adam and Herman. The two men looked more confused than ever the moment they saw her.

Adam blinked rapidly as she approached him with an outstretched hand. "That water bottle was my brother's and I would like it back."

Andor caught her wrist and pulled her arm down as if the two men might be cobras and about to strike her. He held out his hand while turning his body protectively to shield her from the two human males.

"I'm sorry," Adam said. "I don't remember very much of how I got here or why I have this. I didn't steal it." He handed the bottle over to Andor immediately.

"You came here to either kill or hand my woman over to a vampire," Andor explained.

His tone was hard, and Lorraine couldn't help but look up at him. She'd never heard him use that particular voice. He didn't sound in the least sympathetic. *I feel sorry for them, Andor. They clearly don't have a clue to what's going on.*

*Really?* Andor caught her chin and looked into her eyes. Her breath caught in her throat. She could get lost in those eyes, the color of midnight, a velvet violet mixed with a dark, dark blue. *They have memories. Do not be fooled because they are human.*

She didn't want to look into their memories. She'd taught herself at a young age that it was wrong to intrude on other people's privacy. Everyone had secrets, even if they were secret thoughts, and no one wanted others to know what they were. She shook her head.

*They chose to work for Sergey. They are psychic males he found through the Morrison Center. He contacted them and offered them immortality in exchange for their services—meaning whatever he asked them to do. He asked them to get you to bring them inside the safeguards so they could invite the puppet inside. Of course, they did not realize the payment would be the puppet—their friend— eating them alive. Sergey will not bring human psychics into his world unless he intends to make them members of his army. These two would never have made that cut.*

*Why do you say that?* He sounded so matter-of-fact when he was talking about two men losing their lives in a horrendous way. She'd loved that he was so calm and pragmatic, but now, with the lives of Adam and Herman on the line, she wanted him to be emotional—like she knew she was being.

*They did not like their assignment and questioned it, both of them. Once they saw their friend as a puppet, they were horrified. Neither wanted to continue, but of course, they had no choice in the matter. They had been programmed.*

*See?* She jumped on that. *They have good in them. They can be saved.*

*They can never be trusted. They wanted immortality enough to agree to deliver a woman into the hands of a vampire. They knew at the time of the agreement exactly what they were doing in exchange. Sergey likes to make certain his people are aware of what he is.*

Lorraine pressed her fingers to her eyes. She was trying to make Adam and Herman into decent people. She needed them to be decent. *They changed their minds. Sometimes something sounds as if it could be good, but then when you're actually in the moment you realize it's all wrong. People aren't perfect, Andor.*

He leaned down to brush a kiss across her lips. Her heart fluttered alarmingly. She blinked up at him, and he shook his head. *I am not passing judgment on humans for weaknesses, Lorraine. I am very cognizant of the fact that you are holding your brother close to your heart and it hurts that so many think of him as a monster. I do not. I do not think these men are monsters. The fact remains, they were here to harm my woman. They will not get close enough to you to do so again.*

She was all right with that. She nodded to show she was in complete agreement. "What will happen to them?" She whispered it aloud, afraid the way the intimacy of his voice brushing strokes of velvet along the walls of her mind persuaded her that Andor was right in all things.

"We will take them to the compound and Tariq will decide. He has a couple of other human psychics who worked for Vadim now working for him. They are invaluable in that they recognize other men who have aligned themselves with Sergey. They also have a wealth of memories to tap into." He glanced up at the surrounding trees, and Lorraine followed his gaze. Several crows watched with beady round eyes. "Why are we delaying?"

"Isai is not back as of yet," Ferro said. "I reached out to him, but he has not answered. I fear he has run into problems."

Lorraine caught Adam's head movement as he turned toward Herman. She narrowed her gaze on them and stepped closer, in spite of Andor's restraining hands. "What do you know about Isai's disappearance?"

Herman started to shake his head, and she glared at him. "If you lie, they all will know you do. Your master planned for you both to die hideous deaths. You failed in your mission and now he's going to be looking to hurt you both before you die. He's like that. So spill it. Where is Isai?"

Adam shrugged his shoulders. "If he went hunting to the east, a trap was set up to kill one of these men. A campground with a family of five."

Her heart caught in her throat. Instinctively she reached out to catch at Andor's arm to steady herself. "You mean children? You knew Sergey was going to use children to bait a trap for a hunter?"

Again, Adam shrugged, and she wanted to hit him. She took another step toward him and Andor circled her waist with his arm, locking her against him. "You wanted it that much? You would exchange the lives of children for your ticket to immortality?"

"For power," Andor corrected. "For having the power of life and death over others. You chose death for those children and our brother. The thing you might remember, both of you, is that hunters do not die so easily." He turned to the others. "Reach for Isai collectively. All the brethren have exchanged blood with him. We do not need his voice to find him."

"Why would he choose not to send for you or answer you?" Lorraine asked.

"He knows that is expected and they have readied the playing field. They have the advantage when they have set the battleground."

"Then we need to change it up and do the unexpected." That was a direct quote from her father. When an opponent had had the advantage, and known what one of them was going to do, known how they preferred to fight, her father had always told them to "change it up and do the unexpected." This situation called for just that.

*You are thinking of using yourself as bait again.* Andor made it an accusation.

Ferro moved out into the wider meadow, just to one side of where Andor had been so wounded. She couldn't help but stare at him, knowing he was going to do something huge. Something wonderful. Something terrible. She held her breath.

He shifted. One moment, there was a tall man with long flowing hair down to his waist and the next a giant rust-colored dragon. The dragon was magnificent, very beautiful, its scales gleaming in the moonlight. He stretched his neck long and lowered a wing. Beside her, Andor sighed while the two human males gaped.

*Show-off.* Andor whispered it under his breath and into his mind.

He tugged at Lorraine's hand. She was fairly certain she was gaping right along with Adam and Herman. Still, she went with Andor right up to the enormous dragon. Even having seen Ferro shift and knowing it was him, she was apprehensive and more than a little awed. She tentatively touched the scales. They were cool to the touch, hard, but silky smooth, even over the raised bumps she felt within each scale.

The dragon's color was unique, like hematite iron ore, red with grayish overtones—or the opposite, like now, when they were more red than gray. Ferro's eyes were the same color. Like flames burning deep under the surface. The dragon's body looked very much as if a fire burned beneath the scales, the orange and red flames showing through.

Andor climbed onto the extended wing and reached a hand back to help her up. She took a breath and then let him clasp her wrist and pull as she stepped up. *Does it hurt to have us walk on you, Ferro?*

*That is an absurd question.*

She laughed. In spite of the tension, her anxiety over the two human men and what was going to happen to them, and the fact that Ferro had just become a dragon, which made her feel a little faint, he was still Ferro.

Andor settled her in front of him on the neck of the mythical creature. She glanced back at her pack and the two men. "I don't want to lose my parents' or my brother's things." That was a very real fear.

"They will be transported to the compound," he assured.

Ferro began to flap the giant wings, hopping for a moment on his back legs, and then he was in the sky with a surge of power she felt rumbling beneath her. Once in the cool night air, they began to climb. She clutched the dragon's neck and pressed back into Andor, her heart accelerating rapidly. It was crazy. Amazing. Impossible. It was a dream come true and a nightmare of insanity. More and more, she was being drawn into the complexity and fantasy of a world she'd never conceived of.

Had Lorraine been the type of woman to read fantasy and go to that type of movie, she might have thought that the trauma of her family's demise had thrown her deep into her mind and taken her somewhere else, a place she didn't have to deal with their deaths and the repercussions of how they'd died. But she wasn't that woman. She'd always been practical. She wouldn't have believed in the existence of vampires or dragons in a million years.

She tipped her head back to look at the stars as they circled the camp below them. Even up so high, the lights seemed far away, sparkling like diamonds scattered across the deep blue sky. She looked down. One by one, the others shifted, taking the form of dragons, the two human men on the back of what looked like maybe Dragomir.

Ferro led the way. Andor had taken the coordinates of the campground from the minds of Adam and Herman; the humans had set up camp some miles from where Lorraine had been. Below her, she could see the canopy of the forest, trees lifting their limbs toward the sky. Ferro dipped low and set down beside a small lake, shifting the moment Andor and Lorraine leapt from his wing.

Andor had jumped off and then lifted his arms to Lorraine. She didn't hesitate, landing safe against his chest. If he winced on impact, she didn't feel it, but she did feel bad that she hadn't considered it might not be the best idea, jumping on him. For a few minutes, while they were flying through the air, she'd felt elated. Happy. The problems facing them had dropped away with the earth and left her feeling every touch of the wind, seeing every beauty the night provided. The stars overhead had sparkled brighter, and the lake below them had looked like crystal glass, still and untouched. Perfect.

*I wanted to show you my night. There is so much more, sívamet. So many beautiful things that in one lifetime it is impossible to see them all. I want to travel with you, take you to places no other has yet discovered. Caves of crystals. Pools of fresh, untouched water. So much. This will be over soon and we will explore.*

Lorraine knew that "soon" to a Carpathian was very relative. They lived several human lifetimes so "soon" might be the span of an entire human life cycle. Still, she wanted to see those things with him. She knew every minute in his company, in spite of the dangers, brought her steps closer to choosing to be in his world with him.

They moved into the shelter of the trees. Ferro shifted a second time, going from the gigantic dragon to a much smaller bird. He chose a crow, and she knew immediately he planned to spy using its sharp eyes and his own acute senses. He took to the air. Several of the others followed, each going in a different direction.

The moment Dragomir's dragon claws gripped earth, he shifted, dumping both Adam and Herman onto the ground. Instantly, they were whisked into the trees, and sat frozen, unable to move or speak. She didn't protest. There were children's lives at stake.

*The camp is through the trees east of you. There is a meadow right beside the stream running into the lake. They are there. I smell the taint of vampire, and the grass is brown all around the camp area. Flowers are wilted there as well,* Ferro reported.

*I believe there is at least one master vampire orchestrating and running this battle,* Gary added. *He is hidden in the trees, one of two trees. Isai is on the ground not far from the camp. I touched his mind. He has shut down heart and lungs to keep from bleeding out. That was all that was left as a message for us. That and the name Farmington. Does that mean anything to you?*

*I came across his kills more than two centuries ago,* Sandu said. *He is very bloodthirsty and likes to make his victims suffer. He called himself Benard Farmington. He liked the name because he stole it from a family of victims. He had been particularly brutal with them.*

Lorraine closed her eyes. She couldn't think of this vampire surviving so long. She knew he'd survived on the blood of human victims.

*Carpathians as well,* Andor reminded.

Isai wouldn't have been wounded so severely by lesser vampires, even a group of them attacking him. He was wounded so badly he'd been forced to shut down his heart, just as Andor should have done but couldn't once she was with him.

*Gary, can he be saved?* She asked the question she knew none of the others would ask. They were logical about life or death. Either one lived or one died. Worrying didn't make things better.

*I believe so.* Gary gave her the human answer.

Lorraine took a deep breath and nodded. *Thank you. Can you see the children?*

*I caught a glimpse of them when the flap was raised,* Sandu said. *Two boys and a girl. The boys appear to be ten and eleven or so. The girl is more like five. They are very scared and subdued.*

Lorraine glanced toward Adam and Herman. She wanted to punch them. Hard. It wasn't their fault that the family was in danger, but neither of the men, although they'd acted like they'd had a change of heart, had warned the ancients of the danger.

*They were hedging their bets. If we lost the battle, they could tell Sergey how loyal they were. If we won, they could fall back on the fact that they didn't want to invite the puppet into the circle of safety.*

*I'm beginning to think they were more worried about the puppet eating them alive than giving me to it.*

*I believe you are correct.*

She wished she'd kicked Adam a little harder. Andor took her hand and brought it to his mouth, kissing her knuckles. His lips felt cool and firm against her skin.

"Let us start this. Everyone is in position."

"How many are there?"

"The brethren counted six pawns. Four underlings and, of course, the master vampire."

Lorraine stopped in her tracks. "Oh my God, Andor. That's eleven of them. *Eleven.* How can we fight so many and protect the campers at the same time?"

Andor put his hand gently over hers. "Take a breath, Lorraine. You know how to do this. You have been trained from the time you were a child to fight opponents larger and stronger than you, some even better equipped than you. We will win because we have no choice. That is what you tell yourself. If we fail, those monsters will kill those children. That is unacceptable."

She nodded. She knew Andor, like the other Carpathian males, had assessed their chances and knew, with him so wounded and now Isai injured, they would need everyone to aid them. They wanted to win quickly and decisively. The longer the battle raged, the more the odds swung in the favor of the vampires.

"Are you ready?" Andor prompted.

"Yes."

"If they have a child hostage and try to get you to give up your weapons, the only thing possible to do, Lorraine, is to attack. Giving up your weapons will not save the child. More than likely, they will kill a hostage in front of you after you have complied. I have seen it happen century after century. Vampires live for torture of any kind. They know women, in particular, are very sentimental when it comes to children. Oftentimes it is an illusion that they have a child in their custody."

"In this case, we know they do have them." She wanted to be clear on that.

He nodded. "You have to be ready for that tactic. If you do not think you can hold out, you must stay here and allow me to go to them alone."

"That's not happening, so just forget it," she said. "I can do this if you can." Deliberately, she poured confidence into her tone, when she didn't feel it.

*Ferro will battle the master vampire. Sandu and Dragomir will take on the stronger of the rest. There are four, I believe. Gary, Lorraine and I will destroy the lesser vampires,* Andor clarified to all of them. *Gary, we will need your healing abilities and your knowledge of humans to work with this family.*

*I understand.*

It was the logical thing to do, Lorraine knew. Each of them had a job to do. Gary was the best at healing and they would need him for Isai, and most likely others. Andor held out his hand to her and she put hers in it, feeling his fingers close around hers, enveloping her smaller hand. Instantly, she felt his strength and that gave her the confidence she needed.

They began their walk through the trees, avoiding the small rolling slope where Isai lay so quietly. They strolled, murmuring to each other, knowing that they were being watched.

"Do I have other family members of yours to meet to get their approval?" she asked.

"The brethren are my family. Dragomir, Isai, Sandu, Ferro and three others you haven't met as of yet. Fane, who has found his lifemate. We hope to get them to relocate with us. Petru, who is at the compound guarding Tariq, along with Benedek. There were eight of us who stayed there over the years. Several others joined and then left, but these men are my core family."

She sent him a small smile. "Lots of family, then. And intimidating."

"They would never harm you, *sívamet*. They might, however, tell you what to do."

She laughed, keeping her voice very soft. It took effort not to look around her. The forest felt different. She'd spent a great deal of her life camping. Every summer, her family had camped. Often, during the winter. Her father had liked the wide-open spaces and had also wanted Theodore and Lorraine to be prepared to survive in any type of weather.

She felt at home in the forest, or just about anywhere outdoors. Now, there was a different feel altogether. A frisson of dread crept down her spine. Fear settled in the pit of her stomach. Nothing felt the same, not the birds moving from branch to branch, or the ground beneath her feet. There seemed to be an inordinate number of flying insects.

Squirrels chattered at them in alarm. Little lizards scrambled up the trunks of trees, and snakes slithered through leaves and vegetation on the ground. Andor didn't appear to notice. He kept walking, and she took her cue from him. Still, it wasn't difficult to see the way fronds curled back, brown and withered. The way the carpet of grass that should have been green was as shriveled as the older leaves and needles on the ground. Trees wept black tears of sap that ran down their trunks and pooled in tarry collections at their roots.

Lorraine found herself holding her breath, trying not to breathe in the noxious air. There was a heaviness to it, a tainted smell, much like rotting eggs—or meat. Her heart skipped a beat.

*Do you think they have another puppet waiting? Scaring that family?*

He glanced down at her sharply. *Why would you ask that? What are you thinking?*

*I smell one. I can barely breathe with that scent so strong, and it's getting worse.*

Andor inhaled. *I scent vampire. They are rotten inside and out. Their bodies are decaying. That is what you smell, but that is not to say they haven't created another puppet. It is possible.*

She didn't like the way he glanced away from her. He knew there was a puppet close by. If she could tell by the horrible stench, then he could as well. *Why don't you want me to know for certain? I don't like you trying to deceive me.*

*I do not know for certain,* he protested. *No one has caught sight of a puppet, and they are difficult to hide. Still, the odor has permeated the entire area, so I suspect there may be a second one. Or the first was held nearby for some time before being sent to you.*

Lorraine's stomach lurched. She'd rather face a vampire than the puppet. Knowing all along that it had once been human sickened her. Knowing that it wanted to feed on the blood and flesh of another human being horrified her. "Is anyone watching Adam and Herman?"

He nodded. "Ferro sent sentries, animals, to watch over them. We are all needed."

She had to be satisfied with that. If the master vampire knew they were close—and, of course, he did—he might send someone or something to kill them. As long as they were alive, they might be of use to the Carpathians.

*Did Ferro question them?*

*Of course he did. He extracted a tremendous amount of information from both of them. That was how we knew they were more concerned for their own lives than yours.*

*What more use would they be if Ferro got all the information already?* She could see the tent now. It was pitched out in the open away from the trees. She stared at it, trying to will the occupants to move around. A grown man sat in front of a fire pit that he'd dug and carefully stacked rocks around. He kept glancing toward the forest and then toward the tent. His wife sat beside him and it looked as if she was crying. The man put his arm around her and leaned close to speak to her.

*Sergey has recruited others like them, and we need to be able to identify the human males. If they get jobs in the nightclubs or try to infiltrate Tariq's security force, they could do a lot of damage.*

Andor gripped her hand, swung it up to his mouth and pressed a kiss to the inside of her wrist. "Ready, *csecsemő?* Stay close—if necessary, we will be back-to-back. We will get the prisoners free and the others will deal with the remaining vampires."

"I'm ready." She had to steel herself in order to face the puppet—and she was certain that smell meant that one was close, probably in the tent.

*Gary?*

*Drifting on the wind. I want to get close enough to know what is happening inside. Give me another moment or two.*

Lorraine closed her eyes and tilted her face up to feel the wind. It was drifting in the direction of the tent. No more than a slight breeze, it was cool and felt nice on her warm face. She waited, her heart pounding.

*Good, the flap is still up. Children inside. Puppet is there, and even while I watched, the vampire had to stop it from taking more bites out of the oldest boy.*

More bites. That meant the puppet was already trying to feed on the child. That sickened her, but it also steadied her. She wasn't standing around waiting while some horrible creature was terrifying a little boy. They had to get the other children and their parents to safety so Gary could help the oldest child.

"Let's go, Andor."

He began their walk out of the forest. They strolled together, hand in hand. The pair at the fire pit saw them immediately, and the male shook his head several times, trying to warn them off. He even used a hand signal, waving them off, attempting to communicate danger. They kept walking. The mother jammed fingers into her mouth to keep from sobbing aloud.

"Hello," Andor called. "We were hoping to find fellow campers nearby. We smelled your fire."

*And your puppet.* Lorraine pressed down the small bout of hysteria that wanted to well up in spite of her resolve.

The man tried again with a small shake of his head, but he gestured toward the fire. "Welcome. We're just about to start cooking dinner. You're welcome to eat with us."

Andor indicated to Lorraine to keep the couple between her and the tent at all times. They'd gone over that safety issue already, so she knew what to do, but she nodded her head to reassure him.

"Thank you," she called out aloud. "We'd be happy to join you. We didn't bring anything to contribute, though."

"We have plenty," the man assured.

Andor kept walking, although Lorraine halted a little distance from them, pretending to tie her hiking boot. She stayed crouched low, giving her ample opportunity to study the ground around the tent. Insects crawled on the brown shoots of grass, looking a little drunk. They moved in circles, and some fell over as if they couldn't get their legs to work properly.

"I am Andor, and this is my girlfriend, Lorraine."

Lorraine was shocked. He hadn't even hesitated. He sounded smooth and very modern, although he hadn't used a contraction the way most people would have. She looked up from her shoe-tying and waved.

The man stepped forward to shake Andor's hand. "I'm Neil Bennet, and this is my wife, Carol." He leaned closer. "You have to leave now. Get your girlfriend out of here. There's a madman—"

A bellow of rage and a child's high-pitched scream had Neil swinging around toward the tent. His wife tried to run toward it and he caught her around the waist, just as the canvas shredded and all of them saw the three children, two huddled together and one struggling as a puppet tore at a shoulder with jagged teeth.

What appeared to be a man stood slowly. "You were told not to warn them," he said as he came forward. "You knew the sacrifices." He gestured toward the puppet and the thing began to drag the boy away.

Carol and Neil both tried to get to their son, but the man held up his hand and both jerked to a halt. He smiled, showing his teeth. They were dark, stained with blood. He bowed toward Lorraine and Andor. "I am Jannik Astor."

*I recognize the name. Fridrick and Georg took the name Astor. They turned with the Malinovs. Several cousins turned with them. This must be one.* Andor filled her in on Carpathian sharing pipeline.

*We have to stop the puppet, he'll kill that little boy.*

*Gary will free the child. Concentrate. I am going to move the two children farther away from this Jannik. I have to be subtle. Hold his attention. Let me get closer again to the father.*

"Jannik," Lorraine said, moving out from behind Andor.

She kept back, so that the couple was still between her and the vampire, but she stepped out just enough to be seen. She needed his attention focused on her. The vampire thought he had the upper hand and would be able to get Andor and Lorraine to do anything he wanted in order to keep the other two children safe. "No doubt, you already know my name. Has your master told you to bring me to him?"

The vampire's eyes glittered a deep red when she'd mentioned his "master." Apparently, he wasn't quite as happy serving under the leadership of Sergey. He had thought his master was Sergey's brother Vadim, and that was a far more distinguished master, so much so that the vampire's expression told her he was far from pleased to be reminded. She knew, from all the times she'd looked into the warriors' minds, that vampires were vain.

"Sergey Malinov is a worm. Do you know what the ancients call him right before they laugh? He is known as *kuly*. In case it has been long since you spoke your own language, that means intestinal worm. Or better yet, a tapeworm. Or a demon who possesses and devours souls. He probably prefers the last to what he truly is, which is an intestinal worm." She kept her voice low and even. Low, so that Jannik had to listen with all his concentration. "You must detest working for a tapeworm."

Out of the corner of her eye, she saw Andor moving slowly. Inch by inch. He was beside Neil, who held his sagging wife in his arms, refusing to allow her to put herself in danger trying to rush to the two remaining children, or after the puppet who'd carried off their oldest.

Lorraine saw Andor touch Neil's arm, a brush of his fingertips, no more, but it got him the man's complete attention.

"How could you work for him? Jannik, clearly, you're so much more intelligent. Where is he? He sends his best to do his battles because he can't fight them himself. Why have you aligned yourself with this worm?" She poured flattery and interest into her voice.

"He is indeed a worm. I am slowly recruiting others who understand that just because he carries the Malinov name, doesn't mean he is one of them. They were leaders. He crawled on the ground for them, eating their table scraps. He inherited their mantle of leadership. Even now, he waits on his brother."

She felt Andor stiffen. The reaction was in her mind and echoed by all the ancients, Dragomir in particular. She didn't understand why, but she pursued it. "I don't know what that means. What brother? You have to remember, I don't know very much about why your master would want me. Is it his brother who does?"

"He is *not* my master. Vadim was. Vadim had a vision for all of us. We cannot find our lifemates, but we can have women to serve us. To give us children, an army of them. We will have human males serving and protecting us as well. It was to be our century. We were poised on the very brink of destroying the Carpathian people."

"Vadim did that?"

Jannik nodded. "Not his brother, the miserable worm. Vadim must be a prisoner. No one sees him but Sergey. Now Sergey has demanded we get his slave back and along with her, you. He wants two women for himself."

"I am very confused." Andor was now close to the children and between them and the vampire. She wanted to jump up and down for joy. "I thought it was Vadim that wanted women for all of you."

"It was his plan. His woman has been taken by one of the Carpathians. She is pregnant with his child, the first of its kind. I will free Vadim and retake his woman. That child is the beginning of our army and symbolizes that we are not rotting flesh and worms."

"I don't think anyone is called that but your master."

She could see Andor weaving a protection circle around the two children. They sat quietly, looking up at him without fear. She knew he had taken control of them, distancing them from what was happening. That was the first step for the two of them. The second step, before they engaged the vampire, was to encircle the parents and make it clear to them that no matter what happened, they couldn't leave until Andor or one of the others said it was safe.

Gary had to defeat the puppet and rescue the oldest boy and then place him in a protective circle. He needed to get to Isai, heal him and give him blood so he could make the journey home. The others each had specific tasks, but until Andor, Lorraine and Gary ensured the children and their parents were safe, no one could engage in battle. If they did, it would trigger Jannik into making his move, and they weren't ready.

"I told you, he is *not* my master." Jannik's voice, all sweetly pitched before, turned nasally and whining. Spittle ran down his face and he forgot to wipe it clean. Fury twisted his features into a malevolent mask. He jerked at his hair with one hand and a huge tuft came off. He looked at it as if puzzled.

"That's right, of course he's not. How could he be? I'm so sorry, Jannik." She kept her voice appeasing. "I didn't mean to make that same mistake."

Out of the corner of her eye, she caught sight of Andor weaving his safeguards around the couple. Neil had coaxed his wife to sit on the ground. He kept his arms around her and rocked her gently, but both of them had their gazes on the distant forest.

When Andor was finished he turned to face the couple. "Your children are safe. A friend is securing your oldest son and destroying the abomination that took him. Stay where you are no matter what is happening around you. If you move, you will die and so will your children."

He strode over to Lorraine's side. "*Tè kalma, te jama ńiŋ3kval, te apitäsz arwa-arvo*—You are nothing but a walking maggot-infected corpse, without honor. I have come to free you."

Lorraine stepped back to give Andor fighting room. More, she did as he'd suggested earlier and went back-to-back with him, facing outward toward the forest, knowing the others would come.

# II

*The children are secure.* Andor's voice moved in his mind and Gary Daratrazanoff breathed a sigh of relief.

He waited in the cool of the forest for his prey. The scent of blood was strong as the puppet dragged the screaming child toward him. The boy was tough because he was giving the creature a difficult time. Puppets as a rule were slow and lumbering, but they were unusually strong. Kicking and punching, raining blow after blow, the boy made it difficult for the puppet to drag him. It was good for the boy, but bad for Gary, as the puppet continued to struggle with him and finally came to a halt a good forty feet from Gary's position.

The puppet ripped at the child, and the boy's cries sent birds reeling into the air in alarm. Droplets of blood spewed into the air, further maddening the creature. Gary waved his hand toward the vampire's handiwork while he emerged from the forest, bursting out with the frightened birds. The brains of the puppets were so far gone, most of the time magic and power didn't work very well on them. Gary only wanted him slowed enough that the boy had the opportunity to run.

The puppet jerked its head around, as if on the strings of a master, facing him as he came in for the attack. His hands went slack, enabling the child to rip free and stumble a distance away. Gary shifted at the last moment, more to reassure the child than out of necessity. He sent soothing waves of comfort and support to the boy, and took the pain from the child at the same time.

He had been given the easiest job in order to free him to heal Isai. He slammed his fist into the puppet as he drove straight into the creature. Ignoring claws tearing at his body and teeth driving into his shoulder, he extracted the heart, tossed it aside and stepped back. Lightning forked in the night sky and then one whip hit the heart, incinerating it. The sizzling white-hot streak of energy leapt to the puppet, destroying it in a dazzling display of flames.

Gary went straight to the boy. The child stared up at him as he crouched beside him. "I'm Gary. What's your name?"

He put a hand on the boy's shoulder where the puppet had torn chunks of flesh from him. The wounds were painful, but superficial. The vile creature hadn't had time to get started on the boy. Gary called up the healing light in him and brought it through his hands so that the child felt heat, but not so hot that it burned on top of the painful bites and tears.

"Tommy." The boy sniffed. "What is that?"

"We call them puppets. I am going to construct a safety ring for you. If anyone tries to get you to come out of it, you ask them to say the safe word. If they don't, you stay very still inside. They won't be able to get to you."

The boy nodded, his thin body trembling. "I think they got my brother and sister. Maybe my mom and dad." A sob welled up but he choked it down.

Gary shook his head as he began to weave the safeguards necessary to keep the boy safe. "Friends of mine have them safe in the same type of circle I'm giving you. There are still several of the bad people around, and we have to make them leave. You have to do what I say, Tommy, or you won't be safe."

The boy nodded. Gary wanted to send him to sleep, but if he was killed in a battle, no one would be able to rescue the boy. He had no choice, he had to take the chance.

"The secret phrase is '*Curious George likes his bike.*' Can you remember that?" It wouldn't mean anything to a Carpathian or vampire, but it would to a human child. All of them had heard of *Curious George*. The books were very popular and beloved by children.

The boy nodded again, his eyes lighting just a little bit. "Yes. I can remember it." He repeated the phrase for Gary.

"No matter how scary things look, you just stay right there. I'll come for you." He turned away, but then turned back. "If someone comes looking like your parents, they still have to say that phrase. You can't be fooled by these things."

Tommy nodded his head again. "I won't."

*Last child secure. The phrase to remove him from the safety circle is "Curious George likes his bike."*

It was the best Gary could do. He needed to get to Isai and see to his wounds. He turned from the boy and sprinted his way back to the forest. The moment he was in the clear and the child couldn't see him, he took to the air, covering the distance between him and his patient fast.

Isai lay in a small depression he'd clearly opened for himself. Gary's heart jerked when he saw the vampire bending over the Carpathian. The vampire drew back his hand to plunge it into Isai's chest. Gary was there, catching the wrist, preventing the movement that would kill the already badly wounded ancient.

Gary spun the vampire around and drove his fist into the chest, fingernails like talons, digging through muscle, cutting through bone, until his fingers could surround the prize. The undead raked at him with both hands, tearing open his chest. The vampire leaned forward and tore at his neck with his teeth—or tried to. Gary whipped his body around to avoid the jagged, piercing teeth and as he did so, he withdrew his arm fast.

Tossing the heart, he called down the lightning. The vampire dove toward the heart, hand outstretched. It was impossible to outrun the bolt of white-hot energy as it struck. Vampire and blackened heart incinerated almost immediately. Gary bathed his arms and hands in the sizzling heat and then hurried to Isai.

The Carpathian was wounded in several places. Like Andor, he had attacked the undead right in their nest, knowing it was a trap, but trying to rescue the humans anyway. Gary constructed a circle of safety around the ancient warrior. There would be no one to guard him while he worked, and he couldn't afford to have a vampire come upon the shell of his body while he was attempting to heal Isai's wounds.

Once he had the circle of safety safeguarded, he shed his body and moved into Isai, looking to see what he was working with. The wounds were severe, and had Isai not shut down his heart and lungs, he would have died. Gary began the slow healing process.

*The children are secure.* That was Andor.

Still Sandu waited, feeling the cool heat that moved through his body in anticipation of a battle. Gary needed to hurry. They had only so much time before the vampires realized their trap hadn't worked, and Andor was in control at the camp. Sandu and Dragomir had drifted with the night breeze, looking for the vampires and marking their hiding places. The lesser vampires were so much easier to locate than those who had been around a few years.

*Last child secure. The phrase to remove him from the safety circle is "Curious George likes his bike."*

Sandu nodded to Dragomir and the two sprang into action. They both had targeted a lesser vampire, ones close to two of the much more dangerous undead. They wanted to kill the two lesser pawns as quickly as possible. Clearly, from what they saw and overheard, the one calling himself Jannik was one of the four more dangerous vampires. That left one they hadn't found. Sandu dove through the trees in the form of a crow. Dragomir and he had sat there with the master's spies and no one had noticed.

He shifted just before he struck the lesser vampire who was moving back and forth in anticipation of joining Jannik. He waited for a signal that hadn't yet come. Sandu was on him fast, slamming his fist through the unwitting vampire's chest and dragging out the heart before the creature knew what had happened. He had the organ burned and was turning when the one he'd not seen yet hit him hard, spinning him and driving him toward the ground.

Sandu dissolved and burst through the night air, streaming around the vampire and once more shifting back to his form. He sent the vampire a small salute. "Good of you to join me. It saved me hunting you."

"I have not seen you before, yet you appear to have been in many battles."

Sandu bowed slightly. "I am one of the brethren from the monastery. Are you so young you do not recall those locked behind the gate of the monastery to spare the world their power?" He held up his hand and allowed the magic accumulated from centuries to show on his skin. For a moment, it was a dazzling display, electrical pulses sizzling over his skin, and then he appeared normal. "You are?" he prompted.

The vampire looked uneasy once he heard Sandu's claim of having been held within the boundaries of the monastery. Every Carpathian had heard of them. They were ancient warriors and stories of their battles had been sung around the campfires before modern times. Sandu was certain this vampire had been one of those singing.

"Karl." The vampire circled to his left and glanced up toward the branches of the trees, as if looking for help.

Sandu casually sent a burst of flames toward the flock of birds staring down at them with beady eyes. The birds shrieked and took to the air. Sandu whirled his fingers in the air and, in spite of how large they were, the crows were sent tumbling, falling from the sky end over end. While the vampire was transfixed by the sight of the master's spies dropping through the air, Sandu attacked.

He was a blur of motion, so fast the vampire didn't see him before it was too late. He tried to dissolve, but Sandu's fist was in his chest, holding his form. Talons scraped while acid blood poured over the Carpathian's arm, burning it to the bone. The vampire retaliated, attempting to drive his fist into the hunter's chest. It was far, far too late. Sandu had the heart and nothing would deter him. He yanked the prize from the chest of the undead and sent it flying a distance. One of the crows made an attempt to rescue it, but the lightning hit crow and heart. Sandu bathed his arms to get rid of the acid blood and then took to the air to get to the next vampire.

Dragomir sat in the very midst of Sergey's spying crows. He studied each of them, looking for a leader, but none seemed to be a vampire in another form. He waited patiently for the signal. He wasn't happy that Vadim was still alive. Vadim Malinov had led the vampire army in San Diego. They had established a stronghold beneath the city. He recruited human psychic males found through the Morrison Center for Psychics. They had them now around the world. A secret human society actually ran it— those dedicated to killing vampires. They believed in them when the rest of the world thought they were crazy.

The Malinov brothers were intelligent enough to hack the database for psychic men and women. The men they recruited would help them in various ways. They could be out in sunlight and do things vampires couldn't. Vadim had seen the use for them and instead of using them exclusively for food, he promised them all sorts of things in exchange for their aid. He could look into each individual mind and offer their heart's desire.

The psychic women he wanted to give to the vampires in his upper ranks, telling them they could have children to build their powerful army. To do such a thing that was deemed impossible would only give them more status, helping to recruit newer vampires. It wasn't easy to get vampires to follow another. They were vain and narcissistic. Vadim had found the perfect way to entice them to his army.

Dragomir's lifemate, Emeline, had suffered for weeks, acid blood eating her and her child from the inside out. The baby's cries had affected her. It had been impossible to sleep because Vadim would command her. It had been an impossible situation. She'd been unable to take the chance and tell the Carpathians just in case they wanted to harm her child. She'd been uncertain what to do but knew she had to make a decision soon when Dragomir had come onto the scene and heard her speak. He'd known instantly, by the way his emotions and the brilliance of colors had returned to him. Emeline was his.

It had taken a while, but with the help of Gary, he had completely rid both mother and child of any part of Malinov's blood. They thought Vadim had been killed, although a question mark had been raised. Now they knew: Sergey had kept him alive for some reason of his own. Dragomir didn't like the idea of having to go home to his woman and let her know Vadim still lived. They wanted the child—his child now. The baby was a girl, and she was definitely Dragomir's daughter—not Vadim's.

*Last child secure. The phrase to remove him from the safety circle is "Curious George likes his bike."*

Beside him, Sandu made his dive toward the lesser vampire he'd targeted. Dragomir did the same. The two lesser vampires were the pawns to help protect the ones working their way toward being considered master vampires. Neither hunter wanted the pawns at their back when they were battling a more skilled opponent.

He hit the vampire hard, rolling him to the ground, and was on him before the undead knew what happened. As he plunged his fist deep, he was hit from behind. His warning radar went off just before a vampire tried to punch through his back to get at his heart. He turned just enough to throw the vampire off. Still, the fist went deep enough for him to feel it.

In one motion, he extracted the heart and threw it a distance away, calling the lightning at the same time as he whirled to face his new opponent. This one wasn't the more skilled vampire he expected to face, the one he'd watched for a time. This was a second pawn, which told him the vampire he'd targeted was probably closer to being a master than he'd counted on. They often surrounded themselves with sacrificial pawns that helped them win a battle and aided them in escaping.

The sizzling whip of white-hot energy incinerated both the heart and the lesser vampire, but then some unknown force wrestled with Dragomir for the power of the energy. He nearly smiled. Emeline had returned his emotions to him, and he could see the humor in the more skilled vampire thinking he had the advantage. Still, it was never a good thing to feel when one was fighting. He couldn't think about Emeline or anything else.

He loosened his grip on the lash of lightning as the demon vampire ripped at it with a powerful summoning spell. The fork snapped back at the vampire, whipping and flogging the sky, whirling in a circle to surround the undead. Dragomir dropped the coils of white-hot energy right over the vampire's head, making certain that each spiral laid perfectly around his body, one loop right over his heart. He pulled it tight, so the sizzling energy cut right through the vampire, incinerating him and his heart as well.

Dragomir turned to face the lesser vampire. Overhead, lightning crackled ominously. The vampire glanced uneasily at the sky, and Dragomir was on him, smashing through muscle to reach the heart. He straightened, the heart in his hand, when Sandu materialized beside him, preventing a third, lesser vampire from striking him. The vampire waited a few seconds too long, wholly concentrated on Dragomir. He never saw Sandu.

Both men tossed the hearts to the ground and called down the lightning.

Dragomir shook his head. "This is too easy. These vampires are newly made. They have little skills. I don't understand it."

"I agree." Sandu glanced toward the trees where the crows watched silently. "There is more here. Something we are not seeing. How could these men have *no* battle skills? All Carpathians are taught from birth to fight. Battles are often given from father to son. Lorraine has more skills than these vampires."

Dragomir stared out into the meadow where the humans had been camping. "These could not have been Carpathian before they became vampire, Sandu. That is the only answer."

***

Jannik stared at Andor, shock on his face. "What did you dare to say to me? What did you call me?"

"*Te kalma, te jama ñiŋ3kval, te apitäsz arwa-arvo*—You are nothing but a walking maggot-infected corpse, without honor. I have come to free you," Andor repeated. "I interpreted for you, just in case you are no longer able to speak Carpathian. I have no idea how long it has been since you chose to give up your honor. Since you betrayed your people and your lifemate."

Jannik sputtered, spit, clenched his fists and then began to sway. "A lifemate only makes you less, not more. I can have a woman and children without a lifemate forcing me to do things I would not normally do. You keep your lifemate, but she will die with you."

Andor pointed to the vampire. He could see the undead had some skills just in the way he moved, but he didn't have the skills Andor had. He beckoned. Jannik's shock showed on his face when he took a step toward Andor and then another. Each subsequent step was jerky as the vampire fought to stop himself from obeying Andor's summons.

He called out, lifting his hands into the air to muster aid. Andor's other hand came up and he made a small circle with his fingers only and then twisted his wrist. The crows flying toward the meadow from the forest in answer to Jannik's call flew into one another.

"You are *sapar bin jalkak*—coward, refusing to go to your death with honor." He forced the vampire to continue toward him, one step at a time.

Lorraine hissed out a small warning. The lesser vampire appeared out of the sky, dropping down almost at her feet.

"I've got this," she assured.

He had to trust her to keep his mind on his opponent. She had handled herself well, and he was right there if she got into trouble.

Lorraine didn't take her eyes off the new threat. She wasn't fighting just for her own life, but those of the humans locked in their circles of safety as well as Andor. She wasn't going to fail. Already, she made certain her mind was strong, the barricades there extremely strong in case the vampire tried to attack her that way.

He planted his feet in the soil and glanced past her to Jannik and then the humans. A sneer twisted his face. He lifted his hand and pushed air toward her. She felt the assault in her mind first and realized the attacks often began there. Because she refused to flinch, keeping her shield strong, the push of air didn't send her flying backward into Andor as the vampire intended. It did rock her, but not enough to throw her to the ground.

She whipped out her gun, squeezed off three rounds, hitting him in the eye, the middle of his forehead and his throat. The force of the rapidly fired bullets took him a couple of steps back and tilted his head as well.

Before he could recover, she yanked out the flamethrower Andor and the others had managed to conjure up for her.

The vampire's one good eye widened and he turned to run. Vaguely, in the back of her mind, she thought that was strange. In all the battles she'd encountered in the minds of the ancients, vampires shifted. They created illusions. They dissolved into mist. They didn't turn and run.

The steady stream of flames enveloped the vampire and he jerked to a halt, spun around in a strange, three-point turn, much like a marionette, and came straight at her with halting, lurching steps.

*Andor.* She hated to distract him from Jannik. Something wasn't right. She kept the flames pouring straight at the oncoming vampire's heart. She backed up until she was nearly right on top of Andor.

*He's possessed by another. We wondered where the fourth vampire was, and now we know.*

Lorraine didn't know—she wanted to turn and run herself—but she was all that stood between Andor and this maniac coming to burn them both alive. She had to incinerate his heart, so she kept the flamethrower steady right over the place she knew it had to be. Heat brought beads of sweat out on her forehead and had them trickling down her chest. Fear made her heart pound, but she held steady. The vampire was close now, just feet from her, close enough she thought the flames would reach her, but then he began to topple.

He fell to the ground, his arms blackened and charred but stretching out toward her. It was all she could do not to fling the flamethrower at him and run. He was like something out of a horror movie—he refused to die. He dragged his blackened body toward her. Now he was only two feet away. The fire burned hotly, the flames reaching for her along with hideous arms that were now falling apart. Chunks of ashes rolled away from his arms. Her stomach lurched, but she kept her eyes glued to his chest and the spot where his heart was.

"Please, please, please," she found herself chanting and then was horrified that she was all but praying that someone would die.

*Not someone, Lorraine. He is vampire. He chose to give up his soul. He survives by killing others.*

She closed her eyes briefly and then, embodied by Andor's calmness, sucked in air again, this time standing over the creature so she couldn't fail to hit her target.

Andor wanted to help her, but he knew he couldn't afford to break concentration. Jannik stood in front of him, commanding his attention, but he wasn't alone. Another vampire was hidden and helping him. He had taken possession of the lesser vampire, sacrificing him in order to attack Lorraine.

Keeping his eyes on Jannik, Andor raised his hands into the air. "*Mu-onìak te avoisz te*—I command you to reveal yourself." Very few hunters could command a vampire to that level of obedience if the vampire had been around for more than a couple of centuries. He was ancient as were the other brethren. As years passed, power grew. That was what made them secret themselves from others. They knew they were dangerous and could turn should they continue to kill, even though each kill was honorable. "Reveal yourself and come to me." He snapped his fingers and pointed to the ground in front of him as if he might have been commanding an animal.

He was safe because he had Lorraine. Dragomir was safe because he had Emeline. Sandu, Ferro, Isai, Petru and Benedek were all at risk, as was Gary. He hoped by binding themselves to Lorraine and him, at least Sandu, Ferro and Gary had bought themselves a little more time.

To his right, a vampire emerged from the dark. He had been part of a small boulder, but now he was snarling like a wild beast and crawling toward Andor.

*I'm moving three steps to the left. Move with me. I cannot allow them to put us between them. In fact, now that the lesser vampire is dead, stay close to the two circles. I have closed the children's minds so they cannot witness any of this and will remove it all from the parents as soon as we defeat those battling.*

Lorraine sent a small protest to him. *I am not leaving you to be safe elsewhere. I'll stay right here and guard your back.*

His woman. A pain in the ass. He launched himself at Jannik while the vampire was watching his companion crawling. There was contempt twisting his face. The moment Andor came at him, he took to the air.

Immediately he ran into a barrier, slamming his head hard, the blow knocking him back to the ground. He fell, rolled and kicked at Andor, who was on him in seconds.

The moment Andor had his fist inside Jannik's chest, the other vampire got to his feet and started toward the hunter. Lorraine shot him with a gun, just as she had the lesser vampire. This one turned his attention toward her with a sickening smile. He waved his arm and the gun wiggled in her hand, trying to fly away. Then it began to turn toward her.

"You aren't in my head, you lousy excuse for a Carpathian!" She shouted it at him, hurling the insult but knowing he wouldn't even understand it. Still, it helped shore up her defenses. She flicked the flamethrower on and shot a steady stream at him, still clinging to her gun, just in case.

The vampire shrieked, leaping into the air, hitting the same ceiling Jannik had. He fell to the ground, enveloped in flames. Rolling to put the fire out, he took to the air again, this time staying low. He tried to dissolve, but ashes fell and were scattered by the wind. Little embers showed up in the few flames still burning on the ground. The moment Andor spotted them, he waved his hand toward them, still extracting Jannik's heart with the other hand. The vampire fell a second time, this time landing about twenty feet from Andor.

Lorraine glanced over her shoulder and saw Andor covered in blood. Jannik fought back, determined to keep the hunter from taking his heart. He tore at the ancient's face and chest, licked at the blood in an effort to get stronger and tried for the heart. She couldn't let the other vampire come back, and he was already rolling over. She took off running toward him, the flamethrower in her hand, finger on the trigger.

*No, Lorraine, get back here where you're safe.*

She skidded to a halt, and then, keeping her eyes on the vampire who was slowly climbing to his feet, she began to walk backward. A crow squawked. The others took up the macabre chorus, all of them shrieking obscenely. She didn't dare take her eyes from the vampire to look, but she heard the birds leave the shelter of the trees.

Heavy wings beat around her. Everywhere she looked there were large crows. They flew in circles around her. It was disorienting. Several times one flew right into her, knocking her sideways. Then one struck the back of her head with its sharp, wicked beak. She felt the stab as the curved mandible cut a wicked slice into the back of her skull. It felt like fire. The pain was ferocious. She hit at it with the butt of her gun, knocking into the heavy body. It beat at her with its wings, tore strips from her skin with its talons as it dug for a purchase and then it was off her, rising into the air.

She triggered the flamethrower, shooting the stream into the air in a circle around her. It took a minute to get her bearings. Lightning lit the sky, the forks sizzling brightly as one slammed to earth, signaling Andor had killed Jannik and was incinerating his heart and body. She kept backpedaling, trying to find the vampire who had gotten lost in the attack by the crows.

She knew if she'd stayed close to Andor, the ceiling he had raised to prevent Jannik Astor from escaping via air would have protected her. It was a hard lesson. Her head hurt so bad she wanted to vomit. Instead, she tried to find the vampire in the dark. The crows returned to the trees so she turned off the flamethrower and ran back to the safety of her lifemate.

*"O jelä peje teräd, emni,"* Andor said aloud. "Sun scorch you, woman," he repeated in English. "What were you thinking?"

"I was thinking I wanted to keep that thing off you until you killed the other one."

He was silent a moment, moving first one way and then the other. "Thank you, Lorraine. We will work on our teamwork at a later date. You have done very well. Are you injured?"

She realized he hadn't seen the back of her head. "One of those birds pecked me, but otherwise, I'm okay." She was going to have to sit down very soon. The pain made her dizzy. "Do you still want me to sit between the parents and the children out of your way?" She kept her voice very meek, hoping he would attribute her sudden cooperation to her making a mistake and not weakness.

"Get down," Andor called and dove past her.

Lorraine obeyed, not looking to see the danger. She'd discovered that by the time she looked to see what was wrong, it was already too late. Reacting was far better. Vampires and Carpathians moved far too quickly. She squeezed her eyes closed briefly, trying to breathe through the pain from the laceration in her scalp. When she opened her eyes, she was looking at her lifemate.

She'd watched countless tournaments, men and woman who fought, their bodies fluid and well-trained. Athletes, every one of them. Andor moved in a completely different realm of athleticism. Every muscle in his body performed to its greatest potential. There was no fear when the monster came at him, all teeth and raking claws, nails the size of a grizzly's. There was no hesitation in him.

He went straight at the creature and then, at the very last possible second, whirled to one side and sliced through the chest with a casual sweep of his hand. She closed her eyes again as black blood dripped to the ground, smoking where it hit, the little drops of acid containing several wiggling worms.

Lorraine opened her eyes again and there was more of the black blood on the ground, this time from a stroke around the throat. She knew what he was doing, weakening his opponent. All fighters knew the technique. The difference was, he was so casual about it, as if he was merely dancing, rather than in a life-or-death fight. His feet glided smoothly, his body appeared at ease. There was no tension. No strain.

Andor suddenly struck with one hand and whirled around, slamming his fist deep into the vampire's chest. She would never get over that sight—a hunter's arm buried deep in a chest, black blood pouring over his skin, burning it, dripping to the ground. She would never forget the sound, a terrible sucking noise as he extracted the blackened, wizened organ, clutching it in his fist, fingers closed tightly around it while that black blood dripped. Then there was the sound of the vampire screaming, the shriek hurting her ears as Andor tossed the heart onto the ground and a blazing lash of lightning incinerated it and then jumped to the still writhing vampire.

Andor turned back toward her. *We have to wipe the memories from the minds of these humans and heal any wounds on them before we leave.*

---

*Last child secure. The phrase to remove him from the safety circle is "Curious George likes his bike."*

Ferro had waited for what seemed forever to hear those words. He had already found the place the master vampire had hidden. The forest was cool and should have felt fresh. Instead, the air was heavy and unnaturally silent. There were no cicadas making their music. No lizards or mice scurrying in the leaves. Animals had fled the area. He hadn't found one within the three-mile circumference he'd scanned. An abomination was close.

He stayed very still, waiting for one mistake. Eventually, the master vampire, depending on his age, would make one. Right now, Ferro had narrowed his search to a small group of trees. Leaves seemed wilted. An abundance of needles had dropped. Black sap ran down three of the trees, and one trunk was split. All of those things indicated an abomination of nature was close, or had been there.

He studied the split trunk carefully. It was very possible the master vampire had hidden himself in the tree, but his presence had cracked the trunk before he wanted to emerge so he'd left that one open and dying. There was an abundance of insects crawling on the tree closest to it and also along the roots that were bare along the ground. Several of the tree roots looped naturally up into the air. Even in the dark, Ferro could see without hindrance, and there was movement in those roots.

The hunter shifted the wind minutely, just enough so that the turn wouldn't be noticed as anything but natural. He shifted into mere molecules floating on the breeze, allowing it to carry him close to the suspect tree. As he neared his destination, he could see the dark hole at the base of the tree. A wild boar had dug, exposing the roots and feasting on some of them. Inside the hole was a mound of black, stinging insects that were no more natural than the sap running along two of cracked limbs overhead.

He moved into position. For centuries, the inside of trees was often a favorite spot for a master vampire to hide while he sacrificed his pawns to a hunter. Ferro had seen it too many times. He had also seen traps the master vampire set up, one such as this, cleverly done, where the hunter would believe the undead was in one tree, when in fact, he was in another.

Ferro waited, seeing with more than his eyes. He was a dangerous fighter, much more so than any other hunter he had encountered, and his brethren were the best among them. He wanted the fight over as soon as possible. If he lingered, the nothingness inside him always yawned wide, threatening to engulf him.

"*Muonìak te avoisz te*—I command you to reveal yourself." He spoke in the ancient language, words of great power. Those words rarely worked on a master unless the hunter uttering them was far more powerful. All those who had locked themselves away in the monastery held such power.

The master vampire emerged slowly from the split tree, right where Ferro had positioned himself, guessing correctly that the other trees had been set as a trap. Suddenly he rushed Ferro. The vampire would have done much better had he simply kept to his slow pace when he emerged from the tree. Coming so fast allowed Ferro to slam his fist home using the momentum from the undead's attack. His fingers settled around the heart while the master vampire hissed and roared, fighting like a madman, tearing at Ferro's face and chest.

Ferro felt nothing at all. Nothing. The vampire tore at his belly and chewed at his neck. Ferro didn't relent. Not when those teeth sank deep and tore chunks of flesh. Not when the undead ripped through his chest to get his own heart. He had cut himself off from the others, especially Lorraine with her shining light. He couldn't afford to have her in his mind while he fought—and yet cutting himself off made the torment of nothingness far worse.

He extracted the heart and tossed it a distance from the vampire, keeping the creature locked to him while he summoned lightning. He took his time incinerating the heart as well as the undead and then cleaning the acid blood from his body. He spent more time destroying the insects the master vampire had created and then healing the trees and shrubbery, restoring as much of the damaged forest as possible, wanting it clean and untainted for any inhabitants.

⁂

"Isai is ready for travel," Gary said. "I healed the oldest boy and brought him back. Have you examined the others for wounds?" He was very pale.

Sandu immediately offered him his wrist. "Take what I offer freely."

Gary's sharp eyes moved over him before he bent his head to accept the offering.

"All of them are healed," Andor assured. "Dragomir is removing their memories now. I restored their campsite and removed all signs of vampires from the area. The land will regrow without a problem. One of the crows slashed a nasty gash into the back of Lorraine's head. I would ask that you take a look at it. The others offered to heal it, but something about it disturbs me." Andor couldn't quite shake the feeling that she had been specifically targeted.

"I looked," Dragomir added, "but wasn't certain what I was looking for. It looks like a laceration to me."

"Perhaps the healer should wait until we are safely within the compound," Ferro suggested. "He is already weak, and we need him at full strength. Andor and Isai are both in need of his skills."

They weren't the only ones, Andor decided, looking at Ferro, but he wasn't going to say so. A vampire could do a tremendous amount of damage in a very little time.

"We have done all we can do here," Dragomir agreed. "We need to get back to the two human traitors and make our way home."

Andor wasn't certain where home was, unless it was wherever Lorraine wanted to be. He took her hand and they walked with the others back to where they had left Adam and Herman.

The two human psychic males both sat with their backs to a tree just where they were left. Where before they had been bound without rope, now they had barbwire wrapped around their arms, shoulders and torsos. It was pulled so tight the barbs were embedded deep in their skin. That wasn't the worst. Crows sat on their bodies, pecking at them so that neither had eyes and there were holes in their faces and torn into their chests.

Andor turned Lorraine into him, hiding her face. "It is best not to look." He lifted his gaze to the others. "These two knew something we missed. Something Sergey did not want us to find." As he spoke he led Lorraine away from the men, careful to keep her from seeing. She didn't try to fight him, which he was grateful for. He didn't want to ever force her compliance, but in this instance, he would have.

"We are missing something extremely important," Ferro agreed. "Sergey sacrificed a lot here today, and there has to be a reason. He lost four very good fighters, vampires with good chances against anyone but the eight coming out of the monastery and Gary. There were too many of us here. He lost a master vampire as well."

"I cannot hope to understand Sergey Malinov," Sandu said with a small shrug. "Nor do I want to understand him and his reasons. I just want him dead."

"Let us go now," Dragomir added, glancing up at the sky.

The crows had lifted into the air when they got close, settled like silent, dark wraiths on the tree branches above them. Ferro flicked his hand toward them, and several burst into flames. The others took to the sky and raced away.

# 12

Tariq Asenguard leaned across the table, a slight frown on his face. "You should be in the ground healing, Andor, not sitting in on this meeting. Dragomir can represent you. The fact that you're alive is a miracle, and all of us know that. Your woman must be . . . extraordinary in order to pull you back from the dead."

Lorraine swallowed hard and dug her fingers into Andor's thigh. He pressed his hand over hers to give her reassurance. They were both concerned. Worried. So were all the other brethren who had been with them.

"Gary and the others did the work," Lorraine offered.

"Just the fact that all three of them bound themselves to you makes you extraordinary," Tariq said.

Andor couldn't help the flash of pride he felt in Lorraine. She *was* an amazing lifemate. She'd stood with him during attack after attack of vampire and puppets.

"It makes no sense that Sergey sent so many of his pawns after us," Andor said. "At first maybe, when he knew I was mortally wounded and there was only a human woman to fight them off, but after? Three ancients from the monastery and a Daratrazanoff. Even if he didn't know who they were, he would have recognized the way we moved and Gary's features. It is unmistakable. We have to know why he was willing to sacrifice so many."

"Do any of you have any ideas?" Tariq asked.

Gary stood behind Andor and Lorraine, his fingers pushing aside her hair to examine the laceration the crow had ripped so deep in her scalp. He didn't respond, not even when Andor glanced at him.

"None of us know," Sandu said. "But he killed the two human males we were bringing back to the compound. They were aware of something he did not want us to know. We should have taken more time examining them, but we were trying to get back here and do everything in the safety of the compound. We knew he was biting at our heels."

"We also believe he is turning psychic males to build his army," Ferro said, his voice grim.

Tariq sank back in his chair. "They would have no battle experience."

"They did not," Dragomir said. "At. All. They were obviously newly made. They were given very rudimentary skills and sent out against ancients. Sergey knew they would all die, but he still sent them."

"If he sent human psychic males, newly turned, he was not having to sacrifice his vampires, the ones with less battle experience, but still valuable," Tariq mused. "That would make sense. He has to be running out of men and he can't keep throwing them at us and watching them all fall."

"Exactly," Andor said. "I can see him sacrificing the six newly made vampires. But the others? There were four that would have been good soldiers, and a master vampire. The five of them could have cost us had they been up against others not so battle-worn or if they came across one of us alone. I took on seven of his men. He knew we were skilled and yet he kept coming at us, even after the other brethren joined Lorraine and me."

"Gary?" Tariq asked.

The room went quiet. Around the table were the other Carpathian hunters. Maksim, Tariq's partner in the nightclub business. The triplets, Tomas, Matias and Lojos, renowned for their fighting skills. Dragomir and Sandu and Benedek and Petru, all brethren from the monastery.

Isai and Ferro were deep beneath the soil in the healing grounds. Nicu Dalca, an ancient who moved like lightning. Valentin Zhestokly, his eyes as black as ice in a violent storm, sat quietly across from Tariq and with him, Afanasiv Balan, an ancient who was considered extremely dangerous by those at the table.

Gary straightened and shook his head. "The wound is deep and vicious. I should have taken the time to heal this before we took to the air."

Lorraine shook her head and then winced. "You had already spent time on Isai," she pointed out. "We all just wanted to get here before Sergey sent more after us."

Andor pressed her palm deeper into his thigh, feeling her tremble. The brethren hadn't cared about getting there fast, other than to get Lorraine to safety. They lived to hunt. He had done so as well, for so many centuries. Now, he lived for his woman. He had blocked the pain for her, so she felt no discomfort.

"Lorraine, I will have to heal this from the inside," Gary said. "Maksim and Sandu, I could use your help."

Andor knew what that meant. Gary was going to try to find anything that the bird might have planted in her before they were put in the healing grounds. The fact that he had requested Sandu and Maksim meant he was as concerned as they were. Andor wanted to be the one to make absolutely certain nothing evil had touched Lorraine, but the fact remained, he needed healing himself.

"Rather than Sandu," Tariq said, "I will aid you."

Gary shook his head. *If something was planted that could possibly attack one or all of us, you cannot be in the line of fire.*

Tariq all but ground his teeth, but he didn't argue. Andor knew he could never be in Tariq's shoes. The man had been a hunter for centuries. Now, he was the one they all protected, kept behind a wall of warriors in order that he lead. Andor understood it was necessary, and he knew Tariq did as well, but it didn't make the transition any easier.

Gary didn't wait, but shed his body. Maksim and Sandu did as well. Lorraine held herself very still. They all felt the way she steeled herself. She wasn't Carpathian and this method of healing was new to her. Having others inside her body, moving through her with only the white heat of their healing spirits, had to be frightening for her.

*I am with you, Lorraine,* he assured.

*As am I,* Sandu and Gary echoed.

Gary divided the work into three sections. Her arteries and veins, the blood supply running through her body. That was Maksim's territory. Sandu took the organs. It was Gary's job to look at the brain. The problem was whatever the crow might have injected into Lorraine could be so tiny that no one could spot it. It could be anywhere, even a sliver along her bones. A tiny foreign object was difficult at best. With someone like Sergey planting it, it might be impossible to find.

Sandu was meticulous, and Andor monitored all three the entire time. He didn't want any part of the master vampire in his woman. He was certain if Sergey had left behind a splinter of himself, Gary would find it. That was what they all feared the most. Vadim had been adept at splintering. It was a dangerous practice, because if that splinter was found and destroyed, a part of the person leaving it behind was destroyed as well.

Time passed slowly, no one speaking in the conference room. Sandu emerged first, looking exhausted and pale. At once, Benedek was there, offering him his wrist and murmuring the ritual words to him. *I offer freely.* It was an age-old ritual, meaning one life for another if necessary.

Maksim and Gary returned to their bodies at the same time. Gary looked strained, as if he was stretched thin from all the healing he had been forced to do in the last few days. Andor knew that besides Isai, the healer had also attended everyone's wounds, including Ferro's. Once back at the compound, he had worked on Andor again.

"Your verdict?" Tariq said.

All three shook their heads. "She appears to be clean of anything Sergey's servants may have left behind," Gary said.

"But?" Lorraine asked. She was tied to Gary soul to soul and she could read him just as well as the others tied to him.

"I don't like it, Lorraine." Gary gave her the respect due her, telling her the truth. "Would you mind if we replay exactly what happened so all of us could see?"

She moistened her lips with the tip of her tongue, giving away the fact that she was nervous. That wasn't characteristic of her. She also tried to pull her hand out from under Andor's. He pressed her palm tighter to his thigh. *I am with you, sívamet. No harm can come to you in this place.*

*I know. It's just that when we were out there, in the mountains, even with vampires and puppets coming at us, I didn't feel different from you. Here, I do.*

He detested that, but he didn't object. He tried to go over every reason she might feel that way. She was surrounded by male Carpathians. All were hunters. All held power. Only three had lifemates—not counting him. It came to him then. They had continually used the word *human* to differentiate the psychic males, putting humans on one side and the Carpathians on the other. Of course, she would wince each time that word was used.

*You are my lifemate, Lorraine. We belong together, no matter which of our cultures is chosen. It is the two of us together always. Know I stand with you. If you open your mind, you will see that Ferro, Sandu and Gary stand with you as well. The other brethren will. I believe, in spite of what might be a danger to the compound, Tariq, Maksim and the others will hold you as one of theirs, no matter human or Carpathian.*

*They all say the word* human *with disgust. All of you look down on us.*

*You are wrong. There are humans living in this compound and they are loved and respected. A human security force has aided Tariq more than once in fighting for those he loves. They are respected. Gary was human and he was revered by our people. Did we have respect for Adam and Herman? No, sadly, they were traitors. They were willing to trade your life for immortality.*

"Lorraine?" Tariq prompted. "Does our seeing this battle upset you?"

She took a deep breath. Andor felt the way she steeled herself to answer. He'd felt it before. He saw that Sandu came alert. He'd felt that as well. He glanced at Gary. The man looked impassive, but he had moved closer to Lorraine, just as Sandu had done mentally.

"Tell me how to do it."

"You have to open your mind to your lifemate, and he can replay it for us all."

She glanced up at Andor. He leaned into her. *I am extraordinarily proud of you, hän sívamak. You handled that battle as if you were a warrior with years of fighting experience.*

*Yes, until I made that mistake and ran out from under the ceiling you'd constructed to prevent the very thing that happened.*

Was that what worried her? That everyone in the room would see her mistake and blame her for the fears they were now dealing with? *Sívamet, few would have had the courage you displayed. You were fighting for your life-mate.* He let her hear and feel the pride he had in her.

She just nodded and closed her eyes. Those long feathery lashes fanned her cheeks, drawing his immediate attention. She took his breath with her bravery and he was just now registering that, aside from the fact that no matter what, to him, she would always be the most beautiful woman in the world, she was probably considered beautiful by the human world as well.

He took the fight from her mind and replayed it for the others, using their common telepathic pathway. Tariq lifted a finger when it was over and did a short spin. Andor replayed the sequence a second time. When the scene reached the part where Lorraine ran out to confront the vampire and the crows swooped down on her, Tariq held up his hand and Andor instantly paused the unfolding events.

All of them studied the birds surrounding her. The crows were close, wings outstretched, some striking her, but no other talon or beak was close to her.

"If they were attacking her, wanting to harm her, as they should have been," Tariq said, "more than one bird would have used its beak. Definitely their talons. Beaks and talons do the most damage. We've seen attacks from the vampire's creatures before. They shred flesh whenever they can. They look to do the most mutilation possible."

Siv nodded his assent, studying the frozen moment in time. It was difficult not to want to shield Lorraine from all the warriors' scrutiny. "Andor, show us the next frame and stop. I want to see the bird that actually attacks her. Or more precisely, what the rest of the flock does when that one crow approaches."

Andor felt Lorraine shudder. He slipped his arm around her stiff shoulders. She tried to hold herself away from him. He understood. The others watched what happened to her with eyes that had seen so many battles, and they were unemotional. He could tell her repeatedly that they truly couldn't feel, but she couldn't experience that and to have them watch what had transpired—her personal nightmare—while so detached had to be difficult for her.

Andor wrapped his arm around her in spite of the way she stiffened. He pulled her beneath his shoulder, his thigh touching hers, their chairs not a paper's width apart. He wanted the physical closeness with her. More, he wanted the intimacy of the two of them, mind to mind.

*Sívamet, I know this is difficult. Touch me. My mind. Slide into me and feel me surround you. These men seek to maintain your well-being. They do not want to take the chance of anything harming you.*

*They seek to find whatever Sergey left behind in me, if anything, just in case I'm a threat to them.*

His breath caught in his throat. *It is not like that at all. Regardless of what he left, you are no threat and they know it. Do you really believe Ferro and Sandu would abandon you? Or that I would? Even if Sergey planted half of himself in you, we would fight for you.*

There was a moment of absolute stillness, and he knew he'd made a terrible mistake. The rest of the warriors around the table knew something happened. They all looked up, their gazes no longer turned inward to study the replay.

"What is it?" Tariq asked.

Everyone could hear Lorraine's accelerated heartbeat and her shallow breathing. They could feel the raw burning in her lungs as she tried, unsuccessfully, to pull in air. She began to struggle, as if she might free herself from him, but Andor held on tight.

"*Csecsemő*, take a breath. Feel me breathing and breathe with me." He locked her to him and then took her hand and placed her palm over his heart. "Feel my heart beating. Slow down and let your body follow mine." He willed her to listen to him. In her mind, there was chaos. Fear mounting to terror. All he saw was a jumble of puppets feeding on children. Tears swam in her eyes and dripped off her lashes.

"What is it?" Tariq asked again. "How can we help?"

"I have to leave. I have to go." She struggled against his hold.

Andor knew he couldn't let go of her. She was far too skilled in martial arts. If she actively fought him, he would have to subdue her in other ways so she wouldn't get hurt. "Lorraine." He spoke her name with the command and power of centuries of being a predator. "Stop this right now."

She subsided immediately, succumbing to the power and authority in his voice.

"Now, breathe with me. Let your heart follow mine." He knew it was a panic attack and whatever he'd said to trigger it had to be discussed. "Whatever you are afraid of, I am right here with you. I can help."

Lorraine shook her head, but her breathing was beginning to get under control and her heart was already following the lead of his.

He let her calm while the others waited patiently. Gary and Sandu had moved even closer, as if by their presence she would feel safer, but Andor knew this wasn't about her safety.

"Talk to me. Tell me what is wrong."

"You said even if he left half of him behind in me, you would stay. You and the others. The way you said it, you meant it."

"I am your lifemate. Nothing would induce me to leave you."

"The brethren would surround you, Lorraine," Sandu explained. "Sergey will not get you."

"I would work until we got to him," Gary said. "It would not be the first time, although had he actually splintered himself in half, he would be greatly diminished and easy to vanquish so there is no chance he did that."

Her breath came out in a little sob. "But he can put something of himself into me. That's what you're saying. Just like he did the psychic males. He can make me do things to hurt others . . ."

"Stop." Andor said it in the same commanding voice. "You keep forgetting to breathe. First, Lorraine, think logically. No matter how hard any of the vampires or the psychics tried to get inside your mind, you were able to resist. Even if that crow planted a sliver of Sergey into you, and we didn't find evidence of it, he could not make you do something to harm others. Your shields wouldn't allow it."

"But if he's in me . . ."

"Puppets are not made that way. There is blood given by the vampire. There are . . . other things given. You cannot be made into a puppet."

"I just want to go away from here." There was panic in her voice. "When we came in together, I heard the sound of children. I know there are several people here." Her gaze jumped to Dragomir's face. "Your life-mate is pregnant. Do any of you really think I would stay when you so obviously believe me to be a threat?"

"No one thinks you're a threat, Lorraine," Tariq countered, his voice gentle. "We all have seen the way you fought with Andor and the others. You're needed here. Your skills as well as that fierce determination. We want our women to learn those skills, and you would be a tremendous asset. I know you have been learning combat since you were young."

"It isn't the same."

"It is," he countered. "It is a skill set. A mind-set. Once the muscles remember those moves, battle experience can be drawn on, but not until then."

The other warriors nodded, and Lorraine's protest died on her lips.

"We are trying to discern what Sergey is up to," Tariq continued. "Vadim, his brother, planted slivers before, but in the end, that weakened him and I believe Sergey wouldn't do that to himself. He needs his strength to run his army, to hold them to him. If the conversation you had with Jannik is anything to go by, I would say there is dissention in the ranks. Please stay and let us figure this out together."

Andor could see why the man was a leader. He didn't order Lorraine. He appealed to her logic and her belief that the women and children as well as the men should learn to defend themselves. Tariq was speaking with total sincerity, which came through.

*He is a good man in an impossible situation,* Andor added. *He believes it is necessary for all the women to learn to fight the vampire, but some of the men still oppose him. We are ancients and most come from a time when women were cherished and protected.*

*We can be cherished and protected and still learn to defend ourselves should we end up in trouble.*

He had to admit, that snippy little note in her voice sent blood rushing just a little too hotly through his veins. "Are you ready, Lorraine?" He didn't want to wait and let her think too much on whether or not slivers of vampires were hidden in her body somewhere.

She nodded. "Yes. I'm sorry I freaked out."

He would ask her later what *freaking out* was. It was a term he was unfamiliar with. He pushed the fight scene into everyone's mind and paused it just as the large bird flew right at the back of Lorraine's skull. Talons dug into her back, holding the crow to her while the beak slashed deep. The picture was frozen in their minds.

Andor, like the others, studied it. Crows surrounded her, cutting her off from escape. Cutting her off from the vampire she had rushed out to stop before realizing it was a mistake. They were in the air, the entire flock, circling her, wings outstretched, talons ready, but not one other actually appeared to be attacking her.

"They are herding her," Siv said. "Straight to him. The big one."

"In some way, they are also protecting her from the vampire," Sandu noted. "The one on the ground."

Nicu nodded. "Look at it closely. The vampire was furious. She had bested him, and he has been around for centuries. She should not have had a chance against him. He had been careful, I suspect, to keep from killing her and that gave her the advantage. When she took it, see his face? His eyes? How contorted he appears? She burned him. Nearly killed him. A human and a woman at that. He wanted to kill her and had every intention of doing so. Look where some of the birds are."

The others were silent. Tariq drummed his fingers on the tabletop. "They dove at him, while the others separated them. He wasn't supposed to kill her."

Beside him, Lorraine tensed up again, but she didn't say anything, just listened to them discussing the battle. Andor didn't blame her for feeling upset. He wouldn't want Sergey to put a splinter of himself inside him. Anything vampire was vile. Having something that could be an asset to the undead inside one's body, where the vampire could spy, was sickening.

"Okay, now go one frame further," Tariq said.

Andor had to have that interpreted for him. Tariq was very at ease in the modern, human world. Andor had only been involved with them all a short time. He was still trying to play catch-up. He looked to Gary, who, in another life as far as Carpathians went, had been human.

"Freeze it the next movement."

Andor complied, and they all once again studied the rather large bird as its beak drove down into Lorraine's skull. At the same time, its talons scraped the skin of her back open and the wings beat hard to keep it in place so the beak could do damage, stabbing deep. The wounds on her shoulders and back were almost superficial, and compared to the curved, wicked piercing of the beak, they were nothing. The healing had to be done to her skull.

"She was targeted, but I saw nothing in its beak. If it had something, the transfer was made from the mouth to her skull," Tariq said. "Is that agreed?"

The warriors nodded, all in agreement. Andor had been very careful to watch. "Did anyone see that crow before the battle began? You all flew over the area repeatedly in order to spot the enemy. I looked at the flock of crows often, but never saw one that size."

"I was in the forest with them," Sandu said, "and I didn't see it."

"We took the form of a crow and sat among them," Dragomir volunteered. "That large one would definitely have caught my eye. It was not there."

"It was somewhere watching," Andor said. "That had to have been Sergey. He directed the entire battle, and we didn't know."

"All of you are ancients and yet you didn't sense his presence. That doesn't bode well for us," Tariq said.

"There would have been no way to know who was there and who wasn't," Dragomir said. "That explains the master vampire. Sergey knew we would have sensed his presence had he not brought that kind of powerful vampire with him. He was the ultimate sacrifice."

Gary nodded. "Ferro had no trouble ferreting out his trap. He told me he knew the undead he fought couldn't have been a master vampire for too long because, although he did wound him and the wounds were severe, the fight didn't last long at all."

Tariq sighed and drummed his fingers again on the table. "Another sacrifice in order for Sergey to be there at the battle. He was determined to orchestrate it and participate when the time was right. A master vampire and four lesser vampires was a huge sacrifice. He was up to something that was very important to him."

Gary nodded. "I think it best if we try again. This time each of us will trade places. Sandu, you take the brain, I'll take arteries and veins. Maksim, you take her organs, and this time we will add Dragomir. You inspect her bones."

Andor felt Lorraine's instinctive retreat, but she didn't protest. This time she leaned into him. *What if they don't find anything? Should we leave? I can tell that all of you believe he planted something in me.*

*We know what a sliver looks like. Dragomir and Gary have dealt with them. Every ancient has seen them and at one time or another had to remove them. If it is there, they will find it. Have no worries. There are four of them looking.*

Andor wanted to reassure her. If they found nothing, he didn't want her panicking and deciding she had to run from them. He wasn't going to allow her to leave the compound until he knew she was safe. Until he knew what Sergey had done to her, or what he wanted from her, Andor wasn't about to let her set one foot out of the safety area.

He joined with Sandu so when the ancient shed his body and once more slipped into hers as nothing but pure spirit, he could see and feel as well what they encountered. The light from Gary was so bright and hot it illuminated every part of Lorraine's body. Dragomir and Maksim added to that white heat. Sandu was even more meticulous, worried now, as were all the others.

After watching the crow attacking his lifemate, there was no doubt in Andor's mind that she had been specifically targeted. Knowing that Sergey had sacrificed a master vampire so the ancients wouldn't detect his presence made the entire thing even more worrisome. More than anything, Andor wanted to convert his woman and get her into the healing earth. He knew her skills in battle would triple just from becoming Carpathian.

As carefully as Sandu inspected every fold of her brain, every valley and hill, the slopes and shadows, he found nothing that even faintly resembled a splinter. Andor knew slivers were tiny and could embed in the tissue, so that it appeared to be part of whatever it attached itself to. Still, even wriggling to fasten itself to the surface, the sliver had to be lying on the exterior and there would be a tiny dark spot, as if the tissue was in shadow whether light shone on it or not.

Andor had found more than one, always a mage sliver, in the centuries past that he had searched someone for them. He knew Sandu was well aware of exactly what to look for, as were the others searching through Lorraine's system.

*I found nothing.* Sandu should have sounded reassuring, but he didn't.

When the others emerged, as pale and exhausted as Sandu, they all shook their heads. Andor glanced at Tariq and saw him exchange a long look with Gary and knew Tariq was communicating privately with his protector and adviser. Gary shook his head even as he took the wrist offered to him by one of the triplets. Tariq sighed.

"I understand you have not completed the ritual bond," Tariq said.

"Not as yet," Andor said, his tone warning the other man to back off. It was one thing to choose to follow him and protect him, it was another to have the man telling him what to do. He, as well as his brethren, didn't acknowledge any authority over them. They still were uncertain whether or not the ruling prince was worthy of that position.

"I understand." Tariq sat back in his chair. "You can have the use of the smaller house just beside the lake. The soil is excellent, Andor, and Lorraine will be comfortable in it while you rest and heal."

Andor winced. That was a reminder that his woman would be alone and vulnerable while he was beneath the ground. No, while they all were beneath the ground. He detested that for her. He could plant a suggestion to sleep, if she allowed it, but that didn't mean she would. Or he could force sleep, and that was the last thing he ever wanted to do. Lorraine would forgive many things, but he doubted if she would forgive force.

"Charlotte's friend Genevieve watches over the children, as do another couple who stay within the compound. They would be glad for the company," Tariq added.

Lorraine took a deep breath and stood, pushing back her chair as if she couldn't wait to get out of there. He didn't blame her. She had been the subject of their scrutiny for a long while.

*They still suspect Sergey found a way to plant something in her.* He sent that straight to Sandu. He knew the man was bound to Lorraine's soul and only finding his lifemate would break that bond. In the meantime, he could touch her mind and feel her emotions. That would help to sustain him until he found her.

*Do you not suspect this also?*

Of course he did. Not only did he suspect, there was no other explanation.

*You must convert her. Once her blood is replaced with ours, and her human body dies, whatever he planted will be far more vulnerable.*

He knew that. Tariq knew that. The leader had been close to pointing that out to Andor, but Andor didn't want Lorraine to make her decisions based on anything but what she truly wanted. She'd been traumatized enough. Conversion wasn't easy, even with others aiding them, and then she would have to accept things such as sleeping beneath the soil and surviving on the blood of others.

He took her hand and walked out. Once out of the house and into the night air, he lifted his face to study the sky. The night seemed to be passing too fast. He knew, by the little shiver that ran through her, that she felt it, too.

"It's beautiful here," she commented.

"It is. I especially like that he found land where water and forest come together, yet it is clearly a modern estate." The brethren had talked about how Tariq had situated his home for defense. He then bought up property all around his main compound with the idea that other Carpathians could settle close, making their protected world much larger and safer for their lifemates and hopefully any children that came along in the future.

Lorraine glanced at him, a quick little grin coming and fading just as fast. "Look at you, sounding all modern."

"I could have pointed out the fact that this place is very easily defensible against any threat. Land, water or air."

"I did notice that."

She walked with him toward the house situated closest to the lake. It was far smaller than the main house and just a bit more so than the other homes on the property. The detail was attractive. All the houses were smaller replicas of Tariq and Charlotte's home. He especially liked the porch. It looked cool and inviting. He would much rather be outside than inside, or rather, that had always been his preference until he found Lorraine. Now, he would be anywhere with her and be happy.

"What was Tariq going to say when you stopped him?"

His gaze flicked to hers. She wasn't looking at him, but up at the exterior of the house. There was no lying to one's lifemate. Avoidance might be a better way to go. "Lorraine." He sighed when her gaze jumped to his and he found himself looking into those green eyes of hers. "Sometimes, it is better to let things be. You have been through a lot in a very short amount of days. We do not have to do everything at once."

"No, but I would very much like to have all the information available to me. I'm like that, Andor. I need to know everything to make informed decisions. It takes a little while for me to process and then I feel like I've done the best I can with what I know."

He took her hand and led her up the stairs. When he waved toward the door, it opened inward invitingly. He stepped inside and felt the wave of power under his feet and around him. This structure was protected. That made him feel better.

He tugged at Lorraine's hand. She stood just on the threshold looking into the dark interior. Immediately he waved toward the inside, and lights sprang on. Hardwood floors gleamed. There was furniture in the room he could see. She took a deep breath and stepped inside. He watched her face and saw her look down at the floor. She felt that surge of power as well.

"The house is safeguarded. It allowed us in because Tariq gave us his blessing," he explained, but he knew her hesitation came from the nightmare she'd stepped into when she'd returned to her family home from college.

She moved past him and stood in the front room, turning around to inspect everything. "I will be very grateful for a bathroom and an actual bed. Thank you for remembering my backpack."

He saw that her pack was lying up against the wall where someone had put it when they had arrived. "The things in it matter to you."

She sank down into what appeared to be a very comfortable sofa. He sat down beside her and when she shivered, he waved his hand at the fireplace. It immediately sprang to life, the flames flickering and dancing, adding warmth to the room.

"Please tell me, Andor."

There was no resisting Lorraine when she wanted something. She didn't whine. She just asked politely, and he could tell it mattered to her, just like those things in her backpack.

"By converting you, all traces of human would be lost. Carpathian blood would flow in your veins. If Sergey left something in you—"

"All of you believe he did, and so do I," she interrupted.

He nodded. "There is no other reasonable explanation. So, whatever he left would have a difficult time hiding. Carpathian blood does not mix well with anything vampire. Also, you would be with me during our sleep cycle and I could better protect you."

She sat for a long time looking down at her hand, specifically her left hand. He reached for it and slid his palm gently over her fingers.

"What is it?"

"I have my mother's wedding rings. I always thought I would wear them. There are no rings on any of your fingers. Is that because you shift, or because that is a human ceremony?"

Was there regret in her voice? He didn't want her to regret anything. "What each Carpathian pair has is different, because we are all different. You are *my* lifemate and I am yours. If we choose to wear rings, shifting with them is no hardship."

She moistened her lips with the tip of her tongue, and for the first time, genuine happiness crept into her eyes. "Then I suppose you had better get on with it."

He frowned. "I missed something."

"You told me it takes three blood exchanges. We have only had one. If we're to do this by tomorrow night, you'd better take the second exchange now. Tomorrow you can convert me, right?"

"Lorraine, you haven't had time to process. You like to take things slow."

"I've been thinking about it since you first told me I would have to become Carpathian. What do I have left to me? My family is dead. All of them. I have no friends. No other relatives. I have you and Ferro and Sandu. I have Gary. I hope to fit in here, but if I don't, and you're willing, we can go somewhere else together. I know I want to be with you."

Andor couldn't stop himself from gathering her into his arms. In spite of wanting to make certain, so that she would never have regrets, he nuzzled her neck with his mouth. "*Csecsemő*, I want this for us, but you have to be so sure. There will be pain during the conversion. I can be there through it with you, so will the others to try to take most of it, but we cannot prevent all of it."

"The alternative isn't that great. Besides, I've had this taste in my mouth all night and I want to see if it's as good as I remember."

His tongue slid over her pounding pulse. His teeth scraped gently over the spot beckoning him. More than anything, he wanted to make love to her, but his body needed healing and he wasn't a man to do things by halves. He sank his teeth deep, allowing her to experience more of that erotic bite, the flash of pain giving way to nothing but pure pleasure.

He hadn't known how erotic feeding from one's lifemate could be. His body nearly went up in flames, his blood pooling hotly in his groin. His mind found hers, and she was slick with need, her nipples pebbling, pushing against his chest while her body moved restlessly. He took his time, savoring every drop. Her taste was the finest he'd ever experienced and the craving was difficult to resist, but he forced himself to stop when he'd taken enough.

It was her turn, and his entire body clenched in anticipation. The moment her mouth moved on his skin, he threw his head back and roared. She had his entire body hard and hungry. So needy. This, then, was what sex was all about. The craving. The hunger. The drive that was so strong there was no resisting it.

*We had better turn you fast, sívamet, or we both will not survive the taking of blood.*

Her fingers stroked caresses over his skin, along the walls of his mind and, sun scorch the woman, over his groin.

*You are not helping.*

*Oh no, was I supposed to be helping? I thought I was supposed to be showing you what we're missing. You need to heal fast. That's all I'm saying here.*

Her fingers kept stroking, and the sane part of him knew he needed to stop her. Mostly he wasn't sane at all.

# 13

*You're clearly wearing too many clothes.*

Lorraine's voice brushed along the walls of his mind so intimately Andor's cock threatened to explode. She was right—he was wearing far too many clothes. He needed the physical touch of her fingers against his rock-hard flesh. Her hand slid over him, rubbed right over his trousers, and he felt the jerk and throb of pure need.

He waved his hand and he was completely bare to her. He couldn't take the feel of her clothing rubbing on his skin. He wanted her naked as well. It took less than a second to achieve that. Her laughter was gentle, teasing in his mind.

*That was not the plan. It was supposed to be you naked and needing me. Now it is both. How do we get out of this?*

He gently inserted his hand between her mouth and his chest when he knew she had taken enough for a full blood exchange. His heart beat faster at the knowledge she was one step closer to his world—and to him. His body felt on the very edge of control. Even though she was no longer taking his blood, he needed her more than ever.

She obeyed the small command to stop feeding, but kissed her way down his chest to his belly. Everywhere she kissed, she left behind a trail of fire. Her hair brushed over his thighs as she slid to the floor, wedging herself between his legs, her mouth continuing its travels. The feeling of that silky mass sweeping over his body sent more hot blood rushing to his cock until he was so full and thick he felt it all the way to his toes.

He bunched her hair in his fist so he could see her face. He needed to watch her as she kissed her way over his groin. That hungry, intense desire was in her eyes. He loved that look. He knew he would keep that image with him always. She dropped her head lower, and he felt her breath, warm, against the crown of his cock. Small droplets leaked out, enticing her. For a moment, he thought she might swallow him down, but instead, she licked up his balls and then his shaft.

His entire body shuddered with need. He tightened his hold in her hair, this time to guide her where he needed her most. She lifted those long lashes, and stared up at him with sparkling green eyes. Teasing. She was teasing him. His cock jerked in anticipation. Life with Lorraine was always going to be an adventure because she did the unexpected.

*We need to be very careful,* she reminded. *The healer told you to go to ground immediately. He was worried about your wounds.*

He'd forgotten he had any wounds. Blood pounded through his cock. His heartbeat centered in his groin. There was a strange roaring in his ears. Every cell in his body felt alive. Anticipating. Waiting. He found he was holding his breath until his lungs burned.

"Lorraine." Her name was a command. A powerful one. It came out hoarse. Almost desperate. Not nearly as authoritative as he thought it should have, as desperate as he was.

Her warm breath slid over him again so that his muscles tightened. Her eyes laughed happily and that caught at him. In that moment, there was only the two of them, the rest of the world locked out. Every problem. It was Lorraine and Andor.

Then her mouth engulfed him and there was no sane thought. Her mouth was hot and wet, sliding over him tightly. Her tongue danced and stroked. She did some kind of humming that sent vibrations right through his shaft, blowing out the top. It was the sexiest thing he'd ever seen, her mouth moving over him as she knelt there between his legs.

"Keep your eyes on mine, *sívamet*."

Watching her watch him, as she gave him so much pleasure, was just plain erotic. That was another image he never wanted to lose. Those green eyes devoured him the way her mouth swallowed him. Tight and hot. Her tongue stripped him of thought so he was pure feeling. His hips began to move, small thrusts, taking him deeper. He was careful and very gentle, but his centuries of control and discipline were gone with every stroke of her tongue.

Flames teased at the base of his cock—sizzled at the base of his spine. Her mouth slid over him again, so tight. So hot. Flames rushed up from his toes, his calves, and then danced up his thighs to lick at his balls. The heat was tremendous. The fire burned up his spine, coiled in his belly, and burst into a firestorm as his cock erupted like a volcano. Jet after jet. Rope after rope. The hot seed exploded from him. He threw back his head and roared, even while he fought to stay in eye contact with her.

She sank back onto her heels wiping at her mouth, her eyes smiling at him. *Apparently, you like sex, Andor.*

*Like* was not the word he would use. His pulse struggled to return to a calm, steady beat. He waited until he could breathe before answering her. "Apparently, I love sex. I have learned a lot over the centuries. We study everything in order to please our lifemates. I think I can manage to please you as you have me."

"The healer said you needed to go to ground."

"The healer can go to ground. I still have some night left and I intend to make use of it." He was watching her carefully and saw the small hint of apprehension. "What is it, Lorraine?" He beckoned to her and pointed to the spot between his legs. She hesitated, but she moved forward again. Her breasts brushed against his thighs and then his groin. A jolt of awareness teased his cock. Her skin was like satin. "What is it, *csecsemõ*, you have only to tell me."

Her hand moved. Fingers slid over the inside of his thigh and caressed his shaft. She had no trouble touching him or putting her mouth on him, but now, she was unexpectedly shy.

"I didn't expect to have sex with you, Andor. Not right away. I know that you've been wounded and I thought I had time . . ." She trailed off with a small frown.

He rubbed the curve of her mouth with the pad of his thumb. "Are you afraid?" She wasn't afraid of very much, and she'd been the one to initiate oral sex on him.

She shook her head. "I've been camping. There aren't a lot of chances to get clean. You just wave your hand and you're all fresh and smell like heaven. I'm pretty certain I smell like a skunk or something equally horrendous."

He wanted to laugh. She could do that so easily. That faint humor in her voice told him, although it mattered to her, she still was able to laugh at the situation and herself. More reasons to fall harder for her.

"I was thinking you could do more hand waving, but toward me, this time."

Now her laughter was in her eyes. He couldn't help responding. The hand wave came, but she didn't need it. She never did. To him, she smelled earthy and perfect. He tipped her face up to his and bent to take her mouth. Kissing her was another kind of heaven he hadn't expected. There was that fire in her mouth she'd spread over his cock. He burned with her for a few minutes and then he gathered her into his arms and floated them to the main bedroom.

The bed was already made up in anticipation of Lorraine's arrival. He made a mental note to thank Charlotte for her welcoming of Lorraine into the compound. The bedding was soft and he lay his woman right in the center, coming down over top of her, feeling the give in the thick comforter but the firmness of the mattress beneath. Her hair spread across the white comforter, looking more red than brown, the golden tones gleaming from the moonlight spilling in through the windows. Her green eyes were steady on his. Those lashes, feathery and dark, tipped with gold, fluttered, drawing attention to the beauty of her face.

Andor framed her face, his hips wedged between hers, his gaze moving over her possessively. He had never felt possessive in his life. He was all about duty and honor. Material things meant little or nothing to him. Carpathians acquired wealth to use as tools. He knew they owned several planes to take them from one continent to the another. That required money, but keeping up with the modern world meant they had to have the means to do so. Right now, the only possession that mattered, the only thing in his world he would die to keep, was Lorraine.

*I am not a possession, silly man.*

The tenderness in her voice nearly undid him. Emotion welled up, sharp and terrible, a love so strong and intense, it was unlike anything he'd ever felt or experienced.

*And if you died to save me, we would not be together, so no dying,* she added.

There was that humor. He had that. He was given that. A woman so beautiful inside and out. A warrior of true measure. Intelligent and possessing a sense of humor. She had it all and somehow, the universe had deigned to give her to him.

Her gaze drifted over his face, touching him with love. He felt it. She didn't need to say it, because it was there in the way she looked at him.

"Kiss me again, Andor. I love when you kiss me."

She sounded both needy and wanton. Tempting him. His little siren. He kissed her because there was no resisting her, and he didn't want to. He craved her kisses. He loved the way she made his body hard and demanding. He let that take them both, a slow burn that started with just worshiping her mouth. Nibbling. Biting. Licking. Tracing that sensual bow. Breathing and exchanging breath.

Lying over her body, her skin sliding under his, so soft, sensations crashed through him until he felt every inch of her inside and out. He framed her face with his hands, that face that made him ache with need, burn with hunger and soar with emotion, with love for her. He dipped his head and pressed kisses up her throat and over her chin to the corners of her mouth. He tugged at her bottom lip with his teeth, very gently, savoring every awareness of his body and hers—as well as the differences between them.

He kissed her again and again, conveying without words what was in his heart. He had no idea a man could feel so much for a woman. He had lived long, century after century, and he had touched the minds of men in love. He had even shared, for a moment, Dragomir's love of Emeline. Still, that hadn't prepared him for the way he felt toward Lorraine.

When he had uttered the ritual binding words, tying them together for all time, he had given her his heart. He had given her his soul. He hadn't thought what those words meant until that moment, kissing her, absorbing her into his mind and body. Her taste. Her feel. Every inch of her. He had been created for her. He knew that with absolute certainty.

*You're going to make me cry.*

*You worried that I did not choose you, that you would not have been my choice. You worried you would never know love.*

*You see too much.*

He lifted his head to look down at her, his gaze drifting over the beautiful bone structure and feathery lashes. Over the woman who owned his heart and soul—who always would have them in her keeping.

*I see you, Lorraine. Never think for one moment that you are not my choice. That you are not in my heart. I cannot see anything or anyone but you.*

He could have spoken aloud, but it was so much more intimate speaking telepathically. She would feel his heart, his love for her, with every stroke along her mind his words created. Tears glistened on the tips of her lashes and he took them off with his lips.

*I see only you, Andor,* she replied. She arched up, pressing her breasts into his chest, her hips bucking a little as if her body was as equally hungry for his.

He could hear the truth of her words—and also the little hint of surprise. He liked that as well, the flavors in her voice. She hadn't expected to love him so quickly. She didn't understand the pull of lifemates, but she knew it was there. More importantly, she had deliberately studied him, once he told her about the concept and that she was his. Lorraine had gone into his mind and tried to learn who and what he was—what he was about. He could have told her. His character was wrapped up in one word—*honor.*

She nipped his chin with her teeth. *Loyalty as well. Honor and loyalty. There are so many more, Andor, all good, all traits that appeal to me. I believe in honor and loyalty as well.*

He knew that. He dipped his head to the temptation of her breast. The moment his tongue flicked her nipple, she jumped. He lifted his head to look at her quickly, judging her reaction. "You're very sensitive."

"In a good way."

He smiled at her and once more ducked his head toward her breast. He took the time to know every inch of both breasts. The curves were very pronounced, those round mounds that came to a peak he liked to flick and tease with his fingers before he suckled, pressing her nipple to the roof of his mouth and stroking with his tongue until she cried out and writhed beneath him.

He touched her mind to feel what she was feeling. Her body was slick and hot with desire, needing him. Just as she had made his body come alive, every nerve ending on fire, he was doing the same to hers. He kissed his way back to up to her mouth as he reached for one of her legs, wrapping it around him, opening her more fully to him. He took the other leg, lifting it, encouraging her to do the same with her left one, until she had hooked her ankles at the small of his back.

He touched her mind once again. There was no trepidation. His woman was fearless and eager. Needy. He circled the heavy girth of his cock with his fist, fitting the broad head against her slick entrance. The heat scorched him. Drew him. He needed, too. He pushed deeper and both shuddered at the same time as the overwhelming sensation threatened to drown them in pleasure.

Her tight muscles fought him, and then slowly relented, allowing him to push deeper so that he felt his cock was gripped firmly in a silken, hot fist. He threw his head back, savoring that feeling, filing it away with so many others she'd given him. This was the ultimate, that slow burning heat surrounding him, welcoming him, trying to keep him out, yet pulling him in. Beckoning. Tempting. The sensations poured over him. Into him. Filling him. Filling all those tattered and torn places in him until he was whole.

He threaded his fingers through hers and pushed her hands into the mattress beside her head, looking down, straight into her eyes. He held her that way, pinned beneath him, his eyes holding hers captive. *Tet vigyázam.* He repeated it so she would hear him. Understand him. Never doubt again. *Tet vigyázam.* He dipped his head to brush a kiss across her mouth. At the same time, he thrust his hips hard, burying himself deep, driving through her thin barrier to claim every inch of her. Wanting body, heart and soul.

She gasped and went stiff, frozen beneath him. He kept still as well, refusing to release her gaze. *Tet vigyázam means I love you, Lorraine. And I do. My language or yours. Any language. I love you. I do not want there to be any doubts in your mind. Not now. Not ever. Whatever happens, we do this together.*

He felt her body slowly relax around his. That vise gripping him eased enough for him to move. Her smile was tentative, but it was there. *I know I am falling in love with you, Andor. Everything about you, even the fact that you will want me to sleep beside you in the ground.*

He wanted that. He did. When she was beside him, no harm could come to her. He set a rhythm. Gently. Tenderly. His heart had turned inside out. His soul, that part of it she had guarded through centuries for him, shone a light so bright and hot, so strong, he felt as if he was burning from the inside out.

She loved him. She chose him. She was choosing his life, his world. Their hearts beat a little wildly—but together. Her breathing turned ragged, his was labored, but each time he bent his mouth to hers, they exchanged breath, exchanged air. His mind remained firmly in hers, feeling every stroke of his cock, stretching her, claiming her, while she surrounded him with a sheath of pure fire. The friction as he rode her was phenomenal. Artistry. Pure beauty.

Lorraine was everything he had ever thought a lifemate could be, and yet so much more. "*Tet vigyázam.*" He couldn't say it enough. He tightened his fingers around hers, holding her beneath him, staring down into her eyes, his body on fire, in paradise.

Already, far too soon, that feeling was starting in his toes and moving up the backs of his calves, flames licking up his legs, threatening to ignite a firestorm. Her breathing was ragged, labored, her hips moving to match his, her sheath gripping so tightly it felt as if he had been swallowed alive and was being strangled by that silken, scorching hot fist.

"Come with me, *hän sívamak*." It was a command, nothing less.

Her gaze clung to his, and he saw what he'd needed all along. Her complete trust. She let go, her hips bucking, the waves intense, so strong her sheath clamped down on him, and then the flames reached his balls and the seed boiling there. As if she'd touched a match to a stick of dynamite, he erupted, a long explosion, jet after jet splashing the walls of her sheath, triggering even stronger ripples in her.

They rode it out together, soaring, shuddering, their hearts keeping that same wild rhythm. Andor realized that he liked being out of control. He'd spent so many centuries with complete discipline, he never thought that he would be able to let go the way she made him. There was such freedom in feeling, in emotion.

When he could get his breath back, he kissed her, tasting her pleasure. Tasting the way she loved him. He savored that as well, locking it in his mind to take out and look at at a later date. There were so many new sensations. So many overwhelming desires and emotions. "Thank you, Lorraine. I cannot say that enough." He brushed kisses on her eyelids, on her nose and down to her chin, where he couldn't help but nibble. He could stay there for the rest of the night, although he knew that sunrise was coming all too soon.

"Andor?" Lorraine's voice shook. Her breath suddenly hitched in her voice. "Honey, you have to move right now, get off me."

"What is wrong?" He was puzzled. The quake of fear and anxiety in her voice was very real. He felt it in her mind. He was still reeling from the way his body was feeling. Almost euphoria. Certainly, he had experienced something very close to ecstasy, and it wasn't all about his body. All of him had been involved, his entire being. *"Csecsemő?"*

"I think you're bleeding again. Honey, move right now and let me see." Her hands pushed on the heavy muscles of his chest. "All of them will *kill* me if we opened any of those wounds. They've already given you so much blood and I don't know how many healing sessions. Between you and all the injuries the others sustained in their battles, Gary was exhausted. Just when we were leaving, I heard Tariq order him to go to ground."

Andor smiled down at her and nuzzled her chin with the dark, shadowy bristles on his jaw. He left behind a smear of strawberry so he kissed that little spot on her chin. "Did you catch Gary's response?"

"No."

"It was in Carpathian, and I think he managed as many of the swear words as possible in one sentence. Not that it would deter Tariq from giving him another order. Gary's in the ground right now. So are Ferro, Isai, Sandu and Dragomir."

"How badly was Ferro injured? And don't change the subject." Her hands pushed harder. "Get off, right this minute, Andor."

He laughed. A full-out laugh. He hadn't even known he could laugh that way so the sound was startling. Shocking. "I cannot believe you just ordered me in the same way Tariq gave a command to Gary. I am your lifemate, Lorraine."

She leveled her green gaze at him. "*Exactly.* I took note of those vows you said for both of us when you irrevocably tied us together without my consent. Your body was placed in *my* care, so get off me, you big oaf, and let me care for you."

He was still laughing. Happy. He liked her bossy tone. It made him hard all over again, and the last thing he wanted to do was withdraw from that hot haven of sensual pleasure. She was right, though, he felt the wet slickness spreading across his belly and smearing blood onto her. With a little sigh, he withdrew and rolled over. She sat up immediately, her eyes going wide.

"You *are* bleeding."

It was an accusation. He even wanted to laugh at that. "I know, *csecsemő*, but believe me, it was well worth those few drops of blood."

"Few drops of blood, my ass," she countered him, in the cutest, sternest voice he'd ever heard her use. "Tell me what to do right now. Do you need my blood?"

He noticed her gaze shifted away from the blood on his belly, her aversion rising in spite of her attempt to keep it from happening.

"The healer has been working from the inside out, so most of the damage inside is repaired. What you see is simply surface laceration. It is more cosmetic than anything else. There is no need to worry. I can stop this myself."

"Then do it. Right. Now. Do you need blood?"

"Lorraine, look at it. You are afraid for me and it is not necessary—"

"You nearly *died*. Maybe you did die, I don't know. I only know I had to go to a really dark, cold place to find you, and it was horrible. Everyone said you were gone. Gary and Ferro went repeatedly. Sandu went. Then they told me it was our tie that was the only thread they had to you, so maybe you weren't in a coma and you were dead. It's your world, and your beliefs, Andor, but I saw you. I saw you like that."

The confession burst from her. No, the trauma. He hadn't considered the cost to Lorraine emotionally, that journey his brothers and the healer had chosen to make to retrieve him from the land of the dead and dying. "*Sívamet*, I am sorry you were so frightened for me. There is no need to remain so. I cannot die from these wounds now. They are mostly repaired. The healing soil provided here is extraordinary. It will aid me faster than you can imagine." He covered the seeping blood with the palm of his hand, sending warmth to the injured area where the master vampire so many risings earlier had tried to rip his intestines out of him and nearly succeeded. Light erupted around his fingers, and he felt that burst of shocking heat. "It is closed now. The blood is no more than one would expect if a human scraped a knee when they fell."

She lifted his palm away from the injury and stared down at his smooth stomach. Relief lit her features as she let out her breath. "Okay, I have to admit I panicked a little bit."

He took her hand and wrapped her fingers around his needy cock. She glared at him. "We are done playing until Gary gives you the thumbs-up."

He scowled at her when deep inside he wanted to laugh at the idea that he would allow another man to dictate to him whether or not he could make love to his woman. "That healer is *not* going to have any say in our sex life whatsoever." He growled out each word, making the noise as close to that of a wolf as he could get.

He found himself in a staring match with her. His woman. Love had his heart aching, there was so much there. It spilled over into every part of his body. She sighed, conceding the battle to him. He wasn't about to tell her Carpathians didn't need to blink the way humans did. That would mean, later, when she was Carpathian, she might actually win in a stare-down.

"Everything with you is fun," he said. "Or sensual. Thank you for giving me your trust. I know, after the things that happened and the way your friends turned on you, that trust is not easy, so it is all the more cherished as the gift it is."

"Tell me about Ferro's injuries," Lorraine persisted. "I won't tell Gary on you, and I'm not going to tell you how much I love you because you don't deserve it right now, but I need to know why it's always a hushed-up thing when one of you really gets hurt."

She hadn't let go of his cock and her fist slid up and down his shaft almost lazily, as if she wasn't really aware she was sending heat spiraling right down his spine. He took a breath and tried to think with a clear mind.

"We cut off all pain, Lorraine, so we do not feel it. Therefore, if we do not feel it, pain is not acknowledged. Injuries, even life-threatening wounds, happen in nearly every battle. You cannot fight a vampire and expect to walk away unscathed. These vampires we have been fighting are not nearly indicative of what the undead are capable of doing."

"I felt Ferro's injuries."

"I was afraid you might have. It concerned all of us, Ferro, Sandu and Gary, that you would be able to do just that. I shielded you the moment the pain slipped through. Ferro had tried to keep it from you, but he fought a master vampire. He ended the battle quickly, but in taking the heart, the vampire managed to do damage to him."

She nodded. "I replayed the images I saw when he was battling the vampire."

Andor stiffened. Ferro was extremely powerful. She had no business being anywhere near Ferro's mind. "You cannot ever do that again."

"I wasn't prying," she defended.

Her hand stopped, but her fist tightened, squeezing down, threatening to strangle him. The sensations tore up his body. A firestorm burned out of control in his belly. She propped herself on one elbow, turning her body toward him, leaning over his thigh so her hair brushed over his legs and groin. The silky mass of chestnut teased every one of his senses.

"I caught a glimpse of the battle when he was fighting and then when he was injured. I wasn't in his head. He slipped inadvertently into mine. I kept those images and studied them because I wanted to see technique. I was able to see that he didn't shield his body from the vampire's claws and teeth. He got torn up while he worked to extract the heart."

"It is not easy to remove a heart, so giving the undead something to do while the hunter pries that wretched organ loose makes it easier. I never want you to do such a thing. Not ever." He made that a decree.

A slow smile sent a burn spiraling through his body. "I won't. You don't have to worry. I never want to get that close to one of those things." She gave a delicate little shudder and then sat up, her fingers leaving his shaft.

He caught her hand and guided it back to his cock. "You started something, *csecsemő*, you cannot leave in the middle of it. I want that hot mouth of yours wrapped around me."

"I want to talk."

"Talk with your mind."

"It's distracting to have my mouth on you while I'm trying to talk."

He liked the fact that she was already sliding her thumb over the crown and using her saliva to make him slick so she could easily slide her fist around him and then began that glide that could slowly take his breath from his lungs.

"I cannot talk if I am thinking of other things. I liked the way you sucked so hard and used your tongue. I want to see how much of me you can take."

"As it is, you're stretching my limits," she pointed out.

"You did not have a problem; in fact, when I was in your mind you were enjoying yourself. If I checked you right now, just thinking about taking my cock in your mouth, will I find you hot and slick?"

"We just made love. Without a condom, I might add."

"Carpathians can regulate ovulation. In any case, I made certain you felt fresh and clean, as if you'd had a long bath. There will be no excuses."

She squirmed, the corners of her mouth turning up. "Checking is cheating."

"I want to make certain you enjoy yourself with as much pleasure as you are giving me."

Lorraine smiled at him and then lay out over him, wiggling until he opened his legs for her. Andor stretched, linking his fingers behind his head, propping himself up so he could watch her. "Tell me what you like about having my cock in your mouth."

She licked up his shaft and then swirled her tongue over the head of his erection. Her mouth engulfed him. He watched the way his girth stretched her lips. She had naturally rosy lips and seeing them around his cock sent more steel to his groin.

"Tell me, Lorraine."

*Your taste. I love the way you taste. The feel of you. Like velvet, but then so hard. And hot. So very hot. The shape of you. I've never felt anything like it. I especially love how hard you get, right in my mouth.*

Her tongue swirled up his shaft and then teased under his crown until he thought his head would explode. He couldn't just lie there as he had first planned. It was impossible not to move. He gathered her hair into one hand, holding it up and out of the way so he could see the way he filled her mouth and stretched her lips. Her lashes were down, those two thick crescents that fanned her cheeks. He wanted to see her eyes looking up at him. Nothing was sexier to him.

*How far can you take me?*

His hips moved, gently, but insistent. He pushed an increment deeper with each thrust. He'd been careful before, making certain to stay shallow, but keeping his head was becoming more difficult each time she suckled hard, her mouth a tight fist. Seeing her taking him like that added to the need building.

*I'm working on finding that out. I want to swallow you down. Hold you inside. I love this so much, Andor. I love giving you things you've never had and didn't even know you wanted.*

He wanted to throw his head back and roar like a saber-toothed tiger. Heat enveloped his entire body. Sensations poured over him. It wasn't just about what she was doing to his body, it was about how she loved doing it to him.

*I know I want this now. I will never get enough of your mouth.*

*You asked me to tell you what I like. More than anything, I like making you lose control. Knowing I can. Knowing I can give you so much pleasure you don't know what you're doing.*

His hand slipped to the base of his cock, worried he would thrust too deeply and hurt her. He was right there where she wanted him, on the very edge of his control.

Soft laughter slid into his mind, brushing musical notes along those walls and spreading a tight symphony over his cock like a vise. He could feel that endless well of seed in him begin to boil, as if his balls were two blazing pools of magna.

*Csecsemő.* He tried to warn her. He gripped her hair harder in his fist. *Yes.*

Her long lashes lifted and he found himself staring into her eyes. That was all it took. He erupted again. This time he watched her throat. Watched it move as he poured his essence down her.

Instead of pulling away from him, she very gently licked along his shaft, the tip of her tongue sliding under the crown and then swiping over the top of it. The movements were tender. He couldn't remember having been cared for. Memories were so faded over the centuries of nothing, that he couldn't remember laughter or fun, let alone a tender gesture. The way she attended him felt loving to him.

She looked up at him, those green eyes meeting his. *"Tet vigyázam."* She pronounced it correctly, but more, she poured meaning into the words. "I do love you, Andor, more and more with each minute I spend in your company. I want to show you that. I want to give you things you've never had. I'm very aware, from sharing your mind so often, how little you've ever expected or taken in spite of how much you've given."

"*You* are what I've been given, Lorraine. And you're everything."

She stared at him a few moments, looking up at him over his cock, and then she crawled up the bed, which was something he found sexy as well, but he remained silent while she turned over and lay on her back beside him, staring up at the ceiling. He did file it away that he liked the way she crawled up the bed to him. Her breasts were two perfect mounds, her nipples still erect. They swayed with every movement, calling his attention and memory to the way they looked and felt. He wanted to be healed so they had more time and could be much more adventurous.

"When you've been sleeping, Andor"—Lorraine's voice was uneasy—"I've been sleeping beside you. You weren't all the way in the ground. I know it hasn't been all that long, but for some reason, the thought of being separated from you makes me very uneasy. Unsettled . . ." She trailed off.

He was aware she was an independent woman. The pull of lifemates would eat at her. Disturb her. Just bringing up the subject had to cost her, but he knew the conversation had to come up. He had to warn her.

"That is perfectly normal and to be expected. When I go to ground this sunrise"—and it was only a few minutes away—"I will be buried deep and I will sleep the full sleep of Carpathians. If I do not, the injuries will take much longer to heal. The soil rejuvenates and aids in healing."

"I understand you need the soil, but does your face have to be buried as well? Can't I sleep beside you? That way, if I wake earlier than you, I can watch over you?"

He turned to her, locking his arm around her waist. "Lorraine. In this compound, we are both safe. It will be this one day, from sunrise to sunset. I will send you to sleep . . ."

"No. Absolutely not. You may think we're safe, but I am reserving judgment. You know that horrid bird didn't just peck the crap out of my skull. He had to have put something in my brain. What if it comes crawling out while you're asleep? I need to be alert."

"Everyone looked. Every inch of you was inspected. Organs. Bones.

Blood. Brains. Four of our best examined you, each going over the other's areas repeatedly. They found nothing."

"I know." She put her hand on his chest and rubbed absently. "Do you believe he just sliced me open for no apparent reason? Just to attack?"

He wasn't going to lie to her. "No. I do not know what he intended. Maybe he lost out on time. Maybe whatever it was dropped to the ground before he could implant it. I can only say, they inspected you carefully and it was not there."

Her fingers thumped his chest as if in protest. "Please don't make me sleep. I'm tired, I'll fall asleep naturally, but can be alert if there is a problem."

He didn't like it. "Lorraine, you will suffer. The thought of you suffering unnecessarily bothers me on a level I can't even convey. Our separation will weigh on you. Your mind will continually seek mine. When you cannot find me, you will become afraid that I am dead. That can be dangerous with lifemates when they are not fully bound."

"I know the dangers. You've cautioned me. I'll be prepared. If you have to be covered all the way to heal, I understand. I want you to do it, but I can't be asleep so deeply that I wouldn't wake if there was a problem."

He detested that he understood. That he knew what this request meant to her. Another ancient would do what he thought to be right. Andor gave in because Lorraine needed him to.

# 14

Lorraine woke to the sound of children laughing in the distance. She groaned and turned over, feeling every individual muscle in her body protest deliciously. Frowning up at the ceiling, she let herself get her bearings before moving again. She was at the compound, and Andor was not with her. Her mind reached for his. She'd been slipping in and out of his mind for days, but now, for some reason she couldn't fathom, she was desperate to touch him.

She reached. There was only nothingness. Emptiness. He was gone. Her heart dropped and then reality kicked in. They'd had a conversation about this very thing—how one could become terrified that something had happened, when in fact, Andor was safe beneath the soil, healing as he needed to do.

Her teeth worried at her lower lip. What if he wasn't safe? She didn't know. She couldn't see him. Andor had told her this would happen. She just had to trust in him, have faith that at sunset, he would emerge and she would see for herself that he was alive and well.

She sat up slowly. She'd gone to bed fully clothed, ready for war. Her gun was loaded and in reach under her pillow with only the safety on.

She'd practiced hundreds of times flicking it off and pointing her weapon at the door or the windows. The shotgun was loaded as well and propped against her side of the bed within easy reach. The knife was in a sheath and at her fingertips while she slept. She'd practiced with that as well.

She wanted a shower. Or a bath. Or better, a shower and then a bath. She knew she was clean. Andor had seen to that, cleansing her body and hair, but it wasn't the same as standing under a hot spray of water and letting it wash over one. Nor did it take the place of the luxury of a bath. She stretched, grateful for the roof over her head. She'd been camping for nearly two weeks before she'd run into Andor and was caught up in his world.

Very slowly she got out of bed, feeling every ache. She was making Andor's world hers. Showers and baths would be a thing of the past. A nice comfortable bed would be as well. Where did Carpathians make love? Have sex? Get crazy when the notion took them? She made her way into the bathroom, thankful for modern conveniences. She brought weapons with her. Enemies might find her naked, but they wouldn't catch her unarmed.

She opened the screened window so she could listen to the children as she showered. Their voices were happy, not scared. They sounded like normal kids having fun on the playground. She caught a glimpse of stone dragons sitting on the grass looking as if they were guarding the mini-park that was situated outside of the main house and directly across from a cottage that was a miniature replica of the main house.

She liked the sound of the children playing. She needed it. If she stayed on the course she was on, she might not ever hear it again. She would be deep beneath the ground while they lived and played above. When she was up, they would sleep. She pressed her forehead against the tiled walls of the shower. She'd been so absorbed by Andor, so caught up in the battles against the undead and the tremendous honor he and his brethren had, that she hadn't really thought beyond that to the realities.

The ancients had been so selfless always. They'd been willing to tie themselves to her in order to find Andor, each knowing if they weren't successful in recovering him, they would be caught in that terrible cold, dark place. They had known what they were risking and yet they still went after him—for her. For him. For the man they called brother, and they'd done it out of honor and loyalty.

She'd just gone along with everything because there hadn't been time to think. She'd gotten on the roller coaster and she hadn't been able to get off. She hadn't even considered getting off because she wasn't leaving Andor as injured as he'd been. Now—now she had time to think about what she would be missing if she went through with the last blood exchange.

They hadn't talked about children. Andor said he wanted them, but she didn't know what that entailed. Emeline, Dragomir's lifemate, was pregnant. Perhaps a talk with her might alleviate nerves—and she had them. Worse, just as Andor had warned her, her wayward mind kept reaching out to his and finding—nothing.

She was so used to touching his mind, crawling into it when she was afraid, gathering her courage there and then sliding out when she felt armed with enough knowledge to face whatever was coming at her. But if she was honest, she knew it was far more than just being afraid of monsters she had no knowledge of. Or gathering information for a coming battle. She wasn't lonely. At all.

Lorraine knew she'd retreated from the world when her brother had become a headline, a monster. She hadn't been able to face the accusations and whispers. She didn't dare speak of her brother or parents or aunt and uncle. The couple who'd died trying to help Theodore had a family, sons and daughters who now despised her. She'd dropped out of college and cut herself off from friends who'd already deserted her. She hadn't realized just how alone and lonely she was until Andor filled her mind.

She poured shampoo into her hand and rubbed it into her hair. Who knew that shampooing hair could feel like such a luxury? She'd often thought how cool it would be if she was magic and could wave her hand and instantly have her hair done. It was thick and heavy and took forever to dry. After having Andor or one of the others wave their hand and clean and dry her hair, shampooing and conditioning seemed a luxury. She would be giving that up as well.

She stepped out of the shower, wrapping her hair and body in towels.

Her body felt very sensitive, as if every nerve ending was alive. Wandering over to the window, she looked across the yard. The playground was a distance from the house she occupied, but from her vantage point up high, she could see the children.

There was a boy, who looked to be about fifteen or sixteen. Tall, lanky, all arms and legs. His hair was longish and tied in a very small ponytail at the nape of his neck. He pushed a little girl on a swing. The child screeched and kicked her legs excitedly into the air.

"Higher, Danny, higher."

"This is high enough, Bella," he said. "I don't want to take a chance on you falling."

The little legs kicked higher. "We fly dragons, Danny, we can't fall."

Lorraine leaned her head out the window, shocked at how clear she could see from the distance. Her eyesight and hearing seemed much more acute than normal. She found herself smiling as she watched the boy patiently explain how flying a dragon was different than swinging.

"Your dragon makes certain you don't fall."

She looked at the stone dragons overlooking the playground. It was a nice game, the little girl clearly fantasizing the dragons were real. She might have seen the Carpathian hunters shifting, just as Ferro and the others had. That was one thing she wouldn't mind being able to do—shifting into other forms.

"Does your dragon keep you from falling, Lourdes?" Bella called out as she gamely tried to pump her legs to get more height as Danny pushed her.

The child beside her in the other swing was being pushed by a teenage girl. She looked to be a year or so younger than the boy. Lorraine thought both Lourdes and Bella appeared to be three or four, three by their size, especially Lourdes, and four by their intelligent speech.

Lourdes hung her head way back so she could look up at the teenage girl. "My dragon *always* holds on to me, does yours, Amelia?"

Amelia smiled immediately at the child. "Of course. This is where we practice for dragon rides, Lourdes. Bella, you, too. You have to learn to hold on tight with your hands and use your legs and body to help gain height. If you fall here, you'll bounce on the rubber mats, but if you fell when a dragon was in the sky, you would fall a very long way and get hurt."

"I wouldn't," Bella said, pumping her feet like mad. "Cuz Liv will catch me."

"Liv can't catch you if she's sleeping in the ground like Tariq and Charlotte," Amelia reminded. "So, no riding the dragons without grown-ups around."

"Genevieve," Bella called to a woman sitting on a bench watching them.

Lorraine thought the woman might have stepped off the cover of a magazine. She was truly gorgeous. Her face would never need airbrushing. It was perfect. Her bone structure, her large eyes, her lips and her tall, slender body with her fashionable clothes and elegant boots made Lorraine remember that she'd only packed camping clothes.

She dressed hurriedly, but took time with her makeup and drying her hair. Evidently Tariq and Charlotte believed in making guests feel very welcome. The hair products were top-of-the-line as well as the cosmetics, and they'd provided hair dryers, straightening irons and even curling irons. She especially appreciated the brand-new electric toothbrush. She didn't even feel guilty using it. Well, maybe a little, but she could purchase it from them. She'd already left an envelope with enough to cover the cost of everything she'd used.

Her mind reached out for Andor. She had a million questions. She had a million needs. One of them—the most important—was just to feel him in her mind. Close. Pouring into her, filling empty spaces and removing . . . loneliness. She'd learned she could be with a hundred people and still be lonely. She could be by herself and feel strong and complete—until Andor. He'd changed that. She felt strong. Capable. But she was lonely without him. Her mind kept insisting on reaching for him.

Surely, even sleeping below the ground she could touch him. When he'd slept the sleep of his kind, she'd always been able to see his face and reassure herself that he was fine. No enemy could catch him unawares because she'd been there. Right there. Guarding him. Making it impossible for some monster—or some loved one—to harm him.

Lorraine stared at herself in the mirror. Andor was hers. Her family. The man she chose. Whatever happened, she wouldn't take that back. She had crossed a line somewhere when she'd let him in, and now he was there, deep. She wanted it that way. She wanted him enough to give up the sun and the sound of children playing in play yards. She would choose him every time.

"Andor." She whispered his name. Needing him. Knowing it was better if she didn't call telepathically and awaken him before the soil had a chance to do its work. She straightened, still looking at her reflection in her mirror. "You are capable of going a few hours without touching his mind, so pull it together."

Ruthlessly, she crushed down the need to reach for him. The need to protect him, even from her intrusion when he required healing sleep, helped her focus back on other things. She hadn't eaten anything since that first blood exchange, only drank water. Food seemed repugnant to her. She knew she would have to eat something soon, she was getting weak, but the thought turned her stomach.

Very slowly, taking her time, she dressed, pulling out her last pair of clean jeans, her vintage blues, washed so many times they were soft and pale, with a few worn places, but still acceptable to wear if she was going out. Her T-shirt was old as well and one of her favorites, soft and black with words touting *Fireball Cinnamon Whisky*. She liked the sentiment. Did Carpathians drink whiskey? Any kind of alcoholic beverage? Probably not.

She pulled on her hiking boots because they were the only shoes she had with her. Glamourous, that was her. She was going to look good standing next to the model out there. She'd make a really good impression. Squaring her shoulders, she left the safety of the bathroom and made her way down the stairs to the front door.

The moment she neared the door, she felt a surge of power—of protest. *You better not have tried to lock me in,* she said, reaching for him without thinking, a small bit of laughter bubbling up. She sobered instantly when she realized she was doing it again and then her heart began to pound and she could barely catch her breath—signs of an impending panic attack. Swearing under her breath, she fought her way through it, going for logic.

"He told you that you wouldn't be able to reach him and you would do this. You're smarter than this, Lorraine. You have a brain. You don't need to lean on a man, you're one hundred percent okay without one. You know how to take care of yourself. Never, in your life, did you rely on someone else, other than when you were a child and even then, your parents insisted on you trying things yourself before they helped, or allowed Theodore to help."

She pressed her forehead against the door, one hand on the knob. Theodore. He'd helped her so many times when her parents didn't know. She'd always had a sweet tooth, and sugar was strictly forbidden. She wasn't allowed to eat anything that wasn't healthy and good for her. They practically counted calories for her, watching how much she trained and anything outside her home had to be done in the form of exercise, such as bike riding. That was an acceptable pastime. Running was. Reading was okay, but only for short periods of time, like when she was taking a bath.

Theodore had helped her find ways to get her sugar fix. He'd always brought her candy-coated licorice. They'd hid it, most of the time successfully. She couldn't have gotten it for herself because her parents had watched her so carefully, but Teddy had managed and when she'd gone on reading binges, he'd always brought her some. She never wanted to forget those things about him. The good things. The childhood memories she had of him before . . . What had made Theodore take the steroids? She still didn't know. Maybe she would never know.

She opened the door and breathed in the refreshing air. She'd been outdoors for long enough that being inside felt a little stuffy. There was a feeling of reluctance to step outside, even onto the porch, and she knew that had to be part of Andor's safeguards. Still, she wasn't locked in, and she wanted to go talk to the children and the model.

She gripped the doorjamb, heart accelerating as the feeling of power surged over her and under her feet. The floor seemed to tilt back toward the inside while just across the doorway, for one moment, she could see bands, like heat shimmer. Not bands, bars. Keeping her in? Keeping someone out? Maybe both.

*Andor, I'm heading out to see the compound and talk to the children.* Abruptly she broke off again. What was wrong with her that she couldn't stop? Couldn't remember she wasn't to wake him? To reach for him? Every time she did only made her feel more alone and abandoned. More scared that something had happened to him and she wasn't doing her job of protecting him.

She stepped over the threshold, ignoring the pull on her body to go back inside. She wouldn't retreat, she wasn't that kind of woman. Once on the porch with the door firmly closed behind her, she felt free again. Her eyes immediately burned and wept in protest at the almost blinding light of the sun. Every bit of exposed skin prickled as if it might burn under the rays. She had never worried about sunburn, thanks to her father's complexion, so she ignored that weird sensation on her skin and went down the stairs, wishing she'd thought to bring sunglasses.

The lake gleamed, the water appearing like glass, shimmering with grays and blues, even deeper greens. It was beautiful and inviting. A pier ran out over the water and she was tempted to walk along it. The water added to the eye-burning effect the light seemed to have on her so, reluctantly, she turned away.

The little boathouse caught her attention. Someone clearly lived there. She could see someone moving around inside, and when they noticed her watching, they waved and beckoned to her. She'd taken a single step toward the cute little house when the door opened and a woman appeared. She wore an apron and was drying her hands on the material as she stepped onto her porch. She looked older than Lorraine expected, maybe in her late sixties.

"I'm Mary Walton. My husband, Donald, and I live here. We've been with Tariq for a few years now. Donald is just inside watching over the cookies I'm baking for the children."

Lorraine moved closer so she wouldn't have to shout. "I'm Lorraine Peters. I came with all the others last night." She hadn't been told a lot about those living on the estate. Mary Walton was clearly human. So were the children. She didn't know if they knew about Tariq and the ancients. She should have asked more questions.

"We saw them coming in," Mary said. "Of course, we always worry about their battle wounds. They heal so fast, but when they first get them, the injuries look frightening. I still can't get over wanting to wash out the wound, not put soil in it." She gave a small deprecating laugh. "I suspect it's my age."

Lorraine shook her head. "That's my first instinct as well."

"Are you feeling all right? Can I get you a cup of tea?"

Immediately her stomach protested with another lurch of warning. She shook her head. "Thanks, but I'm okay. I thought I'd go talk to the children. They sound so happy. After all the trauma of seeing things I thought were only in movies, worse than anything in movies, I need simple and happy."

"Don't be deceived, Lorraine," Mary said. "Those children have seen and experienced some of the worst those monsters do. They live here because as long as they stay within this compound, the safeguards surrounding us, the undead can't come inside. They know they're safe and it's the only place that is for them. No schools or shopping or fun like other children. They have us and they have one another. That has to be enough for now."

She knew Mary was warning her that the feeling of safety she was experiencing would go away the moment she left. She smiled. "Andor is here, Mary. As long as he's here, I'll be here. If he leaves, I go with him." She wanted that clear. She wasn't a shrinking violet. If he left the safety of the compound, for any reason, she would be at his side.

"Andor? Are you Andor's lifemate?" Mary looked happy about it and sounded even more so. "He's a good boy. They all are. I'm so glad he found you. I wish the others would find their women. Some of them seem so close to the end."

"I'm definitely Andor's lifemate," Lorraine said. It was the first time she'd actually said the words aloud. The first time she acknowledged to anyone else that their souls had been woven together into an unbreakable bond.

She glanced toward the playground and the woman just getting up from the bench and walking over to the swing set. "Who is that?" She couldn't be Carpathian, not when she was out in the sun. Lorraine doubted if one of the hunters had claimed her, because, although she was wearing sunglasses, she was showing a lot of skin with her designer camisole. She looked sexy and elegant. She wasn't certain an ancient would approve, but then again, she would never allow Andor to tell her what she could or couldn't wear. "I'm not going to lie, she's a little intimidating."

"That's Genevieve. She's one of Charlotte's oldest and dearest friends. She's psychic, but hasn't found her man yet. She's independently wealthy, from France, and yet she stays here looking after the children during daylight hours. I'm quite thankful for her. The children are a handful for Donald and me. Genevieve watches them closely during the day. We take over evenings and nights when she gets tired."

Amelia put her arm around Genevieve and leaned into her. Genevieve's face lit up and she smiled at the girl, wrapping her arm around her waist. They laughed together, the sounds mixing so the notes rose into the air. Lorraine thought she could see musical notes and then they disappeared.

"I love when that happens," Mary said.

"So, I'm not crazy," Lorraine said. "There really were musical notes flying around in the air when they laughed."

"You're not crazy," Mary assured. "I think that's one of Genevieve's gifts. Whenever she laughs with a child, or with anyone, you can see the notes in the air. It looks especially beautiful at night. Of course, she doesn't always do it, but now, when all of us try to give the children something special, that's been happening."

"I love it. She's really beautiful, isn't she?"

"Yes, there's no denying Genevieve is beautiful, but she's also one of the sweetest women I've ever met. She's no fighter like Blaze, Charlotte's other friend. She's more like Emeline, Dragomir's lifemate. Sweet. Kind. Courageous, but you won't find them on the front lines. Which are you?"

"I'm more a front lines kind of woman," Lorraine admitted. "I'm anxious to meet Emeline. I've made up my mind to be with Andor, but I need information. I like to know everything before I make decisions. This one is happening very fast, and I'm on board with that, but it's a little scary. I thought some of the women might help me out by answering questions."

"They will," Mary assured. "Everyone seems very willing to help one another. Are you pregnant?" She was blunt about it, eyeing Lorraine's midsection speculatively.

"No. But I'd like to know if I were to get pregnant what happens to the baby while we're asleep belowground. Are children with us or do they have to be aboveground with someone else?"

"Your man can answer that. I don't honestly know," Mary admitted.

Lorraine flashed her a smile and gave a small wave. She wanted to meet the children and the model. "Is she someone famous I should know?" She indicated Genevieve. "Maybe a supermodel? As you can see, I don't know the first thing about fashion." As a rule, she didn't care, either, it was just that she needed friends, and the model seemed a good beginning.

Mary shook her head. "She's very nice," she assured again. "Run along and tell the children I'll be out soon with cookies." She glanced at the sky. "It will be sunset in another hour or so. They'll be joining us soon after, one by one." She waved again and went back inside, closing the door behind her.

Lorraine stared at the little boathouse, wondering how Mary and her husband came to be on Tariq Asenguard's property. He was a celebrity of sorts with his elegant nightclubs. He was a handsome man and very wealthy. He went to black-tie charity affairs. In her wildest dreams, she would never have equated him with vampires. Even when she'd sat at the big round table, every time she'd looked at him, she'd thought it was absurd that he was there and that he was their leader.

He owned a tremendous amount of acreage. The houses on the property were worth a large fortune, but coupled with the land and the lake, she couldn't imagine what it had all cost. She knew the other Carpathians were purchasing the land around Tariq's. They were building a stronghold with Tariq's property in the center. That way, they knew they had a defensible fortress that enemies couldn't penetrate.

She'd learned that Carpathians were selfless. They didn't think in terms of one having more than another. They shared everything. They helped one another. They put their lives on the line for one another. They considered themselves a family, all of them. She wanted that. She'd lost her family, and it made her all the more protective toward the new one being offered to her.

As she walked up the road toward the main house and the playground, one by one the occupants turned to face her. Danny caught the swing and brought it to a stop. Amelia did the same with Lourdes. They stood, partially in front of the two small children. Genevieve stepped between the children and Lorraine as she came closer. Lorraine noticed that the moment the Frenchwoman put herself in front of them, Danny moved just a little to one side, to ensure he could come to her aid. Lorraine liked him instantly for that.

"Hello," she called, waving, before she got too close. She kept walking, making certain they could see she held nothing in her hands. Her vest and boots covered the fact that she had several weapons on her. "I'm Lorraine Peters. Did Tariq let you know I would be here?" She directed her question at Genevieve.

The should-be model nodded. "Yes. Ferro's lifemate, right?" She smiled sweetly.

Lorraine shook her head. It was a good test. "Andor's lifemate. Ferro is still without one and is *extremely* happy that I am not his."

Genevieve's smile was instantly genuine. "Of course, he would say that, when you're probably very nice."

"I fight vampires."

"Aw. Of course. Ferro would disapprove."

"He was very good to me, though. Mary Walton said to tell all of you that she will be along with freshly baked cookies quite shortly."

"I'm Genevieve Marten." The woman stepped closer, holding out her hand.

Lorraine took it, noting that up close, Genevieve was even more striking. "I've just got to say it, you could be the most beautiful woman I've ever seen."

Genevieve laughed and shook her head. "Thank you, although you haven't seen Emeline yet. She's gorgeous."

"You're intimidating enough. Knowing someone else is that good-looking is just plain off-putting. I think I'll take Andor and go while I'm ahead."

Genevieve laughed again. "By now you know very well these men don't see other women. Not a single one so much as glances at me. They're all pretty hot, too, so it's a tad disappointing and can make a girl lose faith in herself."

Danny stepped forward, nudging Genevieve with his hip. "No worries, woman. I've got your back. If no one claims you by the time you're fifty, I'll step in and give up my freedom." He heaved a tremendous sigh as if the mere thought was difficult for him.

Genevieve batted his shoulder with her hand. A very girlie move. Lorraine instantly wanted to teach her how to hit.

"*Fifty*. I have to wait until I'm fifty before you'll step up?"

"Wouldn't want to give up my freedom too early and settle with the old ball and chain," Danny explained.

Amelia stepped around him and delivered a kick to his shin. He howled and leapt around holding one leg and glaring at his sister.

"What did you do that for?"

"Women are *not* balls and chains. You don't even think that way, Danny, and now Lorraine is going to think you do." Amelia switched her attention to her. "He really isn't nearly as annoying as he sounds. He's actually very nice. Most of the time."

Bella slipped her hand into Danny's. "He's always nice," she corrected.

Lourdes came up on his other side and took his hand. "Yeah, he is," she said accusingly, looking at Lorraine as if she'd made the disparaging statement instead of Amelia.

"Not always," Amelia clarified, but she clearly was bailing Lorraine out of trouble.

Lorraine crouched low so she was eye level with the two little girls. "Mary said she was bringing you cookies. What's your favorite kind?"

"Sugar cookies," both girls chimed at the same time and then looked at each other and burst out laughing.

"I'm Lorraine. Do you know Andor?" She waited until both girls nodded. "He's my lifemate."

"I'm Bella," the little girl who was a bit taller stated.

"I'm Lourdes," the smaller child said.

Amelia rubbed at the grass with the toe of her boot. "Tariq told me that you defended Andor when he was wounded by hitting a couple of assassins with a frying pan. Is that really true?"

"Wait. You knew about her and didn't tell us?" Danny demanded.

Lorraine slowly stood up. All of them were looking at her as if she were a heroine out of a movie. She shook her head.

"You didn't?" Amelia sounded disappointed.

"It was actually a saucepot. I was rinsing it off in a stream when I realized someone was attempting to kill somebody. I should have had my gun with me, but I had no idea anyone was around. So, my saucepot became my weapon of choice."

Danny studied her face. "You went up against two men trying to kill a Carpathian armed only with kitchenware?"

"They'd staked him," she replied without thinking. "And there were three of them. I had to do something."

"What does *staked* mean?" Bella asked.

Lorraine inwardly cursed. She mouthed "sorry" to Genevieve.

Genevieve shrugged. "It's going to happen. We'll let Tariq and Charlotte explain that one, Bella. You and Lourdes can ask them when they wake."

"I want Liv," Bella said. Her voice held a little whine. "I don't like her sleeping all the time." She looked up at her older sister. "I don't want you to do that, Amelia. Don't go away from us like Liv did."

Danny and Amelia exchanged a long look. Amelia clearly was giving her brother an I-told-you-so.

He shrugged. "Bella, you know sometimes it's for the best. Liv was hurting, and it was getting worse and worse. Amelia has a hard time, too. You get to see Liv."

Bella shook her head. "I want her *now*." She stomped her foot. "She never plays with us anymore."

Lourdes leaned close to her, and cupped her hand around Bella's ear. "You did that thing again. Stomping your foot. You have to stop, remember? Tariq said no more."

"He can't tell me what to do, only Danny can," Bella declared.

"I'm telling you to stop that," Danny said, his voice firm. "I mean it, Bella, and stop whining. You aren't a baby."

She looked like a baby to Lorraine. She would have cut the child some slack. "Is Liv a sister?" She tried distracting Danny.

He nodded. "Yes, she was torn up pretty bad by a puppet and a vampire harassed her continually." His gaze shifted to his sister. "Amelia's had a rough time as well. She doesn't sleep well."

That explained the faint dark rings under Amelia's eyes. She wore makeup, but it didn't altogether cover the smudges there.

"All of you are human children," Lorraine said, just to clarify.

Danny nodded. "We all have psychic abilities, but we're human, with the exception of Liv. She was converted. She goes to ground with the others during the day. She has a lifemate. I think it's pretty shocking to everyone that they know already because she's so young, but the circumstances were extreme. He guards her most of the time, but he spends time away hunting vampires."

"Does she mind him being away?" Lorraine couldn't imagine what it would be like for a child to suffer, needing to touch the mind of her lifemate.

"Yes," Genevieve answered. "She becomes uncomfortable, but right now, his position is guardian. He takes it seriously, too. She got into some trouble a few weeks ago and he stood for her, but in the end, he was the one who laid down the law to her. Tariq is her father now, but Val definitely calls the shots."

Amelia rolled her eyes. "He's bossy."

"He keeps you alive," Genevieve said. "You don't bite the hand that feeds you, Amelia."

Lourdes frowned. "Who feeds you, Amelia? I thought you fed yourself. And who did you bite? I haven't bitten in a long time. Charlotte said it was bad."

"I'm going to bite everyone," Bella announced. "Even . . . *Val.*" She made the declaration rebelliously.

"That wouldn't be a good idea," Genevieve cautioned. "You would get into a lot of trouble and not even Danny or Amelia could get you out."

"Then I'll bite them, too," Bella said with even more defiance.

Danny caught her hand. "I guess since you're showing off for Lorraine, it's time to take you home and put you to bed, even though I see Mary and Donald heading this way with the cookies."

Bella let out a wail. Danny started walking, taking her with him. She dug her feet into the grass. "I'm sorry. I was just joking around. I don't bite, Danny. I wouldn't really bite Val."

"She's really upset," Genevieve said.

"She still can't bite," Amelia said. "And we were homeless, living on the street. Now we live in that huge mansion, and Tariq and Charlotte spoil her. They spoil all of us. She has pretty clothes and toys. She has a warm bed and good food. Acting like a spoiled brat because she's upset over Liv isn't okay."

"Of course not," Genevieve agreed. "I was just pointing out that we need to talk to Charlotte and Tariq. They need to reassure her about Liv." She wrapped her arms around her midsection. "I don't know what I'll do when all of you are converted. I'll be out here all day by myself. Mary and Donald are sweet, but they pretty much keep to themselves."

"I'm not certain that's going to happen any time soon," Amelia said. "It seems it's more difficult with boys than with girls. My brother would have to be taken to the Carpathian Mountains, and Tariq would have to go with him. Tariq is needed here. We made a pact that we'd all be converted together. I'm not leaving my brother out here alone."

"You're close to him, then?" Lorraine said, aching as she made the observation.

Amelia nodded and looked toward her brother, who was walking with the two little girls, hand in hand, to meet the older couple coming toward them. "Don't tell him, but he's the best. He took care of us after

Mom and Dad died. He kept us together. We didn't have any relatives, so we ended up on the street. Bella would have been taken and adopted out. We never would have seen her again. They might have taken Liv from us, too. Now we have Tariq and Charlotte, and they're the best." She smiled up at Genevieve. "Along with Genevieve."

"Thanks, honey," she said. "That means a lot to me."

The sky was going orange as the last rays of the sun spread across the sky. Gold, red and orange mixed together in a startling sunset. Lorraine watched the spectacular display, wondering if it would be the last one she ever saw.

*When you wish to see a sunset, Lorraine, we will make it happen.*

Andor's voice brushed through her mind like the stroke of velvet. Relief was so strong, so intense, her knees nearly gave out. She realized she'd been holding it together by a thread, just waiting, silently counting the minutes until she heard his voice. She'd been proud of herself for making certain no one else could see that a part of her was falling apart inside. She didn't like that at all. She wasn't that woman but somehow, being tied to him meant she actually was.

*How? You cannot rise because the sun's rays are still out.*

*I am ancient, sívamet. The older one gets the more difficult it is. However, that does not mean you will never see another sunset. I can bring in fog. Fog can enhance the beauty of a sunset if it is done right. You can rise a few minutes earlier than me. We will find a way.*

*I missed you.* He hadn't missed her. He'd been sleeping.

His soft laughter slid over her. *You cannot be upset with me because I had to go to sleep in the way of my people. I have no control over that.* The very last rays of the sun sank.

*I suppose not, but it doesn't mean I can't be annoyed.*

She smelled him first, the clean, fresh scent that was all masculine. Wild, foresty and all him. Andor. His arms came around her, he turned her into him and then his mouth was on hers.

# 15

Lorraine wrapped her arms around Andor's neck and opened her mouth under his. He felt as if he'd waited a lifetime for her kiss. He lifted her easily, cradling her close, his mouth on hers, and took her into the air. She shifted her body even closer, leaning her breasts against his chest, her mouth surrendering under his.

*You taste even better than I remembered.* He gave her that because it was the truth. Each time he kissed her, it felt as if he was burning alive, her mouth hot, pouring molten fire right down his throat and into his veins. It moved through him, a slow burn that smoldered in his belly and settled in his groin. He felt like all those centuries of living and he'd just now come alive, just since he'd met her.

*Where are we going?*

*Somewhere we can be alone.* He knew the right place, he just needed to quit kissing her and make it happen immediately. He thought they were safe, but it didn't mean they were. Sergey was always scheming and no doubt, his spies were close. He lifted his head and brushed another kiss over her temple. *I'm taking you there now.*

Sergey had been acting so strange, making so many crazy decisions that every hunter—and his own followers—questioned his leadership abilities. The fact that Sergey had prepared for turning by kidnapping Elisabeta ahead of time and stashing her where his brothers had no knowledge of her meant he had the Malinov genius. By taking her, it had allowed him to experience feelings through her.

The other Malinov brothers all had reputations for their battle skills, and yet few talked of Sergey. Through it all, he had appeared to follow his brothers, never vying for leadership. In the end, he had two slivers of Xavier, the high mage, in him. One alone would make him a very real adversary, but two made him more than lethal. He had also acquired slivers from his brother Vadim. Who knew if he held them from his other brothers as well? If so, he could call on any battle expertise they had when he needed it.

Lorraine lifted her face to the wind, eyes wide open, taking in everything as they flew over the canopy of trees. *Tell me we're not headed back to the campground. I didn't find it in the least romantic. I'm expecting romance.*

He tightened his arms around her. *I will give you romance, woman. I thought the campground very romantic. You were there.*

*So were about ten other guys, and not all of them were good ones.*

He had to concede she had a point. He dropped down to the side of the mountain. It was a complete drop-off, but there was a small crack, a jagged fissure that ran along the middle of the rock facing outward. He knew behind that very small opening was a cave that would give them privacy and protect them. More, it was a stunning cave. Spectacular.

They approached the side of the mountain. The rock face bowed out in several places, covering the giant fissure from sight.

*I am not skinny enough to fit inside that crack.*

He heard the laughter in her voice. He liked that she never seemed that afraid. She was curious, but unafraid. He waved his hand toward the crack just behind one of the rocks that jutted outward. Immediately the crack opened for him and he swept inside. The cave was large and opened back a long distance. The sound of her laughter was like music to him. He felt and heard her happiness. As they moved through the cave he waved behind him to close the crack, giving them privacy. At the same time, he lit sconces along the walls of the cavern.

Settling to the ground, he took her hand. "You will like this, Lorraine. There is one narrow section, and then it opens up to a large chamber. There is a natural pool. Water comes in from the side of the mountain away from the drop-off. It is a little cool," he added when he felt her shiver. "I can regulate your body temperature." He did so.

"That part of being a Carpathian will be cool," she said.

"Are there parts you are still concerned with?"

"Yes. I'm committed, but I do have questions. I wanted to meet the other women, but you whisked us away so fast, I didn't get the chance. I'm not complaining," she added hastily. "I would much rather be with you than anyone else."

"Good recovery," he teased.

They reached the narrow hallway. They had to maneuver it single file. He went first. Behind them, the lights flickered out one by one. Ahead of them more candles flickered along the walls. As they passed each, that light went off.

"You know, Andor, if I were afraid of very closed-in places or the dark, this would be a little scary. You could be leading me to my doom."

He stopped abruptly, forced her body up against his and tilted her head back, exposing her neck to his teeth. He scraped back and forth several times. "I *am* leading you to your doom," he whispered in a creepy, theatrical voice. "At last, I have you alone with me and I can do what I wish with you, including bite your neck."

"You were going to bite my neck no matter where we were," she said, but he felt the little shiver running through her again. The tiniest of trembles, and this time, it wasn't because she was cold.

"I do not intend to bite your neck," he clarified. "I had other, much more sensual places in mind." He turned back to continue through the narrow hallway.

"I thought the neck was very sensual," she objected. "At least, it felt that way to me."

"That was only for getting started." He kept walking. "And when we are finished here, I will take you back to meet the women. I cannot convert you here. It has to be done there, where the others will aid in keeping the pain at bay."

He walked out into the chamber and stepped aside, his eyes on her face. She stepped after him and lifted her gaze. Her breath caught in her throat. Her face flushed and her mouth opened, those lips of hers in a perfect round *O*. One hand went to her throat. "This is the most beautiful thing I've ever seen."

Gemstones glittered like stars. Clearly, the mountain, thousands of years earlier, had been part of an active volcano. Diamonds sparkled overhead and along the walls of the chamber. The flickering candlelight picked up the dazzling display and enhanced it. Water poured over more diamonds, enlarging them, so it appeared to be a waterfall of diamonds cascading into a deep pool formed of rock.

"Are those diamonds real?"

"Yes."

"Why hasn't anyone discovered them and mined them? Everything is mined nowadays. Nothing is sacred."

"How would anyone possibly discover this place? It's completely enclosed."

"I can feel a draft, and it's easy to breathe. The flames are high. They wouldn't be like that if there was no air."

"There are plenty of cracks through the rocks. That's how the water gets in and out. The pool doesn't overflow and the water goes out through holes in the rock formation at the back, nearly where it comes in, when it gets so high."

"This is truly beautiful. A person can hike and cave their entire life and never discover something like this."

"It's just as well," he said. "It would be gone if they did."

She nodded and turned to him, her arms sliding around his neck. "It was difficult without my mind touching yours." She leaned her weight into him, her head resting on his chest. "I've always been so independent. It never occurred to me that I'd have such a hard time."

"I am sorry, *hän sívamak*, I really am." He stroked caresses down the length of her hair. "I was afraid it might be bad. We spent so much time together, mind to mind, that we both got used to that so fast. Add that to our souls being woven together and there was every possibility of you having a very difficult time."

"It was unexpected," she admitted.

His heart clenched hard in his chest. He had wanted to bring her to this place, one of the few he had discovered in the United States. He hadn't had much time to explore. Had they been in Europe he knew hundreds, but here, this was it.

He tipped her face up to his and kissed her again. She was giving up so much for him. He had explored her mind on waking and seen her regrets. He hadn't seen one moment where she thought to back away from her commitment to him, but there were things she definitely considered difficult to give up.

When he lifted his head, he rubbed her lips with the pad of his thumb. "Tell me what you're most worried about."

"Children. I want them, but I want to raise them myself. I don't want to be like Tariq and Charlotte, who are apart from theirs. What happens when we have children?"

He hesitated. One didn't lie to one's lifemate, no matter how difficult the answer. "Our women had no problem getting pregnant, going to ground, carrying, giving birth, feeding and sleeping in the ground with our offspring in the old days. Xavier, a trusted mage, ended all that."

He held her tightly against him when he felt that deep inhale and her body start to pull away. "No, csecsemő, it is not all bad news. Quite a few people have been working to find solutions, Gary among them. It was discovered that Xavier introduced what amounted to parasites into the ground where we sleep. These parasites caused miscarriages. The few children born had problems sleeping in the ground, and now, of course, we know why. Babies could not nurse because the parasites were passed from mother to child."

Lorraine tilted her head to look up at him. "That's horrific. How could someone do such a thing?"

"Envy. Need of power. Greed. Xavier betrayed all of us."

"Those parasites are in the ground here?"

"No, they are not. According to Gary, periodic checks are made on both male and female Carpathians in the Carpathian Mountains to ensure that they stay free of the parasites, but it is a constant battle to keep the soil free. They found the source and have eradicated it, but it will take some time to destroy them all."

"So, are you free of the parasites?"

He nodded. "I was in the monastery and the parasites never had a chance to travel that far, so all of us residing there are fine. We heard all this when we left the monastery."

"Can the others carry these parasites from the region where they're from to infect us here?"

He couldn't help running his hand through her hair. It was soft and silky. Thick. The strands caught on his wrist and shirt, weaving them together like the threads tying their souls so irrevocably. "I do not know, but Tariq insists on checks often, and so far there has not been a problem. The soil Tariq has gathered for the healing grounds is clear of all parasites."

"Does everyone use the healing grounds when the sun rises?"

He could hear it in her voice that she didn't like the idea, and he was glad. He shook his head. "No, Lorraine. We are not a trusting lot. We scatter and find hidden places to go to ground. We use our own safeguards even within the gates of Tariq's compound. We were taught to always consider that one without a lifemate could rise vampire. With my brethren here inside the compound, that concern is very real."

She pulled back, her gaze startled. "What do you mean?"

He dropped his arms, allowing her freedom. "We secreted ourselves in the monastery for a reason, *sívamet*. Each of us was at his end and yet we did not believe, after living with honor, that it was honorable to take our own lives. Still, we did not want other hunters to have to attempt to destroy us. We knew we were very powerful and it would be a difficult task. We stayed within the monastery, locked away, so humans and Carpathians were safe. Now we are out and in the world once more. Every battle takes a toll. Killing without emotion becomes . . . easy. It should not be."

She paced away from him and then turned back to face him. "You're talking about Ferro. You're afraid for him."

She was very intelligent and able to read him very quickly. He nodded. "Ferro is the oldest and the most powerful of all of us. His fighting skills are unbelievable. He struggles. He also does little to protect himself in a battle with the undead. He is the ultimate hunter, Lorraine. He would be very difficult, if not impossible, to defeat in battle. If he turns, there will be hunters lost in trying to destroy him. I fear, as do the others, that it would take all of us and many of us would not survive."

"I have touched his mind . . ."

"You touched what he allowed. Ferro would never allow you to see into his mind."

"I thought my soul was bound to his."

"It is. Both our souls are. Sandu and Gary are in that mix now as well. It makes Ferro vulnerable, but just as we can track him, he can always track us. He can find you, Lorraine, anywhere in the world. He will know where you are. There is great danger in that."

"That's why you were upset with me for allowing them to bind us all together." She stood at the wall of rock surrounding the pool of water. When she dipped her hand in, her eyes went wide. "How is this warm?"

"I warmed it for you," he admitted. He had tried to think of everything she could want. "And yes, that was why I was upset. Sandu would be dangerous. Gary also. But Ferro . . ."

"It was his idea."

Few things shocked Andor, but that did. "I thought it was the healer's idea. Why would Ferro suggest such a thing? It makes him vulnerable." It was his turn to pace. "No Carpathian male would fail to protect a female, and you are my lifemate. The pull to save you would be very strong. There would be that. He is my brethren. There is that as well."

His attention was caught when Lorraine lifted her hands above her head, pulling her hair up. The action drew attention to her breasts as they rose beneath her T-shirt. He found that very distracting and lost his train of thought.

She smiled at him. "I need a tie for my hair."

His stomach did a slow roll at her smile. He gave her the tie immediately. She took it and secured the thick mass of chestnut-colored hair in a messy knot on top of her head. For some reason, he found the knot very sexy.

"I thought, with Ferro tied to all of us, he could feel through me and through you. Isn't that possible? Even just a little?"

"In theory. I hope he can. He will also feel Gary and Sandu and their darkness. That will compound his own."

"You're scaring me, Andor. I don't want to lose him."

There was more to it than that, Andor realized. Lorraine's beloved brother had turned into a monster, killing her family. She thought of Ferro, Sandu and Gary as brothers. If Ferro did the same as Theodore and became the very thing they hunted, he would have the potential of killing her new family. It would be history repeating itself, but on a much larger scale.

He didn't point out that the risk to the women and children residing in the compound was great. Or that the risk to Lorraine, in particular, with the three ancients tied to her, was even greater. He forced air through his lungs. He didn't just have to worry about Sergey, and whatever nefarious scheme he had hatched against Lorraine, he had to worry about his own brother—whether or not the ancient could hold out against the ever-encroaching demon.

"None of us want to lose him, *csecsemő*," he assured. He found, now that he could feel again, now that emotions were strong, that the brethren in the monastery were family to him. Brothers. They all knew it, but now, thanks to his lifemate, he felt it. He hoped through his lifemate, at least Sandu and Ferro could as well. Maybe that extended to the healer.

Lorraine pulled her T-shirt over her head, folded it neatly and placed it on a nearby rock. She glanced over her shoulder at him. "I want children. Not right away, but eventually. I want to take care of them myself, Andor, not have an aboveground nanny. I want us to be very clear on that. If I can't be with my own children, then we aren't going to have them. I mean that. To me, a family is being part of something together."

"I understand."

He understood watching her remove her lacy bra had his lungs burning for air. He willed her to turn around. She did so slowly, bending to undo the laces of her hiking boots. The way her breasts curved into two soft mounds, firm and full, swinging with every movement had his mouth watering.

She pulled off her boots and then her socks. "Good. I just want us to be on the same page about this. I need to know our children will live the way we do before we have any. I can't imagine what it is like for Charlotte and Tariq, to know the children they've chosen to adopt can't be with them for more than a couple of hours."

Her hands dropped to the waistband of her jeans. He was mesmerized by that small action. He could have waved his hand so easily and removed her clothing, but watching her peel them off, one garment at a time, was not only fascinating, but sensual. She wasn't even trying to be. If she ever tried, he might not survive.

"I will gather all the information we need, Lorraine," he assured, watching the zipper slide down, almost as if it was happening in slow motion. The air was being squeezed out of his lungs, leaving them burning and raw.

"Thank you. What is Tariq going to do about those children?"

He sighed. "The boy presents a problem. The little ones will be easy enough, now that we know all Carpathians can help ease the way into our world the way it was done for Liv. Amelia needs to be brought in as soon as possible. She's suffering. She does not want to be converted until all of them can be. Danny is male. In order for the ritual binding words to be imprinted on him, the ancient warriors have to judge his worth, give consent and pour into him from the line chosen—obviously Asenguard. They would give him their knowledge and their bloodline. He would be reborn a pure Carpathian from that bloodline with all the same powers and gifts given to them."

"And this has to be done in the Carpathian Mountains? It can't be done here?"

He shook his head. "No, the ritual must take place in the sacred caves.

Tariq plans to travel with the boy to our home and go with him before the prince."

He watched as she shimmied out of the jeans, the material sliding over her hips and down her legs. She pulled them off and then hooked her thumbs in the lace panties. He could see the little tiny reddish curls the lace tried to cover.

"I want you bare so you can feel my mouth on you."

Startled, she glanced up, her gaze colliding with his. At once he saw the dark flush of desire staining her cheeks and darkening the green of her eyes. She licked her lips, the panties halfway down her legs. "Bare?"

He nodded slowly. "Bare." He was decisive. "I want you to feel every lash of my tongue and scrape of my teeth."

"I can't feel that with hair?"

"You will be far more sensitive. Besides, I can see every inch of you. I want that, Lorraine." He didn't take it. It would have been so easy, but he liked getting her consent. Her cooperation. He liked that she gave him what he wanted, and she was going to. The idea intrigued her. She found it as sexy as he did.

She tugged the panties down and placed them with the rest of her clothes, on top of the rock. He was beginning to lose focus for anything but Lorraine. He had woken with the usual hunger, but it was far more acute. He craved her taste. He craved her body. He had fed before going to her, knowing he needed to take the edge off. The idea that tonight would be their first night together, going to ground as Carpathians, had him more than exhilarated.

Andor had brought his lifemate to this beautiful cavern because he wanted to give her a gift. This was his gift to her—a place of natural beauty. He knew she understood. He could see it on her face when she'd first entered the cave and seen the walls encrusted with diamonds. When she'd realized the rock formation was a natural pool and he'd heated it for her. The sound of the water playing over the diamonds in the walls was melodic, and the way the gems looked beneath that cascading water added even more beauty to the cave.

*All right.* Her voice was soft. Whispery. An intimate velvet brushing through his mind.

He waved his hand and the chestnut curls were gone, leaving her skin sleek and bare to him. A woman's form was more beautiful than all the diamonds and waterfalls in the cave. He moved to her as if an invisible magnet pulled him forward. Catching her around the nape of her neck, he tugged until she was forced into him, her face tipping up for his kiss.

His mouth claimed hers. He was gentle, because he was inherently gentle with her, but the kiss was demanding. Commanding. A ruthless takeover. Her mouth was hot and sweet. His was all fire and domination. One hand came up to cup her left breast, his thumb sliding over her nipple, brushing insistently back and forth until she arched into him with a little gasp.

He kissed his way down her throat and then over the top curves of both breasts. His teeth left little red marks, his claim on her skin. Then his mouth closed over her right breast while his fingers tugged on her left. Rolled. Kneaded. She gave a broken little cry and cradled his head to her. His tongue flicked and laved while his hand and mouth and teeth continued to drive her up higher.

Andor could see the flush on her body, and it was beautiful. There was need in her eyes. Heat. Desire. He kissed his way down to her belly button, taking the time to swirl his tongue there and nip with his teeth, to leave evidence of his passing with faint little strawberries.

Lorraine's breath hitched as he dropped lower, crouching, nudging her thighs apart. He guided one foot over his shoulder as he circled her other ankle with one hand and ran it slowly up her calf to her thigh. He followed his hand with his mouth, kissing his way up her leg until he reached the inside of her thigh.

Her fingers dug into his shoulders, and she gave another broken cry when he blew warm breath on her slick sex.

*I have waited for this. Carpathians do not dream, yet I dreamt of this. Of the taste of you in my mouth. Of hearing your shattered cries and feeling that place of absolute pleasure I can take you to.*

He caught her bottom in his hands and pulled her to his waiting mouth. There in the cave, with no one around, Lorraine had no inhibitions and she screamed. He heard the plea in her voice and reveled in it. Now that he had the taste of her in his mouth, he wanted more. He *needed* more. He took his time, devouring her.

She tasted like an aphrodisiac. The more he ate at her, his tongue and teeth busy, adding his fingers to bring her pleasure, the more urgent the demands of his body. His cock had never been so hard. His blood had never run so hot. He felt her muscles begin to clamp down, heard her breath come in ragged, labored pants.

"Not yet," he growled, lifting his head, feeling like a feral animal. His need was worse than hers. He gently put her foot back on the floor, one arm a band around her back while he removed his clothes with a single thought. Then he lifted her. "Put your legs around me."

She complied immediately, her green eyes on his face. There was anxiety there. Hunger. Desire. Everything he was feeling reflected back at him. That need was just as hot, just as all-consuming. He guided his cock to her entrance and slowly began to invade. Those tight muscles didn't want to allow him entry. He loved the way they gave ground reluctantly, gripping at his shaft, massaging the crown with hot, terrible friction.

He threw back his head, a guttural sound escaping. It was ecstasy just being inside her. Wrapped in a scorching hot fist of silk. He kept the pressure steady, unrelenting, pushing through her muscles, inching his way deeper and deeper until he was buried in her, fully seated. Her nails bit into his shoulder and her eyes were wide with passion. Her fingers were linked at the nape of his neck, her arms outstretched, so that he could see her breasts and where their bodies were joined together. It was the most sensual-looking image he could imagine, other than when her mouth was on his cock.

He began to move, slowly at first, listening to the way her breath hitched and she moaned. A musical rhythm punctuated each stroke of his cock as he surged into her. He picked up the pace, going from gentle to a little harder thrust, watching her breasts jolt, watching her body swallow his cock. He had enough girth that she was stretched around him, and bare the way she was, he could see that, see her take him. That added to the sensuality.

He felt her body begin to clamp down harder and harder, squeezing his shaft. Gripping him so tightly he thought he might detonate the cave when he blew. His fingers dug into the cheeks of her bottom, urging her to ride, helping her move on him while he thrust faster, deeper and much harder. Her moans had gone to a fever pitch of music, a crescendo. He heard a roaring in his ears. His balls felt on fire. His legs burned. There was a conflagration in his belly. All of it began to come together into a perfect firestorm burning right through his cock.

Her sheath was an inferno—a blazing inferno wrapped tightly around him. "Andor." A plea. "I can't hold back."

"Then come with me now." He managed to bite out the command through gritted teeth.

The explosion was already sweeping through him, both heaven and hell mixed together so it was impossible to tell which. The storm was brutal, fire lashing at them, consuming them, burning them both alive and leaving them completely spent. He didn't know if the pleasure was that great or the pain that exquisite, but he knew he wanted to experience it again and again—with her.

Lorraine collapsed in his arms, her head on his shoulder, her body completely spent. She'd given everything to him, just as he'd given to her. He simply floated over the rock wall and sank into the water with her still seated on his cock. He found a low ledge and sat, his arms around her, while both tried to find air for their lungs again.

She didn't move or speak for a very long time. He held her, enjoying the way her body fit into his and his fit into hers. It felt as if, for a time, they shared the same skin in the way they shared their minds. She stirred first, not moving her body, but moving through his mind.

*Just checking to see if we're both alive.*

That first whisper of her voice filling his mind always got to him. His heart clenched. His stomach tightened and his cock jerked. She set off a chain reaction with just that one small murmur. It felt intimate. Like the stroke of her fingers. She was brushing his nape with the pads of her fingers, absently caressing his skin, and he felt something similar, but deep inside his mind.

*If not, it was the best way to go.*

*I agree. I didn't have any idea it could be like that, did you?*

He knew her taste would set him off. He had her in his mouth. He wanted her there forever. He needed to take her blood. Not enough for a true exchange, but to satisfy the hunger that refused to be quenched by any other's blood. It was not a physical hunger that he needed to feed. It was erotic. Sexual. Primal.

*I saw others and felt what they experienced throughout the centuries, but like you, could not possibly know what we would be like together. I suspected.*

She pulled back to look up at him, her eyes dancing with mischief. "You are such a pervert. You watched others?"

He shrugged. "How else do we learn? Not Carpathians. If I had tried that, I would not be here today. I told you we study what we need to keep our lifemates happy." He dipped his head to kiss her chin and then blaze a trail of kisses down to her left breast. His tongue swirled there and his teeth scraped back and forth persistently.

"I don't know whether to be turned on by that or horrified."

He nipped at her skin. Felt the jump of her pulse. He closed his eyes, savoring her reaction to him. Lorraine never seemed to shy away from his needs. "Be turned on," he suggested.

"I'm giving it thought."

She pulled back farther to give him better access. One hand came up under her left breast, cupping it. His cock swelled, beginning to stretch that hot, delicious sheath all over again. It was just the way she looked, offering herself to him. He couldn't resist. He sank his teeth deep, hooking into that vein, at the same time, lodging in her mind to feel everything she felt.

She cried out, pain flashing through her. It was erotic, that bite, and a flood of liquid heat surrounded his cock. Then her blood was bursting over his taste buds, filling him with an ecstasy all its own. He shared that with her. The heat. The hunger. The need and terrible craving. The way his body responded. He held nothing back from her.

*You taste exquisite. I have taken blood for centuries, and never once has anything come close to what you taste like. The moment I have you in my mouth, my cock craves you the way my hunger does. It mixes together until I cannot separate one need from another.*

That was pure honesty. He wanted to devour her blood. Devour her special honey, the one spilling from between her legs. He wanted his cock in her. Along with all of that, he wanted to be in her heart and mind. He needed all of those things. It was difficult, with her taste filling him, to stop. He forced discipline and drew his tongue over the twin holes on the upper curve of her left breast.

He rocked and his cock moved in her. Water rose around him, licking at his skin. At hers. He brushed a kiss on top of her head. "You amaze me, the way you have accepted my people and me so readily."

Lorraine rubbed her chin on his shoulder. "I was sort of thrown in at the deep end, knowing those horrible men were trying to murder you. Someone had to save you."

"I am very grateful it was you." He bit her earlobe hard enough to make her yelp.

"Then there is the little matter of Adam and Herman, sent by Sergey to, umm—" She broke off, searching for the appropriate word. *"Acquire* me. He wanted to acquire me. I really thought they were decent men, Andor. I would have been fooled by them. If you hadn't been able to stop them, they would have invited that puppet into the circle of safety you put up and for all I know, I would be dead."

She rocked on his cock, sending waves of pleasure spiraling through him. It was enough to distract him for a moment. Just that lazy movement between them brought with it an indulgence he'd never known. There was no place they needed to be. Nothing imperative to do. They had this time together, just the two of them. They had come together earlier in heat and fire, now the slow burn felt right. Perfection. Just what both needed.

"Honey." She turned her head to nibble on his chin and kiss her way over his throat. "I don't know if I ever thanked you for helping me out during that fight. I was so certain I was right and those men needed help."

"I have been tracking and destroying vampires for centuries, Lorraine. I have a little more experience than you."

"How did Sergey even know about me in the first place? I was camping out there for a little while before I heard those men determined to kill you."

"And you attacked them with that saucepot. Seriously, *csecsemō*, I wouldn't try that again. I can see you are determined to learn to fight these creatures, and I am trying my best to look at all the reasons why it is a good idea that you do learn, but saucepots are out."

She laughed softly, the sound muffled against his neck. The vibration running through her body surrounded his cock, the hot, tight sheath bathing him in scorching liquid and clamping down hard enough that when she moved, the friction set his teeth on edge. The lazy heat was becoming hotter and faster than he expected.

"How did he know I was there?"

"He knew I had attacked seven of his vampires. Two were very good in a battle. *Very* good. They had experience and, although it didn't match mine, Sergey could not have known that. All he knew was that a hunter had taken out seven of his crew. He knew I was wounded and guessed correctly that those wounds were mortal and I was dying. He wanted to finish the job so he sent his spies. Did you see the crows? Those were his spies. He uses birds often. If you look around the compound, outside the fenced-in area, you will see flocks of birds."

She gave a delicate little shudder. He felt that, too. When she moved, sliding around to straddle him, she pivoted on his shaft, and the action sent flames shooting up his spine. His hands went to her waist, fingers biting deep as streaks of fire raced up his cock. The water lapped at her nipples where her breasts floated enticingly. She looked right into his eyes, smiling as she began to move her hips, riding him, sliding up and down, so that the heat and fire consumed him.

"You were talking about birds."

"I want to talk about how you make me feel, but I can barely breathe."

She leaned forward to press kisses over his pulse. "Imagine what I can do when I'm like you. Carpathian. I can take your blood, Andor. When

I'm straddling your thighs and your cock is so deep inside me, I can just lean forward like this and help myself to that delicious taste of yours."

His cock hardened and swelled more, stretching her, lengthening, growing to limits he hadn't known were possible without completely detonating. Her mouth was suddenly on his, and it was like she touched a match to a hundred sticks of dynamite. Everything in him went up in flames. Completely ignited with her mouth on him.

He took over, his cock surging deep into her over and over. He lifted her and pushed her down over top of him, feeling that burn ride up his calves to his thighs. Water splashed over the top of the rock wall. She ground down as he thrust up, adding to the maelstrom of need that took over both of them.

He read that dark hunger in her eyes. Saw it in the flush over her face. Felt it in the gripping of her sheath. "*Tet vigyázam*. I love you, Lorraine. You bring me tremendous joy."

He waited until he heard that singsong music that heralded the arrival of her orgasm. It washed over both of them like a tsunami, taking him with her so that his declaration was nearly lost in the shout of her name. Her soft cry was muffled by his shoulder where she collapsed again, holding him tight, pressing her breasts into his chest and her body down over his.

"I love you because you are you, Lorraine. You. Not because you were chosen as my lifemate. It is you."

"I'm not so freaked out by the lifemate thing anymore, Andor," she admitted. She turned her head to one side, her green eyes looking up at him. "Whatever it is, I know I would choose you with or without it. You were born for me. It was as if someone created you for me and me for you."

He was wise enough not to say that was exactly what a lifemate was.

"I love you, too. I don't know how that happened, but I know I do. I'm going to learn to say it perfectly in your language." She kissed his throat. "Say it again. Teach it to me."

So he did.

# 16

E meline, Dragomir's lifemate, was every bit as gorgeous as Genevieve had said she was. Her hair was a true black with bluish high-
lights shining through when the light hit it. She was definitely
pregnant, although, in Lorraine's opinion, on the small side. Andor escorted Lorraine up the steps to the porch of the home the couple occupied. Dragomir stood behind Emeline, his arms around her, both hands
clasped around her baby bump, as if protecting them both.

"Lorraine," Dragomir greeted. "This is my lifemate, Emeline. *Hän
sívamak*, this is Lorraine, Andor's lifemate. She's a very brave woman and
will be a tremendous asset to the compound." There was a note of pride in
his voice.

Lorraine wasn't certain if the pride was for Emeline, or for her prow-
ess as a fighter. In any case, Emeline burst out laughing.

"Dragomir, there is no doubt that Lorraine will be an asset to the
compound, but it is so like you Carpathian males to put that first." She
turned her attention to Lorraine, although she pushed against Dragomir's
chest with the back of her head, as if nuzzling him with all that long,
glossy hair. "I have no doubt that we'll get along quite well, Lorraine.

Come sit down." She waved toward the comfortable-looking chairs on the porch. "Andor, it's nice to see you again. I'm very happy for you that you found Lorraine."

Andor's bow was almost courtly. "Thank you."

That was all he said. Lorraine looked from Dragomir to Andor. They didn't appear uncomfortable with the women. Dragomir had been one of the ancients who'd arrived to help them at the campsite. He'd given blood to the others and had never once seemed uncomfortable with her. She looked back over her experience and realized only Gary, Ferro and Sandu talked very much to her, and then only after their souls had been tied together.

Andor leaned down to kiss her as she sat in one of the chairs facing the playground. "I am going to talk with Tariq again, *sívamet*. Will you be all right without me?"

For a moment, her fingers, of their own will, clutched at his shirt. She realized what she was doing and forced herself to let him go. It wasn't that she was afraid to be on her own—she wanted the opportunity to talk with Emeline—it was the fact that she didn't want the separation from him.

*You can always reach out to me. Meeting or no meeting, I will always respond.*

The air left her lungs in a little rush. She thought she'd handled him sleeping belowground without a problem, but just this small panic attack made her realize she hadn't. *I'll be fine. Just know that I will expect a full report, especially if I'm in any way the topic of conversation.*

She touched the back of her head where Gary had healed the laceration on her scalp. It was smooth. There was no pain. Nothing at all to make her think Sergey had placed something inside the wound. Her body gave a little shudder. She itched between her shoulder blades as if there was an invisible target on her back. It bothered her more than she wanted to admit that none of the Carpathians examining her had found anything at all.

When Andor had brought her back from the cave, she'd asked that they try again. This time, several shed their bodies and inspected her with meticulous care. Petru and Benedek had joined ancients named Siv and

Val. All four had tried to find something, even a small dark spot some-where inside her that might indicate Sergey had left a piece of him behind.

When the ancients had returned to their bodies, shaking their heads, four more had examined her—again at her own request. She'd made it clear she was uncomfortable being around the children or women, espe-cially Emeline, who was pregnant, if she wasn't cleared. Three more Car-pathians, triplets Tomas, Matias and Lojos, joined the grim-faced ancient she'd been introduced to earlier as Nicu. He had a curved scar on his face. The four of them had emerged some time later shaking their heads.

Andor had brought her to meet Emeline, reassuring her that if she had been a danger, with all of them hunting so aggressively, they would have found it. She watched the two Carpathian males stride across the open grass. Dragomir reached down to swing Lourdes into the air. Andor did the same for Bella. The two little girls squealed with delight. The two men set them on the backs of the stone dragons guarding the playground.

"Dragomir is going to make a good father, isn't he?" Lorraine ob-served.

Emeline smiled. "Yes, he is. He saved us. Our baby. He was patient and kind. I was so beaten down when he arrived. Vadim's blood burned like acid day and night. The baby screamed in pain. I couldn't sleep or eat. I knew I was going to have to tell Tariq, but I was terrified they would want to kill the baby. She was mine. I chose her. I told her I'd protect her. I couldn't go back on my word, but had no idea of what to do. I think being sleep-deprived and hurting every minute took its toll. I really was confused and couldn't seem to make decisions. Thankfully, Dragomir changed all that."

"How does it work? Dragomir's blood has replaced all of Vadim's in both of you, but how does that work now? I don't understand very much about the Carpathian world. Andor told me that the girls would be easy to convert, but that Danny would have to go to the Carpathian Mountains."

Emeline nodded. "My daughter is safe now. Tariq and Charlotte want to convert Amelia and the two little girls. They could do that now, al-though Tariq wants to wait to make certain he has word from the prince and those working to make sure our children survive that Lourdes and Bella can live through the intensity of a conversion at their age. They know Amelia can. Liv is younger, and she did. But Danny . . ."

"The girls won't convert until they all can?" Lorraine confirmed.

"That's what they say. It may take time before Tariq can take Danny to Europe. It would be a fast trip, but we're in the middle of a war with Sergey, and now Dragomir has said Vadim is still alive." Emeline put a defensive hand to her throat. "I wanted to believe he was dead. We all did. Now . . . I'm terrified he might want to come after the baby, although he appears to only want males, not females. He probably is afraid the baby will turn out like her Aunty Ivory. She's a hardcore vampire hunter with a reputation that scares them all. She's also Vadim and Sergey's sister. They want males to shape into the undead like they are."

"Doesn't this all seem too unreal? Like a terrible nightmare you're caught in and can't wake up from? Not the lifemate part, but vampires? Puppets?" Lorraine shook her head. "I never want to see one of those things again as long as I live."

"They have worse, I think," Emeline said. She looked around the compound. "I like to be here, where I feel safer. I know Charlotte sometimes wants to go places and do things. I like being here with the children and creating a home for Dragomir and the baby. Now that I know Vadim is still alive, I might never leave."

"What happens when the baby is born, Emeline? Does the baby go to ground with you or does Genevieve have to watch her aboveground while you sleep?"

Emeline paled. Her dark hair emphasized the nearly pearl skin. "We don't know yet. Some of the babies have been able to go to ground, others no. Vadim transferred parasites to both of us. Dragomir and the healer were able to rid us of them, but that doesn't mean having had them in her, she won't be affected like some of the other children were."

"How would you know ahead of time?"

"They talk to us. She will tell us if she can sleep beneath the ground."

"What will you do if she can't?" It was one of Lorraine's worst fears. She didn't want someone else to raise her children.

"While she is an infant, Genevieve has agreed to watch over her. We hope that by the time she is a toddler, we can take over."

"Genevieve is pretty cool," Lorraine said. "Very selfless."

"We're lucky to have her. The Waltons try with the children, but they can't really handle them very well. The children are growing to love Genevieve." She looked across the lawn at the woman coming toward them. "That's Charlotte. Have you met her yet?"

Lorraine shook her head. "She was with the children the first night, and tonight she was talking to Amelia and Liv in their house. At least, that was what Tariq told us."

Charlotte had real curves, and an abundance of thick, wild, auburn curls. She moved with confidence and stopped to wave at another woman who hurried to join her.

"That's Blaze, Maksim's lifemate. She and Charlotte are good friends, too. Blaze and I go way back. I was a kid on the street and I'd climb into her bedroom through the window on nights when the weather sucked. Blaze and her father lived over the bar they owned. Vadim had her father killed. He had taken the children, and Blaze and I went to get them back. That's how he managed to get his hands on me."

Charlotte and Blaze joined Lorraine and Emeline, making themselves comfortable after introductions. Lorraine looked around the yard. "Where's Genevieve?" She was the only human woman besides herself. She didn't like to think that Genevieve was left out.

"She was tired tonight," Charlotte explained. "She takes care of all the children from sunrise to sunset. That's a long time. Bella is upset because she doesn't have Liv to play with anymore during the day, and she's been a bit of a trial. We had no choice, we had to convert Liv in order to keep her alive. Bella doesn't understand that."

Lorraine had seen evidence of Bella acting up. "Is there any way I can help? I used to teach a martial arts class for very young children. I wouldn't mind doing something like that. It might give Bella something else to focus on."

There was a sudden silence. Lorraine looked at the women expectantly. She wasn't about to apologize or back down. She believed in women knowing how to defend themselves. All of them were in a danger-ous position. What Andor had said about the ancients meant that maybe the compound wasn't as safe as they all thought it was. Tariq would know that. Would he share his concerns with Charlotte?

Charlotte and Blaze exchanged a long look and then both broke out in smiles. "We are *so* glad you're here," Blaze said.

"You have no idea," Charlotte added.

Emeline nodded. "I can't say I'm going to be the best at it, but Blaze has been advocating all along that we need to learn to defend ourselves. Then along you came, Lorraine. Dragomir told me you attacked three men who had staked Andor when he was wounded."

Blaze grinned at her, leaning over the table. "With a frying pan."

"It was a saucepot," Lorraine corrected. "I didn't have time to get my gun. I should have been carrying it, but no one had been around forever and I was making this quick trip to the stream. I didn't want to stop and get it out of my pack. It was really, really stupid of me. From now on, I plan to carry every kind of weapon I can."

"A couple of the men are working with Matt Bennet—he's the head of Tariq's security force," Charlotte explained. "They're experimenting with ammunition and weapons to help all of us better defend ourselves against the undead. Matt was Special Forces, and I think he's a genius when it comes to weapons. In any case, they've come up with a few things that might work for us so we don't have to get too close."

Emeline leaned her elbow on the table and propped her head in her hand. "What we really need to do is teach the children, and all of us, I guess, how to see their illusions and not fall for their traps."

Charlotte nodded her agreement. "I was just discussing this with Amelia and Liv. Amelia was very excited about you joining us, Lorraine. She was impressed with the stories Dragomir told them. She's been want-ing to learn to fight, and she came to me the moment Tariq and I rose seeking our permission to ask you to train her. Blaze has been so busy— the vampires seem to be testing every defense we have. She goes out on patrols with Maksim, so she isn't here to work with us very often."

Lorraine nodded. "I absolutely will train her, that is if Andor wants to stay here, and I think he does. You've heard that Sergey made a concentrated attack on me, right? I just can't shake that he was up to something."

"I wholeheartedly agree," Emeline said. "Sergey and Vadim are both Malinovs. From what the other ancients say, the entire family was brilliant at everything, especially strategy. Sergey wouldn't have wasted all those pawns if he had no reason. He definitely had a plan."

"Well, if he did," Lorraine said, "no one has discovered it as of yet, but I believe I'm going to be the hot topic of the conversation they're all having at the knights' round table meeting."

Charlotte's eyebrow shot up. "Knights' round table meeting?" She echoed.

"Doesn't that big table remind you of the knights and their round table? Every book I've read, or movie I saw, showed a big round table."

The three other women laughed. "I guess you're right," Blaze said. "I've actually called Maksim my knight, but he says if he is one, I have to call him the dark knight."

"I think that's a movie," Lorraine pointed out.

"Absolutely," Emeline said. "And one of my favorites."

"I'll have to tell Maksim," Blaze said, and another round of laughter went up.

*Andor. Thank you for this. I haven't been able to sit around with girlfriends and just talk nonsense and laugh, not since Theodore murdered my family. I didn't think I could ever have this again. You gave it to me, though, and I really appreciate it.*

Lorraine reached out to her lifemate, needing him to know what he'd done for her. What he'd given her. It was big. Enormous. Something beyond any price. She was beginning to understand the value system in the Carpathian world, and it had little to do with money or what they had. It was what they gave to one another.

*I did nothing to give you such a gift. The lifemates of my friends are good women. They are eager to accept you into our world.*

She felt the wash of love from him, brushing caresses in her mind. Again, the burn of tears was close, right behind her eyes, but she refused to shed them. She was happy. She enjoyed the sound of the other women teasing one another.

Charlotte was the funniest and the most outgoing. She put Lorraine at ease immediately. Emeline was the sweetest. Lorraine wasn't certain she had a mean bone in her body. Blaze was the most like her, a bit of a warrior woman.

"Amelia is quite taken with you, Lorraine," Charlotte said. "She told me you were talking together earlier. She wants self-defense lessons, but more, I would like you to really reach out to her and befriend her. She's only fifteen. She recently had her birthday. Still a child, but she's had to become an adult so fast. The past few weeks have been especially hard on her. It would be a big favor to all of us if you could become her friend and get her talking to you."

"She's tried so hard with everyone," Blaze said. "She loves Emeline, and we're so lucky she'll actually open up to Emme, but she needs to feel that all of us are here for her and that she has a much larger family. I'm hoping she looks at me like an aunt and that she'll come to view you the same way."

Charlotte nodded. "They all need to feel as if we're a family, especially Amelia. She's so lost, and sometimes I'm afraid for her."

Emeline nodded, leaning into her hand so she could look Lorraine in the eyes. "Amelia is a sweet girl. This has all taken its toll on her, but she'll come back. Give her time."

Lorraine knew there was a story there, but she wanted Amelia to tell her that story. "I would be more than happy to have another friend. Amelia seems like a wonderful girl. I really do believe in women learning to defend themselves. As for fighting vampires, which I believe is important to learn, all of my experience comes from picking the information out of Andor's and the others' heads."

"Wait." Blaze held up her hand. "What do you mean by that?"

"If you want to know how to fight a vampire, surely that information is in Maksim's brain. You just have to access it."

"You said 'others,'" Charlotte corrected. "As in more than Andor."

She nodded. "I've accessed Sandu, Ferro and Gary's experiences, along with Andor's. I think I'm fairly well-rounded when it comes to knowing battle techniques. I've been sorting through the information in order to see what specifically will work for women."

"How in the world can you see into Sandu's brain, let alone Ferro's and Gary's?" Charlotte asked.

Emeline pulled back in her chair, sitting very straight and regarding Lorraine as if she'd grown two heads.

Lorraine shrugged, trying to be casual. *Should I not have admitted I can see into the minds of others? Such as Sandu and Ferro, or the healer? Is that a breach of confidence?*

*Of course not. The others would not care that those women know.*

"Lorraine?" Charlotte prompted. "How is that possible?"

"When Andor was dying . . . Well, he actually appeared dead. The healer tried multiple times to find him and bring him back. In the end, Gary said it was impossible. He had to find a way to bring Andor back, but there was no following his soul. We weren't bound together at that point, but Andor had explained the concept to me."

"That must have been terrifying, thinking you would lose your life-mate," Charlotte said, laying a sympathetic hand over Lorraine's briefly.

She hadn't known enough about being a lifemate at the time, but she'd known Andor was a lifeline. She'd been alone and drifting without a true purpose. She'd practiced meditation every day, sometimes several times a day, but she'd been unsuccessful in stilling her mind.

She'd walked into her home and found a bloodbath. She'd found her parents, aunt and uncle and another pair of adults she'd known most of her life lying dead in a lake of blood. And Theodore.

"Andor gave me back something I had lost, and I wasn't about to lose him the way I'd lost everyone else in my life," she explained. "I knew we had a strong connection and I asked the healer to let me try to find him. At first all of them protested, but you know, I was taught never to take 'no' for an answer if I knew in my heart I was right. So, I didn't take 'no.'"

"That's incredible, Lorraine," Blaze said. "You went into the scary, between place?"

"I don't know what or where it was, but I told myself he was in a coma and couldn't find his way out. I just had to reach him and I could guide him back. It didn't quite work that way."

Charlotte nodded. "It couldn't have, because you said you checked three Carpathian males' minds for their experiences in battle."

Lorraine sighed. She didn't know how to explain what had happened, but she was going to try. All three of the women were obviously fascinated. "Gary helped me shed my human body and I traveled with him into Andor's body." She gave a small little shudder, remembering the bitter cold. "I couldn't reach him, but we came close. I could feel him. Gary explained it was further than he had gotten and we were running out of time."

She would never forget the urgency she'd felt. She'd nearly given in to a panic attack, but she'd managed to stave it off with deep breathing. She'd idly expressed her regret that she and Gary couldn't be tied together and both of them retrieve him. He would make her so much stronger. She hadn't known what she was doing.

None of the men had said anything for what seemed an eternity. The same urgency that had been on her before had worsened, until she'd wanted to scream. She'd pleaded with Gary to try again. It had been Ferro who'd reluctantly told her they could bind themselves to her and might be able to boost her strength and give her what she needed to pull Andor back. She'd jumped at the chance without knowing the consequences. Gary had tried to tell her, but all she'd cared about was bringing Andor back.

"We performed a ritual to bind our souls together in order to reach Andor," she admitted. "I didn't realize that by doing so, I would have access to their private thoughts and also their battle experiences. Obviously, they can shield their minds from me, but no one does that day and night, twenty-four seven." Looking at their shocked faces, she hastened to try to redeem herself. "I didn't know what that meant. Seriously. I didn't allow Gary to tell me when he wanted to. I just wanted Andor back and didn't think beyond that."

"*Ferro* suggested it?" Charlotte asked.

Lorraine nodded slowly. *This was a bigger deal than you let on to me even when you explained about the danger to everyone.*

*It is done. There is no undoing it.*

That much was the truth. Gary and the others had told her that once bound to her, they couldn't undo the bindings. Only a lifemate could. She hadn't cared. She'd only wanted to save Andor. She'd been very persuasive because the others had been adamant it wasn't a good idea. She'd gotten her way.

"The others tried to stop me," she conceded. "I pushed and pushed until I finally got my way. That place is dreadful, filled with despair. It was just horrible and scary and took its toll on all of us, but in the end, it was so worth it in more ways than one."

"I don't understand how that would work," Emeline said, looking very confused. She looked to the two others as if they had the answer.

"Are your souls still bound?" Blaze asked.

Reluctant to give away family secrets, she just shrugged rather than have to lie.

Charlotte leaned into her. "Lorraine, I admit I'm new to the Carpathian world and I still think in terms of being human, but even I know this is highly unusual. I think, if Tariq knew, he would have told me." She lowered her voice and looked around her. "Something like that is explosive."

She sank back in her chair, and it was clear she was talking with her lifemate. Lorraine had just done so, but having Charlotte consult privately with Tariq made her a little nervous. Having lifemates speaking telepathically as an everyday, common occurrence was just plain cool. Still, Tariq was the leader, and the idea that she'd explained anything incorrectly to Tariq's wife, and perhaps had made more problems for the ancients, upset her.

"He knows," Lorraine said, tilting her chin at Charlotte. "Andor told him immediately."

Charlotte nodded. "He does know. He said he was thinking about the consequences before telling me."

"Consequences?" Emeline asked. "Why would there be consequences?"

Blaze touched Emeline's wrist very gently, drawing Lorraine's attention to the white scars there, as if someone had torn Emeline's skin as deliberately rough as possible. "An ancient without a lifemate is potentially a very dangerous man to all of us. They are our greatest weapons, but should they turn, they would make the worst of all enemies. Tied to the three, Lorraine would be unable to hide from them."

Emeline turned her gaze to Lorraine, not attempting to hide her horror. She'd been tied to a vampire and knew how truly brutal and cruel they could be.

"I think, having the three of them bound to us"—she made certain to include Andor—"gives them the opportunity to feel my emotions when they haven't felt for so many centuries. I'm hoping it gives them more time."

Charlotte started to say something with a little shake of her head but then stopped herself. Lorraine lifted an eyebrow. "What? Just tell me. Sooner or later someone will, and I may as well have the information now."

"It's just that feeling emotion and then losing that ability over and over, as they would when they were away from you, is actually harder on them."

Lorraine frowned. "That doesn't make any sense. They are tied to us until they find lifemates. All three. At any time, they can access emotion. That should make it easier, not harder. Unless they are a great distance away, hunting, which I am certain other lifemates do, they can feel if they tap into my emotions."

"She's right," Blaze said. "I checked with Maksim."

"That should be right, but these are ancients we're talking about. Like truly ancient. I know anything over five hundred years is considered ancient, but this is a huge difference in age. They no longer count age, but all this time they've been building in power," Charlotte said.

Lorraine couldn't help but see why she was fit to be lifemate to the leader. Charlotte was looking at problems from every angle and trying to figure out what could happen to better prepare them all for it.

"So, what do you think is happening, if not the ability to tap into my emotions?"

"I think those ancients are struggling every minute of every rising, and they are going to become more careless in the way they fight. They don't believe in meeting the dawn, so where can they go? What can they do? Emotions without an anchor will mess them up more. Their lifemates anchor them where you can't."

Blaze threw her hands into the air. "Charlotte, I still don't understand. What are you saying?"

It was Emeline who answered. "Blaze, think about what would happen to someone if they hadn't seen in color but now can. It's disorienting. It can actually make them feel sick. The vivid brightness is too much. It's overwhelming. And then add emotions into the mix. They have to sort through them very quickly and choose to use or discard. A lifemate automatically aids with those things. You do it without even being aware that you're doing it. The three ancients cannot possibly assimilate those things without help. The draw to tap into Lorraine's emotions has to be incredible, yet it won't help them. In fact, just the opposite."

The air exploded out of Lorraine's lungs. *Why didn't you tell me?* But she knew why. Andor had explained things in a way that had made her believe the ancients benefited from her pressing them to be tied to her. He wanted her to believe she'd done something good for those she cared about. She already thought of them as family. The last thing she wanted to do was harm them in any way. She wanted to protect them and help them find the lifemates she believed they deserved.

*Breathe, Lorraine. You already knew there was a risk . . .*

*To me. To us. In that they could find us, but the risk to them was only if they turned vampire and you could track them. I never thought by binding them to me, I would make what they suffered more. I thought it would be less.*

*We do not know what is happening to them because they choose not to tell us. I could find out . . .*

*No. Absolutely not. You are not to look into their minds. That would be considered a breach of etiquette.*

She didn't want to look into their minds. She'd discovered too many horrific things. She'd her own nightmare to deal with, she didn't need any more, or to take on someone else's.

"Lorraine." Emeline's voice was sweet.

Lorraine could imagine her holding a baby in her arms and rocking her gently.

"These men have been contending with evil and the fight to stay honorable for a long time. No matter what happens, you remember it was their choice. It is always a choice whether or not they choose to give up their soul," Emeline said.

"How is that possible?" Lorraine fought to understand. The world of the Carpathians was far older than she'd imagined and she had difficulty grasping the complexities.

"There is one clarifying moment, even in a thrall, Dragomir told me, where they have a chance to go back. To take that decision back. Those who are vampire stayed that course. They decided for themselves that they preferred to become the undead rather than go out of this world with honor."

Lorraine bit down on her lower lip. "I'll send up prayers that Ferro, Sandu and Gary don't ever have to make that decision." She meant it, too. After the loss of her family, she wasn't certain what she believed anymore, but she could pray and do it in several languages. Surely, she would be heard and not judged for being angry.

"Honey," Charlotte said, "they make that decision every rising."

That sank in. Mostly, she thought in terms of Andor. He'd been an ancient making his way in the world, searching for her, his lifemate. He'd endured rising after rising and never given in to the persistent voice that tried to lure him to become the undead. Had he been tempted?

*Were you tempted, Andor? Was it as bad as it sounds?*

*Worse. Much worse*, he promptly responded. He was matter-of-fact. There was no bid for sympathy; he might have been discussing the weather. *And yes, I was tempted, but only after the whispers ceased, leaving me with nothing at all.*

Lorraine couldn't imagine his life, but she felt it, she'd sensed emotions coming from him when he hadn't been able to acknowledge them. She'd felt pain when he couldn't. To some it might seem a perfect existence, but she knew better.

*"Csecsemō, we need you here at the warriors' council. You have about fifteen minutes and then you will receive a summons. It is up to you whether you wish to decline or not.*

That didn't sound good. Now the next fifteen minutes were going to crawl by. *Thanks for the heads-up.* She failed to keep the sarcasm to herself.

*I thought you would want time for those strange things you women do.*

*What things?* she challenged.

*Fuss, because you do not think you look good enough, when in fact you look so good your lifemate struggles with control.*

*My lifemate never struggles with control, although sooner or later, I will make certain that it happens.* Deliberately she thought about licking up his shaft. She felt the way his body reacted, a hard jerk of his cock. Instant alertness of his nerve endings. Her little gesture was an immediate success.

*Just remember retaliation is in order.*

She loved the threat in his voice. *Loved* it.

"Lorraine, are you paying attention or drifting off?" Blaze demanded and pointed to Amelia, who had just walked up the stairs.

Charlotte laughed and held out her hand to the newcomer. Amelia went to stand beside her adoptive mother, allowing Charlotte to wrap her arm around her waist.

"She's got that goofy look on her face," Amelia said. "The one you all get when you talk telepathically to your lifemates. The only thing a person can do for self-preservation, if they don't want to see you all mushy, is close their eyes and count to one hundred. Or plug their ears and sing lalala." She rolled her eyes.

"I don't look goofy," Lorraine protested.

"Totally goofy. And gooey," Amelia added. "Bella would say *gooey*." The smile faded and she looked down at her feet.

Lorraine saw Charlotte nudge the teen gently. Amelia lifted her chin and moved a scant inch closer to Charlotte. That told Lorraine a couple of things. The first and maybe most important, Amelia accepted her adoptive mother and trusted her. The second was her gaze continually shifted away from Lorraine's. Either she was very shy, which seemed doubtful, given the way she was when they'd first met, or something had happened to her and she thought Lorraine knew.

"I want to learn to fight vampires." Amelia was abrupt to the point of rudeness, her voice belligerent and almost angry. "Blaze is going to work with me when she has time. I want you to help me as well."

Lorraine steepled her fingers. "I actually think that's a good idea, Amelia. I wish everyone thought the way you do. We can't always count on having someone to protect us. I think, rather than seek them out ourselves, we should understand that eventually, given that we live in such close proximity to the hunters, we are bound to see vampires. They are difficult to kill. Really difficult. Have you exchanged blood with anyone?"

Amelia's entire demeanor changed. She heaved a sigh of relief that Lorraine was taking her seriously. "Yes, Tariq."

Great. The fearless leader. The teen's father. Lorraine didn't know that he would want a child to be running loose in his head. She rubbed the bridge of her nose. "I had hoped to bring this subject up with Charlotte," she admitted, changing her tactic. "Maybe gather the women together, and before you protest, I count you among the women."

"I want private lessons as well," Amelia said staunchly. "I want to learn fast. I'll work really hard."

A red flag went up at the hard belligerence in her voice. "Amelia," Lorraine cautioned. "You can't fight these things alone."

"You did. You fought off three men with a saucepot, and then you protected Andor when he was mortally wounded."

Gossip traveled fast in the Carpathian world. Lorraine knew it was so easy to communicate telepathically, and all Carpathians seemed to use that method. "I didn't fight off vampires by myself, and I certainly am far too intelligent to go seek one out. That would be suicide."

Amelia looked away from her, staring out toward the lake. Since the lake was in the distance, and there was nothing much happening on it, Lorraine took that to mean she didn't want to discuss her reasons.

"I have a responsibility to you, Amelia. To any of the women I teach. Your body is your temple. You take care of it. You put nothing into it that isn't healthy, and you don't contemplate giving up your life, certainly not when you're one of the few people who actually know about the undead. You have an obligation, just as I do, to these three women and all the Carpathians."

Amelia frowned at her. "I'm not a grown-up. What I do doesn't affect anyone but me."

"You know that isn't the truth, Amelia. If something happened to you, what of your siblings? Bella is already terrified and upset over the loss of one sister. That one sister isn't dead. She can still see her and play with her even if that time has limitation."

Amelia shook her head, as if denying the truth, but she seemed calmer and less agitated, as if she were listening in spite of not wanting to.

"I always have tried to live with truth, Amelia. It's so much easier than lying to others or especially lying to oneself. If you're going to study under me, you'll have to trust me enough to give me truth. Do you understand?"

Amelia slowly nodded. "I can do that."

"Saying it and doing it are two different things. I want you to think long and hard about it, and if you still feel the same way tomorrow, we'll have our first lesson."

Amelia flashed a smile that didn't quite clear the dullness from her eyes. "You don't want to start right now?"

"I would, but apparently the council has other plans for me. I have been summoned." Lorraine stood up and pushed her chair in. "Thank you for the wonderful company. I loved every minute of it. It's been a long while since I talked to anyone and I'm so glad it was all of you. Thank you for making me feel welcome."

Charlotte nodded. "It was very nice to meet you. I'll look forward to the ceremony of your conversion later tonight."

Lorraine wasn't exactly looking forward to it, although she was committed. She knew that was part of the problem. "I'm a little nervous about that. I should have just told him to do it right then. But I wanted to have time to go over the details in my mind, and I'm glad I did." That had given her time for processing to take place, so she knew she was making the right decision. She wanted Andor to always feel as if she hadn't been coerced. "But at the same time, I'm super nervous. Still, I'll be looking forward to seeing you tonight."

She left the women on the porch, waving as she went, inexplicably happy that she'd found some friends. She'd missed being able to laugh with other women. She had it in her mind that once they had lifemates, their lives were so wrapped up in their men, they forgot all about women bonding together. Looking at the four of them laughing together, she knew that wasn't the truth.

# 17

Looking down at the very large carved oak table, Lorraine had a sudden urge to laugh. The men were seated around it, although, like gentlemen, they'd come to their feet when she entered the room. There had been no convincing them that she didn't need the recognition. Carpathians were old-school gentlemen. They might rip a man's heart out, but that was okay. Forgetting to stand for a lady was an infraction none of them wanted.

Across the table was a map—and it was huge and hand drawn. There was the location of Tariq's nightclub and his home, clearly marked. Beneath the streets of the city was a labyrinth of marked twists and turns. The map had been drawn by each Carpathian contributing what they knew of the vampires' whereabouts and lairs. They seemed to be everywhere.

Lorraine was a little shocked to see her camping spot so clearly marked. Every encounter the hunters had with the vampires was put on the map. There appeared to be a wide circle with the labyrinth in the center, as if that maze was the very heart of the undead's domain.

"What is this?" she asked. "Aside from the obvious."

Tariq answered. "We were discussing how Sergey is staying in this city. In the past, when hunters came, the vampire fled and took up residence somewhere else. We have evidence to suggest that is no longer true. We send Mikhail, our prince, as much information as we can gather on everything new and different about the undead. If they are doing this here, they have to be doing the same thing there."

Andor reached for her hand and tugged until she was close to him, close enough that she felt his body heat. "They are definitely coming together in South America as well. The De La Cruz brothers sent word to us and continue to do so. We are all keeping track now with maps. They have all been sent to one of our own, Josef, who compiles them into a worldwide map for each of us."

"How can he do that?" Lorraine asked. "What kind of software puts together vampire attacks?"

"One of his own making. Josef creates tools for whatever we need," Gary said. He was seated at Tariq's right hand.

Lorraine looked closer at the two men. She could see a small shimmer arcing from one to the other, as if that seat of power couldn't quite make up its mind.

*They are learning to work with each other,* Andor explained, seeing her look of inquiry. *Sit down.*

*Where?* As far as she could see, every chair was occupied. The only one not present that she knew of was Ferro. *There aren't any chairs open. Where's Ferro? Was he hurt a lot worse than you let on?*

*You could sit on my lap,* Andor offered. There was a mischievous note to his voice.

*Um. No. Not with all these men around and your wandering hands. You might accidentally forget what we were doing. I already know about your forays into voyeurism.*

Andor laughed, and for a brief moment, gazes from around the table flicked from him to her. She felt a blush creeping up her neck to her face. He waved a hand and produced a chair right next to him. Very close. She gave him her sternest look and sank into it. He dropped his hand on her thigh and she immediately realized her thigh was tight against his.

She should have cared, but the truth was, she was glad to be with him again. She'd kept her mind from tuning to him too often, and only when she felt the subject was important, but the toll on her for having to fight her own inclinations had been more than she'd bargained for.

She forced her attention back to the others. Tariq and Gary were new to working with each other. That brought up questions. *Why does Gary have to work with Tariq?*

*The prince asked. When he asks you to do something, you could decline, but no one ever has. Gary is Tariq's adviser, protector and just about everything else in between.*

"Is there word on Aidan?" Tomas asked. He was one of the triplets and had spent some time traveling, she knew.

*Aidan is a Carpathian who has been some time in the States. Everyone believed he would be chosen by the prince to lead in this place, but he is moving to New York. There has been activity reported there.*

Tariq glanced at Gary. "I will let the healer answer."

Gary shrugged. "I went to him to see what I could do to help. His family was there. Darius and his lifemate, the others from the Dark Troubadours."

"Wait. What? The Dark Troubadours? Are they Carpathian?" The band was renowned and working their way into genuine stardom. Everyone she knew was vying for tickets. The band preferred small venues, so it wasn't easy to be one of the lucky ones to get in.

Andor answered for the others. "Yes. Darius is Gary's brother. A Daratrazanoff. That should tell you something right there."

Lorraine didn't know what it was supposed to tell her other than that maybe Darius was a healer like Gary and Aidan's wounds had been fatal, much like Andor's. She felt a sudden kinship with Aidan's lifemate. Through the tie of their souls, had she held him to her in the same way Lorraine had held Andor? She glanced at her lifemate, knowing he was in her mind, just as she was in his. *Did she?*

*Yes, sívamet, she did.*

"He must have been very bad to need two healers," she pointed out.

Now, more than ever, she was worried about Ferro. Why weren't they talking about his wounds?

Tariq inclined his head. "Aidan was caught in a trap. He fought several vampires, destroying them, and the trap was sprung once he was wounded." Tariq turned the full power of his gaze on Andor. "This trap was exactly the same as the one the undead used on you. I've sent the information to every Carpathian hunter to beware. I know that we've always been solitary hunters, and that worked for centuries, but I propose we hunt in twos or threes. We don't have the armies they have. Sergey is making himself an army by turning human male psychics into newly made vampires."

"With no experience," Sandu pointed out.

"Absolutely none," Tariq agreed. "But they are voraciously hungry and have no control. Those two traits alone make them dangerous. We are outnumbered. We can't afford losses. We thought they couldn't, either, but now that we know he's creating an army, we know we are not taking down his numbers."

*That makes it more important than ever that the women learn to defend themselves.*

*Then say it. Tell Tariq what you think. Everyone is allowed an opinion and is encouraged to give it when they sit at this table with him.*

She liked that concept. She lifted her gaze to that of the leader. "I think it's time to teach the women and children to defend themselves against vampires. You should all work with them and share the experience of your battles. If you have new weapons that would even the playing field between a woman and the vampire, they need training in how to use them."

Abruptly, she went silent. Her heart pounded. Her mouth went dry. Ordinarily, she had no problem sharing her opinion, but at the table she was surrounded by Tariq's men, his army, and they appeared larger than life. Very scary and dangerous. Mostly, just plain powerful. Giving them advice or telling them they had missed a great opportunity in training the women seemed a little presumptuous of her. She didn't mean it that way and hoped they didn't take it that way.

Tariq's fingers drummed on the tabletop. "I have considered this for a long time. Blaze has been pushing for this same thing. It breaks with our tradition. Women have always been of the light, and taking a life doesn't come from that place inside of us. Any life. There is a tearing at the soul when one has to kill another being, no matter what it is. That is how it should be. It is the reason we believe the hunter has no emotions after a certain age. He knows it is wrong to kill, yet he has no choice in the matter. He must destroy the vampire."

Sandu nodded his head. "Having a woman in on the battle would divide the attention of the hunter. No matter how good she was at the hunt, we would be unable to forget she was there. The hunter would end up dead and so would she."

"Sandu." Lorraine leaned forward to look him in the eye. "I'm not talking about taking a woman on a hunt. I'm saying she needs to know how to defend herself. If a vampire gets past your safeguards or she is somewhere unprotected, she has to know she has a chance to defeat him. That isn't the same as demanding to go on a hunt."

"Blaze goes with me," Maksim volunteered.

Lorraine wanted to kiss him. He was Tariq's partner and he seemed very relaxed, deceptively lazy in the way he leaned back in his chair, stretching his legs under the table.

"We are all well aware you choose to risk your lifemate," Petru said.

Lorraine's heart sank. She was going up against the ancients and knew that battle wasn't to be won. She'd thought without Ferro sitting at the table she would have had a chance to talk some sense into them.

"I choose to allow my lifemate to be who she is. Who she always must be. You will do the same when you find yours, Petru."

Maksim hadn't taken offense at Petru's pointed accusation. Lorraine was determined to be the same way. She had a temper that she tried hard to suppress—or temper with wisdom. So far, she hadn't achieved her goal.

"Petru, I really am talking about the women and Amelia and Liv. Right here in this compound. The vampires managed to get inside. They could again." She had one ace, and maybe it was time to play it. "It is even possible one of you, one trusted, would turn vampire, and you're already inside. What happens when you go to tear apart one of the girls and the only ones here are the women? All the men went somewhere and you were left to watch over them. What happens then, Petru?"

There was a shocked silence. Most people, men and women, were careful how they spoke to the ancients. Sometimes, it seemed, the ancient hunters were more feral predators than humans. She had to fight to keep from moving closer to Andor for his protection. The others would use that against her. Still, Petru was intimidating with his eyes the color of mercury and his silent stare.

*No one has brought up the threat the ancients present, living here in the compound with us,* Andor explained. *Not even when I was without you.*

Gary moved, drawing the attention to him. It was the slightest of moves, but it was enough when he was usually so still. "This debate has raged in the Carpathian Mountains as well. My brother, Gregori, is categorically opposed to the idea. The prince, however, feels this is something that should be left up to lifemates. He feels forcing a decree, an absolute law, on everyone doesn't account for individuals, and I have to agree with him. No two people are alike. Ivory is an incredible huntress. Blaze is good as well and an asset in a fight. I do not believe a woman such as Genevieve would be."

Lorraine thought he was extremely intelligent to use Genevieve as an example rather than one of the Carpathian woman. Her lifemate might object on principle and the discussion would turn into something altogether different.

"My feeling is that all women should be taught to defend themselves. The children should be taught," Gary continued. "Vampires have evolved, and we have to evolve as well. We're behind because we didn't take advantage of technology. We didn't believe vampires would ban together to fight us, even when we were presented with the evidence. I know it is because Mikhail was struggling just to keep the species alive. I was in that fight. I saw the cost to us, but this is different. If Sergey succeeds, we will be extinct very quickly. It is necessary to change in order to survive."

There were low murmurs as the individuals around the table argued back and forth. Tariq was the one to put a stop to it. "I believe as Gary does. As far as whether or not a woman goes into battle, it is her lifemate's decision with her, not ours. If Maksim tried to stop Blaze from fighting at his side, she would be unhappy. Our purpose is to keep our lifemates happy. It is a vow we take, and there is no other recourse."

"Ferro would never agree to such a thing," Sandu said. "Petru and I will stand with him."

"I would imagine, if that is the case, your lifemates will not be the kind of women who would want to go into battle beside you. If they were, they were not made for you. On the other hand, I see no reason that they not be taught the art of self-defense." Tariq turned toward Lorraine. "I would very much like you to begin training after you rise from the conversion. Blaze will work with you once she is no longer needed on the patrols. And that brings us to another topic and the reason you were asked to join us."

Lorraine inclined her head. "I would be happy to start training the women, but it would be helpful if some of the men volunteered to help us out. I need someone to be an attacker as well as those who would allow the women to see into their minds, to the battles. Gaining experience that way is easier and far more useful. They can see actual battles. I was lucky enough to have Ferro, Sandu, Gary and Andor help me. From their experiences, I was able to choose techniques that I knew applied in the situation I was in, and that I was capable of doing."

Petru and Benedek exchanged a long, shocked look. "Sandu? You did this? You allowed her access to your memories?"

"It was necessary to save Andor's life," Sandu said, with a small shrug.

"And Ferro did this as well?" Benedek prompted.

"Yes." It was Andor who replied, and his answer sounded terse and clipped. "Ferro has great respect for my lifemate. She was cool under fire and aided us greatly."

Tariq nodded. "From all the details, I have to agree with you. Lorraine, we would very much like to go over the attack again, one frame, so to speak, at a time. During that time, some of us would question you. We have been unable to find a single parasite in you, yet we all agree, the entire battle and trap was orchestrated in order to get to you. Even the

campers he chose had children, which would appeal to you and your protective instincts."

Lorraine wanted the entire matter over. They'd gone over this so
many times, yet found nothing. A part of her was trying to believe Sergey
had failed at whatever plan he had. The idea that he hadn't, that somehow
he had put something foreign into her, something vampire, filled her with
repugnance. She also feared she was a threat to those living on the estate.
She'd met them and liked them all. She certainly didn't want to be the one
to bring them harm.

"Of course, I'll be happy to have you go over this again. I want to
be thorough." She bit her lip, glanced at Andor and forced herself to make
the offer. "I would leave if you wanted me to. I would understand."

Andor reached out, took her hand and brought it under the table to
press her palm into his hard thigh. That connection instantly grounded
her. His thumb slid back and forth over the top of her hand in a soothing
gesture of camaraderie. He was standing with her. She knew he would,
but having him show it to her, show he believed in her, meant everything.
She found herself smiling at him, uncaring if her heart was in her eyes—
and she was certain it was. How could she not feel overwhelming love for
him? He trusted her to argue her case without him interfering and making her look weak.

"We don't want you to leave," Tariq said. "You clearly are an asset to
us. We're just trying to figure out what we're missing. Something small
we didn't catch before. Andor, you replay the combat in her mind. Give
us every detail."

She nodded to indicate he could start at any time.

Lorraine watched the battle for the family begin to unfold. She paid
particular attention to the crows this time, because, obviously, that was
what the Carpathians were most interested in. The birds sat in the trees a
distance away from her, which was why she hadn't really felt a particular
threat from them. Occasionally, one would flap its wings. Another crowed
loudly. Two or three took flight, circled the area and returned to the
branches.

"Stop there," Sandu said. He looked around the table. "I was busy fighting my own battles, but I had actually sat among the crows. I remember them flying in a circle and knew they were gathering information. Because they circled the entire battlefield, I didn't equate it with gathering information on Lorraine, as they clearly are doing."

"How is this clear to you?" Tariq demanded. "I see crows flying in a wide circle and returning to their perch. I know they are Sergey's spies, so I am guessing they are recording what they see for him."

"I was there. I *felt* the malevolence. They were definitely Sergey's spies, and when they returned from that mission, they settled on the branches, folded their wings and began talking. I was in a crow's body so I could have listened in, but I didn't. I should have known they were discussing Lorraine by the way they all looked down at her. All of them. Not just one or two. They kept their gazes fixed on her." Sandu lifted his eyes to hers. "I am sincerely sorry, Lorraine. I should have been paying more attention. I didn't catch that detail in the battle, but watching this sequence over and over shows that I failed you."

She gave a little shake of her head. *Never think that, Sandu. We were all fighting for those campers to live. The boy was screaming, and the puppet was tearing at him. All of us had to wait for the signal that all the children were placed safely within a circle before we could move, and that puppet ripping chunks from the boy was terrible to witness. It was awful and nerve-wracking.*

She felt the warmth of his spirt and then it was gone.

"Is it possible for you to pull your memories up and within those memories, access what your crow is hearing?" Dragomir asked.

"I've never tried such a thing." Sandu pulled his version of what happened out of his head and put it into the air in front of them, just as Andor had taken her memory of the incident and everything leading up to it.

Again, they watched the birds flying in a wide circle, dipping low, beady eyes on Lorraine. They never stopped watching her. Lorraine gave an involuntary shudder. It was creepy to have the birds looking at her that way. They looked intelligent and malicious at the same time. The combination terrified her. Andor's hand pressed hers deeper into his thigh, making her aware of all that steel running through his body. He made her feel safe in spite of knowing she was Sergey's target.

"As far as I can tell, they just repeat to one another that she is the one. Watch her. She is the one. Master says do not touch her. That's a very loose interpretation. All those squawks and annoying clicks added things to the conversation I cannot possibly interpret."

Lorraine wanted to throw her hands in the air out of sheer frustration. She was the one . . . what? What did that even mean?

"Keep going, Andor. We want to see everything," Tariq said.

The battle unfolded with maddening slow motion. Occasionally, someone would hold up his hand, Andor would stop the replay and they would try to answer the question to the best of their ability. Lorraine hated the tedious work. For one thing, she knew the attack was coming and every time she had to relive it, she felt what she had been feeling in that moment all over again.

Then the crows took flight, leaving their perches to make a wide circle around her. At the time there seemed like so many, but now she could count them, and there were only fifteen. When they made their pass at her, flying low, one came in so fast and hard, she had to turn away or it might have knocked her flat. She had the flamethrower in her hand, but she didn't use it.

Tariq indicated to freeze the frame there. Crows circled around her, some far closer than others, and she had been unable to return to the safety of the ceiling Andor had created so they all would be out of reach of the crows or anything else coming at them from overhead.

"Stupid mistake," she chanted over and over, putting her head into her hand. "I can't believe I did that. All that time I had the ability to fry those things and I didn't use it."

"It is the same as with Sandu," Andor answered. "In hindsight we can make better choices because we have the opportunity to review things, but at the time, there is no way. Things are happening too fast. You act on instincts and do your best."

"That was my point earlier," Petru pounced. "Women don't have a hunter's instinct."

Lorraine wanted to kick him. "Don't say I don't have the instincts of a hunter," she snapped. "Because I do. I don't honestly know why I left the safety of being with Andor to rush out there like a fool, or why I didn't use the flamethrower."

"I am going to replay the crows flying over and at Lorraine," Andor said.

*Do you have to? This part always makes me feel sick. I don't know if I can go through it again and again.* She had to be honest because her stomach lurched ominously.

Andor brought her hand up to his mouth and pressed a kiss into her palm. "I think this is where they lure Lorraine out into the open. The crows circled in one direction over her head. Then they did a reverse circle. It was so smooth we didn't catch that."

"I caught it," Dragomir corrected. "But I have no idea what it means. It just looked like the crows changed direction several times."

"Yes, they did. They flew low and they flew high. Above and below. They flew clockwise and counterclockwise," Isai pointed out.

"A spell. Sun scorch those birds, it was a spell," Sandu said.

Lorraine stared at the vision of the birds, her eyes narrowing, wishing the crows would go up in flames. "What kind of spell?"

"To compel you to leave your shelter. Of course, they used the vampire to lure you," Gary said. "I suspect, with the way your shields are, it took a tremendous amount of effort on Sergey's part, which is why it was so easy for the rest of us to defeat the others. He couldn't bolster them. His puppet was the easiest I'd ever faced. At the time I questioned it, and thanked my lucky stars that he didn't kill the boy before I could get to him."

"He pulled us all off Lorraine," Andor said. "All those combined years of experience and we still fell for it. Sergey Malinov is one to be reckoned with."

"Did you spot him in the trees?" Tariq asked. "He had to have been there directing the entire sequence of events. He didn't care if his pawns lived or died. He only cared that Lorraine moved out into the open. We have to figure out why."

As Lorraine watched herself stumble out from under the ceiling, and the birds fly at her, the entire attack took on a sinister rhythm she hadn't noticed before. She felt that itch between her shoulder blades again, as if a target had been painted on her back. The hair on the back of her neck stood up. She detested the sight of those crows flying at her, circling her, looking for an opening.

"Stop," Sandu called. "Lorraine, this is important. What were you feeling right then? Emotionally, what were you feeling?"

"That I had to stop the vampire from getting back up."

"Why? What motivation did you have that was strong enough to make you disobey Andor's orders to stay there?" Sandu persisted.

Lorraine didn't like that at all. She hadn't thought about disobeying Andor's orders. She hadn't been thinking at all. She tried to find words to articulate what she felt. "It wasn't like that, Sandu. I listened to everything all of you told me. I knew I had no chance against one of them myself, not without aid and not without the weapons you all created for me. I never, at any time, thought about disobeying Andor's orders."

Andor's fingers curled around the nape of her neck. *Breathe, Lorraine. No one is accusing you. They only wish to get at the truth.*

She knew that. Intellectually she knew Andor was right. She forced herself to calm down and to look deep to see what she had been feeling. It wasn't easy to lose her ego and need to defend her actions, but thankfully, at no time had anyone acted accusatory.

*Follow my breathing. Follow my heartbeat.*

Her Andor. He was right there, breathing for her. His heart ignored her accelerated rhythm and beat a smooth, steady one for her. She took her time, getting herself under control. While doing so, she realized what happened.

"After finding my brother, parents, aunt and uncle and their friends murdered, I've suffered panic attacks. I saw Andor fighting off a particularly difficult vampire and found myself panicking. I needed to help him."

Tariq raised his hand. "You *needed* to help him. Do you feel that need was so strong because you were lifemates?"

She frowned, trying to remember. She wanted to yell at Andor to take the entire sequence down. She couldn't think clearly with it up in the air like a large screen. She pressed one hand to her stomach. "It's affecting me now, Andor."

Tariq and Gary both hitched forward instantly. Sandu was out of his chair and standing beside her as if he would fight off any enemy. Andor wiped the screen clear. "Breathe with me, Lorraine. He can't get to you here."

"He just did. Every time I look at that, I get sick. And it becomes worse with every viewing." She sat up straighter. "But he isn't going to win. Now that I know he's getting to me that way . . ."

"No," Andor said firmly. "Absolutely not."

"He can't win," Lorraine protested. "If he does, I'll fear his power over me every single time. I have to know I can defeat him. He cast a spell and had his crows carry it out. That spell played on my fears of losing Andor after I lost my family. Does that sound about right, Gary?" Deliberately she went to someone she knew was tied to her and was powerful. He was adept with spells. He knew what they could do.

"That sounds right, Lorraine," Gary conceded. "But breaking spells is dangerous. We would have to get back to the crows and look at them repeatedly until we know what we're working against."

"Then let's do it," Lorraine said. "Andor, you know we have to. You can't have me panicking if there is a real fight against this monster and I'm anywhere near him."

"Once she is past this part, we can figure out what he placed in her and how," Benedek added. He rarely spoke, so when he did, Lorraine felt the way Andor reacted. It was a straightening of his spine, a snap to attention. And Benedek had those eyes. Unique. Midnight black, like ink. He could look at you and cut you in two with one flick of his eyelashes.

*You are certain, Lorraine? You do not have to do this.*

*You know I do. I can't live with being a coward. I can't shy away from doing something I think is right because it happens to be frightening. He took one of my worst memories, and he played me. He also may have done something to make me into some kind of walking bomb meant to destroy everyone in this compound. If that is the case, we need to know and figure out how to counter his move.*

Andor inclined his head and then put the memory back up the way one would turn on a big screen. Lorraine forced herself to watch the crows moving into formation over and over. "Why is it so obvious now? I should have been able to notice the pattern. How could I have been so unobservant?"

"We all were," Sandu said. "I sat in the branches with the crows. I saw them fly off. Sergey distracted me with a fight and Ferro with a master vampire. Andor was busy. So was Gary. Sergey is a master at planning. I have to respect that trait in him."

"I think I've got most of the spell," Gary said. "It's simple enough that I think I can take a stab at the rest." He leaned forward and lifted his hands.

*Circle of three I summon thee*
*Each to his own a piece to see*
*Search inside to find the hidden*
*Finding the tie for that which was given*

*Obtain the gift*
*Fasten the thread*
*Raking the claws*
*Now tap the head*

*Choices taken*
*The unbinding done*
*Threads seared*
*By the morning sun*

"That is the spell, or the gist of it," Gary said. "I can see that it still haunts you, Lorraine. I am soul-bound to you and Andor, and I feel the weight on me as well as you." He looked at Sandu. "Can you not feel it?"

"I feel I should have wrung those crows' necks," Sandu said. He rubbed his temple and then nodded. "There is a weight, yes."

"Can you get rid of it?" Lorraine asked. She gave a small, delicate shudder. "I don't want one thing in me or on me or whatever from that horrible vampire."

Andor nodded. "Yes, *sívamet*. We can do that." He lifted his hands and Sandu and Gary joined with him in a chant. The way their hands moved fascinated her.

*I call to Morrighan*
*Washer of the ford*
*She who sees*
*Carrion Crow*

*She who serves to judge the day*
*I seek your power*
*Your eyes*
*Your knowledge*

*Renew the bond, refasten the tie*
*Binding the two so none shall die*
*I call to you to right the wrong*
*Bring forth the power of the Carrion Crone*

*Mend that which has been broken*
*Which is now unsure*
*Reminding two hearts*
*They are bound and pure*

It was shocking how much tension eased out of her. Lorraine hadn't known she was so tight, so edgy and stressed. "I swear I think that worked. Either that or you have the best power of persuasion imaginable."

Gary smiled at her. "I was there, *sisarke*. I should have caught this. He made certain each of us, those who would recognize a spell, was otherwise occupied."

It was the first time he had ever called her *little sister* and something inside her melted, just as it had when Sandu or Ferro called her that. She knew the ancients were hanging on by a thread, and she was grateful that they all considered her family when she no longer had any.

"If you are feeling better, Lorraine," Tomas, one of the triplets said, "we should continue to attempt to find Sergey among the crows."

"What does it matter?" Lorraine asked. "We can't do anything about him now." It really didn't make sense to her.

"Have you noticed the birds surrounding the compound?" Tariq asked, his voice very gentle, as if he thought she needed to be soothed, or comforted.

Maybe she did. She didn't feel sick or panicked, but the entire thing was taking a toll on her. She seemed to be thrown from one trauma to the next and there was no letup. She glanced at Andor's face with those lines carved so deeply. Sandu and Gary had those same lines, as did Petru and Benedek. They had endured so much. Ancients had been in far too many battles, she knew.

*It is our way of life, Lorraine,* Andor said gently. *Do not worry about us so much. We had choices, whether you think we did or not.*

"Let's just do this," she whispered and turned her gaze to the screen.

Without the disorienting, sick feeling she'd gotten when she'd looked at the memory before, it was much easier to watch the crows. "How could you possibly tell one crow from another? I still don't understand why we're doing this."

"We will be able to tell the difference. Remember, he was much larger than the others," Mataias explained. "Once we spot him, each time he takes that same shape—and he will—we will know it is Sergey."

*If I am Carpathian, can I do that as well?* That would make things so much better. Knowing the bad guy no matter which crow he chose to occupy. She liked the idea of it.

*I can teach it to you. He will take many forms, Lorraine. Not just this one.*

*Still, I'll be able to tell it is him if he's a stinking crow, and I can teach the children and other women. That way, there will be more eyes on him, if he is watching.*

They replayed her memory over and over in slow motion several times before the master vampire was spotted.

"There he is," Andor said. "Up high in the pine. He's hidden by most of the branches, but his eyes catch the moonlight every now and then. He's almost directly in front of Lorraine."

She had been so busy watching herself and the crows flying around her that she had forgotten to look in the trees to try to spot the crow Sergey occupied. Now, she took her time, looking carefully through the branches until she found him. He looked bigger and meaner. Definitely more menacing. His eyes were baleful, brooding, staring down at her without blinking.

She shivered, and this time, uncaring the others might see, shifted in her seat to move closer to Andor. He slid one arm along the back of her chair, his hand curving around the nape of her neck. The other, he pressed to her hand on his thigh and just held there.

"Start it very slowly, Andor," Tariq advised.

She didn't know how many times they went over this part. It always left her feeling slightly sick and unclean no matter that Gary had reversed the spell. It was just the sight of those crows coming at her again.

In the replay, the crows flew at her, disorienting her. Some were in her face. She was hit with wings, battered so that she threw her arm into the air to try to protect herself from the large bodies flying around her head.

Then the large crow was there, wings outstretched and flapping, talons digging at her back for a purchase to hold himself on her while he slammed his beak into the back of her skull. He ripped downward viciously with his curved beak. For a moment, she felt that all over again and her free hand flew to the back of her skull. Immediately Andor was there, his palm shaping her head, his thumb and fingers gently massaging.

*This is nearly over, csecsemō, and you are safe here.*

She might be, but what of the others? She might be the vampire's instrument to strike at them. It hurt watching the crow hit her so hard with his beak. She looked at the eyes. He was there. The enemy. The master vampire orchestrating his battle with one thought only—to do this to her. If that was the case, what had he actually done?

"Andor, turn the memory slightly. Can you get a good look inside his beak?" Gary asked.

The others were silent while Andor did as the healer requested. They studied the bird. His mouth was open, the hooked upper beak stuck in the laceration it had created at the back of Lorraine's skull. Lorraine found her heart beating fast. Was there something in the beak? Something besides that tongue? It was black and evil-looking, coming to a sharp point.

"Look at the tongue," she said. "Crows don't have tongues like that. Could he have stabbed me with it and something was on the end of it?" She shuddered at the idea of that wicked tongue touching her, even if it was only on the back of her head.

Several of the Carpathians got up to examine the scene closer. "I do not see evidence of anything on the tongue or in the mouth," Lojos said. "Do you see anything?" he asked Andor.

Andor shook his head. "Tariq, we have gone over this, multiple times, and there is nothing in that bird's mouth, in its beak or on its tongue."

Lorraine, looking at those disturbing, creepy eyes, didn't want them to stop until they figured out the puzzle. She wrapped her arms around her middle. "Maybe we should go, Andor. I don't want anyone to come to harm here. There are children. He managed to cast a spell with crows during a battle. Why would he do that if he didn't have something up his sleeve?"

Tariq shook his head. "Lorraine, leaving is not the answer, especially not this rising. Andor has told me that he plans to convert you this night. The bed of healing soil is the best soil we could find anywhere here in the United States. It was brought in from all over. We know it is free of parasites. We test often, especially before and after every use. All of the Carpathians here will gather to help with your conversion, just as they did when our Liv was converted."

She glanced once more at the birds flying in circles around her in the memory and then looked to Andor to make the decision. She was all out of decision making. It was up to her lifemate to decide what they were going to do.

*There is much pain involved in a conversion, Lorraine. If we go . . . I cannot shoulder it all for you, others have tried and found it impossible. With the others, it will go much easier.*

*Then we stay. But if it looks as if something is wrong, we get out of here fast. I refuse to endanger any of these people, especially the children.*

"We will stay," Andor said. "We will return to convert Lorraine two hours before sunrise."

Tariq nodded, and they all rose. Andor retained possession of her hand as they said their good-byes to the ancients surrounding the table. Her knights. That was how she thought of them. All of them. She knew it was her protective instincts, honed sharper by the loss of her family, but she wanted to take care of them all.

# 18

I'd very much like to show you the night, Lorraine. Is there anything in particular you would like to do or anywhere you would like to go?" Andor asked as they left the main house. His fingers tightened around hers as he pulled her in close to him. They had stopped to briefly confer before choosing a direction.

She nodded toward the carousel sitting out in the open. "I love that. The animals are amazing. They look as if they've been shaped from wood. Does it work?"

"Tariq put that there for the children. He carved all the animals by hand and then painted them. Now, Charlotte helps him. He has dozens of old carousel horses that need restoring and that just happens to be her expertise. They are both a little obsessed." He said the last to get a rise out of her. It was all he could do not to smirk when she scowled at him.

"It isn't obsession to share a passion for something," she reminded, giving him that snippy little note in her voice, the one he loved.

He grinned at her. He hadn't even known he knew how to grin. He took her over to the carousel, and, his hands around her waist, lifted her onto one of the horses. Instead of riding one as well, he stood beside her, his arm around her waist as the platform began to spin and music played. She laughed. He shook his head, because flying was so much better and he was going to show her that as soon as the carousel stopped.

"What is the thrill of this?" he had to ask, because it never made sense to him. Tariq tried to explain it, but he just didn't get it. They were going around and around in the same spot. If one wanted to ride a horse, there were flesh-and-blood horses to ride. He got why children might love the ride, but grown-ups?

"You are an arrogant Carpathian, Andor," she told him. "You think because you can fly, you have the ultimate in entertainment."

"Better than this," he countered.

"Maybe, but don't ruin my fun." She laughed again as the horse rose and fell with the music and the platform spun. "This is a very fine carousel."

"I could do better."

She raised an eyebrow, one arm slung around the horse's neck. "You think?"

She was so beautiful she took his breath. Her hair fell around her face and tumbled down her back. Her green eyes were alight with mischief and a sense of fun he had never known. She gave that to him, that feeling of happiness and excitement he'd been missing for far too many years. He couldn't take his eyes from her.

Andor waved a hand toward the carousel and as she went around, the horse straightened out the direction and took her right off the platform and into the air. It still rose and fell with the same rhythm, but this time it climbed higher. Lorraine gave a little soft cry of shocked elation and clutched at the wooden neck.

Andor rose with the horse, straight into the air, his arm still around Lorraine's waist to prevent any accidents. Below, he could see the compound, the lake shining in the moonbeams. Above their heads was a blanket of stars. Her soft laughter moved over him like the brush of velvet, caressing his skin, making him feel more alive than he'd ever felt.

Her laughter sang across the sky, warm and intimate, surrounding him with joy. He had done that for her. He'd spent so much time in her mind, reliving that nightmare moment when all the joy and laughter had faded from her life. He'd given her back the ability to feel those emotions. She mourned her family—that he couldn't take away—but she'd found a way to laugh again with him, and he was grateful he'd given her that gift.

Andor knew he was bringing Lorraine into a world of danger, but it was also a magical place, with moments just like this one. He spun the horse, changing direction, and Lorraine's hair flew out and around her like a living cloak. Her laughter scattered musical notes of silver and gold all around them. When she realized, her breath caught in her throat and she turned her head to look at him, eyes so bright they rivaled the moon.

"That's so beautiful, Andor. How did you do that?"

He swung up behind her onto the wooden horse as it rocked and swayed, riding up and then down across the sky. His arms went around her, holding her securely so there was no chance of her falling.

"You'll be able to do that," he assured as he nudged the hair from the nape of her neck so he could put his lips there.

"I love the way the notes look, sparkling like that all around us."

"That is the way your laughter feels to me," he admitted. "Have you ever been on a horse when it was bucking? Or rearing?"

He felt her swift intake of breath and then the wooden horse reared up on its back legs, pawing at the air with its front hooves. Lorraine clutched his arms but laughed, scattering more silver and gold notes around them. The horse snorted, its breath great puffs of vapor, leaving a trail behind them as it began to buck, lifting its hind end and dipping its head as it hopped across the sky. Andor settled them back into a more sedate pace, the wooden animal moving with an easy rhythm that sent her body deeper and tighter against his.

"Do you want to fly without the horse?" He whispered the temptation in her ear.

She turned her head to look at him over her shoulder. One arm curved back to wrap around his head, and she leaned to offer him her lips. There was no resisting that invitation. He kissed her and immediately their fire took over, consuming him, taking them both to that place he would never take for granted.

Little tongues of fire licked at his skin and spread embers in the sky all around them. They looked like tiny fireflies of orange and red. Crackles of electricity added to the symphony of their combined music. He kissed her over and over, loving the feel of her body moving against his, her mouth so hot it could ignite a volcano.

*Do that thing.* Her voice was pure seduction.

His heart jerked hard in his chest, but not nearly as hard as his cock. *That thing?*

*The one with the clothes. Wave your hand and they disappear. I want to feel you against me. Like Lady Godiva on her horse. You have heard of Lady Godiva, haven't you?*

Her voice was soft and seductive, purely sensual. What man could resist? He couldn't. He would give her anything she asked for. There was an image in her mind, her facing him, arms around him, the horse moving in that same up and down rhythm as if it was still on the carousel platform and riding in its circle.

He waved, and their clothes were gone. He found himself holding her naked body in his hands, all that soft skin, her curves, her spine rubbing along his front. His cock pressed tight against her, and he cupped her breasts into the palms of his hands. They rode for a few minutes that way, her head back against his shoulder, her body finding that rhythm and relaxing into it.

Andor hadn't known such contentment. He hadn't known there was such a thing as this kind of serenity. Passion rose, but it was a long, slow burning climb, and he let it take both of them. She was content with her head back against him and his thumbs moving gently over her nipples. Small little brushing caresses. Persistent, but not demanding.

Her breath moved in and out. His followed. He slid one hand down her belly, feeling every muscle. Feeling how soft she was. Taking that in. Sliding the pad of his finger around her belly button. Tracing that small circle, mapping her body in his mind. Claiming every inch he could take in with his palm and spread fingers. He found the junction between her legs and his fingers trailed down, curved in, his thumb finding that hot little button that gave him gasps and squirms when he brushed and caressed it.

*You are so hot and slick, Lorraine. I cannot wait much longer to be inside you.* He had enjoyed just rocking with her, going along and allowing their passion to smolder and then burn slowly, but the moment his fingers found her hot cream waiting to welcome him, to bathe him in all that fiery silk, slow had gone out the window.

Again, her soft laughter surrounded them with such joy, his heart turned inside out. *You are so beautiful to me. Everything about you. Thank you, sívamet, for saying yes.*

*What did I say yes to?*

Her hands went to his, the one caressing the junction between her legs. Her fingers surrounded his wrist and she moved her body, sliding on the two fingers curled into her. It was a sensual, heated feeling. He pressed closer to her, his fingers plunging and retreating, his thumb stroking and flicking as if that sweet little bud was the string of a violin he was playing.

Her soft groans moved through him like a lazy melody. Soft. Sweet. Perfection. He nuzzled her neck, wanting to take her blood. No, *needing* to do so. He kissed the small spot over her pulse where it was calling to him. Hot. Wild. Telling him she was as needy as he was.

"What did I say yes to?" she prompted again.

"Me. You said yes to me," he answered and then sank his teeth into the amazing gift that was Lorraine. The taste of her burst in his mouth, rushing through his veins like a freight train. All his. Everything he would ever need.

A fresh flood of liquid heat coated his fingers and she arched into him and pressed her breasts into his cupped palm. She cried out, the sound of her voice adding to the erotic moment, driving his passion up even further. The horse between their thighs rocked and danced through the air, keeping her legs open for him while he indulged his desires.

"I need you in me." She whispered the entreaty, reaching back to wrap her arm around his head. "I love this so much."

*Tell me what you love.*

*The way I'm everything to you. The way you can't conceive of a life without me.* There was the briefest of hesitations. *I feel that way about you.* The admission came in a shy offering.

He wanted more of her blood. So much more, but that had to come later. In the healing grounds, surrounded by his people. He couldn't imagine how he was going to keep his body calm during the exchange, but there was no other way, not when he wanted to lessen the pain for Lorraine's conversion.

He knew others had converted their women without the aid of others and it had been horrendously painful. Rumor had it, some of the women barely made it over to the other side, the process was so agonizing. He didn't want that for Lorraine, not if he could prevent it.

Andor forced himself to stop the flow of her blood, licking across the two tiny holes in her neck to seal them closed and numb them a little more so they wouldn't hurt at all. He turned her head to his and took her mouth. Kissing Lorraine was heady. Passionate. Perfect.

She poured herself into her kisses, taking him straight to paradise. There was no way to become used to that first feeling of her mouth on his. Of her tongue following his. Tangling or dancing with his. The sweet heat. The scorching passion. She gave it all to him.

"Please, Andor."

Her soft entreaty. He loved the way she did that, pleaded for his body, as if he could ever deprive himself. She wasn't a woman to hide her needs. She asked for what she wanted. Sometimes she demanded. No matter, he was more than happy to oblige.

"Do not turn around. I am going to lift you. You use your hands on the base of my cock to guide me inside you."

She nodded. So eager. He loved how she didn't try to hide how much she wanted his cock. He caught her hips and lifted. She held his shaft in her hands and guided the broad head to her entrance. She was slick with need, and he found himself shuddering with pleasure as she slowly settled over him, swallowing him, her tight channel gripping like a vise as he slid inside her.

She didn't stop settling over him until she was fully seated and he was buried in her. He wrapped his arms around her for a moment, holding her to him, his hands cupping the soft weight of her breasts in his palms. He caught at her nipples, tugging and rolling gently. She was especially sensitive there and each pinch and tug of his fingers caused a shudder and more scorching hot liquid to surround his shaft.

The horse moved one way, Lorraine another and Andor was caught in the middle. It was the best place to be. Every small move she made sent heat rushing through him. Her body squeezed and massaged his. Her soft little cries accompanied the gripping and milking, that exquisite torture that had his breathing raw and his body in the throes of passion.

He stood the waves of magic as long as he could and then he picked up the pace, the horse rocking wildly up and down, pushing him deep into her, adding to the weight of him as he thrust harder, feeling that burn through his body. Flames licked at his skin, over him, into him, surrounding his cock as he took her higher and higher.

Her body clamped down hard on his. The strength of those small muscles defeated him every time. There was no hanging on when she did that—surrounded him with her scorching tight sheath and then milked and grasped so greedily. The explosion came from somewhere in the vicinity of his toes and rocked up his calves to his thighs. From there, his balls drew up tight and hot, his seed swirling mercilessly into an explosive volcano. Then his cock was jerking wildly, shuddering and pulsing with absolute need.

Lorraine cried out, calling his name, and his voice, hoarse with desire, muffled by her shoulder, answered with her name. He tightened his arms around her, holding her safe while their carousel horse circled back to find its way home. She sighed contentedly and pressed back against him. He could feel the air moving once again, in and out of her lungs. Her heartbeat began to settle back to normal.

"I am so in love with you, Andor." She stared up at the stars. "I keep thinking I'm going to wake up and find you aren't at all real, that I've been living in my own dream so I wouldn't have to wake up and face the reality of my family's death. Is that possible? That you aren't real? That none of this is?"

He caught the little hidden sob in her voice. He bent his head and found the junction between her shoulder and neck. He bit down. Hard. Hard enough that she yelped. Immediately he let up on the pressure and kissed the spot, licking at it with the healing saliva in his tongue. "You felt that. Would it hurt if this was a dream?"

That wasn't the underlying problem, and he knew it. She felt guilty, afraid she shouldn't be happy when she'd lost the people she loved so much. That was something Andor had often wondered about. His family had died around the same time his emotions had faded. Had that been part of his acceptance of the loss? He couldn't feel that mind-numbing emotion of grief? He didn't have that answer. Only he did know that just being happy didn't say anything about forgetting those one loved.

"*Sívamet*. We take happiness when and where we can get it. One has nothing to do with the other. You know that. Intellectually, you know that is the truth. One can still be grieving and yet have a moment of shared laughter or passion. There is no guilt in living when you have lost so much. You live for them. You make your life count. You live to keep their memory alive. You live for yourself. It's all wrapped up together. We are part of the universe and it is vast. We are small, insignificant in the tapestry, yet we are there. A part of something larger. One false pull of that thread and everything could unravel."

She leaned her weight into him, a smile in her voice. "Sometimes you say things that are so profound, and yet I have no idea what you're really talking about."

"Oftentimes, neither do I, but it made the brethren think I was very important."

She laughed. "I can imagine. Are you going to teach me the song sung about you around the ancient campfires?"

"No. The only reason to sing that song is to drive Dragomir to distraction." His hands settled around her waist. He hated to be out of her, but they were getting close to home and he wanted to clean and clothe them.

He lifted her, cleansing both of them so they felt refreshed. He added clothes, so when they were once more on the carousel platform, they would look presentable.

"Dragomir deserves a song. Why doesn't he have one?"

"He probably does. Or did. They are from ancient times, *csecsemő*, easily forgotten as the older ones of our species die out."

"That's sad."

"It's life. The younger generations don't want to hang on to the old ways because they feel their ways are so much better. Singing songs around a campfire is boring to the younger generation. We have young children already learning technology. That is a good thing, but to have them do both, the singing and learning from their elders as well as embracing new technology, that would be the best of both worlds. That is what we will be teaching our children."

"If you're expecting an argument, you aren't going to get one," she said.

He detested covering up her body, but he had done so. The ride back to the carousel was nice—he still held her close, his body protectively wrapped around hers, but he wasn't in her, where he felt he belonged.

The horse slipped back onto the platform and the music immediately began to wind down. They sat for a moment before Andor slipped off and then gently lifted her to the wooden platform. She clutched at him, staring up at his face, and he could see the stars in her eyes.

"Thank you, that was wonderful."

It was impossible to miss the sincerity in her voice. He kissed her gently. "I loved it, too." He looked around him. "I think we have an audience."

She looked up to see a child watching them. Amelia stood next to the little girl, one arm around her. Both looked at them with speculative too-old eyes. She flashed them a smile and then looked beyond them as a shadow passed overhead. "Andor?" There was no disguising the shakiness in her voice, or the trembling in her body.

"I see it, *csecsemő*. You just walk down to the yard and meet Liv. Clearly, they've been waiting. Make certain Emeline is out of sight. If not, warn her."

Lorraine nodded, not panicking. He knew she wouldn't. She wasn't the type of woman to panic. She glanced at the crows gathering around the fences. "There are so many of them. I've always liked ravens and crows. I thought they were smart, and when the sun shines on their feathers, they're beautiful, although a bit too large."

"Sergey has taken them over. The birds are not bad, just what a master vampire is forcing them to do for him."

"Well, they do look sinister gathered together like that," she pointed out. "It's just like a very scary movie. I've never seen so many of them in one place before."

He caught her chin and kept her looking at him. "Sergey cannot get past the safeguards. He can have his crows follow every move we make and he still cannot touch us."

"Those poor children, though, Andor. What a way to live their lives. It has to take a toll on them."

"They were street kids. They have a good home, clothes, food and a lake to swim in when it's hot. They have dragons to fly and a playground to play in. They have carousels with horses and other animals, and those carousels will do all sorts of fun things. More importantly, they are loved."

She pressed her forehead to his shoulder. "I suppose you're right. It just feels to me as if there must be a way to free those crows from Sergey's hold. They would be free, and so would all of us."

"Even if you can't see his spies, Lorraine, they are there. Always, there are eyes on this place. It is better for us if we see them."

She shook her head. "I disagree entirely. You will get used to them being there. The children will get used to them. Soon, no one will pay that much attention. If you can't see an enemy, but you know he's close, you're going to keep looking, and that makes you all the more aware."

Andor blinked. His woman could be right. "I am not arguing with that. You could very well be right, although I hope not. I know Sergey is determined to make his stand against us. Now, knowing for certain his brother still lives, the only thing I can think to do is plant a spy among his followers. We tried to do such a thing in South America. It is not an easy task."

She gave a delicate shudder. "I can't imagine what that person would have to go through."

"They have parasites in their blood. Their blood is very much like acid. Destiny, a child who was turned by a vampire, endured their blood for a long time, although it wasn't quite as caustic as it is now. Emeline is the only other person who went a very long time with vampire blood eating away at her. It was difficult for her to even think with the presence of the blood in her veins. Still, it can be done. It just is very . . . uncomfortable."

They stepped off the carousel platform and started across the yard toward Amelia and Liv. The two girls were leaning against a large brown stone dragon. Liv had her arm around its neck.

"She is a child, but already her lifemate is aware of her," Andor explained. "Val Zhestokly joined our brethren centuries ago. He wears the tattoo on his skin declaring to the world that he lives for her. He was taken prisoner by Vadim almost immediately after he left the brethren. He was tortured and bears the scars. Young Liv was given to puppets and used to feed vampires. Vadim tried to force Val to join them by first starving him and then offering Liv to him to kill. Instead, he gave her a blood exchange to make her stronger, allowing her to live until rescue came. At that time, although she was barely starting puberty, which is when a lifemate can find another lifemate, he was able to tell that Liv was his. He guards her closely."

"You said it was difficult for a lifemate when they know but can't do anything about it."

He nodded. "It is a torment like no other. Val can see in color, although not bright colors. Liv recently turned eleven. It will be a couple more years before colors brighten for Val. His emotions are there, but not like you experience them. I think it is just enough to feel guilt that he cannot feel more."

They spent time with the two girls, both getting to know them. Andor had been there for a few weeks, but he hadn't talked much to either girl. He found them intelligent and quick, but truthfully, he could feel the terrible weight of darkness pressing on Amelia's shoulders. He knew Lorraine felt it, too. She looked to him as if he could ease her burden. He shook his head in regret. There were things even a Carpathian couldn't undo.

———

The healing grounds were huge and cool beneath the house. The black soil, filled with sparkling minerals, stretched out the full length of the house. Low cement walls ringed the grounds, holding the large posts that set the foundation for the building. Just beyond the cement were wooden boards cleverly joined to make up the walls beneath the basement, yet every so many support beams held cracks to allow moonlight in.

Above the grounds were raised balconies that circled the dark, rich soil, so that the Carpathian people could gather and watch the proceedings below and join in when needed with chants for healing. It was a perfect platform for them when another human woman or child was being converted.

Andor kept Lorraine's hand tight in his as they took up a position in the middle of the healing grounds. He spotted his brethren, all but Ferro, scattered among those present. Val was there, and with him, Gary. He was grateful to see the healer in their midst, just in case. He hadn't heard of even one ceremony going bad, but he didn't want to take any chances.

"I need to remove your clothes, Lorraine," he said. "I am aware that most humans have a problem with nudity, and I can assure you, I will keep it appearing as if you have clothes at all times. Is that okay with you?"

"It isn't that I'm worried about everyone seeing my body," she said, reluctance in her voice. "But when you remove my clothes, it makes me feel vulnerable. With you, I'm okay with that, but to have others see me that way, makes me feel particularly exposed and helpless."

"I will give you my word that they will not see you as naked."

Lorraine touched her tongue to her mouth, moistening her lips. His heart clenched hard in his chest. He wanted her to choose. Eventually, he would have to take that choice from her, but not right away.

She nodded her head slowly. "Tell me what's going to happen."

"I will give you the third blood exchange. Your body will begin the conversion. Sometimes it takes a little longer than others, but once it starts, no one, not even me, can stop it. Not even for you to take a breath. Everyone here will sing the healing chant and bear a part of the pain you would be expected to endure."

"Other women have done this without everyone helping, right?"

He nodded, worried she suddenly wanted to go through it on her own, and he could never agree to that.

She let her breath out. "Okay. I just wanted to know if all these preparations failed, if I could still do it on my own. If others did, then I can. I just would have to be prepared to be a lot less comfortable than we both counted on."

That made sense. He nodded. "You're being very brave, *hän sívamak*, and I'm extremely proud of you."

She flashed a nervous smile. "I'm not that brave. In fact, I'm questioning my sanity. On the other hand, I am looking forward to being able to do all the cool things you can do." She lifted her head to search the small grouping of Carpathians for familiar faces. "Is this the extent of our army, because he had more crows than this."

"Sadly, yes. We are hunters and are used to relying on ourselves. The good thing is, we are true ancients. In our society, anyone living over five hundred years is considered an ancient, after that we do not necessarily count the years. Time flows until it all becomes the same. We do not measure the years after, but it does not mean we do not improve our fighting skills or build in power as time marches on."

"That makes me feel better. Sergey seemed to have a lot of men he could throw away."

Andor sighed. "I talked to Tariq specifically about that and like me, he feels we neglected to consider what to do about the human psychic males. Clearly the Malinov brothers had no such problem. They are recruiting them with promises of giving them whatever they want most. They hook them by providing Carpathian blood, which makes them feel stronger and more alive. Eventually they see the donor, such as Val. He was kept in a cage, drained so he was weak, and the men accepted that they were taking his blood and making him weaker."

"That's terrible."

"That is not the worst. They are introduced to the making of puppets, and over time, they lose their horror of the puppet tearing at a child's flesh. They are mostly grateful it is not them being eaten alive. Those who want immortality are promised it, given it, but then sent out to be used as pawns to be slaughtered by one of us when Sergey needs to have numbers."

"I feel so bad for them. Everyone has failings, and a master vampire could easily get into their heads. He would find a weakness and exploit it."

Andor nodded. "Yes, that is exactly what he would do. Converting a psychic male is difficult and unnecessary until they are mortally wounded on our behalf and we know this is their wish. Ordinarily, they would live out their lives never knowing we existed, and finding true happiness with a woman in their world."

"The Malinovs find them through the Morrison Center, don't they?" Lorraine asked. "They were at my college, which means they could have recruited some of my friends."

"It is possible, but we do not know that as of yet. Josef should be here soon. He is in contact with Tariq and monitors all activity on the database used for any human psychic."

Once more she lifted her head to look at the gathering Carpathians. Andor was in her mind, reading her thoughts. She had pushed the time so close to sunrise, she was afraid they would all be caught out, yet she still couldn't quite make herself give Andor the go-ahead. She wanted to be a Carpathian. She wanted to be with him, but she was very reluctant to slide under that soil.

"You are trembling. If you are not certain, *sívamet*, there is no need to rush this. You can choose another time."

"Everyone is already here."

He shrugged. "They will gather rising after rising until you are ready. You are in no way putting them out, nor will you, if you need more time."

She turned fully to him, one hand sliding up his chest to tug at the vee of the neckline. The pads of her fingers brushed fire over his skin when she nervously pulled at the material. "I want to do this tonight. It's just very overwhelming. I didn't ask Emeline what it's like to sleep beneath the earth. I had such an opportunity. I could have asked her or

Blaze, or even Charlotte, although she's a little like a queen or something, being royalty and all."

Andor couldn't help laughing. "Charlotte would never think of herself as royalty. Not in a million years. It just wouldn't happen. She's very much a part of all of us."

"The blood part, which you'd think would sicken me, actually is kind of hot." Her voice was a whisper, and when she made her confession, it dropped even lower. "If I told any of my college friends that, they'd think I was truly a nut. Sleeping in the ground is worrisome, though. I'm not certain I can get over feeling as if we're being buried alive. I could take it when you were partially covered in soil, but the thought of your head being buried terrified me. It really did. I hated it."

"You should have told me."

She shrugged. "I didn't think the closer I got to this moment, the more I'd think about that. What if I can't do it?"

"I will help you. I helped you get water down a few times when you thought you couldn't because your stomach was too upset. You were unable to eat food and the others helped. Sandu and Gary. Ferro. All three came to your aid."

"They did?" She scowled up at the balcony where the Carpathians were murmuring softly to one another, catching up on one another's lives.

"Yes. They didn't bother to tell you because they are very much ancients."

"What does that mean?" she asked suspiciously.

"It means they are set in the old ways. They may want to embrace the latest technology, but they still believe firmly that a woman is to be cherished, treasured and cared for whether she likes it or not."

"All women would like that."

He smiled at her and shook his head. "They would not like the way we go about it, taking the decision out of your hands. You do not like the thought that they fed you without your consent. You frowned and it was easy enough to read your expression."

"It wouldn't have hurt them to ask me first."

"That is my point, *hän sívamak*, I doubt very much that they will ask their lifemates' permission to do much at all. Ferro especially. He is too old and believes too strongly in what his role is and what that of his woman is." He sighed and rubbed his temples.

Whenever he thought of Ferro, his heart ached. He knew it was too late for his brethren. Ferro knew it as well. He would never embrace a modern woman, and no way would a lifemate be born in this time for him. Even a Carpathian woman brought up in the ways of his people would be exposed to the modern world and the way women were and be discontented.

"What's wrong?" Lorraine asked abruptly. Her fist closed tightly on his shirt. "Tell me."

"Ferro plans to leave when he rises. He will return to the monastery. He will be accompanied by Afanasiv Balan. Everyone refers to him as Siv if you do not recognize the name. He was at the meeting of the ancients. Most consider him extremely dangerous. He will be the gatekeeper as long as he is able."

"Then Tariq will lose two of his best hunters."

She looked close to tears, and his heart turned over. "I am well aware of that, but better Ferro turn far from here where those he cannot feel love for, but that he knows he does love, are away from him and safer."

"You didn't ask him to leave, did you?"

"No one would ever ask him to leave, *sívamet*."

She took a deep breath. "I'm ready. Just do it now, Andor. Before I can think too much more and fear takes hold of me."

Immediately, Andor felt elation rise. In only a short time, she would be wholly in their world. When next they rose, they would rise together as Carpathians. He found a seat on the ground and pulled her onto his lap. He was going to hold her as long as he was able. It was a mere touch of his mind and their garments were gone, but he shrouded them in flowing mist. One hand went to the nape of her neck, anchoring her to him. He kissed his way from the corner of her mouth to the tip of her breast and then back up to the top of the curve. His teeth sank deep, and she cried out.

Her blood held that perfect taste he craved. He took enough for a blood exchange and then opened a line right above his heart across the heavy muscle and pressed her mouth to him. The way she moved her body into his and didn't hesitate to draw his blood into her set him on fire. He let it happen, feeling joy that he responded so completely to her.

When he stopped her from feeding, he lifted her chin, forcing her head up so he could take her mouth in a soul-destroying kiss. He would always crave her. This woman who was giving herself into his keeping even when she had to be terrified.

She had quite a lot of Carpathian blood in her system. The men who had tied themselves to her soul were powerful ancients. That blood would mix with his and the conversion would start rather rapidly, he was certain. He wasn't wrong. Almost within moments, a ripple of unease went through her body.

*Her body is preparing. Already, I feel it.* He sent the alert to the others. At once they responded, their voices swelling with the healing chant. They had been using the lesser healing chant to aid a human woman or in Liv's case, a child, in coming into their world. He shared her mind, entrenching himself there so he could monitor what was happening to her.

Lorraine dug her fingers into Andor's shoulder, nails biting deep as something that felt incredibly like a blowtorch was turned on her stomach. The next pass hit her even harder. Then she was writhing, convulsing as wave after wave of excruciating agony took her without letup. At once he felt the worry of Dragomir and Tariq.

*It was not this severe.*

*It was the combination of the ancients' blood. So many of us,* Gary explained. *I should have considered this might happen. We have powerful blood. She has to be able to accept it.*

She had no way to catch her breath. No way to rest. The waves kept coming, each one worse than the one before. Had he not had her in their sacred healing ground or the other Carpathians surrounding them trying to bear the brunt of the pain, Andor doubted if Lorraine would have survived.

She vomited repeatedly, and the toxins left her body, draining away into the soil. He kept the area clean, but once the convulsions continued, it was all he could do to stop her body from breaking bones with the violence of the seizures.

*Emeline's conversion was not this violent and she had your blood as well as mine, healer.* Andor seconded Dragomir's opinion of the healer's assessment.

*She did not have Ferro's blood.* There was the softest of sighs accompanying that revelation.

Andor closed his eyes. He should have known. The conversion seemed to take an hour or more, each minute seeming like a thousand minutes. Eventually the waves of convulsions and agony lessened enough that he thought it was safe to put her in the ground.

*You have done well,* he praised her, brushing kisses over the little beads of red dotting her forehead. *You did not make a sound, Lorraine.*

*My father always told me to suck it up when I was in pain, but I never want to experience that again. Nor, if asked, would I ever recommend it.* That was a distinct warning.

Andor thanked the other Carpathians, knowing the night was at its end and they needed to find sleeping arrangements. He waved his hand toward his woman and Lorraine's eyes closed, her long lashes fanning her cheeks. Andor breathed a sigh of relief and opened the earth deep. He floated them both down, knowing the sun was already rising and the others hastened to get to their sleeping quarters. Most did not use the healing grounds to sleep. It was reserved for those in need. The Carpathians scattered around the compound as the sun rose, and even beneath the house, Andor winced, feeling the burn of the light against his skin.

He sank into the rich soil, laying Lorraine out gently onto her back. He lay beside her and watched as the earth began to fill in over their legs. Her body moved. Jerked. Andor frowned and leaned over her. She should be in a deep sleep. There it was again, that same jerk, her back moving back and forth as if rubbing into the soil. Suddenly, her eyes went wide, lashes lifting. Shock was there. Horror. He had sent her to sleep, but she was experiencing fear. Not just fear. Total terror. Her eyes stared into his.

"It's loose, Andor," she whispered. The same horror that was in her eyes was in her voice. "It was in his talons and he put it into my skin. Now it's loose in the healing grounds. There's no getting it back."

There was no way to resolve the situation. Andor knew whatever Sergey had managed to release into the healing soil would have carte blanche for a few hours. His first guess would have to be a parasite that would kill all children or the ability for their women to conceive. How had they all missed that? It had been placed into her skin. Right on the surface. The wound had been cleaned and healed. No one, least of all him, had noticed anything amiss.

He closed his eyes and sank into the soil beside Lorraine, urging her to lie her down. *Sleep for now. We will hunt at the next rising.*

# 19

Andor burst from the soil the moment after he checked on his sleeping lifemate. He wanted her to stay asleep, although a part of him feared the parasite would enter her and prevent them from having children. Still, the most important thing was to go on the hunt. All of them.

*We need to know what we are hunting for.* That was Tariq, and he was not happy.

Andor couldn't blame him. They had all checked Lorraine's body repeatedly. She had been patient with them. She had wanted them to check her. He should have paid more attention to the little clues she gave him. She'd even mentioned that her back itched, right between her shoulder blades. He had thought that the itch meant the shallow laceration from the crow's talons was healing.

She had been uneasy. The sight of the crows seemed to bother her more than they should. Even the children hadn't paid as much attention to them. There were warning signs, but he hadn't read them correctly. None of them had. Emotions got into the way.

*O jelä peje teräd.* He swore in his own language. Furious at himself.

Furious that one of the Malinov brothers had managed to fool every one of them. If Tariq had been the target . . . He brought himself up short.

"Go feed before we start this thing. I've called in Matt and his security force. They are willing for us to use them for sustenance when needed. This is a need," Tariq said. He stood on the edge of the healing grounds, looking it over, his hands on his hips.

"You could be the target, Tariq," Andor warned. "It waited until Lorraine was here. Sergey knew I would convert her, and he programmed that thing like a missile to wait until she was in the ground."

"Andor," Tariq said patiently. "Go feed."

Andor cursed again. "You cannot set one foot onto those grounds. Not one. Until your security force, and I do not mean the humans, get here, I am not taking any chances with your life."

"Yet your woman still sleeps beneath the soil."

"If he was targeting her, she is already dead and there is nothing any of us can do. I do not believe she is the objective. If that were so, he would have killed her when he had the chance. He could have used that crow to drive right through her head with his beak. You know that as well as I do."

Gary appeared right beside Tariq and Siv emerged on the other side, both coming out of a mist. Gary inclined his head toward Andor. "I am sorry. We all looked where he knew we would."

"Could it be a sliver of himself? Is it possible to put it in the skin?"

"It is possible, of course, but improbable. It would not be able to control the host at all. He wouldn't have use of her eyes or ears. There would be no point," the healer replied. "You need to feed, Andor."

Andor didn't want one more person to mention that he looked like hell without coming out and using those terms. He sighed and dissolved, hurrying quickly into the air outside where he saw several of Tariq's human security force sitting on the ground or giving blood to one of the ancients. He chose one who looked healthy and fit. The man turned toward him as he approached. It was normal to wave a hand, take control of the mind and just feed. He did so without thinking and only realized after he had taken his fill that the blood had been freely given. He re-awakened the man and thanked him as he helped him to the ground.

At once, Genevieve was there, handing out a glass of orange juice. "Why is everyone so upset?"

Andor realized these humans had thrown their lot in with Tariq. Each of them had agreed to have barriers put in place to keep any vampire from knowing they were part of Tariq's force. Their brains also were shielded from allowing them to talk about vampires or Carpathians to anyone but a recognized part of the security force. Safeguards also had been added. Even Genevieve had shields to keep her from accidentally blurting out what she knew of the Carpathian people.

He wasn't used to living with them, or trusting them. Tariq did both. He trusted them to watch over the compound and his children. Lorraine had asked a good question when she was worried about the babies. If they couldn't go to ground with their parents, who would watch over them? Who would raise them? In that moment, he understood why humans such as Gary had been, before he became fully Carpathian, revered. They had done everything necessary to ensure no harm came to a member of the Carpathian race.

"Lorraine was attacked by a crow during the encounter with the vampires. We realized early on that the entire skirmish had been orchestrated just for that purpose. He had not tried to acquire her, or kill her, so that meant he put something in her to bring back here." As he laid out the scenario to Genevieve, he found it helped to think it through.

"How horrible for her. I can't imagine how she must have felt."

"We searched, all of us, over and over, and we could not find it," Andor continued. "We all came to the same conclusion—that he had to have planted something on her—but none of us, after repeated attempts, could find it. We looked inward, where he was most likely to plant something. A sliver. A parasite. Something that might eventually kill her. We looked at every organ, her bones, her bloodstream. Not one of us thought to look outside her body, in her skin, where he carefully planted what he wanted to get inside."

Genevieve gave a little shiver. She rubbed her hands up and down her arms. "What was it? What is its purpose?"

None of them knew, other than perhaps it was the parasite to prevent them from having children. Still . . . it had waited to infect the ground. The healing ground. If a woman was giving birth, or pregnant, she would most likely rest in that soil, the best they had around them. "I do not know, Genevieve. We hope to find that out. We'll be searching for it, but we have no way of knowing what it is."

"How do you know it's there, then?"

His head snapped up. He flashed her a small smile. "You are a brilliant woman, Genevieve. No wonder you are guarded carefully. We cannot lose your great mind."

He turned and was gone, streaking back to the main house and moving beneath it to where Tariq had set up the healing grounds. The Carpathian hunters had gathered. They didn't want their women near the contaminated soil. It was too late for those already lying beneath it.

"Lorraine might know what to look for. She woke when it escaped her skin. She would have a feel for it, perhaps even be able to identify it."

"If you wake her too early and she isn't ready," Tariq cautioned, "she might still feel the pain of the transformation."

It was a risk. The others waited patiently for him to decide. He let his breath out slowly. He had to make his decision based on what Lorraine would do. She would want to be awakened and apprised of the situation. From there she would be able to tell them whether or not she could help.

"I will wake her," he said. He opened the soil over where his beloved was sleeping, remembering at the last moment to cleanse and clothe her before bringing her to the surface. He caught her up in his arms, cradling her close to his chest. "Awaken, Lorraine. We have need of your help."

Her long lashes fluttered against her pale skin. It took a moment before she lifted them so he could stare into her green eyes. The impact was immediately and nearly overwhelming, a visceral feeling that cut right through him, gutting him. She did that with one look. He smiled down at her, seeing the confusion in her eyes, feeling the wince when she moved her body just slightly. It was too soon and her body wasn't fully healed.

She woke starving, every cell crying out for nourishment. He hadn't considered that, either. She would be waking without control. *I am going to feed you, Lorraine. Take what is freely offered.* He turned his body to try to give her privacy from the others. He was a big man and sheltered her against his chest.

She glanced over his arm and saw the others. "Tell me what is going on."

He looked down at her face. There was nothing there but concern. Certainly, no panic or after the fact wanting to take her decision back.

*I will tell you after you have fed.* He used his teeth to open his wrist. He pressed it to her mouth, giving her no choice but to drink him down.

She caught at his arm, holding it in place, her need pushing aside her fear of anyone seeing her feed. *Tell me. What is wrong?*

*At sunrise, I put you to sleep. The transformation was particularly difficult for you.*

*There was a lot of pain,* she agreed.

*There still is.* He couldn't afford to be weak from blood loss. He had to watch the amount she consumed.

*Not like there was last night.*

To his shock, she swept her tongue across the laceration and sat up in his arms. "Tell me, Andor. Something's terribly wrong for all of you to be gathered together like this, wearing your grimmest faces."

"Do you remember, just as I put you to sleep, what you said to me?"

She frowned, and he couldn't help brushing a kiss across her nose, even though he knew it might be distracting. As he raised his head, her eyes went wide and one hand went to her throat defensively. She remembered. She had that haunted look in her eyes, the one she got every time Sergey was mentioned or she thought about him.

"Yes. I felt something moving on my skin." Her frown deepened and she gave a little shake of her head.

Andor carried her back from the center of the healing grounds to the edge where the others waited. They needed to hear what she had to say.

"No, that's not right. It was *in* my skin, and I knew the moment it moved that the crow had put it there. It felt dark and ugly. When it moved across my back, I could actually feel my cells shrinking away, trying to avoid it."

Sandu nodded. "That is the abomination of the undead. They are soulless creatures and wholly evil. Your body would shrink from all contact."

"Why couldn't I feel it when he put it in my skin? It had to be touching me. I could see, if he'd gotten inside me, how I wouldn't know, but if he planted it into my skin, I should have felt it, right?"

"You actually did," Andor said. "You thought a couple of times that you itched between your shoulder blades but you put it down to being a target. I caught those thoughts."

"Maybe, but it should have been more, something dark and ugly like when it emerged," she argued.

There was a moment of silence and then they all began talking at once to one another, putting out all kinds of theories. It was Petru who held up one hand for silence. When the others quickly subsided, the ancient put forth his own opinion. "She would not have felt this, if at the time it was planted, it was benign."

Andor was stunned. He should have thought of that—considered that whatever Sergey introduced into Lorraine wouldn't in any way appear threatening or harmful. She would have known immediately where it was if it were malicious. She had said her back itched, right between her shoulder blades.

"Lean forward, *csecsemő*, I want to look at your back," he said. He had seen her back before, that smooth, sleek expanse of silky skin.

Lorraine complied immediately, and he pushed her T-shirt up to expose her skin. The others gathered around to stare at the blackened cells. The evidence was damning. They knew something of Sergey's had escaped into the healing soil—it was no longer a matter of speculation.

"Can you tell us what it looks like, Lorraine?" Gary asked.

"I didn't see it. I only felt it."

"I understand that," the healer persisted. "But you had to have felt its size and shape. Call up the memory just as you did when we were trying to find what the crow planted in you."

Lorraine didn't argue. She always seemed ready to comply when it was a matter of urgency. She didn't ask questions or insist on answers they didn't have, she simply nodded and looked into her mind, trying to find the exact moment she was aware of the creature living in her skin.

Andor stayed very still in her mind, waiting to see the memory, hoping to help with the details. Pain crashed through him—through her, only because they both replayed the event in their minds, deliberately calling up exactly how it felt along with the memory.

She took the pain on a quick inhale, drawing air into her burning lungs. Breathing through the constant convulsions, the twisting of her organs as the blowtorch inside continued to reconstruct her body. There was that moment of peace as Andor sent her to sleep. She was nearly there, drifting away from the pain, so thankful it was over.

The moment her back settled into the soil, she felt the other thing and knew it was evil. It was squishy and yet firm, a long skinny creature. The tiny feet felt like a hundred of them, razor sharp, stepping on her, dragging the stinger over her skin. It hurt, but in a different way from the conversion. This hurt her soul. It held a kind of agony all its own.

"I knew immediately Sergey's crow had planted it."

No one, least of all Andor, pointed out the master vampire had been inside the crow. They'd all missed that. He had so many spies, it was impossible to pinpoint a single crow and know it was the head of the vampire army. Now, all of them had studied the crow and would be able to pick it out of any flock, but he doubted if Sergey would use the same trick again. He was too clever for such an obvious mistake.

"It slit open my skin and clawed its way to the surface. The moment the healing soil touched it, it wiggled and slashed as if very excited. I tried to hold it back. It was silly to think that by tightening every muscle in my body, I could keep it from entering the soil, but I did, just in case I could contain it. I couldn't." There was regret and guilt in her voice.

Andor immediately caught her chin and lifted her face toward his. "This is not your fault. Nothing about this mess is your fault. Every one of us failed to consider the crow's talons. To be fair, that laceration in your skull was deep."

"He's so smart," she whispered. "Scary smart."

"We know what we're looking for," Gary said. "Thank you, Lorraine. It's small, about, what do you think? Two, three inches long?"

"Longer. Almost like a small snake. More like six or seven inches, but very, very thin, like a pencil, maybe," Lorraine explained.

Andor remained quiet. Gary had a way of enticing a person to give him more information without realizing he was coaxing more details out of them.

Gary nodded. "But with legs, like a centipede."

Lorraine frowned. "Yes." There as a bit of reluctance in her voice. "I did feel the feet, as if there were a lot of them, but that wasn't necessarily how it moved. It moved more like a snake might, wiggling but . . ." She trailed off.

Gary was silent a moment. Andor breathed shallowly, watching Lorraine's face. It cleared suddenly.

"Sideways, the thing moved sideways, like a sidewinder would move. I could feel the brush of its feet. They were sharp, like a tack might be, but their purpose wasn't to walk. It was more like the creature used them to stop his momentum, turn or rake."

"That's perfect, Lorraine. You've given us a good picture of the creature. We're going to be searching, but this is a huge area for something that small to be hiding in."

"Don't forget it has a stinger. I felt that as well. It didn't sting me, but I remember I was waiting for it to do so."

"It is too bad it didn't tell you where underground it was going," Petru said.

She shrugged. "You just have to figure out its main goal. What its purpose is. Once you know that, you know where it is."

Main goal. Main purpose. Andor turned those words over and over in his head. "What does Sergey desire the most?" He murmured the words out loud.

"Power," Tariq said. "He wants to rule the planet. I believe every Malinov had that goal."

"Wealth," Tomas said. "My brothers and I have often commented on how the Malinov brothers would rather go to the trouble of stealing than work for their gain. They steal lives, they steal money. They steal anything that would benefit them."

"Children," Dragomir guessed. "More than anything, the plan was to get psychic women and force them to have their children so they could have replacements in case of their demise."

"No." Andor shook his head. "We're talking specifically Sergey, not Vadim or any of the others, dead though they are."

"We hope they're dead," Gary said.

Every ancient looked to the healer. "What do you mean?" Mataias asked. "Of course they're dead."

"Not necessarily completely. Suppose they were talked into giving a sliver of themselves to their youngest brother. The brother no one thought had any kind of intelligence when it came to battle strategy. Or any kind of courage. Suppose he cultivated that image from the time he was very young, and the others, individually, were asked for aid. They might help their youngest brother out. Each would do so without the other knowing. If they placed a sliver of themselves in his mind, he would have all of that amazing intelligence as well as the slivers of Xavier. That would make Sergey the most powerful vampire, not only alive, but for all time."

Tariq shook his head but didn't say anything. The others looked a little stunned, or like him, Andor suspected, shell-shocked. It was not only possible, it would explain a lot of things.

"He planned this all along," Andor said. "The entire thing, the underground city, the gathering of the armies, the slow takeover."

"He wouldn't have to take over," Gary said. "That might have happened out of necessity. Vadim might have been catching on to the true genius in the family. Sergey couldn't afford to have his brother know his plans. As long as he was considered the least of the threats, no one would be sent after him."

"So, we're back to the original question," Andor said. "What does he want most? He took Elisabeta before he ever turned vampire. He kept her from his brothers. He kept the knowledge of her from them. There was no trace of her in all those centuries, which means he had prepared places for her. He didn't take her on a whim, it was completely planned out, every single step. I think Elisabeta is what he desires most."

"Is she his lifemate?" Siv speculated.

Andor shrugged. "We have no way of knowing that. We can only try to keep her from him. She is light. He is darkness. She is good. He is wholly evil. I think that creature was sent by him to find her. He needs to know where she lies."

"This is pretty far thinking," Lojos said. "Vampires don't usually have this kind of fixation on a woman. Even if she was his lifemate, she couldn't help him."

"No, but she can give him the things he lacks. Color. Even emotion. It makes sense when we know Sergey has held up so much better than the others," Gary said. "His body hasn't rotted the way his brothers' all did."

Andor had to agree. "Sergey knew Lorraine was my lifemate and human. He also knew I would protect her. He made certain to make us all think that acquiring her was his goal, but he wanted her brought here, to this compound, because when I converted her, she would be put in the healing soil, where Elisabeta was already lying in a deep sleep."

"Do you really think a vampire is capable of that kind of planning? To use a wounded ancient and his potential lifemate to bring a weapon or beacon right into the Carpathian stronghold?" Lojos asked. "This turns everything we know about vampires on its head."

"I believe it absolutely," Andor said. "And the more time we take discussing it, the more time it has to find her."

The ancients looked at one another. "How do we best use this information, providing it is correct?" Petru asked.

"We open the earth around her," Tariq said. "Search it first and then isolate it if the creature isn't found."

He floated above the healing soil and began cutting out a wide cube toward the left of the center. The cube moved up into the air, and was set squarely on the cement pad away from the wide expanse of healing soil.

"Who else is in the ground?" Andor asked, setting Lorraine carefully on the cement pad a short distance from the cube.

"Ferro. Liv normally sleeps here as well, but she awakens before the rest of us do. She enjoys playing with her siblings," Tariq answered.

"It will be impossible to tell where Ferro went to ground," Benedek stated. "Even within the monastery, we never knew where he slept. He is always careful."

"We should consider waking him," Tariq said as he paced around the room.

Before he could say another word, or the others could respond, the soil on the right side, above where Andor was certain Elisabeta slept, spouted up like a geyser. Great columns of fine dirt sprayed into the air. Ferro shot up and then turned and dove across the cement barrier, back into the deep soil in the healing grounds.

"The creature. I saw it just for a moment," Andor said, and followed Ferro's example. He chose a place just ahead of where he thought the hideous little organism, half reptile, half anthropod, wholly evil, might be.

Behind him, the other ancients fanned out, each choosing a side of the ring, forming a large circle where they hoped to corral Sergey's servant. Andor began to quarter the area he had chosen to protect. Each of the ancients sent Ferro their coordinates. He was the active pursuer. No one knew exactly what shape he was in, but it didn't matter. The creature had disturbed his sleep, and he was already hunting it.

*Make certain each quarter of the soil you take to search, you leave behind the sacred spell so he cannot enter it. He is small to hide in this vast complex,* Ferro cautioned.

*Did you know you were sleeping so close to Elisabeta?* Andor asked curiously. Ferro sometimes knew things others did not. He could have had a premonition that Sergey would try to strike at her.

*I did so on purpose.*

Andor took that as confirmation that Ferro had some kind of precognition that Elisabeta would be targeted by the master vampire. He moved through the earth, sifting it carefully, hoping if he did find the creature, if he couldn't catch it, he could push it back toward Ferro.

*We knew he would eventually make a try for Elisabeta.* Tariq joined in the conversation. *We thought he would have to wait until she was once more awake.*

*He calls to her,* Ferro said. *His foul voice permeates the healing ground. I think the creature is sending out signals in the hopes of waking her.*

*Maybe so,* Gary said, *but from what Lorraine described, the vile thing is more than a homing device and wake-up alarm. It has a stinger and can use its feet to slash at an enemy. I would imagine there is a poisonous substance on each of those feet or the end of its stinger.*

*I felt the lash of that stinger,* Ferro agreed. *It injected some concoction into me, or tried to, the moment I felt its body come up against mine. I knew it was something foul Sergey sent to try to get to Elisabeta. I moved fast, but unfortunately, the creature is like lightning and I was still partially paralyzed. My wounds were . . . grave.*

*Do you believe he wants to kill her? That he would rather she be dead than leave her to us?* Tariq asked.

*It is always possible, but I do not think so,* Ferro said.

Andor had to agree with him. Sergey had had too much time to kill Elisabeta. When she'd been found in the cage, he could have chosen that moment to end her life, but he hadn't. He had allowed the Carpathians to save her. Perhaps, at the time, he didn't believe they would be able to free her from the cage. Her prison had disappeared and became part of the background, but with the aid of a young mage, they had found the correct spell to bring the cage back into the open and eventually they were able to free her.

*Ferro, perhaps it would be wise to leave the hunt to others and allow Gary to heal your wounds properly,* Tariq ventured.

Andor thought it was significant that Tariq was careful with Ferro. It showed the man was a good leader, very aware of everyone around him. Even by those who didn't know him, Ferro needed respect given. It was his due and he wore that just as easily as he wore his skin.

*Perhaps when I have found and destroyed this evil creature so there is no threat to our women and children,* Ferro replied.

Andor wasn't surprised by his response. Ferro would never consider himself or his well-being before the safety of others. He was tied to Gary and could feel the others' concern, although Gary couldn't feel it, nor could Sandu or Ferro. He understood better what Lorraine had tried to tell him. It wasn't that they didn't have emotions, no matter how old they were, there was a disconnect, which meant they couldn't feel them.

Andor knew better than to try to dissuade Ferro from his decision. They all just had to do their part. He sifted through the dirt—and there was a lot of it.

*Why is Ferro so sad?* Lorraine's voice caressed him, brushed him with the velvet of her voice, the silkiness of her growing love for him.

*I do not detect sadness.*

*He hides it from even himself. You feel exactly what he feels, which is nothing, but go deeper, Andor. He is very sad. A great sorrow. I don't like it. Do you think he plans to sit out in the sun?*

He couldn't imagine Ferro doing such a thing. *As I said before, he plans to return to the monastery.*

Andor couldn't see Lorraine, but he knew exactly what expression would be on her face. He wanted to hold her. *There is no stopping Ferro once he has made up his mind, csecsemō.*

*How will he find his lifemate?*

*He no longer believes it is possible.*

*Of course, it is possible. You found me. Or I found you. Whatever. We found each other. If he secrets himself away, he will die of pure boredom.*

*Some of us have learned to meditate.*

*Meditation is for the birds. Seriously, Andor, I tried it multiple times and it doesn't work. I found myself so bored I wanted to fall asleep. I may have.*

*It takes discipline.*

*I think monks lied about meditation and its benefits in order to keep the ones who liked to talk from chattering too much and driving the others crazy. I'm going to talk to him.*

Andor had to admit to himself that for some reason, his brethren accepted Lorraine when they barely trusted anyone else. There were very few allowed into their circle. She had an influence on the other ancients. They certainly respected her. It was possible she might persuade Ferro to stay when no other could. On the other hand, if he knew he was too close to that edge of danger, of turning, then it would be far better for him to leave.

*Don't think that. Not even for a moment.*

*Sívamet, you have no way to understand how bad the torment can be. Ferro does not believe even should he find a lifemate that she would be able to live with him.*

*Do you know how utterly ridiculous it is to think that?*

*We are from ancient times when things were far different.*

*Yes, you are. Andor, you are from those times and we found each other. I'm modern. Dragomir is from ancient times, and Emeline is modern. You told me that lifemates complete their other half. That whatever one needs the other provides. How exactly can you or Ferro think that he would have outlived his lifemate's needs?*

His woman was intelligent. And right. He couldn't stop himself, he shared her thoughts with Ferro. *What do you think?*

*I think your woman is making you soft. Hunt for that hideous bug. Drive it toward me.*

Still, for all of Ferro's seeming rejection of Lorraine's theory, Andor felt as if the ancient listened. At least it was out there, and maybe he would give the hunt for his lifemate as much attention as he was the reptilian creature Sergey had sent their way.

*O jelä peje terád,* Sandu's voice snapped, on the common Carpathian path. *That thing tried to sting me. I kicked it accidentally.*

Sandu's position was just to the right of Andor. He moved very slowly in that direction, feeling with his senses, not his eyes. A faint displacement of soil came from the right as if something very small slithered toward him. He went very still. It came closer and closer.

*Sandu, make some noise. Petru, you, too. Just a little as if you're trying to be sneaky.*

*I was sneaky, but that didn't turn out to be such a good thing when I found it.*

Andor suppressed the need to laugh. He was listening intently, feeling for the thing now. He'd been determined on driving it toward Ferro so the other Carpathian could capture or kill it, but now, he devised a plan to grab the thing. He was aware of the razor feet and stinging tail. He needed something besides his hands to scoop it up.

Sergey's spy dug through the soil, coming right at him. In his mind, he created a thinly meshed screen that could snap down as the creature entered a small cage. When he was certain it was only inches from the long, thin cage, he froze.

*Ferro, now, come toward me fast.*

Ferro reacted instantly, pushing hard through the soil. Andor heard the creature hit the end of the cage and he slammed the mesh down to lock it in place. *Got it. Coming to the surface. Lorraine, you stay far back.* Andor burst through the dirt, the cage swinging from his hand.

The sound the reptile made was horrendous—a high-pitched shriek that could only be a warning to its maker that it hadn't accomplished its mission. Andor silenced it immediately with a wave of his hand. It stared at him with malevolent eyes. Pulling back its lips to show wicked, needle-like teeth, it hissed at him. The sound was muffled, impossible to hear other than a scant foot from the cage.

Ferro emerged, his gaze on the snakelike reptile Sergey had sent. "It has feet, just as Lorraine said."

They all watched as it began scissoring the feet back and forth in a frantic attempt to saw through the floor of the cage. "What is it?"

"I think a homing device," Andor said. "I think the reptile is the delivery system and will do anything to get to Elisabeta."

"Of course he wants Elisabeta." Ferro turned from staring at the strange creature to Andor. "His greatest desire. He would not want to lose her. She has sustained him all these long years."

When he turned, Andor could see the extent of his injuries. There were two that were clearly mortal wounds and needed repairing. He glanced at the healer. Gary was looking at the wounds, not the ancient. He knew healers had a difficult time being around the wounded without aiding them. Apparently, Gary was no different.

Andor studied the big Carpathian with concern. He had been torn up by the master vampire. The undead had definitely put up a fight for survival.

He knew few ancients without lifemates would accept the help of another. Not unless the situation was so dire they had no other choice but help or death. By the looks of him, Ferro had chosen death, yet here he was, sitting in the middle of the healing grounds.

"I thought Gary had seen to your wounds," Andor said.

"I did the best I could to get him back here," Gary answered when Ferro remained stubbornly silent. "He went straight to ground."

"Ferro, we have need of every hunter right now," Tariq chastised, his voice mild.

Ferro flicked him a look.

"Do not be such a baby," Andor snapped. "Big deal—a healer has to help you. I had three mortal wounds. You have only two. I doubt you will have nearly as much need of him as I did."

"Stop whining. Your lifemate has turned you into an old man, wizened and soft."

"Do not be jealous that I had much more severe wounds and yet suffered them stoically."

"I thought the wounds on both of you were mortal," Lorraine said. "Doesn't that mean that both of you would die from them? How can one be considered more mortal than another?"

Gary shed his body and went into Ferro's before the ancient could protest.

"They cannot," Ferro said.

"Of course they can," Andor said. "The master vampire I fought nearly eviscerated me. Believe me, having your guts ripped out is no fun."

"Your guts were not ripped out," Sandu pointed out. "And it just means you are slower."

Lorraine's ripple of laughter was worth making a fool out of himself with trying to distract Ferro while Gary healed him.

The nasty little creature's feet hadn't stopped moving the entire time and the claw marks on the cage floor were deep now. Andor shook his head. "You are not going to get away."

The moment he uttered those words, the reptile stared at him in silence. The feet ceased to move. The tail with the venomous stinger on it whipped up and hit itself in the back. The mouth opened in a silent scream and the thing fell over on its side.

"It must have poisoned the ground," Ferro ventured.

"I doubt it. It had one purpose, and that was to get to Elisabeta," Andor said.

"She has to be Sergey's lifemate," Sandu said.

Ferro shook his head. "That is impossible."

"Why would you say that?" Andor asked. "It fits. Why else would he target her even when she was a young Carpathian? She couldn't have been more than a teenager when she disappeared. Her brother, Traian, was frantic by all accounts. Sergey must have had a reason for taking her."

"I believe he did," Ferro said. "She has gifts. But she is not his."

"You can't possibly know that."

"I can, because she is mine. Elisabeta is my lifemate."

# 20

Lorraine lay across the bed in the house Tariq had graciously lent them. Outside, the water from the lake lapped at the shore. The moon spilled her light through the open window right onto Lorraine's very bare bottom. Andor had a difficult time keeping his mind on the subject she was so intent on talking about when just the sight of her gave him other ideas.

"I don't understand. If he knew that Elisabeta was his lifemate, how could he possibly consider going to that ridiculous monastery where you were all locked away with no chance whatsoever of finding your lifemates?"

"As I understand it, Elisabeta's cries were muffled beneath the soil, and he heard her voice then and knew when he went this last night into the soil to heal. He shifted his position to lie closer to her, in an attempt to give her comfort. That was why you felt such sorrow in him. He felt her pain. He shared that pain, more emotional than physical."

Andor drew his hand down her hair, feeling the slide of silk in his palm. "He will rise with her and try to aid her. She hasn't known any other but Sergey in all these centuries. She had only his company, his care.

He told her what he wished her to know. He fed her. Took care of every need, and demanded who knows what in return. It will be a long road back for her."

Lorraine nodded. "I know. She'll be so frightened of everyone, having no interaction with others. I hope Ferro has endless patience."

"He is her lifemate."

"Are we going to stay here?"

"I think they need us here. Why?" He bent his head to slide his tongue over the nape of her neck, tasting her skin. She shivered and her hips squirmed, drawing his attention once more to her bare bottom.

"I'd like to help her if at all possible. I know her instincts will tell her to get back to Sergey, even if she doesn't want to. She really will be so afraid. Once Sergey realizes she has a lifemate, my guess is, he'll want to kill Ferro. They'll both need friends."

"You've given this a lot of thought." He should have known she would. Lorraine had a lot of compassion in her. Others would just look at the surface, judging Elisabeta; they had no idea of what the real damage several lifetimes of living as a slave to an evil man would be, let alone a vampire.

"Yes. I feel like we're a family. You. Me. Sandu, Gary and Ferro. I know that sounds silly, given they're ancients and don't feel the same about me. Us. Maybe you don't, either, but I want Ferro to know we'll help him in any way we can."

He kissed her right in the middle of her spine and then added more kisses until he got to the small of her back. He loved her. It was impossible not to love Lorraine. "I think you are wrong about the others, *sívamet*. They have a deep respect for you. As much as we can call someone family when we do not know what that is exactly, they call you family."

Those long lashes swept her cheeks and then her green gaze was steady on his face. "I worry that Ferro will overpower Elisabeta. Just looking at him can scare me, so you can imagine what it will do to her. Is he going to stay, do you think? Now that he knows she's here and needs him?"

"I believe he will. It is difficult to say with Ferro. He goes his own way. Even if he stays, *csecsemő*, this does not guarantee them a happy ending. She has to be pretty damaged and he is . . . different."

"Then it's more important than ever for us to stay and help them."

He slid his hand down the smooth expanse of her spine. "You cannot interfere between lifemates. That is a sacred law in our world."

She scowled at him. "I have no intentions of interfering. Guiding maybe, but not interfering."

Andor found himself laughing. The real thing. The laughter spread happiness through his entire body. Joy had colors and they danced in the air around his woman. Her little scowl turned into a slow, beautiful smile that shook him.

"*Tet vigyázam*, Lorraine. Always. I had no idea I could love so much. It seems to grow with every rising. You bring me such gifts."

She smiled at him, her heart in her eyes. "I love you more than I thought it was possible to love, Andor. She rolled over onto her back. "Kiss me. Right here." She pointed to her mouth.

He kissed her eyelids. When he lifted his head, her long lashes fluttered against her cheeks so he kissed them as well. Then he left trails of kisses on either side of her mouth. He loved her mouth. The shape of it. The texture. That sweet fire she poured down his throat when she kissed him back. The scorching heat she surrounded his shaft with when she took his cock into her mouth and brought him pleasure beyond measure. The way she laughed, her white teeth flashing at him, teasing him, coaxing the joy that seemed to spread through him. Her mouth did all of that. That perfection.

He kissed her, cajoling her lips apart with the tip of his tongue until she gave him entry. At once, it was there, all of it, the beauty of her response, instant, fiery, her taste exquisite and just for him. All his. She kissed him back, her arms circling his neck, her body melting into his, giving him everything—giving him her.

He spent time on her mouth, letting the need for her, that terrible hunger, take him over. The brutal urgency swept through his entire body like a wildfire he knew only she could put out. He kissed his way down her throat, leaving marks of his possession because this rising was his. Theirs. She had risen fully Carpathian.

After keeping her in the healing soil for three days, he knew her body was completely, wholly Carpathian. She was strong. She embraced his world. His soul was intact, and that mattered to him. Living mattered to him.

He kissed his way to her breasts. He loved their shape and size. The feel of them. Soft, responsive. He made certain to take advantage of that fact, and spent time there as well. Kissing. Using his teeth and tongue. Waiting for her to squirm, her hips bucking. Her breathing changed, a ragged, labored sound that was music to him.

He kissed his way to the junction between her legs. She widened her thighs at his urging, and drew up her knees at his command. He loved that about her, too. She was always ready for him, always responsive and willing to go where he wanted to go. She made her own demands just as readily, stopping him to drag him up for more kisses, or holding his head to her breast. Now, her moans started, a soft melody of need.

She had a hunger that matched his and she was ferocious about it. He loved that, too. She was his match in every way. Her breathless cries told him she was close, so he stopped abruptly, lifting his head to watch her face. He saw hunger there, all for him. All his. It had been a long road, but he had her now.

"Turn over, Lorraine. I want you on your hands and knees."

She flicked him a look that said he'd better hurry, but she turned over readily. Before she could comply with his order, he bunched the thick mass of hair in his fist and tugged gently. She turned her head obligingly. He kept tugging until her head rose and then she was on her elbows looking over her shoulder at him. He sat very still on the side of the bed, holding her hair like reins, admiring the way her full breasts swayed, nipples dragging along the sheets.

"Are you looking at something in particular?" she demanded, her voice miffed.

He grinned at her because he couldn't help it. "Yes. I am looking at the love of my life." Her body was flushed a beautiful rose color. Her green eyes were slumberous. Sexy. Her bottom was up in the air, waiting for him, while her breasts swayed gently in temptation. She squirmed. Bucked her hips. Did a slow circle with them.

"I'm waiting here."

"I see that." His palm caressed her right breast. Teased at her nipple, tugging gently. He watched the beauty that happened. How her face changed. Her expression. The swift intake of breath. Using her hair, he guided her mouth to his. The fire had gone hotter than ever.

He took his mouth off hers, barely a scant half inch. "Do not move, Lorraine. I want you just like this."

"You'd better hurry, or I'm going to try out one of the many Carpathian spells you all whip up on a dime."

He wasn't certain what that meant, and in any case, he didn't feel the need to hurry so he took his time moving around behind her. Gathering her hair again, he pulled her head toward him until her back was down and her bottom was up. One handed, he pushed her thighs farther apart. Keeping her hair tight in his fist so she couldn't move, he began using his fingers and occasionally dipping his head down to use his mouth, teeth and tongue, driving her up where he wanted her, but keeping that fire from igniting.

"Andor." His name was a wail. A groan. He smiled and added his fingers, just to keep that burn right on the edge. "Do something. Anything. Hurry, honey."

He liked the way she gave him an endearment. He liked the way she pleaded, that soft moan that told him she was very, very close.

He entered her fast and hard, a deep thrust that sent her right over the edge. Immediately his cock was surrounded with her scorching hot sheath. She was liquid fire, tight gripping muscles, paradise taking him in. He moved, feeling the streaks of fire racing up his spine, racing up hers. He closed his eyes to savor the heat, the experience unlike anything else, but she was there as well, behind his lids, her body writhing around his.

She cried out as the ripples grew, so intense, spreading through her body, so that her tight sheath massaged and gripped his shaft as he pounded into her. He thought *gentle* in his mind, but his body betrayed him, taking charge, giving both of them what they wanted—and needed. He held out against the wild waves crashing through her and around him.

And then her body clamped down viciously, a vise of perfection, wringing him dry.

Andor came down over top of her as she collapsed under him. She lay breathing hard, his body weighting her down, blanketing her. He knew he should move, but he couldn't find the energy. It took minutes to control his heart and breathing because, honestly, he wasn't trying very hard. He enjoyed everything about making love to Lorraine, even this aftermath, where their hearts beat out of control and their lungs burned raw.

He threaded his fingers through hers on either side of her head. She had her eyes closed, and when he lifted his head enough to set his chin on her back so he could watch her, those lashes of hers did the flutter thing he found mesmerizing.

"I'm too tired to go teach self-defense. I think Bella could kick my butt," she murmured.

"Who do you plan to teach first? The women or the little ones?" He rubbed his jaw along her back, and then watched with satisfaction as her skin turned pink from the tiny stubble shadowing his jaw.

"If the little ones are still up when I get out there, I'll give them a lesson. Genevieve said if I tired them out for her, she'd pay me top baby-sitting wages."

"Um, *csecsemő*, you have no more need of money. We are very wealthy by human standards."

"I'm not really going to take her money, silly. She was teasing me. And I do need a bank account. All of you should have one if you're going to appear human."

"It is bad enough that Tariq is photographed so widely," he objected. "Sooner or later he must appear to grow old, and he will have to move on so as not to be discovered."

"Leaving your property to yourself, to an identity you choose before you pretend to die, can be done over and over. I don't see that it will be harmful as long as he's careful. I need air. Are you going to move?"

"No." His hand smoothed down her hip, over her butt and down one thigh. "You have to learn to regulate your breathing. You are not going to suffocate. Think of filling your lungs with air. It will come to you."

"I see. This is training."

"Yes. And you are doing very well, Lorraine. So far you have not panicked."

"There are other ways to train me in filling my lungs various ways, you know."

Again, he closed his eyes at the suggestive temptation in her voice. The moment he did, he found her there, the image of her on her knees in front of him, his cock down her throat, holding there while she learned air could find her lungs when needed. His cock stirred all over again. It hadn't taken much. The thought of that mouth surrounding him with heat and fire made him harder than ever. His hand stroked her bottom again and then slid lower, between her legs, fingers whispering over her sensitive clit.

"Are you trying to get out of teaching those little girls?"

"Yes. Absolutely. If you give me a training lesson, no one can say anything about me being late. I have a really good excuse. I can start their training tomorrow night, unless I don't get this first lesson right away."

Her hips moved, pressing her pelvis deeper into the mattress. He smiled against her back. "I do not know. This lesson may be too advanced. I doubt very much if you can get it in one try."

"I'm willing to do my best."

He slid off her back and rolled over, one hand circling his thick shaft. His erection felt heavy, his need growing. He liked the way she played. The way she made everything fun. Making memories where he had very little. They were all about her. His lifemate. He had no idea how he'd survived without her. When she knelt in front of him, took him into her mouth, swallowing him deep, lips stretched around him and her green eyes staring up at him, he didn't know if he would even survive with her.

# APPENDIX I

## Carpathian Healing Chants

To rightly understand Carpathian healing chants, background is required in several areas:

1. The Carpathian view on healing
2. The Lesser Healing Chant of the Carpathians
3. The Great Healing Chant of the Carpathians
4. Carpathian musical aesthetics
5. Lullaby
6. Song to Heal the Earth
7. Carpathian chanting technique

## 1. THE CARPATHIAN VIEW ON HEALING

The Carpathians are a nomadic people whose geographic origins can be traced at least as far as the Southern Ural Mountains (near the steppes of modern-day Kazakhstan), on the border between Europe and Asia. (For this reason, modern-day linguists call their language "proto-Uralic," without knowing that this is the language of the Carpathians.) Unlike most nomadic peoples, the Carpathians did not wander due to the need to find new grazing lands as the seasons and climate shifted, or to search for better trade. Instead, the Carpathians' movements were driven by a great purpose: to find a land that would have the right earth, a soil with the kind of richness that would greatly enhance their rejuvenative powers.

Over the centuries, they migrated westward (some six thousand years ago), until they at last found their perfect homeland—their *susu*—in the Carpathian Mountains, whose long arc cradled the lush plains of the kingdom of Hungary. (The kingdom of Hungary flourished for over a millennium—making Hungarian the dominant language of the Carpathian Basin—until the kingdom's lands were split among several countries after World War I: Austria, Czechoslovakia, Romania, Yugoslavia and modern Hungary.)

Other peoples from the Southern Urals (who shared the Carpathian language, but were not Carpathians) migrated in different directions. Some ended up in Finland, which explains why the modern Hungarian and Finnish languages are among the contemporary descendants of the ancient Carpathian language. Even though they are tied forever to their chosen Carpathian homeland, the Carpathians continue to wander as they search

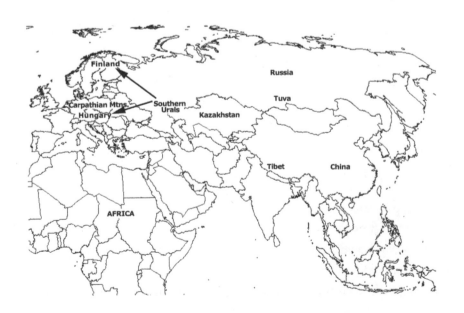

the world for the answers that will enable them to bear and raise their offspring without difficulty.

Because of their geographic origins, the Carpathian views on healing share much with the larger Eurasian shamanistic tradition. Probably the closest modern representative of that tradition is based in Tuva (and is referred to as "Tuvinian Shamanism")—see the map on the previous page.

The Eurasian shamanistic tradition—from the Carpathians to the Siberian shamans—held that illness originated in the human soul, and only later manifested as various physical conditions. Therefore, shamanistic healing, while not neglecting the body, focused on the soul and its healing. The most profound illnesses were understood to be caused by "soul departure," where all or some part of the sick person's soul has wandered away from the body (into the nether realms), or has been captured or possessed by an evil spirit, or both.

The Carpathians belong to this greater Eurasian shamanistic tradition and share its viewpoints. While the Carpathians themselves did not succumb to illness, Carpathian healers understood that the most profound wounds were also accompanied by a similar "soul departure."

Upon reaching the diagnosis of "soul departure," the healer-shaman is then required to make a spiritual journey into the netherworlds to recover the soul. The shaman may have to overcome tremendous challenges along the way, particularly fighting the demon or vampire who has possessed his friend's soul.

"Soul departure" doesn't require a person to be unconscious (although that certainly can be the case as well). It was understood that a person could still appear to be conscious, even talk and interact with others, and yet be missing a part of their soul. The experienced healer or shaman would instantly see the problem nonetheless, in subtle signs that others might miss: the person's attention wandering every now and then, a lessening in their enthusiasm about life, chronic depression, a diminishment in the brightness of their "aura" and the like.

## 2. THE LESSER HEALING CHANT OF THE CARPATHIANS

*Kepä Sarna Pus* (The Lesser Healing Chant) is used for wounds that are merely physical in nature. The Carpathian healer leaves his body and enters the wounded Carpathian's body to heal great mortal wounds from the inside out using pure energy. He proclaims, "I offer freely my life for your life," as he gives his blood to the injured Carpathian. Because the Carpathians are of the earth and bound to the soil, they are healed by the soil of their homeland. Their saliva is also often used for its rejuvenative powers.

It is also very common for the Carpathian chants (both the Lesser and the Great) to be accompanied by the use of healing herbs, aromas from Carpathian candles and crystals. The crystals (when combined with the Carpathians' empathic, psychic connection to the entire universe) are used to gather positive energy from their surroundings, which then is used to accelerate the healing. Caves are sometimes used as the setting for the healing.

The Lesser Healing Chant was used by Vikirnoff Von Shrieder and Colby Jansen to heal Rafael De La Cruz, whose heart had been ripped out by a vampire as described in *Dark Secret*.

### *Kepä Sarna Pus* (The Lesser Healing Chant)
*The same chant is used for all physical wounds. "Sívadaba" ("into your heart") would be changed to refer to whatever part of the body is wounded.*

*Kuńasz, nélkül sívdobbanás, nélkül fesztelen löyly.*
You lie as if asleep, without beat of heart, without airy breath.

*Ot élidamet andam szabadon élidadért.*
I offer freely my life for your life.

*O jelä sielam jörem ot ainamet és soŋe ot élidadet.*
My spirit of light forgets my body and enters your body.

*O jelä sielam pukta kinn minden szelemeket belső.*
My spirit of light sends all the dark spirits within fleeing without.

*Pajńak o susu hanyet és o nyelv nyálamet sívadaba.*

I press the earth of our homeland and the spit of my tongue into your
 heart.


*Vii, o verim soɲe o verid andam.*

At last, I give you my blood for your blood.


To hear this chant, visit: http://www.christinefeehan.com/members/.


## 3. THE GREAT HEALING CHANT OF THE CARPATHIANS

The most well-known—and most dramatic—of the Carpathian healing
chants is ***En Sarna Pus* (The Great Healing Chant)**. This chant is reserved
for recovering the wounded or unconscious Carpathian's soul.

Typically a group of men would form a circle around the sick
Carpathian (to "encircle him with our care and compassion") and begin
the chant. The shaman or healer or leader is the prime actor in this healing
ceremony. It is he who will actually make the spiritual journey into the
netherworld, aided by his clanspeople. Their purpose is to ecstatically
dance, sing, drum and chant, all the while visualizing (through the words
of the chant) the journey itself—every step of it, over and over again—to
the point where the shaman, in trance, leaves his body, and makes that
very journey. (Indeed, the word *ecstasy* is from the Latin *ex statis*, which
literally means "out of the body.")

One advantage that the Carpathian healer has over many other shamans is his telepathic link to his lost brother. Most shamans must wander
in the dark of the nether realms in search of their lost brother. But the
Carpathian healer directly "hears" in his mind the voice of his lost brother
calling to him, and can thus "zero in on" his soul like a homing beacon.
For this reason, Carpathian healing tends to have a higher success rate
than most other traditions of this sort.

Something of the geography of the "other world" is useful for us to
examine, in order to fully understand the words of the Great Carpathian
Healing Chant. A reference is made to the "Great Tree" (in Carpathian:

*En Puwe*). Many ancient traditions, including the Carpathian tradition, understood the worlds—the heaven worlds, our world and the nether realms—to be "hung" upon a great pole, or axis, or tree. Here on earth, we are positioned halfway up this tree, on one of its branches. Hence many ancient texts referred to the material world as "middle earth": midway between heaven and hell. Climbing the tree would lead one to the heaven worlds. Descending the tree to its roots would lead to the nether realms. The shaman was necessarily a master of movement up and down the Great Tree, sometimes moving unaided, and sometimes assisted by (or even mounted upon the back of) an animal spirit guide. In various traditions, this Great Tree was known variously as the *axis mundi* (the "axis of the worlds"), Ygddrasil (in Norse mythology), Mount Meru (the sacred world mountain of Tibetan tradition), etc. The Christian cosmos, with its heaven, purgatory/earth and hell, is also worth comparing. It is even given a similar topography in Dante's *Divine Comedy*: Dante is led on a journey first to hell, at the center of the earth; then upward to Mount Purgatory, which sits on the earth's surface directly opposite Jerusalem; then farther upward first to Eden, the earthly paradise, at the summit of Mount Purgatory; and then upward at last to Heaven.

In the shamanistic tradition, it was understood that the small always reflects the large; the personal always reflects the cosmic. A movement in the greater dimensions of the cosmos also coincides with an internal movement. For example, the *axis mundi* of the cosmos corresponds with the spinal column of the individual. Journeys up and down the *axis mundi* often coincided with the movements of natural and spiritual energies (sometimes called *kundalini* or *shakti*) in the spinal column of the shaman or mystic.

### *En Sarna Pus* (The Great Healing Chant)
*In this chant, ekä ("brother") would be replaced by "sister," "father," "mother," depending on the person to be healed.*

*Ot ekäm ainajanak hany, jama.*
My brother's body is a lump of earth, close to death.

*Me, ot ekäm kuntajanak, pirädak ekäm, gond és irgalom türe.*
We, the clan of my brother, encircle him with our care and compassion.

*O pus wäkenkek, ot oma śarnank, és ot pus fünk, álnak ekäm ainajanak,*
*pitänak ekäm ainajanak elävä.*
Our healing energies, ancient words of magic and healing herbs bless
my brother's body, keep it alive.

*Ot ekäm sielanak pälä. Ot omboće päläja juta alatt o jüti, kinta, és szelemek*
*lamtijaknak.*
But my brother's soul is only half. His other half wanders in the
netherworld.

*Ot en mekem ŋamaŋ: kulkedak otti ot ekäm omboće päläjanak.*
My great deed is this: I travel to find my brother's other half.

*Rekatüre, saradak, tappadak, odam, kuŋa o numa waram, és avaa owe o*
*lewl mahoz.*
We dance, we chant, we dream ecstatically, to call my spirit bird, and to
open the door to the other world.

*Ntak o numa waram, és mozdulak; jomadak.*
I mount my spirit bird and we begin to move; we are under way.

*Piwtädak ot En Puwe tyvinak, ećidak alatt o jüti, kinta, és szelemek*
*lamtijaknak.*
Following the trunk of the Great Tree, we fall into the netherworld.

*Fázak, fázak nó o śaro.*
It is cold, very cold.

*Juttadak ot ekäm o akarataban, o sívaban és o sielaban.*
My brother and I are linked in mind, heart and soul.

*Ot ekäm sielanak kaŋa engem.*
My brother's soul calls to me.

*Kuledak és piwtädak ot ekäm.*
I hear and follow his track.

*Saɣedak és tuledak ot ekäm kulyanak.*
Encounter I the demon who is devouring my brother's soul.

*Nenäm ćoro, o kuly torodak.*
In anger, I fight the demon.

*O kuly pél engem.*
He is afraid of me.

*Lejkkadak o kaŋka salamaval.*
I strike his throat with a lightning bolt.

*Molodak ot ainaja komakamal.*
I break his body with my bare hands.

*Toja és molanâ.*
He is bent over, and falls apart.

*Hän ćaδa.*
He runs away.

*Manedak ot ekäm sielanak.*
I rescue my brother's soul.

*Alɘdak ot ekam sielanak o komamban.*
I lift my brother's soul in the hollow of my hand.

*Alɘdam ot ekam numa waramra.*
I lift him onto my spirit bird.

*Piwtädak ot En Puwe tyvijanak és saɣedak jälleen ot elävä ainak majaknak.*
Following up the Great Tree, we return to the land of the living.

*Ot ekäm elä jälleen.*
My brother lives again.

*Ot ekäm weńća jälleen.*
He is complete again.

To hear this chant, visit: http://www.christinefeehan.com/members/.

## 4. CARPATHIAN MUSICAL AESTHETICS

In the sung Carpathian pieces (such as the "Lullaby" and the "Song to Heal the Earth"), you'll hear elements that are shared by many of the musical traditions in the Uralic geographical region, some of which still exist—from Eastern European (Bulgarian, Romanian, Hungarian, Croatian, etc.) to Romany ("gypsy"). These elements include:

- the rapid alternation between major and minor modalities, including a sudden switch (called a "Picardy third") from minor to major to end a piece or section (as at the end of the "Lullaby")
- the use of close (tight) harmonies
- the use of *ritardi* (slowing down the piece) and *crescendi* (swelling in volume) for brief periods
- the use of *glissandi* (slides) in the singing tradition
- the use of trills in the singing tradition (as in the final invocation of the "Song to Heal the Earth")—similar to Celtic, a singing tradition more familiar to many of us
- the use of parallel fifths (as in the final invocation of the "Song to Heal the Earth")
- controlled use of dissonance
- "call and response" chanting (typical of many of the world's chanting traditions)

- extending the length of a musical line (by adding a couple of bars) to heighten dramatic effect
- and many more

"Lullaby" and "Song to Heal the Earth" illustrate two rather different forms of Carpathian music (a quiet, intimate piece and an energetic ensemble piece)—but whatever the form, Carpathian music is full of feeling.

## 5. LULLABY

This song is sung by a woman while a child is still in the womb or when the threat of a miscarriage is apparent. The baby can hear the song while inside the mother, and the mother can connect with the child telepathically as well. The lullaby is meant to reassure the child, to encourage the baby to hold on, to stay—to reassure the child that he or she will be protected by love even from inside until birth. The last line literally means that the mother's love will protect her child until the child is born ("rise").

Musically, the Carpathian "Lullaby" is in three-quarter time ("waltz time"), as are a significant portion of the world's various traditional lullabies (perhaps the most famous of which is "Brahms' Lullaby"). The arrangement for solo voice is the original context: a mother singing to her child, unaccompanied. The arrangement for chorus and violin ensemble illustrates how musical even the simplest Carpathian pieces often are, and how easily they lend themselves to contemporary instrumental or orchestral arrangements. (A wide range of contemporary composers, including Dvořák and Smetana, have taken advantage of a similar discovery, working other traditional Eastern European music into their symphonic poems.)

### Odam-Sarna Kondak (Lullaby)

*Tumtesz o wäke ku pitasz belsö.*
Feel the strength you hold inside.

*Hiszasz sívadet. Én olenam gæidnod.*
Trust your heart. I'll be your guide.

*Sas csecsemõm; kuńasz.*
Hush, my baby; close your eyes.

*Rauho joņe ted.*
Peace will come to you.

*Tumtesz o sívdobbanás ku olen lamt3ad belső.*
Feel the rhythm deep inside.

*Gond-kumpadek ku kim te.*
Waves of love that cover you.

*Pesänak te, asti o jüti, kidüsz.*
Protect, until the night you rise.

To hear this song, visit: http://www.christinefeehan.com/members/.

## 6. SONG TO HEAL THE EARTH

This is the earth-healing song that is used by the Carpathian women to heal soil filled with various toxins. The women take a position on four sides and call to the universe to draw on the healing energy with love and respect. The soil of the earth is their resting place, the place where they rejuvenate, and they must make it safe not only for themselves but for their unborn children as well as their men and living children. This is a beautiful ritual performed by the women together, raising their voices in harmony and calling on the earth's minerals and healing properties to come forth and help them save their children. They literally dance and sing to heal the earth in a ceremony as old as their species. The dance and notes of the song are adjusted according to the toxins felt through the healer's bare feet. The feet are placed in a certain pattern and the hands gracefully weave a healing spell while the dance is performed. They must be especially careful when the soil is prepared for babies. This is a ceremony of love and healing.

Musically, the ritual is divided into several sections:

- **First verse**: A "call and response" section, where the chant leader sings the "call" solo, and then some or all of the women sing the "response" in the close harmony style typical of the Carpathian musical tradition. The repeated response—*Ai Emä Maye*—is an invocation of the source of power for the healing ritual: "Oh, Mother Nature."
- **First chorus**: This section is filled with clapping, dancing, ancient horns and other means used to invoke and heighten the energies upon which the ritual is drawing.
- **Second verse**
- **Second chorus**
- **Closing invocation:** In this closing part, two song leaders, in close harmony, take all the energy gathered by the earlier portions of the song/ritual and focus it entirely on the healing purpose.

What you will be listening to are brief tastes of what would typically be a significantly longer ritual, in which the verse and chorus parts are developed and repeated many times, to be closed by a single rendition of the final invocation.

### *Sarna Pusm O Mayet* (Song to Heal the Earth)

*First verse*
**Ai, Emä Maye,**
Oh, Mother Nature,

**Me sívadbin lañaak.**
We are your beloved daughters.

*Me tappadak, me pusmak o maγet.*
We dance to heal the earth.

*Me sarnadak, me pusmak o hanyet.*
We sing to heal the earth.

*Sielanket jutta tedet it,*
We join with you now,

*Sívank és akaratank és sielank juttanak.*
Our hearts and minds and spirits become one.

*Second verse*
*Ai, Emä maγe,*
Oh, Mother Nature,

*Me sívadbin lańaak.*
We are your beloved daughters.

*Me andak arwadet emänked és me kaŋank o*
We pay homage to our mother and call upon the

*Põhi és Lõuna, Ida és Lääs.*
North and South, East and West.

*Pide és aldyn és myös belső.*
Above and below and within as well.

*Gondank o maγenak pusm hän ku olen jama.*
Our love of the land heals that which is in need.

*Juttanak teval it,*
We join with you now,

*Ma ye ma yeval.*
Earth to earth.

*O pirä elidak weńća.*
The circle of life is complete.

To hear this chant, visit: http://www.christinefeehan.com/members/.

## 7. CARPATHIAN CHANTING TECHNIQUE

As with their healing techniques, the actual "chanting technique" of the Carpathians has much in common with the other shamanistic traditions of the Central Asian steppes. The primary mode of chanting was throat chanting using overtones. Modern examples of this manner of singing can still be found in the Mongolian, Tuvan and Tibetan traditions. You can find an audio example of the Gyuto Tibetan Buddhist monks engaged in throat chanting at: http://www.christinefeehan.com/carpathian_chanting/.

As with Tuva, note on the map the geographical proximity of Tibet to Kazakhstan and the Southern Urals.

The beginning part of the Tibetan chant emphasizes synchronizing all the voices around a single tone, aimed at healing a particular "chakra" of the body. This is fairly typical of the Gyuto throat-chanting tradition, but it is not a significant part of the Carpathian tradition. Nonetheless, it serves as an interesting contrast.

The part of the Gyuto chanting example that is most similar to the Carpathian style of chanting is the midsection, where the men are chanting the words together with great force. The purpose here is not to generate a "healing tone" that will affect a particular "chakra," but rather to generate as much power as possible for initiating the "out of body" travel, and for fighting the demonic forces that the healer/traveler must face and overcome.

The songs of the Carpathian women (illustrated by their "Lullaby" and their "Song to Heal the Earth") are part of the same ancient musical and healing tradition as the Lesser and Great Healing Chants of the warrior males. You can hear some of the same instruments in both the male warriors' healing chants and the women's "Song to Heal the Earth." Also, they share the common purpose of generating and directing power. However, the women's songs are distinctively feminine in character. One immediately noticeable difference is that, while the men speak their words in the manner of a chant, the women sing songs with melodies and harmonies, softening the overall performance. A feminine, nurturing quality is especially evident in the "Lullaby."

# APPENDIX 2

## The Carpathian Language

Like all human languages, the language of the Carpathians contains the richness and nuance that can only come from a long history of use. At best we can only touch on some of the main features of the language in this brief appendix:

1. The history of the Carpathian language
2. Carpathian grammar and other characteristics of the language
3. Examples of the Carpathian language (including the Ritual Words and the Warriors' Chant)
4. A much-abridged Carpathian dictionary

## 1. THE HISTORY OF THE CARPATHIAN LANGUAGE

The Carpathian language of today is essentially identical to the Carpathian language of thousands of years ago. A "dead" language like the Latin of two thousand years ago has evolved into a significantly different modern language (Italian) because of countless generations of speakers and great historical fluctuations. In contrast, many of the speakers of Carpathian from thousands of years ago are still alive. Their presence—coupled with the deliberate isolation of the Carpathians from the other major forces of change in the world—has acted (and continues to act) as a stabilizing force that has preserved the integrity of the language over the centuries. Carpathian culture has also acted as a stabilizing force. For instance, the Ritual Words, the various healing chants (see Appendix 1) and other cultural artifacts have been passed down through the centuries with great fidelity.

One small exception should be noted: the splintering of the Carpathians into separate geographic regions has led to some minor dialectization. However, the telepathic link among all Carpathians (as well as each Carpathian's regular return to his or her homeland) has ensured that the differences among dialects are relatively superficial (e.g., small numbers of new words, minor differences in pronunciation, etc.), since the deeper, internal language of mind-forms has remained the same because of continuous use across space and time.

The Carpathian language was (and still is) the proto-language for the Uralic (or Finno-Ugric) family of languages. Today, the Uralic languages are spoken in northern, eastern and central Europe and in Siberia. More than twenty-three million people in the world speak languages that can trace their ancestry to Carpathian. Magyar or Hungarian (about fourteen million speakers), Finnish (about five million speakers) and Estonian (about one million speakers) are the three major contemporary descendents of this proto-language. The only factor that unites the more than twenty languages in the Uralic family is that their ancestry can be traced back to a common proto-language—Carpathian—that split (starting some six thousand years ago) into the various languages in the Uralic family. In the same way, European languages such as English and French belong to the better-known Indo-European family and also evolved from a common proto-language ancestor (a different one from Carpathian).

The following table provides a sense of some of the similarities in the language family.

**Note:** The Finnic/Carpathian "k" shows up often as Hungarian "h." Similarly, the Finnic/Carpathian "p" often corresponds to the Hungarian "f."

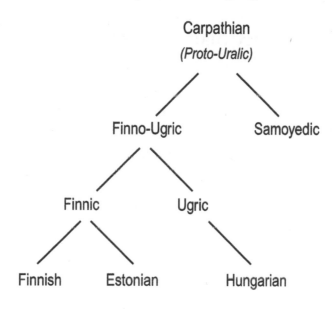

| Carpathian (proto-Uralic) | Finnish (Suomi) | Hungarian (Magyar) |
|---|---|---|
| *elä*—live | *elä*—live | *él*—live |
| *elid*—life | *elinikä*—life | *élet*—life |
| *pesä*—nest | *pesä*—nest | *fészek*—nest |
| *kola*—die | *kuole*—die | *hal*—die |
| *pälä*—half, side | *pieltä*—tilt, tip to the side | *fél, fele*—fellow human, friend (half; one side of two) *feleség*—wife |
| *and*—give | *anta, antaa*—give | *ad*—give |
| *koje*—husband, man | *koira*—dog, the male (of animals) | *here*—drone, testicle |
| *wäke*—power | *väki*—folks, people, men; force | *val/-vel*—with (instrumental suffix) |
| | *väkevä*—powerful, strong | *vele*—with him/her/it |
| *wete*—water | *vesi*—water | *víz*—water |

## 2. CARPATHIAN GRAMMAR AND OTHER CHARACTERISTICS OF THE LANGUAGE

**Idioms.** As both an ancient language and a language of an earth people, Carpathian is more inclined toward use of idioms constructed from concrete, "earthy" terms rather than abstractions. For instance, our modern abstraction "to cherish" is expressed more concretely in Carpathian as "to hold in one's heart"; the "netherworld" is, in Carpathian, "the land of night, fog and ghosts"; etc.

**Word order.** The order of words in a sentence is determined not by syntactic roles (like subject, verb and object) but rather by pragmatic, discourse-driven factors. Examples: *"Tied vagyok."* ("Yours am I."); *"Sívamet andam."* ("My heart I give you.")

**Agglutination.** The Carpathian language is agglutinative; that is, longer words are constructed from smaller components. An agglutinating language uses suffixes or prefixes whose meanings are generally unique, and which are concatenated one after another without overlap. In Carpathian, words typically consist of a stem that is followed by one or more suffixes. For example, *"sívambam"* derives from the stem *"sív"* ("heart"), followed by *"am"* ("my," making it "my heart"), followed by *"bam"* ("in," making it "in my heart"). As you might imagine, agglutination in Carpathian can sometimes produce very long words, or words that are very difficult to pronounce. Vowels often get inserted between suffixes to prevent too many consonants from appearing in a row (which can make a word unpronounceable).

**Noun cases.** Like all languages, Carpathian has many noun cases; the same noun will be "spelled" differently depending on its role in a sentence. The noun cases include: nominative (when the noun is the subject of the sentence), accusative (when the noun is a direct object of the verb), dative (indirect object), genitive (or possessive), instrumental, final, suppressive, inessive, elative, terminative and delative.

We will use the possessive (or genitive) case as an example to illustrate how all noun cases in Carpathian involve adding standard suffixes to the noun stems. Thus expressing possession in Carpathian—"my lifemate," "your lifemate," "his lifemate," "her lifemate," etc.—involves adding a particular suffix (such as "-*am*") to the noun stem (*"päläfertiil"*) to produce the possessive (*"päläfertiilam"*—"my lifemate"). Which suffix to use depends upon which person ("my," "your," "his," etc.) and whether the noun ends in a consonant or a vowel. The table below shows the suffixes for singular nouns only (not plural), and also shows the similarity to the suffixes used in contemporary Hungarian. (Hungarian is actually a little more complex, in that it also requires "vowel rhyming": which suffix to use also depends on the last vowel in the noun; hence the multiple choices in the cells below, where Carpathian only has a single choice.)

| | Carpathian (proto-Uralic) | | Contemporary Hungarian | |
| --- | --- | --- | --- | --- |
| **person** | **noun ends in vowel** | **noun ends in consonant** | **noun ends in vowel** | **noun ends in consonant** |
| 1st singular (my) | -m | -am | -m | -om, -em, -öm |
| 2nd singular (your) | -d | -ad | -d | -od, -ed, -öd |
| 3rd singular (his, her, its) | -ja | -a | -ja/-je | -a, -e |
| 1st plural (our) | -nk | -ank | -nk | -unk, -ünk |
| 2nd plural (your) | -tak | -atak | -tok, -tek, -tök | -otok, -etek, -ötök |
| 3rd plural (their) | -jak | -ak | -juk, -jük | -uk, -ük |

**Note:** As mentioned earlier, vowels often get inserted between the word and its suffix so as to prevent too many consonants from appearing in a row (which would produce unpronounceable words). For example, in the table on the previous page, all nouns that end in a consonant are followed by suffixes beginning with "a."

**Verb conjugation.** Like its modern descendents (such as Finnish and Hungarian), Carpathian has many verb tenses, far too many to describe here. We will just focus on the conjugation of the present tense. Again, we will place contemporary Hungarian side by side with Carpathian, because of the marked similarity between the two.

As with the possessive case for nouns, the conjugation of verbs is done by adding a suffix onto the verb stem:

| Person | Carpathian (proto-Uralic) | Contemporary Hungarian |
|---|---|---|
| 1st singular (I give) | -am (andam), -ak | -ok, -ek, -ök |
| 2nd singular (you give) | -sz (andsz) | -sz |
| 3rd singular (he/she/it gives) | — (and) | — |
| 1st plural (we give) | -ak (andak) | -unk, -ünk |
| 2nd plural (you give) | -tak (andtak) | -tok, -tek, -tök |
| 3rd plural (they give) | -nak (andnak) | -nak, -nek |

As with all languages, there are many "irregular verbs" in Carpathian that don't exactly fit this pattern. But the above table is still a useful guide for most verbs.

## 3. EXAMPLES OF THE CARPATHIAN LANGUAGE

Here are some brief examples of conversational Carpathian, used in the Dark books. We include the literal translation in square brackets. It is interestingly different from the most appropriate English translation.

**Susu.**
I am home.
["home/birthplace." "I am" is understood, as is often the case in Carpathian.]

**Möért?**
What for?

**csitri**
little one
["little slip of a thing," "little slip of a girl"]

**ainaak enyém**
forever mine

**ainaak sívamet jutta**
forever mine (another form)
["forever to-my-heart connected/fixed"]

**sívamet**
my love
["of-my-heart," "to my-heart"]

**Tet vigyázam.**
I love you.
["you-love-I"]

*Sarna Rituaali* (The Ritual Words) is a longer example, and an example of chanted rather than conversational Carpathian. Note the recurring use of *"andam"* ("I give"), to give the chant musicality and force through repetition.

**Sarna Rituaali (The Ritual Words)**

**Te avio päläfertiilam.**
You are my lifemate.

*Éntölam kuulua, avio päläfertiilam.*
I claim you as my lifemate.

*Ted kuuluak, kacad, kojed.*
I belong to you.

*Élidamet andam.*
I offer my life for you.

*Pesämet andam.*
I give you my protection.

*Uskolfertiilamet andam.*
I give you my allegiance.

*Sívamet andam.*
I give you my heart.

*Sielamet andam.*
I give you my soul.

*Ainamet andam.*
I give you my body.

*Sívamet kuuluak kaik että a ted.*
I take into my keeping the same that is yours.

*Ainaak olenszal sívambin.*
Your life will be cherished by me for all my time.

*Te élidet ainaak pide minan.*
Your life will be placed above my own for all time.

*Te avio päläfertiilam.*
You are my lifemate.

*Ainaak sívamet jutta oleny.*
You are bound to me for all eternity.

*Ainaak terád vigyázak.*
You are always in my care.

To hear these words pronounced (and for more about Carpathian pronunciation altogether), please visit: http://www.christinefeehan.com /members/.

*Sarna Kontakawk* (**The Warriors' Chant**) is another longer example of the Carpathian language. The warriors' council takes place deep beneath the earth in a chamber of crystals with magma far below it, so the steam is natural and the wisdom of their ancestors is clear and focused. This is a sacred place where they bloodswear to their prince and people and affirm their code of honor as warriors and brothers. It is also where battle strategies are born and all dissension is discussed as well as any concerns the warriors have that they wish to bring to the council and open for discussion.

## *Sarna Kontakawk* (The Warriors' Chant)

*Veri isäakank—veri ekäakank.*
Blood of our fathers—blood of our brothers.

*Veri olen elid.*
Blood is life.

*Andak veri-elidet Karpatiiakank, és wäke-sarna ku meke arwa-arvo, irgalom, hän ku agba, és wäke kutni, ku manaak verival.*
We offer that life to our people with a bloodsworn vow of honor, mercy, integrity and endurance.

*Verink sokta; verink kaŋa terád.*
Our blood mingles and calls to you.

*Akasz énak ku kaŋa és juttasz kuntatak it.*
Heed our summons and join with us now.

To hear these words pronounced (and for more about Carpathian pronunciation altogether), please visit: http://www.christinefeehan.com /members/.

See **Appendix 1** for Carpathian healing chants, including the *Kepä Sarna Pus* (The Lesser Healing Chant), the *En Sarna Pus* (The Great Healing Chant), the *Odam-Sarna Kondak* (Lullaby) and the *Sarna Pusm O Mayet* (Song to Heal the Earth).

## 4. A MUCH-ABRIDGED CARPATHIAN DICTIONARY

This very-much-abridged Carpathian dictionary contains most of the Carpathian words used in the Dark books. Of course, a full Carpathian dictionary would be as large as the usual dictionary for an entire language (typically more than a hundred thousand words).

**Note:** The Carpathian nouns and verbs below are word **stems**. They generally do not appear in their isolated "stem" form, as below. Instead, they usually appear with suffixes (e.g., *andam—I give*, rather than just the root, *and*).

**a**—verb negation (*prefix*); not (*adverb*).
**aćke**—pace, step.
**aćke éntölem it**—take another step toward me.
**agba**—to be seemly; to be proper (*verb*). True; seemly; proper (*adj.*)
**ai**—oh.
**aina**—body (*noun*).
**ainaak**—always; forever.
**o ainaak jelä peje emnimet ŋamaŋ**—sun scorch that woman forever
    (*Carpathian swear words*).
**ainaakä**—never.
**ainaakfél**—old friend.

**ak**—suffix added after a noun ending in a consonant to make it plural.

**aka**—to give heed; to hearken; to listen.

**aka-arvo**—respect (*noun*).

**akarat**—mind; will (*noun*).

**ál**—to bless; to attach to.

**alatt**—through.

**aldyn**—under; underneath.

**alə**—to lift; to raise.

**alte**—to bless; to curse.

**amaŋ**—this; this one here; that; that one there.

**and**—to give.

**and sielet, arwa-arvomet, és jelämet, kuulua huvémet ku feaj és ködet ainaak**—to trade soul, honor and salvation för momentary pleasure and endless damnation.

**andasz éntölem irgalomet!**—have mercy!

**arvo**—value; price (*noun*).

**arwa**—praise (*noun*).

**arwa-arvod**—honor (*noun*).

**arwa-arvod mäne me ködak**—may your honor hold back the dark (*greeting*).

**arwa-arvo olen gæidnod, ekäm**—honor guide you, my brother (*greeting*).

**arwa-arvo olen isäntä, ekäm**—honor keep you, my brother (*greeting*).

**arwa-arvo pile sívadet**—may honor light your heart (*greeting*).

**aš**—no (*exclamation*).

**ašša**—no (before a noun); not (with a verb that is not in the imperative); not (with an adjective).

**aššatotello**—disobedient.

**asti**—until.

**avaa**—to open.

**avio**—wedded.

**avio päläfertiil**—lifemate.

**avoi**—uncover; show; reveal.

**baszú**—revenge; vengeance.

**belső**—within; inside.

**bur**—good; well.

**bur tule ekämet kuntamak**—well met brother-kin (*greeting*).

**ćaδa**—to flee; to run; to escape.

**čač3**—to be born; to grow.

**ćoro**—to flow; to run like rain.

**csecsemõ**—baby (*noun*).

**csitri**—little one (*female*).

**diutal**—triumph; victory.

**džinõt**—brief; short.

**eći**—to fall.

**ej**—not (*adverb, suffix*); *nej* when preceding syllable ends in a vowel.

**ek**—suffix added after a noun ending in a consonant to make it plural.

**ekä**—brother.

**ekäm**—my brother.

**elä**—to live.

**eläsz arwa-arvoval**—may you live with honor; live nobly (*greeting*).

**eläsz jeläbam ainaak**—long may you live in the light (*greeting*).

**elävä**—alive.

**elävä ainak majaknak**—land of the living.

**elid**—life.

**emä**—mother (*noun*).

**Emä Maγe**—Mother Nature.

**emäen**—grandmother.

**embɛ**—if; when.

**embɛ karmasz**—please.

**emni**—wife; woman.

**emni hän ku köd alte**—cursed woman.

**emni kuŋenak ku aššatotello**—disobedient lunatic.

**emnim**—my wife; my woman.

**én**—I.

**en**—great; many; big.

**en hän ku pesä**—the protector (literally: the great protector).

**en Karpatii**—the prince (literally: the great Carpathian).

**enä**—most.

**enkojra**—wolf.

**én jutta félet és ekämet**—I greet a friend and brother (*greeting*).

**én maɣenak**—I am of the earth.

**én oma maɣeka**—I am as old as time (literally: as old as the earth).

**En Puwe**—The Great Tree. Related to the legends of Ygddrasil, the axis mundi, Mount Meru, heaven and hell, etc.

**engem**—of me.

**és**—and.

**év**—year.

**évsatz**—century.

**ete**—before; in front of.

**että**—that.

**fáz**—to feel cold or chilly.

**fél**—fellow; friend.

**fél ku kuuluaak sívam belső**—beloved.

**fél ku vigyázak**—dear one.

**feldolgaz**—prepare.

**fertiil**—fertile one.

**fesztelen**—airy.

**fü**—herbs; grass.

**gæidno**—road; way.

**gond**—care; worry; love (*noun*).

**hän**—he; she; it; one.

**hän agba**—it is so.

**hän ku**—prefix: one who; he who; that which.

**hän ku agba**—truth.

**hän ku kaśwa o numamet**—sky-owner.

**hän ku kuulua sívamet**—keeper of my heart.

**hän ku lejkka wäke-sarnat**—traitor.

**hän ku meke pirämet**—defender.

**hän ku pesä**—protector.

**hän ku pesäk kaikak**—guardians of all.

**hän ku piwtä**—predator; hunter; tracker.

**hän ku pusm**—healer.

**hän ku saa kuć3aket**—star-reacher.

**hän ku tappa**—killer; violent person (*noun*). Deadly; violent (*adj.*).

**hän ku tuulmahl elidet**—vampire (literally: life-stealer).

**hän ku vie elidet**—vampire (literally: thief of life).

**hän ku vigyáz sielamet**—keeper of my soul.

**hän ku vigyáz sívamet és sielamet**—keeper of my heart and soul.

**hän sívamak**—beloved.

**hängem**—him; her; it.

**hank**—they.

**hany**—clod; lump of earth.

**hisz**—to believe; to trust.

**ho**—how.

**ida**—east.

**igazág**—justice.

**ila**—to shine.

**inan**—mine; my own (*endearment*).

**irgalom**—compassion; pity; mercy.

**isä**—father (*noun*).

**isänta**—master of the house.

**it**—now.

**jaguár**—jaguar.

**jaka**—to cut; to divide; to separate.

**jakam**—wound; cut; injury.

**jälleen**—again.

**jama**—to be sick, infected, wounded or dying; to be near death.

**jamatan**—fallen; wounded; near death.

**jelä**—sunlight; day, sun; light.

**jelä keje terád**—light sear you (*Carpathian swear words*).

**o jelä peje kaik hänkanak**—sun scorch them all (*Carpathian swear words*).

**o jelä peje emnimet**—sun scorch the woman (*Carpathian swear words*).

**o jelä peje terád**—sun scorch you (*Carpathian swear words*).

**o jelä peje terád, emni**—sun scorch you, woman (*Carpathian swear words*).

**o jelä sielamak**—light of my soul.

**joma**—to be under way; to go.

**joŋe**—to come; to return.

**joŋesz arwa-arvoval**—return with honor (*greeting*).

**joŋesz éntölem, fél ku kuuluaak sívam belsö**—come to me, beloved.

**jotka**—gap; middle; space.

**jotkan**—between.

**juo**—to drink.

**juosz és eläsz**—drink and live (*greeting*).

**juosz és olen ainaak sielamet jutta**—drink and become one with me (*greeting*).

**juta**—to go; to wander.

**jüti**—night; evening.

**jutta**—connected; fixed (*adj.*). To connect; to join; to fix; to bind (*verb*).

**k**—suffix added after a noun ending in a vowel to make it plural.

**kać3**—gift.

**kaca**—male lover.

**kadi**—judge.

**kaik**—all.

**käktä**—two; many.

**käktäverit**—mixed blood (literally: two bloods).

**kalma**—corpse; death; grave.

**kaŋa**—to call; to invite; to summon; to request; to beg.

**kaŋk**—windpipe; Adam's apple; throat.

**karma**—want.

**Karpatii**—Carpathian.

**karpatii ku köd**—liar.

**Karpatiikunta**—the Carpathian people.

**käsi**—hand.

**kaśwa**—to own.

**kaδa**—to abandon; to leave; to remain.

**kaδa wäkeva óv o köd**—stand fast against the dark (*greeting*).

**kat**—house; family (*noun*).

**katt3**—to move; to penetrate; to proceed.

**keje**—to cook; to burn; to sear.

**kepä**—lesser; small; easy; few.

**kessa**—cat.

**kessa ku toro**—wildcat.

**kessake**—little cat.

**kidü**—to wake up; to arise (*intransitive verb*).

**kim**—to cover an entire object with some sort of covering.

**kinn**—out; outdoors; outside; without.

**kinta**—fog; mist; smoke.

**kislány**—little girl.

**kislány kuŋenak**—little lunatic.

**kislány kuŋenak minan**—my little lunatic.

**köd**—fog; mist; darkness; evil (*noun*). Foggy, dark; evil (*adj.*).

**köd alte hän**—darkness curse it (*Carpathian swear words*).

**o köd belső**—darkness take it (*Carpathian swear words*).

**köd elävä és köd nime kutni nimet**—evil lives and has a name.

**köd jutasz belső**—shadow take you (*Carpathian swear words*).

**koj**—let; allow; decree; establish; order.

**koje**—man; husband; drone.

**kola**—to die.

**kolasz arwa-arvoval**—may you die with honor (*greeting*).

**kolatan**—dead; departed.

**koma**—empty hand; bare hand; palm of the hand; hollow of the hand.

**kond**—all of a family's or clan's children.

**kont**—warrior; man.

**kont o sívanak**—strong heart (literally: heart of the warrior).

**kor3**—basket; container made of birch bark.

**kor3nat**—containing; including.

**ku**—who; which; that; where; which; what.

**kuć3**—star.

**kuć3ak!**—stars! (exclamation).

**kudeje**—descent; generation.

**kuja**—day; sun.

**kule**—to hear.

**kulke**—to go or to travel (on land or water).

**kulkesz arwa-arvoval, ekäm**—walk with honor, my brother (*greeting*).

**kulkesz arwaval, joŋesz arwa arvoval**—go with glory, return with honor (*greeting*).

**kuly**—intestinal worm; tapeworm; demon who possesses and devours souls.

**küm**—human male.

**kumala**—to sacrifice; to offer; to pray.

**kumpa**—wave (*noun*).

**kuńa**—to lie as if asleep; to close or cover the eyes in a game of hide-and-seek; to die.

**kuŋe**—moon; month.

**kunta**—band; clan; tribe; family; people; lineage; line.

**kuras**—sword; large knife.

**kure**—bind; tie.

**kuš**—worker; servant.

**kutenken**—however.

**kutni**—to be able to bear, carry, endure, stand or take.

**kutnisz ainaak**—long may you endure (*greeting*).

**kuulua**—to belong; to hold.

**kužõ**—long.

**lääs**—west.

**lamti (or lamt3)**—lowland; meadow; deep; depth.

**lamti ból jüti, kinta, ja szelem**—the nether world (literally: the meadow of night, mists, and ghosts).

**lańa**—daughter.

**lejkka**—crack; fissure; split (*noun*). To cut; to hit; to strike forcefully (*verb*).

**lewl**—spirit (*noun*).

**lewl ma**—the other world (literally: spirit land). *Lewl ma* includes *lamti ból jüti, kinta, ja szelem*: the nether world, but also includes the worlds higher up *En Puwe*, the Great Tree.

**liha**—flesh.

**lõuna**—south.

**löyly**—breath; steam. (related to *lewl*: spirit).

**luwe**—bone.

**ma**—land; forest; world.

**magköszun**—thank.

**mana**—to abuse; to curse; to ruin.

**mäne**—to rescue; to save.

**maɣe**—land; earth; territory; place; nature.

**mboće**—other; second (*adj.*).

**me**—we.

**megem**—us.

**meke**—deed; work (*noun*). To do; to make; to work (*verb*).

**mić (or mića)**—beautiful.

**mića emni kuŋenak minan**—my beautiful lunatic.

**minden**—every; all (*adj.*).

**möért?**—what for? (*exclamation*).

**molo**—to crush; to break into bits.

**molanâ**—to crumble; to fall apart.

**moo**—why; reason.

**mozdul**—to begin to move; to enter into movement.

**muonì**—appoint; order; prescribe; command.

**muonìak te avoisz te**—I command you to reveal yourself.

**musta**—memory.

**myös**—also.

**m8**—thing; what.

**na**—close; near.

**nä**—for.

**nâbbŏ**—so, then.

**ŋamaŋak**—these; these ones here; those; those ones there.

**nautish**—to enjoy.

**nélkül**—without.

**nenä**—anger.

**nime**—name.

**nókunta**—kinship.

**numa**—god; sky; top; upper part; highest (related to the English word *numinous*).

**numatorkuld**—thunder (literally: sky struggle).

**ńûp@l**—for; to; toward.

**ńûp@l mam**—toward my world.

**nyelv**—tongue.

**nyál**—saliva; spit. (related to *nyelv*: tongue).

**ńiŋ3**—worm; maggot.

**o**—the (used before a noun beginning with a consonant).

**ó**—like; in the same way as; as.

**odam**—to dream; to sleep.

**odam-sarna kondak**—lullaby (literally: sleep-song of children).

**olen**—to be.

**oma**—old; ancient; last; previous.

**omas**—stand.

**ŏrem**—to forget; to lose one's way; to make a mistake.

**ot**—the (used before a noun beginning with a vowel).

**ot (or t)**—past participle (*suffix*).

**óv**—to protect against.

**owe**—door.

**päämoro**—aim; target.

**pajna**—to press.

**pälä**—half; side.

**päläfertiil**—mate or wife.

**päläpälä**—side by side.

**palj3**—more.

**palj3 na éntölem**—closer.

**partiolen**—scout (*noun*).

**peje**—to burn; scorch.

**peje!**—burn! (*Carpathian swear word*).

**peje terád**—get burned (*Carpathian swear words*).

**pél**—to be afraid; to be scared of.

**pesä**—nest (*literal; noun*); protection (*figurative; noun*).

**pesä**—nest; stay (*literal*); protect (*figurative*).

**pesäd te engemal**—you are safe with me.

**pesäsz jeläbam ainaak**—long may you stay in the light (*greeting*).

**pide**—above.

**pile**—to ignite; to light up.

**pion**—soon.

**pirä**—circle; ring (*noun*). To surround; to enclose (*verb*).

**piros**—red.

**pitä**—to keep; to hold; to have; to possess.

**pitäam mustaakad sielpesäambam**—I hold your memories safe in my
  soul.

**pitäsz baszú, piwtäsz igazáget**—no vengeance, only justice.

**piwtä**—to seek; to follow; to follow the track of game; to hunt; to prey
  upon.

**poår**—bit; piece.

**põhi**—north.

**pohoopa**—vigorous.

**pukta**—to drive away; to persecute; to put to flight.

**pus**—healthy; healing.

**puwe**—tree; wood.

**rambsolg**—slave.

**rauho**—peace.

**reka**—ecstasy; trance.

**rituaali**—ritual.

**sa**—sinew; tendon; cord.

**sa4**—to call; to name.

**saa**—arrive, come; become; get, receive.

**saasz hän ku andam szabadon**—take what I freely offer.

**sas**—shoosh (*to a child or baby*).

**saɣe**—to arrive; to come; to reach.

**salama**—lightning; lightning bolt.

**sarna**—words; speech; song; magic incantation (*noun*). To chant; to sing;
  to celebrate (*verb*).

**sarna hän agba**—claim.

**sarna kontakawk**—warriors' chant.

**sarna kunta**—alliance (literally: single tribe through sacred words).

**śaro**—frozen snow.

**satz**—hundred.

**siel**—soul.

**sieljelä isäntä**—purity of soul triumphs.

**sisar**—sister.

**sisarak sívak**—sisters of the heart.

**sisarke**—little sister.

**sív**—heart.

**sív pide köd**—love transcends evil.

**sív pide minden köd**—love transcends all evil.

**sívad olen wäkeva, hän ku piwtä**—may your heart stay strong, hunter (*greeting*).

**sívam és sielam**—my heart and soul.

**sívamet**—my heart.

**sívdobbanás**—heartbeat (*literal*); rhythm (*figurative*).

**sokta**—to mix; to stir around.

**sõl**—dare, venture.

**sõl olen engemal, sarna sívametak**—dare to be with me, song of my heart.

**soŋe**—to enter; to penetrate; to compensate; to replace.

**Susiküm**—Lycan.

**susu**—home; birthplace (*noun*). At home (*adv.*).

**szabadon**—freely.

**szelem**—ghost.

**ször**—time; occasion.

**t (or ot)**—past participle (*suffix*).

**taj**—to be worth.

**taka**—behind; beyond.

**takka**—to hang; to remain stuck.

**takkap**—obstacle; challenge; difficulty; ordeal; trial.

**tappa**—to dance; to stamp with the feet; to kill.

**tasa**—even so; just the same.

**te**—you.

**te kalma, te jama ńiŋ3kval, te apitäsz arwa-arvo**—you are nothing but a walking maggot-infected corpse, without honor.

**te magköszunam nä ŋamaŋ kać3 taka arvo**—thank you for this gift beyond price.

**ted**—yours.

**terád keje**—get scorched (*Carpathian swear words*).

**tõd**—to know.

**tõdak pitäsz wäke bekimet mekesz kaiket**—I know you have the courage to face anything.

**tõdhän**—knowledge.

**tõdhän lõ kuraset agbapäämoroam**—knowledge flies the sword true to its aim.

**toja**—to bend; to bow; to break.

**toro**—to fight; to quarrel.

**torosz wäkeval**—fight fiercely (*greeting*).

**totello**—obey.

**tsak**—only.

**t'šuva vni**—period of time.

**tti**—to look; to see; to find.

**tuhanos**—thousand.

**tuhanos löylyak türelamak saγe diutalet**—a thousand patient breaths bring victory.

**tule**—to meet; to come.

**tuli**—fire.

**tumte**—to feel; to touch; to touch upon.

**türe**—full; satiated; accomplished.

**türelam**—patience.

**türelam agba kontsalamaval**—patience is the warrior's true weapon.

**tyvi**—stem; base; trunk.

**ul3**—very; exceedingly; quite.

**umuš**—wisdom; discernment.

**und**—past participle (*suffix*).

**uskol**—faithful.

**uskolfertiil**—allegiance; loyalty.

**usm**—to heal; to be restored to health.

**vár**—to wait.

**varolind**—dangerous.

**veri**—blood.

**veri ekäakank**—blood of our brothers.

**veri-elidet**—blood-life.

**veri isäakank**—blood of our fathers.

**veri olen piros, ekäm**—literally: blood be red, my brother; figuratively: find your lifemate (*greeting*).

**veriak ot en Karpatiiak**—by the blood of the prince (literally: by the blood of the great Carpathian; *Carpathian swear words*).

**veridet peje**—may your blood burn (*Carpathian swear words*).

**vigyáz**—to love; to care for; to take care of.

**vii**—last; at last; finally.

**wäke**—power; strength.

**wäke beki**—strength; courage.

**wäke kaða**—steadfastness.

**wäke kutni**—endurance.

**wäke-sarna**—vow; curse; blessing (literally: power words).

**wäkeva**—powerful; strong.

**wara**—bird; crow.

**weńća**—complete; whole.

**wetc**—water (*noun*).